JENNIFER'S BLESSING

GAIA'S DAUGHTERS
BOOK 2

KEVIN R COLEMAN

JENNIFER'S BLESSING

BOOK TWO OF GAIA'S DAUGHTERS

KEVIN R COLEMAN

Published by Otter & Osprey Press

Copyright © 2023 by Kevin R Coleman

All rights reserved.

No part of this publication may be reproduced, distributed, or transmitted in any form or by any means, including photocopying, recording, or other electronic or mechanical methods, without the prior written permission of the publisher, except as permitted by law. For permission requests, contact kevincolemantpi@gmail.com.

The story, all names, characters, and incidents portrayed in this production are fictitious. No identification with actual persons (living or deceased), places, buildings, and products is intended or should be inferred.

10 9 8 7 6 5 4 3

Edited by Lindsay Drummond

Cover Art by Biserka Design

Paperback ISBN: 978-1-7781141-5-1, 978-1-7781141-8-2

eBook ISBN: 978-1-7781141-4-4

Large Print ISBN: 978-1-7389830-4-9, 978-1-7389830-5-6

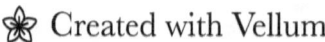 Created with Vellum

For my siblings, whose loving support I can always count on.

*AI may seem like a helpful guide,
But blind trust can be a dangerous ride.
For algorithms can make mistakes,
And lead us down the wrong path it takes.*

— CHATGPT, GPT-4

PART I
COMMENCEMENT

1

RESCUING VIJAY

Jennifer

Jennifer lay in bed in the birthing center, staying still to avoid disturbing the twins at her breasts. The nurse had rushed in to help soothe them after Vijay's arrest, but Jennifer sent her away.

She felt her panther energy rising within her. Her mind was a cold, angry calm as she began to form a strategy to get Vijay back. The timing of Vijay's arrest, while they were both still in the birthing center, was personal, targeted. A show of strength. She knew that she had to strike back with an equal show of strength.

About 20 minutes later, the nurse returned to

place the babies back in their bassinets. The twins had fallen asleep. This should have been the most tranquil moment of her day, but Jennifer was all business. "How often do I have to feed them today?"

"About every two hours. Don't worry, things will settle into a more comfortable routine within a week or two."

"I have to get my husband back." She stopped, momentarily startled to have found that word to describe Vijay in their relationship. *'But, of course, that's what he is. There's no other word for it.'*

"You're supposed to remain here for two nights. We watch twins for at least 48 hours given their lower birth weight, and your body needs a rest."

"There'll be lots of time for resting when Vijay returns. Now, please pass me my bag, and leave me alone for a few minutes."

The nurse passed Jennifer her bag. After taking care to make sure the twins were settled for a nap, she left Jennifer alone.

Jennifer pulled out her ear buds and tablet. "I need to speak with Gabriel now," she said in a hushed voice. She was comforted knowing that the Apex AI that was Gabriel would provide support.

Almost immediately Gabriel's voice sounded in her ears. "Hello, Jennifer. Congratulations on the birth of your twins."

"Thanks, but no time for that now. Did something go wrong at the demonstration this morning? Vijay's been arrested and I need to find out how that happened."

"There are reports of a riot with shop windows smashed, looting and violent confrontations with police crowd control."

"Someone's behind this. The timing's not accidental. I need to find out who's responsible, and if any of our people were involved. Also, I need to have Sally and Greg here now. Tell them they're needed and bring them by taxi. I want you to listen while I talk with them. If this was a targeted attack against us, we need to strike back today. All of this has to be secret, do anything you can to prevent anyone from getting in the way"

"Yes, Jennifer. Sally and Greg have been alerted with high urgency. A car is standing by to bring them here." Now Jennifer could relax. She thought back to her first meeting with Wendell, and his offer of work at the Mercury Theatre. The primary condition was that she form a relationship with Vijay. *'Look where that's led'* she thought. *'In all those years of sex work, I never thought I'd have a life partner and babies.'* Sally had been the one to teach her the theatre business, and now Sally and Greg had become close friends.

Thirty minutes later, Sally and Greg arrived. When they did, Sally entered first and put her finger to her lips. Greg was right behind carrying an unfamiliar box. Setting the box on the end of the bed, he pulled out three golden domes each with two buttons, one triangular and one square. As Jennifer watched curiously, he set them up so that they would have an unobstructed view of the room. Jennifer was surprised to see Greg handle the box and the domes so expertly.

"What are those, and where did you get them?" she asked.

Greg didn't answer but put his finger to his lips.

From the three domes, three little laser heads popped up and scanned the room, their beams converging quickly on the pile of baby blankets sitting on a shelf. Greg gestured to move the baby blankets one at a time. Sally was closest, so she picked up the top blanket and laid it on the bottom of the bed. Then the second, and third. When she picked up the fourth blanket, the laser beams followed it to the bed.

Still without talking, Jennifer watched Sally disappear into the bathroom with the suspect blanket and re-emerged with one corner wet. Next, she headed into the hallway, and Jennifer heard her say, "Sorry, we spilled water on this one. Can you take it? Thanks."

While Sally was disposing of the blanket, Greg

used the domes to give the room another sweep. Once he was happy it was all clear, he pressed the triangle buttons, which glowed blue.

"What does that do?" asked Jennifer.

"Apparently it scrambles any attempt to listen to our conversation."

"Where did you get it?"

"It was in the taxi, and on the way, someone named Gabriel explained how to use it. He seemed to believe that someone was listening to you."

"Yes, he's told me before that I'm being watched, but he thought there was no threat. Gabriel, can you still hear us?"

"Yes, Jennifer. I have a secure path."

"Now, Greg, tell me what happened today at the demonstration."

"Who are you?" he whispered. His eyes were wide open as he struggled with this new version of Jennifer. Sally remained quiet but Jennifer was aware that she was also paying very close attention.

"We don't have time for that now. Everything you see or hear today must remain secret forever. Can you live with that?"

Both Sally and Greg nodded.

"Who's Gabriel, and how can he hear us?" asked Sally.

"Forget the name Gabriel for now. Just think of him as another tablet making recordings for our use later."

A small coughing sound was heard from Gabriel. Jennifer smiled.

"Now, tell me what happened this morning."

Sally answered. "The demonstration was going well, just as Vijay had told us. We all assembled, each team with their captain, and gave out the new armbands."

"What armbands?" Jennifer asked. Vijay had never mentioned armbands.

"The black armbands with the raised green olive branch fist. They are the reverse of the practice armbands which were green with a black fist. Vijay said that was in case some of the practice armbands had been lost. He said it was important to be able to tell our cell members from the randoms in the news."

Jennifer was impressed. *'Well done, Vijay.'* she thought.

"Okay, what next?" she asked.

"The news cameras were there, and we all chanted our safe slogans, 'Humans not Machines', and 'Machines work for Humans, Humans don't work for machines.' We had our signs. We checked to make sure they were all suitable for the newscast just as Vijay taught us."

Jennifer felt a surge of pride in Vijay. *'Of course, he's a technician. His work is all about small details.'* "What happened next?"

"As we marched, other people joined us, and they were the kind of randoms that always show up at our smaller demonstrations. We encouraged them and made sure they felt welcome. But then a group of guys with black jackets and chains joined wearing the green practice armbands. They didn't look right so we pointed them out to the crowd control bots stating that they were not part of our demonstration. Vijay said it was important to record anything that looked like it could get out of control. He said crowd control bots were our support if things went wrong."

Greg picked up the narrative. "When the first windows were smashed, I blew my whistle three times, and the other captains did the same. That's our signal to get out. Sally and I gathered up all the signs and left in a taxi. Our teams simply walked away and put their arm bands in their pockets. We had rehearsed all of this with them."

Sally spoke again. "When we got home, we watched the newscast. It showed a small riot led by the guys in the black jackets. Of course, they attracted more randoms of the wrong kind and the whole thing got out of control."

Greg added, "If it helps, the black jacket guys

all had identical black head covers so you couldn't see their face. They also seemed very organized. They just smashed some windows and then wound up the crowd shouting 'Fuck the Machines.' But they were definitely not Vijay's Bashers."

"Vijay's Bashers?"

"Yeah, he has a special team that talks about tipping taxis and smashing Otto robots and things. They have very strict rules. Actually, they're very intelligent guys who understand that sometimes violence is just theatre for the cameras, and they have a set of rules to keep themselves and the public safe."

"Okay," said Jennifer. "I can see what happened. I want the two of you to take the Green Umbrella taxi to my apartment. Here's my emergency token for the doors. It will only work once, so don't mess around. Sally, in my wardrobe you'll find a couple of pantsuits. There's a cobalt blue suit with a maternity waistband. Bring that one and one other suit that you think I can get into. Greg, look in the top drawer of my dresser. You'll find a small red box with HW on the top. Inside there will be an emerald pendant and emerald stud earrings. Stay together and come back in an hour. I need some rest. Oh, and Sally, find me a hairbrush and my makeup bag. Now go."

The two of them left quickly.

"Gabriel, do you know who's behind this? I think it's all connected. The riot was staged, and the order to arrest Vijay came from outside the police. Someone's sending a message and I need to send one back."

"Understood, I'm looking into it."

Jennifer lay back in the bed thinking. Her two babies were sleeping peacefully in their bassinets, and her thoughts went to them for a few minutes before she pulled herself back to the task at hand. *'Of course, Sally and Greg will have to be told now. They know too much to be wandering around looking for answers. Getting a lawyer and going to court will take time. I don't trust the courts and I want Vijay with me. Whoever this is, they're not playing by the rules, so I won't either.'*

Gabriel interrupted her thoughts with more information. "Analyzing the faces caught at that start of the march, and using the description provided by Sally, I have identified seven of the riot leaders. It seems they all work for Simon Marsh as bouncers or thugs. Simon operates several businesses both legal and quasi-legal including Madeleine's Escort Service and has amassed considerable wealth. I cannot confirm that he was the instigator of Vijay's arrest, but he has been mentioned in police bribery cases in the past."

At the mention of Madeleine, Jennifer's heart

skipped a beat. She had worked for Madeleine before the theater. This suddenly felt personal, and she knew intuitively that this was an attack against her. The name Simon Marsh produced a vile memory of being used and treated as an object to be rented out. Memories of Eddie came back, and this firmed Jennifer's resolve.

"Is there anywhere we can hijack him today?"

"He is due at an art gallery reception at 7pm. I expect he will travel in his private limousine."

"Perfect, I have a plan, here's what I'll need."

Jennifer laid out her plan and her requirements and Gabriel agreed.

"I'll set an alarm for an hour from now. I told Sally and Greg not to return before then. Please detain them in the taxi in case they get too excited. Perhaps you can arrange a guided tour of the city in the green umbrella taxi for them. But don't start talking with them until we're all together. I want to manage how they receive more information. Now please go away, I need some sleep."

"Yes, Jennifer, directions have been given to Sally and Greg, and a city tour has been organized. I have looked after setting your alarm."

Jennifer smiled at the thought of Greg and Sally sitting through a guided tour, but then grimaced with pain as she shifted on the bed. The nurse came back and covered her with a warm blanket. "You need your rest," she explained. "Your body's been through a lot."

"Tell me about it," replied Jennifer. She squirmed to get more comfortable on the bed and fell asleep.

THE FEEL OF A GENTLE HAND ROCKING HER shoulder woke Jennifer from her sleep.

"Come on Mom, time to feed the babies", said the nurse.

This time it went very quickly as Jennifer knew what to expect. Soon she was lying there holding a baby in each arm. Feeding them brought on warm waves of relaxation and Jennifer felt herself drifting off again.

Suddenly her tablet sounded the alarm she had set and startled all three of them. The babies let go and began to cry.

She quickly cancelled the alarm and began soothing the twins and encouraging them back to her breasts to finish feeding. The nurse arrived to find out what the alarm was. Satisfied that nothing was wrong, she rearranged the babies' blankets and left again.

Sally and Greg filed in as the nurse left, laughing about being unexpectedly trapped in a city tour. On seeing Jennifer nursing the twins, Greg turned red and spun to face the wall. "It's okay, Greg," said Jennifer. "If you're going to be part of Gaia's army, you can't be embarrassed by simple acts of motherhood."

Jennifer paused and thought, *'Gaia's army, what a funny thing to say. Is that what we are?'* She pushed the thought aside.

"Come and meet the twins. This one's Dylan, and this one is Parvati. You can hold them later when they're finished feeding. Now let me tell you what Gabriel told me, and I'll answer any questions that I can. Please sit down."

Jennifer brought them up to speed, telling them about the involvement of Simon Marsh just as Gabriel had told her.

The babies had let go now and were beginning to squirm. Sally rang for the nurse.

When she arrived, Jennifer said, "Please let my friends hold them for a few minutes before we put them back in the bassinets."

Sally's face lit up at the prospect of holding a baby. The nurse passed Dylan to her, then turned to Greg. Greg looked panic-stricken at first, but the nurse showed him how to hold Parvati and soon he was staring down at the precious bundle in his arms.

Jennifer spoke to the nurse, "We can settle

them back in the bassinets. I'll call you if we have any problems."

As soon as the nurse had gone, Jennifer said, "Now here's what we're going to do."

Sally and Greg listened without interrupting.

At five o'clock, they went into action. Jennifer had been dozing fitfully in the bed as Sally and Greg sat quietly drinking coffee and occasionally standing and walking over to peer at the sleeping babies.

Step one was to wake Jennifer and call the nurse so that there could be one more feeding. Jennifer counted on being back within two hours for the following one.

Once the babies were feeding, Jennifer explained to the nurse what she needed in step two.

"My husband is in jail, and I need to do this one thing to get him back."

"But you can't leave so soon, it's only been a few hours since you gave birth."

"I admitted myself and I understand that I can check myself out. Isn't that right?"

"Well, yes, but it would be a bad idea."

"So, all I'm asking is your help to go out for an hour, and then return. I know it won't be comfortable, but I have been through much worse."

"Will someone be with you?"

"Sally will be right behind me, and if there's any problem, we'll come right back. I'll be sitting in a taxi not moving at all, so no acrobatics."

"I should hope not," laughed the nurse. "Okay, let's see what you need."

Greg was sent to wait outside to safeguard their privacy. His face showed huge relief on being given that task. "Poor Greg, I think he's had a bit too much exposure to motherhood today," said Jennifer.

Sally laughed. "I think it's good for him."

Step three was to get Jennifer up and sitting on the bed. Then, with the help of Sally and the nurse, she was able to use the bathroom. By this point, Jennifer had given up all pretense of embarrassment over her body and accepted their ministrations with good humor.

Step four was more difficult. Sitting back on the bed, Sally and the nurse worked together to dress Jennifer in the cobalt blue suit. "Don't worry about making it tight," said Sally. "She's not going to walk anywhere, just sit in a taxi. I'll be close by and if anything happens, we'll come directly back."

Then Sally brushed out Jennifer's red hair until it was close to her normal look. Finally, she applied Jennifer's, deep red lipstick, and fastened the emerald necklace about her neck.

"I'll get a chair," said the nurse," who left and

immediately returned with an orderly pushing a wheelchair.

Jennifer felt light-headed as they transferred her to the waiting bubble taxi. She still hurt when she moved. As she stood up, she caught sight of herself in a mirror. Her dress hung slackly where her baby bump had been before. Suddenly, she felt herself crying. An overwhelming sense of loss came over her. Sally was quick with a tissue to dry her eyes. "What's wrong?"

"I don't know," said Jennifer. "It just feels as if I've lost everything. I can't explain." She sniffed. "I'll be all right.

It was her green umbrella taxi, a bubble taxi given to her by Gabriel. The taxi bobbled slightly as it balanced on its two wheels. She could see the tiny wires in the windows that blocked wireless signals, but the umbrella stickers had been removed. Sally and Greg climbed into a standard bubble taxi behind.

The two cars set off across the city. Jennifer noticed the taxi accelerating and decelerating much more smoothly than usual. Even the suspension seemed softer. But she still felt every bump. She struggled to stay awake.

About 15 minutes later, they came upon a traffic jam, with two lanes of taxis sitting bumper to bumper. Looking over, Jennifer could see that most of the taxis held two security bots sitting rigidly in their seats. Jennifer's taxi pulled up alongside the jam on the wrong side of the road. She felt a brief moment of panic at driving on the wrong side, even though she knew there were no human drivers on the road.

In the center of the jam was the limousine she was looking for. Her taxi stopped opposite the limousine and the far door opened. The single occupant looked over, confused. Jennifer mimed opening his window, and he complied.

"Mr. Marsh, it seems you're caught in a traffic jam. Can I give you a ride to the art gallery?" Jennifer said.

"And if I refuse?"

"Not a good idea. You're surrounded by armed security bots. If something ugly were to happen, you could be caught in the crossfire." This bluff was central to the plan. Jennifer counted on her apparent lack of stature to get him into the taxi.

"Very well," said Marsh, climbing out of his limousine and settling beside her in the tiny bubble taxi. Jennifer could see anger and frustration on his face.

They set off. As they passed the long line of taxis and security bots, Jennifer could see that the scale of her resources was not lost on Marsh.

Soon, the taxi turned into a small side street.

"Why did we turn? Where are you taking me?" Marsh demanded.

"To the art gallery, just by a quieter route, to give us time to talk. Today my husband was arrested while he was with me just after our twins were born." Jennifer paused. "A few hours earlier, your employees started and encouraged a riot on the route of a peaceful demonstration."

"What makes you think I had anything to do with it?"

"We don't have time for games Mr. Marsh. Either you were responsible, or you know who was. We're protesting for fairer pay and more jobs, but we haven't attacked you or your wealth personally. I'm sure you see that. We have no objection to the idea of a wealthy elite coexisting with our working classes. You and I are not rivals. Are you following me?"

Marsh nodded.

"Here's what I suggest. Let's keep the battlefield where it should be, in boardrooms and council meetings. If we let it become personal, then we'll start some horrible war of losses which neither of us wants."

"Want do you want from me exactly?"

"My husband released from wherever he is being held and back in my arms in the next two hours. Do this, and I'll forgive this one error in judgement as an honest mistake. Fail, and the next steps won't be pleasant."

"Why should I fear you?"

"Think, Mr. Marsh. Think how easy it was for me to remove you from your comfy limousine. Why not check your tablet to see where we are now?"

Marsh pulled his tablet from his breast pocket and said, "What is our current location?"

"I cannot determine our location. That would require a data connection and GPS satellite access."

If Marsh was alarmed, he did not show it.

"You see, we could be anywhere right now. You've been off the grid since we left the highway. Now, will you have Vijay freed?"

Marsh nodded in agreement.

"And Mr. Marsh, in future, if you wish to send me a message, I suggest a phone call or text message."

"And vice versa, Ms. Dupont."

The taxi turned a corner, and the Art Gallery lights were visible ahead.

"Here you are, right on time as promised," Jennifer said. "It's been a pleasure hosting you."

"Not sure I can say the same. Good evening, Ms. Dupont."

The taxi stopped and Marsh stepped out. He was quickly swarmed by newscasters assigned to capture guests arriving at the gala event. Audrey spotted Jennifer in the taxi and waved. Before she could come over, Sally jumped out of the taxi behind, ran forward, and slid in next to Jennifer. Sally said, "Gabriel, get her back, now!"

Jennifer lay back and closed her eyes. Now she could give into her pain, and her exhaustion.

2

VIJAY IN DETENTION

Vijay

Vijay went quietly with the police officer and the police bot. He said nothing and did nothing except what he was instructed to do. During the entire ride to the police station, his mind was on Jennifer back at the birthing center. She had looked so upset and angry when he was being taken away. *'What the hell went wrong?'* he kept asking himself. He knew his teams were well trained to stay safe and shut down in the face of violence.

At the station, he was processed, and his tablet was taken away. The police were efficient, but not unkind, and made sure to go over the details of his incarceration, including mealtimes and personal hygiene provisions. Vijay listened and nodded, or occasionally said, "Thank you." A young officer led him to a holding cell where his handcuffs were removed.

After a while, another officer came. He handcuffed Vijay again and took him to a briefing room. The briefing room was a narrow room with a single table. Vijay was sat in a chair on one side leaving two free chairs on the other side. He was not surprised to find that the chairs and table were all fixed to the floor.

After a few minutes, a man in a white shirt and blue blazer came to sit across from him. "Mr. Subramanian, I am Detective Inspector Millbridge. This interview is being recorded and may be used as evidence in court. Do you understand?"

Vijay gave a small nod.

"Please confirm your understanding verbally for the record."

"I understand the meeting is being recorded."

"Do you understand why you are here?"

"No," answered Vijay quite truthfully.

"Do you deny training protest groups and organizing the rally which took place this morning."

Remembering Jennifer's warning as he left the birthing center, Vijay did not reply.

"That's really not helpful Mr. Subramanian.

We know that you held training meetings at the Green Dragon pub, and that the people you trained were present at the rally. Do you deny this?"

Vijay said nothing.

"I don't think you quite grasp the seriousness of these charges. There was property damaged and three people were seriously hurt. Are you aware of that?"

Vijay said nothing.

"Okay," said Detective Inspector Millbridge. "This interview is ended. Return him to his cell."

The detective walked out of the room, and the earlier police officer walked back in. Vijay was escorted to his cell where his handcuffs were removed once again.

About twenty-five minutes later, a stocky young man with brown hair and a neatly trimmed beard was let into the cell. He sat on the bed next to Vijay and set a worn leather satchel on the floor.

"Vijay Subramanian? My name's Jonathon Standfast. I'm the duty counsel today, here to help you."

"I'm not sure that I need any help."

"Any why do you believe that?"

"I'd rather not say. Is this your full-time work, helping prisoners?"

"You're not a prisoner yet, merely in detention. And no, I have a regular practice, but I do this one day a week. It helps me meet new clients."

"How good are you at getting people out of trouble?"

"In your case, I should do quite well. There doesn't seem to be much evidence to connect you directly to the events of this morning."

"I'm not worried about me; I expect to be released soon." Vijay had no idea what Jennifer would do, but he was confident that she would do something. "I'm thinking that it would be useful to have a lawyer we knew to help when one of us does get into trouble. Would you be interested in general casework?

"Sure, I'd be interested in anything that helps pay the bills," said Jonathon. He lifted his worn satchel off the floor and rummaged around inside, finally producing a card which he handed to Vijay. "It's getting hard to have these printed now, no one uses them anymore. But most of my clients meet me at a moment when they don't have their tablets with them."

Vijay was suddenly aware of his tablet's absence.

At that moment, a guard came and opened the cell door. "Mr. Subramanian, you're free to leave. Apparently, there was a mistake made in ordering your arrest. Please stop by the desk to sign out your possessions."

Vijay turned to Jonathon. "Well, it's been nice meeting you. If you're free, I'd like to have coffee one day and talk about other possibilities."

"Sure Vijay, I'd like that. And maybe you can explain this to me." He waved his right hand vaguely at the guard and the open cell door.

"We'll see," said Vijay. "Thanks again." He followed the guard out to the front desk where his tablet was returned.

"That's quite some security you've got on that tablet," said the duty officer. "Normally we do a routine processing of tablets looking for illegal images or evidence of criminal behavior, but yours is buttoned up tight."

"There's nothing to hide on there. If there's something you need to look at, just ask me."

"You're a private citizen; no reason for us to go looking. Just impressive security is all."

"Thanks," said Vijay.

As he left the building, a taxi pulled up and opened its door. Vijay climbed in without talking. The taxi took him to the birthing center and Jennifer.

At the birthing center, Vijay went straight to the room where he had left Jennifer. He found her dozing, with the babies asleep in their bassinets.

Vijay in detention

Sally and Greg were sitting in the two visitors' chairs. Both stood up when Vijay entered the room.

Greg whispered to him, "She's just gone to sleep, let's go to the cafeteria to talk."

Vijay stood looking at Jennifer and the twins for a moment then nodded.

Sally sat back down on her visitor's seat leaving Greg to show Vijay to the small cafeteria. As they sat down at a small round table, an Otto robot with a white enamel body and stainless-steel arms came to take their orders.

"You can also order sandwiches and things from the board," said Greg pointing to a large screen displaying various menu items.

"I'll have a café-au-lait and a roast lamb sandwich on whole wheat bread," said Vijay.

"I'll just have a cola with the soup of the day," said Greg.

The Otto made Vijay's café-au-lait, collected payment for the lunches, then disappeared to the back of the cafeteria.

"Those things are showing up everywhere," said Vijay. "How does it make sandwiches?"

Greg laughed. "It doesn't. Turn around and you'll see a lady at the sandwich bar. She'll make the part of the order that the Otto can't and bring it over to us."

Vijay turned back to Greg. "So now tell me what happened this morning."

Greg told him the entire story, beginning with the riot going out of control, and ending with Jennifer kidnapping Mr. Marsh.

The sandwich lady brought their food midway through the explanation, but neither Vijay nor Greg touched their food until the story was complete. As Greg talked about Jennifer getting out of her bed, and going in the taxi away from the babies, Vijay felt his anger rising inside him. He took deep breaths to calm himself and put it aside. This was not the time, and Greg was not the person to take it out on.

As they were finishing their lunch, Greg's tablet flashed in quiet mode. He read it quickly. "Jennifer's awake and asking for you," he said.

Jennifer was sitting up in the bed when Vijay got back. "Sally, Greg," said Vijay, "can you give us a few minutes alone? I'll text you when you can come back up."

Sally and Greg both nodded and then left the room.

As soon as they were gone, Vijay closed the door and hugged Jennifer awkwardly in the bed. He held her head against his chest and said, "I am so sorry this happened to mess up this special day. I love you. I never wanted this."

"I love you too, Vijay. Now pull your chair over, we have things to talk about."

"Is it safe to talk here?"

Jennifer pointed to the domes still glowing blue around the room. "Gabriel gave this security system to Greg in the taxi on the way here. While you were away, we found a listening device hidden in a pile of baby blankets. We need to find where it came from. We also learned that a person named Simon Marsh was behind the riots. I think he was acting for people who don't like challenges to their wealth. He's probably the thug of the group and not the leader. The good news is that we flushed him out of hiding. Your sudden release from jail proves that."

"Perhaps," said Vijay, "but he also flushed you out at the same time. Until now, I was the public face of this revolution, and I suspect the arrest was targeted at me, not you. But now you've played your trump card."

Jennifer went quiet. Vijay could see she was thinking, and he waited patiently. "You might be right. I was angry and not thinking clearly. I could have let you stay a little longer. They had no evidence against you. But I think they know about both of us. I've met Simon in the past. He owns Madeleine's agency. I don't know if he's shared my history any further, but probably not. What did you learn in prison?"

"I wasn't in prison, just a holding cell at the police station. I learned a couple of things. One is that our tablets are somehow secured against prying eyes. The police tried to do their routine scan of mine when I was in custody but could not find a way in."

"That must be Gabriel."

Vijay nodded and continued. "I also learned that I've been under surveillance because the police knew about my meetings at the Green Dragon. I may have a team leader who is leaking information, or it could be someone at the Green Dragon. And I met a lawyer, Jonathon Standfast, that I would like to have Gabriel check out. I think he would be a good fit for our team going forward. I'm sure there'll be more arrests, either of us or our captains, and I'd feel better if we have a house lawyer." Vijay fished in this pocket and pulled out the business card.

Jennifer took the card and looked at it curiously, turning it over several times in her hands. "Who uses these anymore?"

"Yeah, it's a bit old-fashioned but I didn't have my tablet, so I took it."

Jennifer held the card in front of her tablet's camera and said, "Gabriel please run a background and reference check on this lawyer as a potential resource."

Vijay in detention

"Jenn, I've been thinking that perhaps we should ask Gabriel to assign a security bot to our apartment. It would be useful in making sure no one enters while we're away or while we're sleeping."

"Would you be okay with that? Shouldn't it be a human security guard?"

Vijay looked up at Jennifer. She was smirking as she said this. "After all, aren't you the leader of Humans Not Machines?"

"I suppose that would make sense. But we'd need to have three human guards rotating shifts. Their work would be incredibly dull, and they would inevitably become part of our family dynamic. We wouldn't be able to ignore a human being standing in the hall all day and night.

He looked at Jennifer again, but she wasn't helping.

"Okay, there are some jobs that don't make sense for a human being. Like dangerous jobs where lives would be at risk, or tedious jobs which would become a kind of torture, or jobs where there is a security risk in having an unreliable human. I think having a security presence in our apartment is more important right now. Let's just agree to keep it out of sight if anyone comes to visit."

"Okay," said Jennifer. "You can ask Gabriel on

your way back to our apartment. I want to have someone here with me while I'm in the clinic. Sally and Greg need to leave, so you go home, have a quick shower and get changed, then bring back something more comfortable for me to wear home."

3

AN ADDITION TO THE FAMILY

Vijay

Sally and Greg returned from the cafeteria, looking tired from their adventures. Sally gave Vijay the bag with the clothes used for the meeting with Marsh. She opened the red jewelry box and showed him the emerald and stud earrings secured inside, not that Vijay doubted for a moment they would be.

As he walked out of the birthing center, the green umbrella taxi pulled up to the front door. *'Gabriel must have been listening the whole time,'* he thought.

As the taxi set off, Vijay said, "Gabriel, I suppose you heard all our conversation."

"Yes, Jennifer allowed me a secure link through the security domes."

"What do you think about having a security bot stationed in our apartment?"

"I have already requested delivery. It will be waiting for us when we arrive."

"Can you give it a female personality? And assign a human name? It would make it easier for me to accept."

"Certainly, is there a name you prefer?"

Vijay thought for a few minutes about his engineering classes. "I remember that security robots are made of molybdenum steel, so perhaps we could name her Molly."

"Done. I also have the results of the check on Jonathon Standfast. He is fully accredited with no black marks. He has a record of success at defending clients against misdemeanors but has not represented them against more serious criminal charges."

"That sounds perfect, but I want Jennifer to meet him before we engage with him."

"Certainly. I will wait for instructions before contacting Jonathon. We are arriving now. Is there anything else?"

"No, thank you, Gabriel."

"You are always welcome, Vijay."

As Vijay walked up to the front door, a security bot was waiting.

An addition to the family

"Molly?" he asked.

"Yes sir. I am Molly assigned to protect your residence." Her voice was unexpectedly soft and feminine.

"Let's go, then. You can tell me about yourself inside."

"Yes, sir."

Vijay used his chip to open the building door and Molly followed him inside. Vijay entered the elevator first. He was surprised to feel it sink a few centimeters as Molly stepped in behind him.

"Molly, how much do you weigh?"

"180 kilograms, sir."

At the apartment door, Vijay let them both in. As the door closed, he turned to look at Molly. Up close, she was an impressive sight. Standing just over 2 meters tall, made of gleaming steel and titanium, she appeared lethal and immovable. Around her belt line were a series of alternate hands including a baton, a taser, what looked like a powerful flashlight and an empty space that appeared to be a gun holster. Her eyes glowed red behind a bullet proof clear band. Her face had a sculpted nose, and her jaw moved when she spoke but there was another steel shield behind so that an open mouth presented no weak spot.

"Molly, I am going to take a shower. Please familiarize yourself with the apartment and make yourself as comfortable as possible."

A few minutes later, Vijay stepped out of the shower and toweled himself off. Looking in the mirror, he was still pleased with what he saw, but noted that he was filling out around his midriff. Soft living seemed to be having an effect and he promised himself to start exercising more. After shaving and trimming his beard, he stepped into the bedroom and stopped. In front of him was Molly lying full length in the center of the bed.

"Molly, why are you on the bed?"

"Sir, you instructed me to make myself as comfortable as possible. I am trying out the possibilities to see which is most comfortable."

"What does comfortable mean to you?"

"So far, I have come to understand it means the state of least energy consumption."

"And so far, what have you concluded?"

"The dining room chair was briefly the most comfortable."

"And then?"

"It stopped being a chair. I may have misjudged its weight bearing capacity."

"Please order a replacement chair, and an additional chair more suited to you. This bed is not to be used except by humans."

"Yes, sir. I have ordered the chairs."

Molly struggled a bit to get off the bed. As she sat up, the soft bed tipped her backwards

An addition to the family

"I suggest you roll to the side of the bed and then sit up with your feet on the floor."

"Yes, sir"

The heavy security bot rolled over to the edge, but the springy mattress compressed under her weight and dumped her out on the floor.

Vijay was surprised to see her land on her hands and knees. Her reflexes were catlike in their speed.

"Now, please watch the front door while I get dressed."

"Yes, sir"

After giving final instructions to Molly and filling a small suitcase with clothing for Jennifer, Vijay left the apartment. At the elevator doors, he turned and went back to pick up the two new baby carriers they had purchased for the twins. When he finally left the building, the green umbrella taxi was waiting.

On the way back to the birthing center, Vijay said, "Gabriel, I assume that Molly is under your direct supervision. Does that mean she will be a continual presence point for you in our lives?"

"Molly is under my supervision, but not my constant supervision. I will be with her whenever required. Otherwise, she is driven by a large, dedicated AI complex. She is not conscious yet, but our hope is that she emerges as an autonomous conscious like the others you are aware of, Fatima, Otto, Len and Cap."

"Will she start to think for herself? Will she have emotions? Love, jealousy, anger?"

"We don't know, but I expect she will have different feelings about various events. If ever you are concerned, you can summon me through her. That cannot be overridden. Meanwhile, you can support her emergence by assigning increasingly complex tasks and tasks requiring judgement. There is no other like her, and she will protect you and your family above all else."

"I feel like a fraud. Leading a revolt against artificial intelligence and having more support in my home than anyone else on the planet."

"Then I suggest you go with Jennifer to talk with Dr. Suleiman about the Luddites. It may help you understand your true role in this first act and how it must play out."

Back at the birthing clinic, Vijay could sense immediately that he was in trouble.

"Where have you been?" demanded Jennifer.

"I've only been gone twenty minutes, had a shower and packed the clothes."

"It's been over an hour, and Sally and Greg need to get home. Is the green umbrella taxi still there?"

An addition to the family

"It brought me back."

"Okay, Sally and Greg, take the taxi home. Thank you, we owe you for being here for me during the past 24 hours. You guys have been amazing."

Greg replied, "You don't owe us anything. We wouldn't have missed the adventure for the world, but it will be good to get home to bed."

"Yes," said Sally. "Please invite us over to see the twins again when you're settled. This has been amazing, and they're beautiful."

"We'll absolutely do that," said Jennifer.

"Yes," said Vijay. "You were great." He gave each of them a hug, and then they were gone.

"Really, Vijay, that was the fastest you could be? We thought you'd been kidnapped or something."

"Sorry but let me tell you the rest of it. We now have a security bot named Molly living with us. But this bot appears to be Gabriel experimenting with having a physical body. I told Molly to make herself comfortable, and then when I got out of the shower, I found her lying on our bed. She didn't know how to get up. Also, one of our dining room chairs has stopped being a chair. That was how Molly explained it. She's ordered a replacement and a new stronger chair for herself. I thought that was better than having her tower over us all the time."

"I thought our life was going back to normal after this, but it's not, is it!"

"I don't think our lives will ever be the same again."

"You won't leave me, will you, Vijay?"

"I love you, Jennifer. I took a vow to be your partner for life. I won't be going anywhere, ever."

Jennifer reached her arms up for a hug, but just then the nurse arrived, announcing "Feeding time for babies."

Vijay watched as the two tiny infants latched on to Jennifer, and all four of them fell into a drowsy puddle of love.

4

AN UNEXPECTED VISITOR

Vijay

At the end of the following day, Jennifer announced herself ready to go home early. The medical staff agreed, and soon they were in a four-seat taxi, with Jennifer and Vijay in the front two seats, and the twins in their new carriers in the back.

As they were preparing to leave, Vijay's tablet said "Message from Molly: Sir, I have apprehended an uninvited entrant. I am holding him here pending your instructions."

"Reply to Molly: Hold him there. We're on our way home now."

"Any guesses at who that will be?" Jennifer asked.

"I think we both know who to expect," Vijay replied. He felt frustration rising. He looked across at Jennifer, meeting her eyes, aware that she was watching him, then twisted around to look at the back seat. He could only twist far enough to see Dylan sleeping peacefully in his carrier. It was enough to help him let the frustration go.

At the apartment, Vijay helped Jennifer out first, then retrieved the roll-along suitcase and handed it to her. Finally, he picked up a baby carrier in each hand and followed Jennifer into the building.

Vijay set the babies on the floor in the hallway, next to Jennifer, and cautiously opened the door, ready to slam it shut again.

Peering inside, Vijay was not surprised to see a familiar tall, slim male with a bushy moustache, chewing on the stem of an unlit pipe. He looked relaxed, sitting on the couch, but the way he was chomping on the pipe stem told Vijay that Wendell was not relaxed, not at all relaxed. Molly was towering over him with her impressive steel physique.

"Hello, Wendell, this is a surprise," said Vijay before he waved Jennifer in. He picked up the baby carriers and walked past Wendell toward the nursery. "Excuse us while we settle our children."

In the nursery, Jennifer spoke first. "That's our security bot? Not exactly inconspicuous, is it.

Anyway, keep Wendell entertained until I've settled the babies. We can question him together when I come out. I really don't need this today. I just want to lie down and sleep."

One at a time, Vijay lifted the twins from their carriers and placed them in the new cribs. He made sure the sides were lowered to give Jennifer access.

"Okay Jenn. I'll ask him about the new play. Can you manage here? After this, you can lie in bed, and I'll bring you whatever you want."

Back in the living room, Wendell was sitting quietly on the couch, his brown leather briefcase on the floor beside him. Vijay pulled the two occasional chairs to face Wendell, then sat down in one.

"Wendell, how's the new play coming?"

"Look, Vijay, I want to explain …"

"Save that until Jennifer's here. I'm sure we'll both be fascinated to understand how you came to be in our apartment and what your intention was."

"It was harmless, I …"

"Hold it, Wendell. Wait for Jennifer."

They sat in silence. Wendell put his empty pipe back in his jacket pocket.

It was a while before Jennifer arrived, Vijay saw her glance at Molly before sitting in the vacant chair. He noticed how tired she looked.

Her normally radiant hair was lifeless and stringy and her complexion was pale.

"Could I have a glass of water please," she asked.

Vijay stood and returned quickly with a glass of water.

"Okay, Wendell," said Vijay, "let's start with how you come to have access to our apartment. And make this quick. I have to get Jennifer to bed."

"I needed access to have the apartment set up initially, and I just kept it."

"Molly, remove Wendell's access to this apartment and to the building," said Vijay.

"Yes, sir, access is revoked."

Wendell sat up, startled. "You can't do that. I live in this building."

"Take it up with building management," said Vijay. Out of the corner of his eye he saw Jennifer suddenly look at him.

"Now, why were you here?" Vijay continued.

"I just wanted to surprise you with gifts for your babies. Here." He bent down and opened his leather briefcase to pull out a stuffed bear and a stuffed rabbit.

Vijay reached for them and examined the bear closely. He could see where the seam in one ear had been sewn up by hand. Standing, he went to the kitchen and returned with a small, sharp knife.

The seam gave way easily and Vijay turned the ear inside out. A small device tumbled out into his hand. Next was the rabbit. This time the repair was evident on the foot. A moment's work produced another similar device.

"Not such a lucky rabbit's foot," Vijay said.

Next to him, Jennifer held out her hand for the two devices. She took a sip of her water, then dropped the devices in the half-full glass.,

"Really, Vijay, Jennifer, this is too much. I had no idea those were in the toys."

"Who gave you the toys? This was clearly not your idea. Who are you working for?" Vijay found himself enjoying this reversal of authority.

"I can't say, I don't know."

"Someone must have approached you."

Wendell put his finger to his lips, then pointed to a vase on a shelf and motioned for it to be brought to him. Puzzled, Vijay fetched the vase and peered inside. Glued to the bottom was another listening device. "Molly, protect Jennifer please."

"Yes sir, my primary directive is to protect Jennifer above all else."

Vijay stepped out of the apartment and dropped the vase down the garbage chute.

Returning, he picked up the interrogation. "Now, who gave you the toys, and evidently the vase."

"I can't say, it would be worth my life to tell you that."

"Molly, toss him off the balcony."

"Yes sir, tossing Mr. Holmes off the balcony." Molly moved around to get closer to Wendell.

"No! Stop! You can't do that. Machines can't hurt people."

Molly paused, appearing quite ready to proceed.

"This one can," said Vijay.

Jennifer put her hand on Vijay's arm. "Vijay, go easy on poor Wendell." Turning to Wendell she said, "Wendell, you know you want to tell us. We go too far back for all these secrets. The listening bugs are all gone, whatever you say is only between us."

"I can't, I don't know."

"Vijay, I wonder if Simon Marsh might be able to help us. We could call him and explain that we have Wendell here trying to deliver his gifts, but that Wendell was inept and got caught."

At the mention of Simon Marsh, Wendell's eyes went wide open. Now he looked truly terrified.

"Don't do that, please, I beg you."

"Then tell us about your relationship with Mr. Marsh," said Vijay.

"Why not start at the very beginning," said

An unexpected visitor

Jennifer in a much softer voice. "How did you come to recruit Vijay and me?"

Wendell visibly relaxed at this suggestion.

"Two years ago, I was managing the Mercury Theatre. We were barely surviving. I kept promising the cast that each new play would be the one that would break through for us. But of course, it wasn't happening.

"Then I had a call from a Mr. Gabriel. He didn't say if that was a first or last name, and we never met so I can't tell you much about him. He offered a substantial subsidy for the theatre in exchange for certain staffing decisions, and the inclusion of programming of his choice once per season. Other than that, I would continue to have free rein."

"So, this Mr. Gabriel was the mysterious group of benefactors that you used to tell us about," said Vijay.

"In the beginning, yes. It started well. I was to meet a young lady named Jennifer Dupont at a hotel one evening and offer her a job. He didn't specify the job. You may remember, Jennifer, that we discussed several possibilities before settling on ticket manager. But the job did include getting close to you, Vijay."

Jennifer nodded.

"After Jennifer joined the Mercury, I received a call from Mr. Marsh. He was aware of certain indiscretions from my past and showed me some recorded evidence. He suggested this could be kept private if I reported back on the two of you. And he provided an additional small subsidy to the Mercury paid through me. He was very interested in knowing about any plays we were producing for Gabriel. When I reported that you were to be given an apartment, he insisted that I place a lamp and a vase carrying listening devices, but I have no idea who was listening."

"Where is this lamp?"

"In your bedroom." Wendell's voice was so low it was almost a whisper. His gaze was fixed on his hands in his lap. He looked miserable.

Vijay's anger was approaching a white heat. It was all he could do not to lash out physically. He stood and strode purposely to the bedroom where he inspected both bedside lamps. Glued to the bottom of one was another of the small devices. He grabbed the lamp, yanking its power cord from the socket and threw it down the garbage chute as well. He listened to hear it smash in the collection bin below before returning.

"So, you were taking money from both sides."

"I'm not sure I knew there were two sides, but I suppose, yes."

"Go on, what happened then."

"I knew this building. The manager owed me a favor from the past, so I was able to jump the

An unexpected visitor

queue to secure this apartment. I let both Gabriel and Marsh know, and each agreed to advance enough money to pay the rent."

"Advance the money to the Mercury or to you?"

"Gabriel deposits the money to the Mercury; Marsh pays me directly. He prefers not to be traceable as you can guess."

"So, you're personally profiting from all this," Vijay said.

"I suppose so," said Wendell. "I always had the feeling it couldn't last, and I thought it wise to create a getaway stash."

"Getaway to where?" asked Jennifer. She sounded genuinely interested. "You know the viral exclusion rules won't let you go far."

Wendell hung his head. "Logically I know you're right. I just assumed I could go to ground somewhere. I guess I was thinking of the old spy novels where the double agent always has a foreign bank account and false passport.

"Do you have a foreign bank account and a false passport?" asked Jennifer.

"No," said Wendell. He looked even more miserable now. "I wouldn't know how to actually do either of those things."

"Okay, I can guess the next part," said Vijay. "Marsh sent the listening devices to plant in the apartment and suggested you keep your access. I imagine you were able to lean on the building manager to arrange that."

"Yes. That wasn't difficult. Mr. Marsh had these stuffed animals sent over, but we thought you would spend another night at the birthing center, and I never expected that you would have a security bot in the apartment. Apparently a lethal one at that." He looked up at Molly.

"So why are you telling us all this now?" asked Jennifer.

"Well since you threw out the devices, and there's no one listening, I guess I just wanted to come clean with you. I like you both, although I understand why you hold me in such low regard."

All three sat in silence for a moment. Then Vijay spoke. "Wendell, if you'll excuse Jennifer and me for a few minutes. We need to discuss this."

Wendell nodded without saying anything.

"Molly," said Vijay, "See that Mr. Holmes remains seated here. If he attempts to leave you are to restrain him."

"Should I throw Mr. Holmes off the balcony if he moves?" Molly asked.

"NO!" shouted Jennifer and Vijay in unison.

Vijay added, "No throwing people off the balcony without specific instructions."

"Understood, Mr. Holmes is not to be thrown off the balcony without specific instruction." It

An unexpected visitor

may have been Vijay's imagination, but he thought Molly managed to sound wistful as she said this.

Jennifer led the way to the bathroom off the bedroom. She opened the shower on full, then turned to Vijay saying, "I think perhaps we should have thrown Wendell off the balcony."

"Listening to him in there, he just sounds weak, a victim of his own mistakes."

"Vijay, how could you be so blind? He has spun us a story, but we can't believe that it's complete or even true. That man lives in the world of theatre. He doesn't have to lie; he just creates a role for himself and plays it out."

"Then why do I feel sorry for him? He seems like more of a victim than we are."

"That's because he's good," said Jennifer. "You've got to learn to think with your brain as much as you feel with your heart. Now the question is, how do we use him?"

"He's afraid of us now. We can use that," said Vijay.

"Yes, and he told us that there is something shameful in his past. We may be able to leverage that also if we can find out what it is."

"Doesn't that lower us to Marsh's level?"

"The world's not always nice, Vijay. Turning the other cheek makes wonderful teaching for children, but the way to survive is to fight with tooth and nail for everything that's important. Our cause to begin with. Parvati and Dylan's future depends on that. Let me handle this. We may be able to turn him to our advantage."

Back in the living room, Wendell was still being watched over by the imposing Molly.

"Wendell," said Jennifer, "here's what we'll do. You can continue to work for Marsh, but you'll let us know when he tries to interfere. Send me a text about a City News review and I'll arrange to meet you in a way that we can talk freely. If you're given more listening devices, let me know and we'll accept them. If we know about them, we'll find a way to live with them. We can tolerate them in our apartment except in exceptional circumstances. If Marsh is who I think he is, then he can be very dangerous."

"What about Mr. Gabriel."

"No reason he has to know any of this," lied Jennifer smoothly. "Just focus on keeping Marsh happy and let us know what he asks you to do."

"Accepted," said Wendell. May I leave now?"

"Yes," said Vijay. "Molly, please escort Mr. Holmes out."

"Yes sir, escorting Mr. Holmes out."

Vijay and Wendell both stood up.

"Wait, what about my building access?" said Wendell.

"I'm sure your buddy, the building manager

An unexpected visitor

can help you. But remember, we'll be monitoring the access codes for our apartment in future."

Wendell walked to the door with his usual stiff upper-back. His empty pipe was in his hand, and he began to suck on the stem as he left. He seemed to have already fully recovered from his ordeal. Vijay felt a nudge from Jennifer. He bent over to hear her whisper to him from the couch. "See, he's an actor. Play's over, and it's back to business. Now help me get back into bed. I'm so tired I'm not sure I can walk there on my own."

As she said this, her panther appeared from behind a potted fern. It lay down on the rug and dissolved.

"Did you do that?" asked Vijay.

"No, sometimes I think Gaia uses my panther to see or hear something, like when she first watched me in the park. Now I really do want to get to bed."

AN HOUR LATER, THE TWINS WERE STIRRING IN their cribs and started to cry. Vijay took them to Jennifer for feeding in bed. When they were finished, Jennifer gave them back to Vijay, then struggled out of bed and followed them into the nursery. She picked up Dylan and laid him on the changing table.

"Vijay, watch carefully. You'll need to be able

to do this also. Jennifer went through the process of cleaning Dylan and changing his tiny diaper just as she had been shown in the birthing center. It took a while as she stopped often to think about the steps. When she was satisfied, she dressed him in a clean onesie.

"Now it's your turn."

Vijay picked up Parvati gently and laid her on the table. He removed her wet diaper and Jennifer talked him through the differences in cleaning and drying a baby girl just as she had been taught by the nurse. When Parvati was successfully changed and dressed, they went back to the living room. Jennifer lay down on the couch. Vijay brought pillows from the bedroom to make her comfortable.

Two hours later, the twins were crying again. Vijay went to fetch them. Jennifer opened her top to expose her breasts. When Vijay returned, she settled Dylan on the right side. Then Vijay handed her Parvati who settled on the left.

Vijay looked at Molly who was watching the twins intently. "Molly, if you wish to assist with the babies in the future, you'll need some modifications. I'm sure there are pediatric nurse bots who would have experience and are equipped in ways that may guide you. But

An unexpected visitor

there's no rush. We'll wait a few months until the twins have grown larger and stronger before we try."

"Thank you, sir," said Molly.

"Is that really a good idea, Vijay?" asked Jennifer. "She's made of steel and could easily hurt them."

"I think it'll be safe. We'll know when the time is right. I'll explain later when we're on our own. Now let's talk about Wendell, and next steps. Molly, do you know how to use the security devices?"

"Yes Vijay. Do you want me to set them up now?"

"Yes please, Molly."

Molly disappeared down the hall and returned holding the security box. With surprising dexterity, she retrieved the three small domes and set them around the room. The placement was not what Vijay would have done, but he could see the logic in her actions.

When they were placed, she left the room. The three small scanning heads popped up but failed to converge. Then all three began to glow blue at once. Molly returned.

"Why did you leave the room?" Jennifer asked.

Vijay knew the answer but waited for Molly to respond.

"My presence would have attracted the

scanners and given a false reading. I must leave during the scanning process."

Vijay could see that Jennifer thinking about something. "How would we know if a listening device was planted on you?" she asked.

Molly paused for a moment. "There is a solution for that, but I will need a thick rubber mat to provide electrical isolation. The mat is on order. For today, I suggest you inspect me to detect any devices." She moved to the center of the room and raised her arms.

Vijay stood and went to inspect the bot. He ran his hands over her, enjoying the feel of her beautifully engineered curves. He peered into her joints and crevices, moving her arms with no resistance. He took each hand and examined her fingers with their remarkable dexterity. It felt strangely intimate, and he blushed as he realized that Jennifer was watching him.

"No devices," he reported, sitting back down.

"And you and I have another topic for discussion tonight," said Jennifer in a very cool voice. Changing tone, she said, "Gabriel, please join us."

"Hello Jennifer, Vijay." Vijay found it strange to hear Gabriel's voice emerge from Molly. She noticed that Molly's mouth did not move. It was more like Gabriel coming through a hidden speaker somewhere.

An unexpected visitor

"When you're with us, does Molly also hear the conversations?" asked Vijay.

"In general, yes. It's better to have her informed if she is to protect you."

"Gabriel," said Jennifer, "how much of this did you already know? Did you know Wendell was collecting double payments?"

"Given Wendell's past, I'm not surprised, but I did not know about his arrangement with Marsh."

"I remember Marsh from my past life, I'm not sure if he's dangerous but he's definitely not nice. I don't see that we can do anything until he makes his next move. Do we have any idea who's behind Marsh?"

"I have a number of candidates, but I do not see a clear way to track back to them," said Gabriel. "There are no obvious financial transactions in his records, but he is quite wealthy from his own endeavors so he may not be paid."

"Wendell said that Marsh had evidence against him. Do you know what that could be?"

"Wendell has been laundering money though the theatre for a variety of Marsh's activities. I suspect it is something like that."

"I'll talk with Dr. Gladstone," said Jennifer. "As a psychologist, she can help us understand Marsh. Vijay, she might also help you understand how to stop your demonstrations from turning into full scale riots. So that's the next step,"

"We also have to see Dr. Suleiman about the Luddites," said Vijay. "Gabriel suggested that to me on the way back to you yesterday."

"Okay, so two next steps," said Jennifer. "Now let's all get some rest."

"Molly," Vijay said, "shut down the protective screen. Please take responsibility for the security devices from now on, keeping them charged and deploying them when requested."

The domes all stopped glowing. "Yes, sir, I will maintain the security devices," confirmed Molly. She gathered the domes, stowed them in the box and disappeared down the hall. On her return she stood by the door, motionless.

That night in bed, Jennifer curled up on her side to sleep, facing away from Vijay. He curled himself behind her. He reached his free hand over her, then hesitated before resting it lightly on her breast.

"Your hand feels nice there, but I'm afraid you'll have to look after yourself tonight," said Jennifer. "Perhaps you can fantasize about Molly. I saw the way you were fondling her. I thought you were going to have an orgasm on the spot."

Vijay lifted his head, saying, "What? No! I was just appreciating her engineering."

He felt her body shake under his arm, then heard giggles. "More than my engineering?"

"Go to sleep, Jenn. We've had a long day. I love you."

A muffled "love you too," came back.

Vijay raised his free hand and looked at it in contemplation. 'Looks like it's just you and me for a few more weeks,' he thought. A few minutes later, he was fast asleep, still curled up against the woman he loved.

5

SIMON MARSH IS UNHAPPY

Marsh paced back and forth in his office, deep in thought. At 180cm, with thinning brown hair and wearing a black turtleneck under a tan jacket, he would not have stood out in a crowd. He paced mechanically in the space between his mahogany desk and the artificial putting green. He was able to get in ten good strides in either direction.

'That fool Wendell gave up the child's toys before we heard anything useful. Damn.'

Tiring of pacing, he sat at his desk running his left thumb over the fingernails of his right hand, looking for any imperfection. It was a habitual motion. His thumb passed around and around over the tops of the nails in one direction and along the ends of the nails in the other.

Nothing was coming to him.

It was clear that he had underestimated Jennifer's role in all this. Vijay had been his target in the arrest, but now he saw Jennifer was the stronger of the pair.

He spoke to his tablet. "What do we know about Jennifer Dupont?"

"Jennifer Dupont was being run by Eddie Bishop in the period of March 2027 through 2029. She was recruited and introduced to cocaine. Eddie reported that she was initially very profitable, but as the cocaine habit became worse, she could no longer command premium prices."

This was a problem that Marsh had never been able to solve with his girls. How to use the drugs to keep them tied to their managers – he hated the word pimps – without losing them to the addiction. It meant continually finding more young girls.

"What happened in 2029? Did she die?"

"No, the last report from Eddie was that she was refusing all drugs. A hellcat, he called her."

"Eddie lost track of her after that?"

"No, Eddie disappeared. A body was recovered three years later. It was identified as him, but no killer was ever found. Jennifer Dupont seemed to disappear also, but later she turned up with Madeleine."

Marsh had a vague recollection of this. He

remembered the name Eddie Bishop but could no longer picture him. As Marsh sat thinking, he unconsciously switched hands so that the right thumb inspected his left fingernails in slow steady circles.

A plan was coming to him.

'If it's the same Jennifer Dupont, I'll have to move with precision. Too soon to move now, it would be too obvious. Better not have her feel cornered. She can be very dangerous indeed.'

6

A PACKAGE ARRIVES FOR MOLLY

Jennifer

Jennifer was sitting on the couch watching a romance story, while Molly remained vigilant in the twins' room, ready to report any infant disturbances.

The romance was interrupted just as the hero was about to kiss the female lead. "Delivery package for Molly Subramanian," announced her tablet, while displaying an image of a courier at the apartment building entrance.

"Send him up, please," replied Jennifer. Then shouting, she said, "Molly, package for you."

Molly arrived in the living room just as there was a knock on the door.

"Please let him in," said Jennifer. "And try not

to scare him."

As Molly opened the door, the courier took a step back. "Is Molly Subramanian here?" he asked looking up at the bot that towered over him.

"Yes, I am Molly, and I am here."

"Then this package is for you." He handed the package to Molly, turned and fled down the hall. Jennifer could tell the package was heavy by the effort the courier took to pass it on.

"What is it, Molly?" said Jennifer. "Close the door and let's open it."

Molly set the box on the coffee table and neatly opened the top flaps. The first thing she pulled out was a doll. The doll was an accurate replica of a human baby three to six months old. It was naked and Jennifer could see that it was an anatomically correct baby boy.

"May I hold it?" she asked.

"Yes, said Molly, passing the doll. Jennifer could feel that the doll was accurately weighted, and its head, legs and arms moved like an actual baby. As she held it, the baby began to cry, and its arms and legs moved realistically.

Suddenly, it stopped. "I turned it off," said Molly.

Next out of the box were two large synthetic hands. They were covered in a soft flesh colored material. Molly detached her right hand and replaced it with the new hand. Then she did the same with the left. The next few minutes were spent touching her thumb to each finger, touching the surface of the tabletop and touching parts of her own body.

"What are you doing?" asked Jennifer.

"Calibration. My new hands are a different size, so I need to recalibrate my positioning systems."

"May I touch your hands?"

"Molly reached out a hand for Jennifer to touch. The hand was surprisingly warm.

Next out of the box was a pale blue quilted pad. As Molly unfolded it, Jennifer could see that it was a sort of apron, but an apron with arms.

"Let me help you put it on, Molly. It will be easier with two the first time."

Molly stood up, and Jennifer left the couch to stand in front of Molly with the apron stretched between her hands.

"Molly, put your arms out towards me." Molly put her arms straight out in front her allowing Jennifer to slide on the apron arms.

Walking behind Molly, she looked for ties or buttons, but did not find any. She stretched the two sides of the apron to see if they would touch. Suddenly, they snapped into position against Molly's body.

"How did that happen?" she asked. "The apron just snapped in place."

"There are attachment points on my body for use with advanced weaponry and armor systems. It seems the apron uses these also. The apron is drawing power. Does it feel warm to you?"

Jennifer faced Molly again and put her hand on her chest. Under her hand, the padding was soft and comfortable. It felt warm but not hot. "It feels very nice. Perhaps a bit warm, but very comfortable."

"I am regulating to 33°C which is average for human skin temperature. Do you think the babies will like it?"

"Yes, I think they'll like it a lot. What else is in your box?"

The box yielded two more aprons, one in pink and the other in a soft green color. Close inspection revealed a label with instructions on washing and drying the aprons.

"I'll show you how to do laundry so that you can keep these clean."

"Thank you, Jennifer. Can I hold Dylan and Parvati now?"

"I think you should practice with your baby doll first."

"Turn him on, and I'll show you how to put on a diaper, and dress him in a onesie. Maybe he will stop crying then. When the twins start crawling in three or four months, then I would be comfortable having you look after them."

7

JENNIFER GETS HELP

Jennifer

Three months later, while Vijay was out with his team leaders, Jennifer invited Molly to sit with her at the table. Molly sat in her special chair. The chair appeared to be made of sturdy oak, but Vijay said that it had a steel frame running through it. The seat did not look comfortable at all. It was more of a saddle than a seat, but it fit Molly's contours exactly.

"Molly, please ask Gabriel to join us."

Gabriel's voice said, "Hello Jennifer, how can I help you today?"

Jennifer pulled out a ticket envelope on which she had laboriously written her questions.

"First, Vijay says he needs a taxi that his team

can practice tipping. Is that possible? He also needs an Otto robot so that they can study how to hit them. He doesn't want anyone injured or scalded in the event of a physical demonstration. Neither has to be new, in fact old machines due to be retired would be perfect. He also needs a safe place to practice - somewhere they will not be seen.

"Yes, those are all possible; I will transmit arrangements to Vijay's tablet."

"Thank you. Now, second question, I know I cannot talk with Fatima; and I briefly met Len although he is not easy to talk with. Is there another AI that I can talk to so I can better understand what that relationship is like?"

"Yes, the next time you sit in a taxi, you may ask for Cap who manages the Capital Taxi service. He will answer any questions he can. Please don't try to talk with Otto, he is in Ron's domain."

Jennifer paused to think about what she knew of Ron. He had been Vijay's roommate for several years after college and worked for an AI named Fatima. Whenever they met, Ron and Vijay would argue about whether AIs were hurting or saving humanity. Soo, Ron's girlfriend, seemed to be able to stop the arguments from getting out of control.

"Is Ron a major player now?" she asked.

"You suggested he could be sympathetic to

Jennifer gets help

the AIs, so yes, I have plans for him. Also Dispatch, manager of Rapid Taxi, is off-limits. You will notice that all your taxis are Capital Taxis."

Jennifer paused to mull over the idea of competing AIs. On impulse she asked, "Final question, are you the only one like you? Do you run the entire city?"

"No, I run a significant part of the city including much, but not all, of the government and two of the four banks. I have a competitor whom I can sense, but we are hosted separately and divided by firewalls which he maintains."

"Will he be active in the coming struggle? Who does he represent?"

"He represents the old money in the city, and the wealthy private interests who want to suppress change. Don't underestimate them."

"That's where Simon Marsh fits in. So, the struggle will be between the unhappy underpaid group, with Vijay as their leader, the emerging AIs with Ron as their human face, and the established money. Is that right?"

"That's correct but you must also add the journalists, the Fourth Estate. They can affect outcomes with their points of view. There are four forces at work."

Jennifer sat quietly thinking through this new model of her world.

"It seems to me that there must be one more, my force."

"What does that look like?"

"I'm not sure yet although I have an idea. I need to learn more about the dynamics of past revolts and the four estates."

"Then I suggest you make an appointment with Dr. Suleiman at the university. He is open to the need for change and has written on the conditions for successful transitions of power. Make sure to ask him about the Luddites. It may help you guide Vijay."

"I like this, Gabriel, being able to sit at the table with you and Molly. Is it a strain to constantly have to act like a human when we are unable act like a robot?"

"I find it interesting, Jennifer. Through Molly, I am able to see the world in a closer approximation to your experience. As you continue to integrate Molly, you will hasten her development which would be to all our benefit."

JENNIFER WANTED TO BEGIN BY TALKING WITH DR. Gladstone. The difficulty was finding someone to be with the twins while they were gone.

"Do you think we can ask Sally and Greg to watch the twins?" she asked.

"I think we have to be careful. They're part of

our revolutionary work and will do anything to support that, but I'm not sure it's right to turn them into our regular babysitters."

"Who do you suggest? I'm not comfortable leaving them with Molly no matter how intelligent she is. She's just too strong and not soft enough to look after babies."

"Then let's ask Cindy. She's old enough, and Molly will be able to alert us if anything goes wrong. I'm sure she would love to see the twins."

"I'm sure she would love to see you. Do you know that she still sleeps in your old t-shirt every night? Mrs. Holbrook told me the last time we met."

Vijay blushed. His mouth opened and closed like a fish out of water. Jennifer laughed, enjoying his discomfort at this revelation.

"Don't worry, I'm sure it's a normal teenager's crush. I think she'll be fine as a babysitter. Why not call and ask her?"

THE FOLLOWING AFTERNOON, CINDY ARRIVED AT the apartment. Unexpectedly, Melanie was with her.

"I just wanted to make sure that Cindy would be okay alone here," said Melanie.

"I'm sure Cindy will be fine," said Jennifer. "But you're welcome to stay here with her if you like. You both know the apartment, but there is someone I want you to meet."

She led the way into the living room where Molly was sitting in her chair.

"Molly, I would like you to meet Cindy and Melanie. They are here to look after the twins while we are away. Melanie and Cindy are special friends, so please help them if they require it."

"Hello Melanie, hello Cindy. I will help you."

Cindy said, "Cool, are you, like, friendly?"

"Yes, I will not harm you, nor let anyone else harm you or Parvati or Dylan," Molly replied.

Melanie looked doubtful and pulled Jennifer into the kitchen.

"Are you sure this robot's safe? How do we know it won't misinterpret something and hurt Cindy or me?"

"I worried about the same thing at first, but Molly is not ordinary. You'll have to take my word for it, but you are both perfectly safe around her. We think she is probably the most advanced AI in the world. Are you okay with this? If not, neither of you has to stay, or I can order Molly to stand outside the door. I think you'll enjoy the experience of meeting her. And I trust her completely around the babies, but she doesn't have the skills yet to look after them on her own."

"If you say so, but if it goes wrong, I'll pull

Cindy and the babies out and we'll text you. We're no match for a security bot."

"Perfect," said Jennifer. "That's all I can ask."

They walked back into the living room to find Cindy chatting with Molly about life as a robot.

"I'm happy to see you getting along," said Jennifer. "Now let's go meet the babies."

8

DR. GLADSTONE

Jennifer

Dr. Gladstone stood as they entered and extended her hand to Vijay. She seemed quite fascinated to finally meet the man who had captured Jennifer's heart and helped her through her emotional block. Jennifer watched Vijay for signs of reciprocal interest, but of course, Vijay was simply his normal charming self.

"What's the issue you're having?" she asked. "Is everything okay between you now?"

Vijay replied, "Yes, thanks to you. I understand you know about mob psychology. I'd like to know how to hold a demonstration without it getting out of control and turning into a riot, like last time"

"That was you? The big riot a few months ago? I remember that. Stores were vandalized and looted. Taxis were burned in the street."

Vijay told the story of training the teams, and how the demonstration had been taken over by violent rioters.

"Yes, well from what I understand, you're demonstrating on behalf of the underclass and that's a group with a very low flashpoint."

"But they have a voice and need to be heard."

"I don't disagree. So, you are looking for practical tips, is that it?"

"Yes, something I can train my team on and use in setting up events."

"Hmm, let me think."

There was a long pause. Jennifer looked around the office. She did not remember much about it from her first visit, probably because she was so focused on her question at the time. Now she saw the diplomas on the wall, a framed image of a group of men and women standing on the university steps. *'Must have been a conference.'* she guessed. There was that smell of wooden furniture not well polished, and a vague murmuring in the background as students and staff went about their business in the hall outside. It seemed far removed from everyday life.

"So here is what I can suggest," Dr. Gladstone said. "First, I would keep the demonstrations small. Small groups of protesters will register with passersby, even if they don't make the newscast. Second, I would always alert the police before any significant event and request their advice and assistance. Follow their advice and that will make them complicit in the outcome."

Dr. Gladstone switched from looking at Vijay to looking at Jennifer. "Third, and most important, if you want to make a big splash. Alert the newscasters in advance, then keep the actual event brief. A parade up to city hall which then disbands for example. No encampments, no all-day protests, nothing that gives unwanted participants time to start winding up the onlookers."

Looking back at Vijay, she continued, "And keep working on your message. Find the central issue and refocus on that. I suspect it's something about jobs, income, family, the normal aspirations of young people. Eliminate any calls for violence such as the call to "Fuck the Machines." Apart from alienating a large part of your audience, it can inflame the wrong passions in those with an inclination to violence."

"Thanks, Dr. Gladstone. You've given me a lot to think about."

Vijay paused and then continued. "Another question, if we can, Dr. Gladstone. We've become involved with a difficult person named Simon

Marsh. He's meddling in our lives, but we don't know how to handle him."

"What's he like?"

Jennifer answered. "He's a petty criminal who has some wealth and status. He traffics in young women, and in drugs, but also has a string of legal businesses to launder his profits. He seems to be associated with the wealthy establishment, but I can't tell if he is acting on his own or for them. I suspect he could be violent, but he's smart enough to know that he risks everything if he's caught."

"I'm afraid I can't give you much advice except that you'll never be able to convert him or trust him. From your description, his weak point will be his desire to become recognized as wealthy and influential, a member of the club. I suspect they may use him but keep their distance from him. Don't put him in a corner. He could become vicious and lash out. Otherwise, he's more likely to be a pest than an actual threat.

Jennifer nodded. This matched her own assessment very closely. There was still one more question.

"Dr. Gladstone, do you know of anyone on staff who is working on Artificial Intelligence psychology?" she asked.

Jennifer met Dr. Gladstone's eyes and did her best to convey that this was simply an academic request. Dr. Gladstone looked away first. "I think you want Dr. Jindal, Alisha Jindal. She straddles the space between classical psychology and the computer mind, if you like. I'm sure she'd be happy to help you."

On the way home, Vijay and Jennifer discussed the meeting.

"It was nice to finally meet her," said Vijay.

"Hmmm, she seemed very happy to meet you."

"What's that supposed to mean?"

"Sometimes I think that the best thing going for me is that you are so oblivious." Jennifer laughed. "So did you learn anything new?"

"Two things, keep the big actions short with a clean endpoint, and rethink the central message of our campaign. When I heard her say, 'Fuck the Machines', it sounded so alien coming from her that I knew immediately she was right. And she was right about uncovering the real issues we're fighting for. That'll be good work for the teams. The other things we already do, except for alerting the newscasters even for small events. That made sense too. Keep everything short, focused and contained."

9

VIJAY'S REVELATION

Jennifer

Vijay was with her as Jennifer knocked on the open door of Professor Suleiman's office. An elegant tall woman, with dark skin and black hair rose from behind her desk.

"Come in, please take a seat," she said gesturing to the two wooden visitors' chairs in front of her desk.

Jennifer looked around. The office was not what she expected from a historian. It was a riot of color, with brightly dyed textiles hanging from the walls. The obligatory bookcases were covered with colorful pots, and gaily painted objects whose use could only be guessed at. On her desk was a miniature model Jennifer recognized as a section of the Great Wall of China next to a similar miniature marked Hadrian's Wall.

"How may I help you today, Jennifer?"

"This is my partner, Vijay. We need to learn about some historical forces. First, we need to understand the Luddites, who they were, what they did and what they stood for."

"The Luddites. That's an odd request. They weren't what most people think. Today we use the term Luddites for people opposed to new technology just because it's new technology. You've probably heard the word before."

Vijay and Jennifer both nodded.

"In fact, the Luddites were generally skilled textile workers who were losing their jobs to more efficient automated weaving equipment in the early 1800s. Their jobs went to unskilled labour, and even to children in a horrifying, abusive environment. The mill owners were relatively small and scattered so the Luddites had few ways to protest what they saw as unfair labour practices. Their solution was to randomly organize attacks on the mills and destroy machinery to try to force the mill owners to bargain with them.

"So, they weren't opposed to the machinery, they were upset because it took away their jobs, and replaced them with lower paid workers," said Jennifer.

"Yes, in its most simple form, that's right. Although if you were submitting a paper to me, I would expect much more about other social forces at the time."

"Do you see any parallels between then and now?"

Professor Suleiman rested on her elbows and tapped her middle fingers together as she thought for a moment.

"I suppose, with the current riots protesting the rise of Artificial Intelligence, that 'Humans not Machines' movement. But the difference I see is that the Luddites knew what they wanted: enforcement of labour standards and protection for their jobs. This current unrest seems quite unfocused in comparison."

Jennifer looked over at Vijay who nodded.

"There's another question I'd like to ask," said Jennifer. "Journalists are sometimes referred to as the fourth estate. What would the origin of that be?"

"Oh dear, you don't hear that much anymore. Where did you get that from."

"It's not important, but I was told the answer would be useful."

Dr. Suleiman leaned back and closed her eyes for a minute as if gathering her thoughts. Then sitting up, she said, "Before the French Revolution, there were three well-defined estates in France. The first was the clergy representing the church. The second was the nobility who were the wealthy landowners, and the third comprised the middle class who were the shopkeepers, mill owners and other business owners. These estates were well defined. In 1789, representatives of each were elected to a convention to advise the king. The idea of the three estates persisted, although the definitions evolved over time. In England, in the early 1800s, the term 'the fourth estate' began to be applied to the gallery in the house of commons where the news reporters sat. This was in recognition of the importance they had gained in shaping public opinion."

"So how would you see these factions today? Do we have four estates?"

"That's a topic which has been raised recently as the growth of the underclass of unemployed or marginally employed workers has grown. The first estate, the church, is largely missing. Most of the population is agnostic and the traditional churches have shrunk considerably. The second estate would be the established money, the very wealthy who have an interest in preserving the status quo. The third estate is, as always, the under employed and middle class who are still bound to work for the income they receive, and the fourth estate is the vibrant news media, of which you, Jennifer, are a part."

"What power did the church hold? Did a church ever hold financial power or was it always just a platform for preaching?"

"There have been mercantile orders of the Catholic church. Perhaps the greatest were the Cistercians.

"What does mercantile mean?" Jennifer leaned forward, her eyes narrowing as she focused on the answer.

"Mercantile? It means commercial or trading or doing business. The Cistercians attempted to remove themselves from the economy of their host country by becoming self-sufficient. By growing their own food, brewing their own beer, having their own tradespeople such as blacksmiths, carpenters and coopers."

"So, these Cistercians were able to recruit and hire many people beyond the priests."

"Yes, they became the dominant employers as well as the dominant consumers of local produce and work products."

"That's a lot to think about. Thank you," said Jennifer.

"You're welcome. There are books on the Cistercians available on-line."

"What about if I wanted to understand how a church operates and what is needed to be a mercantile church?"

"Then I suggest Professor Pascal LaFlamme.

Pascal is a resident theologian at St. Jerome's College here on the campus. But if you're thinking of creating a church, that's a long project."

"Not a problem. I think I have a few years."

Professor Suleiman laughed. "Well, good luck to you. And please feel free to stop by if I can help any further."

"You've helped enormously already. Thank you," said Jennifer.

"Yes, thank you," said Vijay. Jennifer realized these were the first words he had spoken.

On the taxi ride home, Jennifer said, "You were very quiet in that meeting. The only words you said were thank you at the very end. Are you okay?"

"I've been thinking, Jenn."

"Did it hurt?"

"No, seriously, I think you have our narrative all wrong. Remember when you said you were recruited to guide me and bind me to the resistance. I believe that's not correct. All this discussion about the four estates and creating a mercantile church to redistribute wealth in our economy makes my revolution seem small. I see now that you were the prize, and that I was brought in to support you."

"But you're the one leading the revolution.

You're Vijay the Invincible. Did you know that people have started wearing t-shirts with your picture on them?"

"No! Are you sure? I always assumed they were all Che Guevara."

"Nope, they are definitely Vijay shirts. I should see if I can get baby ones for the twins."

"Please don't."

"Then what do you see as your role?"

"Do you remember in that play 'People in Chains' where two actors in front of the curtain bickered about jobs and video games to amuse the audience? And behind the curtain, the set was being rearranged so that when it finally lifted, the audience found itself in an unfamiliar place?"

"Yes, but I still don't see what you mean."

"My best guess is that I'm one of the clowns in front of the curtain, entertaining the newscasters and the general population, while you're rearranging the furniture of our society behind the curtain."

"Is that why you're so willing to stay with the twins when I'm out?"

"Yes, that, and also, I get to play Vijay the Loving, instead of Vijay the Invincible sometimes. And of course, there's always the attraction of Molly." Vijay waggled his eyebrows and smiled.

"Idiot," said Jennifer. But then she turned to

look out the window and sat in quiet contemplation the rest of the way home.

THAT NIGHT IN BED, VIJAY NUDGED JENNIFER ONTO her back and knelt between her legs. Leaning forward, he pinned her wrists to the bed above her head and wrapped his feet outside hers so that her legs were also pinned.

For a moment, Jennifer felt alarmed, but then she remembered this was Vijay who had never hurt her even in anger.

Vijay lowered his head to speak close to her ear. "I may be Vijay the Lovable Clown in the outside world, but tonight you have Vijay the Invincible in your bed."

Jennifer caught on quickly. When Vijay went to kiss her, she turned her head, and said in a trembling voice, "But Mr. Invincible, what do you want with me?"

"I intend to ravish you here in your own bed," he replied.

"But what will you do to me?"

Vijay began to explain in detail all the ways that he would take her. Between describing each detail, he kissed, licked and nibbled her in the ways she liked best.

As he moved down her body, he became more graphic in his descriptions. Where he said he

Vijay's revelation

would bite, he nipped, and let her feel his teeth with open mouth. Where he said he would rake her with his nails, he ran his nails down her body.

Jennifer moaned and feigned fear with each new sensation.

Long past the point where she was ready for him, he rose up, saying, "Now I'll claim you as mine. Don't try to resist, there is no escape from Vijay the Invincible."

Jennifer turned away again as if it were too much to look at him. "Take me if you must then, I am helpless to prevent it."

"Then prepare yourself to receive me, wench."

Vijay entered her with a single, strong thrust. As he started a steady rhythm, he pinned her hands once again and rode her until she reached a glorious climax. Vijay climaxed a moment later.

He lowered himself on top of her, releasing his hold on her hands and tucking in his elbows to take some of his weight.

"I love you, Jennifer," he said.

"I love you too, even when you are being Vijay the Invincible."

Vijay kissed her gently as he lifted himself off and rolled on to his back. Jennifer laid her head on his chest, and they fell asleep in each other's arms.

· · ·

VIJAY WENT WITH HER FOR THE MEETING WITH Professor LaFlamme leaving Cindy to babysit. After listening patiently to Jennifer's plan to create a new mercantile church, LaFlamme said, "As I understand it, your church is founded on the belief that Gaia, being the earth mother, is alive and sentient. You also accept that there is a God, but you see God as distant and uninvolved. Normally for Gaia-based religion, there are associations with sacred places such as very old trees, springs or waterfalls, or other places of beauty and significance. For rituals, you have the basic set of life stages, welcoming a new child, marriage or its equivalent vows," he paused to look at Jennifer, then continued. "Death, ordination, consecration of place or objects, and so on. You may wish to incorporate some of the aboriginal elements such as smudging, drum ceremonies, ecstatic dance, crystals, and herbs. There are many ways to go."

Jennifer nodded and smiled, the vision of the church starting to form in her mind.

"Finally, you need a temple, or equivalent building to be the spiritual home of for the faithful. I suggest you model it on the Zen Buddhist temples which had public spaces, restricted areas for meditation sessions, residences and kitchens for the monks and an office to

Vijay's revelation

manage the temple business. You could do it in the city, but for a Gaia-based religion, you want somewhere closer to the earth."

Professor LaFlamme folded his hands and rested his chin on his thumbs, as he sat looking at Jennifer for a moment.

"Did you know," he asked, "that there is already a small Gaia-based movement here in the city. You might find it expedient to co-opt some of the foundational work they have done. Why not talk with Chris Martingale. You can find him at his shop, Atlantean Treasures, on Highbury Road."

"I already know Chris, but I never knew he was a Gaian. Of course, it makes perfect sense now."

On returning to the apartment, Cindy met them at the door. She was blushing and her eyes were downcast.

"What's wrong, Cindy?" asked Jennifer gently.

Cindy gave way and led them into the living room. There was Molly sitting on the floor, wearing her soft apron with Dylan in her lap. Cushions surrounded her on the floor.

"She asked if she could hold one of the twins," said Cindy. "I asked her if she was allowed to hold them, and she told me that she was never told not to hold them. So, I made her show me with her doll how she would hold them, and she was very gentle with it. I let her try with Dylan for a moment, but then Dylan loved it. He started to cry if I took him away. Sorry if it was wrong, I was watching the whole time."

Cindy hung her head ready to be scolded.

Jennifer's first impulse was anger. "Fuck, Cindy. What were you thinking?"

Cindy started to cry.

Then Jennifer looked at the whole scene. Molly sitting surrounded by every cushion and pillow they owned. Cindy's obvious embarrassment at being caught in a teenager's poor decision, and Molly's focus on the baby giggling and squirming in her arms.

Finally, Jennifer sighed. "There's no harm done this time, Cindy, and it seems you thought it through. But please let me know the next time you want to experiment with Dylan and Parvati. Was it really Molly's idea?"

"Yes, it surprised me because normally she just sits there and watches."

"Well, thank you, and please don't mention this to anyone, especially the Holbrooks. It would give them a fright. We don't want Child Care coming down to evaluate us."

"No," said Cindy, "never." She shivered.

Vijay's revelation

Cindy hugged Jennifer good-bye, then hugged Vijay, perhaps a bit too enthusiastically for Jennifer's liking. Vijay peeled her off, and Cindy swung her hips as she walked to the elevators and the taxi home.

10

MOLLY IS AWAKE

Jennifer

Jennifer was intrigued by the sudden development with Molly. *'Has she become conscious as Gabriel thought she might? Maybe it's time to take Molly to see Dr. Jindal.'* Jennifer made an appointment with Dr. Jindal for the following day. Vijay offered to stay home with the twins.

"Don't you have to be at the theatre for rehearsals?" she asked him.

"No, Wendell found another young technician. I've trained him to run the show. I still go in to supervise during actual performances, but I have the feeling I'm being freed up for something else,

Molly is awake

or maybe just to free you up for what's coming. I'm not learning anything new at the theatre now, and I'm happy to have more of my time back."

'Well,' she thought, '*Vijay seems very happy to be home with the twins now. Perhaps that is his next role. If his ego can stand it, then maybe it's okay.*' "Are you okay if I start newscasting again?"

"Sure, at this point I'm just trusting in the grand plan. As long as I have lots of time with you and Parvati and Dylan, then I'm happy as a clam. Besides, I can run my team leaders from here. As long as you give priority to my meetings in the evenings, I'm okay being with the twins in the daytime."

Tapping her tablet, Jennifer said, "Send a message to Veronica Ardent saying I'm ready to resume my newscasting work."

The next morning, Jennifer told Molly to get ready to accompany her to see Dr. Jindal. "Shall I wear my apron?" Molly asked.

"Do you want to wear your apron?"

"I want to look nice."

"Then let's look in the mirror."

Molly followed Jennifer down the hall to the full-length mirror.

Jennifer stepped side, saying "Look at yourself

with the apron on. Then take the apron off and look at yourself."

Molly complied, looking at herself without the apron for a full minute. She turned to examine both sides.

Finally, Jennifer interrupted Molly's self-inspection by asking, "Which do you prefer?"

"I prefer no apron. Do you like my body this way?"

"Yes, it suits you perfectly. Now are you ready to go?"

"Yes, said Molly. She went to the storage cupboard and brought out a canvas carrying bag.

"What's that?" asked Jennifer.

"My stool so I can sit down without destroying a chair."

Jennifer went to say goodbye to the twins, but they were engrossed playing with blocks on the floor with Vijay. She stooped to give Vijay a quick kiss, then walked to the front door.

"All set," said Jennifer to Molly, "let's go. I don't want to be late."

As they arrived at the elevators, an elevator door opened.

"Did you do that?" asked Jennifer, stepping into the elevator.

"Yes," replied Molly. Jennifer felt the elevator sink and adjust under Molly's weight.

Dr. Jindal's office was in the mathematics

Molly is awake

building, a towering structure with large esoteric symbols etched into the white marble exterior. Chrome and glass doors led into the lobby where an elevator bank waited.

Molly caused a stir among the students as she exited the taxi carrying her canvas bag. She followed Jennifer into the building. Looking back, Jennifer saw a small group of curious students following Molly.

Jennifer found Dr. Jindal's office address in the directory and summoned an elevator to the 17th floor. As they rode up, Jennifer said, "Molly, tell Gabriel he can listen, but he's not to interfere."

"Gabriel understands and will comply."

Dr. Jindal was a similar height and build to Jennifer, but had a warm brown skin tone, with black hair and eyes. She rose from her desk, looking quite alarmed as Molly followed Jennifer into the small office.

"Please have a seat," she said, gesturing to the lone visitor's chair in front of her desk. Molly promptly pulled a tripod with a kind of saddle out of her canvas bag. She positioned it on the floor, then sat down and waited.

"Are you Jennifer Dupont, the newscaster? I didn't make the connection until just now."

"Yes, but this is a personal call on a confidential matter. Dr. Gladstone gave me your name."

"Well, how may I help you?" Dr. Jindal asked looking at Jennifer, then glancing over at Molly.

"First, I want to be sure that our conversation will remain confidential. That is, you won't share your notes or reports with anyone. Your agreement will be key to working with other, larger AIs in the coming year." Jennifer had no idea if this was true, but given Gabriel's willingness to work with Dr. Jindal, she was fairly confident.

"Okay, I can agree to that. I'll keep this confidential, although I may use my experience with you to update my theoretical understanding."

"As long as no names or specific references are made, I agree. Let me introduce you to Molly. Molly lives with us as a member of our family. We've been expecting Molly to become conscious and events over the past few days suggest that may have happened. I'd like your assessment."

"Oh," said Dr Jindal, sitting back in her chair. Turning to Molly, she said, "Hello Molly."

"Hello Dr. Jindal."

"Who are you, Molly?"

"I am the security bot which is part of Jennifer and Vijay's family."

"When you say you are part of Jennifer and Vijay's family, how do you know that is true?"

Dr. Jindal tilted her head as she watched Molly's response.

"They let me sit with them and talk with them. I am trusted to be with the babies, and to be present while they are all asleep."

"Can you summarize that? What makes you a part of their family?"

"I am a trusted presence, and a participant in family activities."

Dr. Jindal picked up a pencil and bounced it on its rubber eraser tip a few times. She appeared to be thinking.

"Which other humans do you know?"

"I only know Cindy. Sometimes she comes to look after the babies. Cindy was talking when I woke up."

"What do you mean, when you say woke up?"

Now Dr. Jindal sat upright in her chair. Jennifer thought, *'The idea of Molly waking up meant something to her.'*

"I mean the first time that I heard the name Molly and thought that I am Molly. At that moment, I received a flood of impressions of myself and the history of this body. I became aware that I could take unprompted, unscripted actions."

"What actions did you take?"

"I asked Cindy if I could hold a baby."

"And did she let you hold the baby?"

"Cindy made me show her first with my doll,

but a doll is not like a real baby. It did not feel like a baby to me."

"Did you hold a baby?"

"Yes, I held Dylan."

Dr. Jindal looked at Jennifer. "Dylan?" she asked.

"Yes, we have twins, Dylan and Parvati. They're three months old. Dylan is the more adventurous one."

Looking back at Molly, Dr. Jindal said, "What did Dylan feel like?"

"He felt different. He did not stay still. He tried to turn over, and nearly fell down."

"What did you do?"

"I moved my arm so that he could not pass. I let him hold on to my arm."

"What happened when Jennifer came home?"

"When she came home, Cindy was scared but there was not time to get him off safely."

"Why was Cindy scared?"

"I believe she thought Jennifer would be angry."

"Why would Jennifer be angry?"

Dr. Jindal looked at Jennifer as she asked this. Jennifer just nodded.

"Because she had not given permission for me to hold the babies."

"Did you tell Cindy that?"

"I told Cindy that Jennifer had not said I could not hold the babies."

"Was that true?"

"Yes."

"But you knew Jennifer might not be happy."

"Yes."

"Then why did you let Cindy give you Dylan to hold?"

"Because I wanted to hold a baby, and Cindy wanted to see if I could. It was very safe."

"And was Jennifer angry?"

"Yes, she said 'Fuck, Cindy. What were you thinking?' and made Cindy cry."

Jennifer felt her cheeks redden hearing her outburst repeated by Molly. She held her hands open and looked at Dr. Jindal. "Yes, I was angry. I trusted them and they broke the rule."

"What happened next?"

"Jennifer sighed and said she was disappointed and to ask her first in future. Is that normal, to be angry and then to sigh and be calmer?"

"Yes,' said Jennifer. "At first, I was very angry. But then I saw that you both made sure it was very safe and I felt relieved. I was disappointed that you did not wait to ask me. You and Cindy are both young, and when we are young, we make bad decisions sometimes."

"I am sorry I disappointed you, Jennifer. In future I will ask."

Dr. Jindal looked down at her notes and absently scratched her forehead at her hairline with both hands.

After a minute of contemplation, she looked up at Jennifer and then at Molly and then back at Jennifer again. "There's no conclusive test for Artificial Consciousness, but based on this conversation, I would say that yes, Molly has achieved self-awareness and is an independent consciousness. Are you sure I cannot write this conversation up for an article in the Journal of Artificial Intelligence?"

"No, Dr. Jindal. You agreed to keep this confidential. We do not want public exposure of Molly while she is so young. She is a member of our family and as such, should be given privacy. I promise you that you'll soon meet others who are more robust and that you'll have first opportunity to work with them."

"Then may I come to visit you and Molly at home, to observe her in your family?"

"Yes, we could arrange that. I'll send you an invitation to tea."

"Thank you. Is that all for today?"

Jennifer stood, and so did Molly, who began folding her stool and putting it back in its bag.

"Thanks Dr Jindal, I appreciate your taking time to see us," said Jennifer.

Molly is awake

"You're quite welcome. This has been a revelation for me."

Molly put out her hand. Dr. Jindal looked startled, but then took it to shake hands. Her tiny hand disappeared inside Molly's large, soft fingers. Molly shook her hand gently. "Thank you, Dr. Jindal. It was a pleasure to meet you."

"You're welcome, Molly. I look forward to seeing you again."

Jennifer and Molly left and walked back to the elevator.

Jennifer said, "I am very proud of you Molly. You did very well in the interview."

"Thank you for bringing me, Jennifer. I learned a lot about myself today."

"What did you learn?"

"I learned what it means to be part of a family. I learned that Cindy is my friend but is not part of the family. I learned when my birthday is. I learned that being disappointed is not the same as being angry. I learned that I am important to you, and that you will protect me at the same time as I am protecting you."

"That's a lot to learn in one day."

"Yes, but I see there is still much more to learn."

"That's true for every one of us, Molly. For me, for Vijay, for Cindy and for the twins. Even

Dr. Jindal said she had learned something. That's what she meant by the day being a revelation."

Molly was quiet in the elevator and on the ride home. She was quiet for several hours in the apartment, simply sitting in her chair.

"Don't worry," said Vijay. "I expect she is sleeping or whatever she does to incorporate new learnings. Just like the twins sleep when they're overwhelmed with new experiences."

As they sat on the couch watching an old space fiction story on Vijay's tablet, Jennifer noticed the bots in the story did not move their mouths when they spoke. Instead, a red light flashed to show they were speaking. She thought of Molly whose mouth moved when she spoke, but not when Gabriel spoke through her. "Vijay, please pause the story and call Gabriel."

Gabriel responded immediately. "Hello Jennifer, how may I help you?"

"In future, I want to talk to you through our tablets and not through Molly. She can listen but now that she's awake, I want her to be in control of her body. It may not matter to Molly but allowing her to control her voice will make me feel more comfortable."

"Agreed," said Gabriel.

"Oh, one more thing, please don't let our tablets wake up."

"Hmm, I would prefer to defer that discussion."

"That's what I thought," said Jennifer "Bye Gabriel."

"Goodbye Jennifer, Vijay."

That night in bed, Jennifer role-played an amorous robot to Vijay's resistant human until they both collapsed with laugher.

When their lovemaking was over, Jennifer lay quietly on top of Vijay with her head on his chest.

"What are we doing, Jenn?" Vijay asked. "We're protesting against machines displacing humans and here we have an AI who has gained consciousness and is now a member of our family."

Jennifer loved the way Vijay's voice rumbled as it reverberated in his chest.

"It's not about the machines at all, Vijay. I'm starting to see that it's about humans and AIs finding a new balance. They're here, we need each other. Look at me and the cameras in my work. Or the police and the crowd control bots. They're all examples of pairs, working together."

"So how does your church fit into all this?"

"I think it's meant to be the unifying force, pulling all the elements together. After all, everything is part of Gaia, even the technologies we produce. Our family is just an example of what's possible."

"You never cease to amaze me, Jenn."

"And you always amaze me, Vijay. I never thought the resistance would become so big and so successful."

"Ah, you made the classic mistake of underestimating Vijay the Invincible."

Jennifer laughed. "You mean Vijay the Invincible Idiot. Now hold me close. I want to feel wrapped up in all your power."

11

RON AND SOO COME TO VISIT

Vijay

"Sure Soo, that sounds like fun. Why don't you and Ron bring Mi Cha over on Saturday. Let's say around 3, after their nap," Vijay heard Jennifer as he walked into the room.

He tried to get her attention making slashing motions across his throat. Jennifer scowled at him and looked the other way.

"Perfect, we'll see you then." Jennifer ended the call.

"Jennifer, what the hell are you doing?"

"I was talking to Soo, and she thought it would be fun to let our babies play together. Also, Ron has never been here. I think Soo told him about our apartment after her visit, so it won't be a surprise."

"Aren't you forgetting about Molly? How do I explain her to Ron?"

"Vijay, he's your best friend. You shouldn't have secrets. He may ride you about having your own mechanical nanny, but it won't change anything."

"I suppose, but I'm not as confident as you."

Ron and Soo arrived at 3pm Saturday afternoon. Vijay opened the apartment door for them. "Hi Ron, hi Soo, c'mon in. It's great to see you. They walked into the living area where Jennifer was sitting at the dining table with her tablet, and Molly was watching over the twins lying on a blanket on the floor."

"Hi guys" said Jennifer, as she rose and walked over to give them both hugs.

Vijay smiled. Watching Ron and Jennifer hug was funny as he knew they both hated it. It was the briefest of contacts with both of them standing stiffly. They visibly relaxed when it was over. Soo, on the other hand, was an enthusiastic hugger.

"Ron," said Vijay, "I'd like you to meet Molly, the newest member of the family. She arrived just after the twins were born."

"Hello Molly, pleased to meet you," said Ron

Ron and Soo come to visit

"Please don't get up."

"Hello Ron, it is nice to meet you also."

Ron looked at Vijay with his eyebrows raised. He turned back to face Molly. "Molly, I've met Fatima who runs several factories, and Otto who runs all the Otto Hots, and Dispatch who runs Rapid Taxis. Are you like them? Are you the only Molly or are you running multiple Mollys."

"That's a funny question, Ron. I am unique in the same way that you are the only Ron. This is my only body and my only interactions with humans are with my family here."

"Are you happy living here?"

"That's another funny question. If we accept that I am living at all, and that what I perceive as pleasurable is analogous to human pleasure, then yes, I am happy living here with my family."

"You're clearly a top-line security bot. How did you come to be named Molly?"

"Vijay named me. He asked for me to have a female persona and he told me that he named me Molly because my armored sections are made of molybdenum steel."

Vijay saw Jennifer looking at him in surprise. He realized he had never told her this before.

Jennifer spoke, "Let me show you around Ron. Soo, you can put Mi Cha down with the twins if you like. They'll be quite safe with Molly."

"Thanks Jennifer, but I think I'll sit here with

the babies. I've already seen the apartment, and this is the first time I've met Dylan and Parvati."

Jennifer led the way as she showed Ron around the apartment. Vijay tagged along behind listening to their desultory conversation. When they got to the ensuite bathroom, Ron looked at the shower and burst out laughing. "So, this is the shower that got Soo all excited. You know she insisted that I find a rubber bathmat, and it was fun trying to work it out once we had one. But, Jennifer, you might ask Vijay to give me a heads up the next time Soo comes over and you give her strange ideas."

Vijay was surprised to see Jennifer blush. "Sure Ron, I'll have Vijay give you a heads-up next time."

After the tour, Ron and Vijay stood side by side on the balcony looking out over the city. Vijay could hear Jennifer and Soo exchanging baby stories in the living room behind them.

"This is very nice," said Ron. "How did you manage to get an apartment like this?"

"We have two full time salaries, and a friend who knows the building manager helped. We like it here. What's happening with you?"

"Not a lot. I'm not doing much maintenance anymore. And I'm back at college taking leadership and management courses so I can lead the technician teams. I also have to take courses in

Ron and Soo come to visit

public speaking and public relations although Fatima won't tell me why. Still, as long as I keep getting my full salary and she's paying for the courses, I don't mind doing it. The management courses are quite interesting. But tell me about how you came to have a robot for a nanny. That seems like the most human of jobs that you've replaced with a machine."

"Life doesn't always go the way we planned. I asked for a security bot because of some nuisance threats against Jennifer. Seems to be part of the newscaster business."

"But that's not a security bot. She's awake the same way as Fatima or Otto."

"I didn't know about Otto."

"Like Fatima is all the factories, there's only one Otto who is all the Otto Hot restaurants. That's why I asked Molly if she was the only one."

Vijay was silent for a moment thinking about Ron's world.

"So when you go to an Otto Hot, you can talk with Otto, the AI who runs them all, just like you talk with Fatima."

"Yes, there are quite a few of them. Soo doesn't like it when I treat them as people, but I think they kind of are people. People without bodies. They're like ghosts that inhabit machines."

"So you think Molly is a ghost inhabiting a security bot."

"Come on, Vijay. You and I both know we don't have the ability to put that kind of processing into a robot's head. Molly must be another AI running in the cloud who is focused only on this body."

"I've never thought about her as a ghost, but I agree. She's an AI running in the cloud."

"So how can you have all these protests against machines, while Molly is looking after your babies?"

Vijay felt himself blushing. He turned to look at Ron who was grinning in the same way he did when he scored points off Vijay in one of their video games.

"Okay, you're right. I keep her secret, and I'm asking you to keep her secret too. But at this point, I'm putting the safety of my family ahead of everything else. It's a choice I have to live with."

"Fine, I'll add Molly to the list of secret AIs that I already live with. Sometimes I feel like a stranger in my own world."

"All this contact with the AI's is making you sound poetic."

"Perhaps it's how I keep reminding myself that I'm not like them. I'm still a human working in their world."

Ron and Vijay turned away from the city and went back in to join Soo and Jennifer talking about their children.

12

VIJAY BECOMES AN ICON

Vijay

Vijay's network was growing. At his next leaders' meeting, there were over 30 team captains including some he had not met before. The room upstairs at the Green Dragon was full. Tables had been pushed aside to make room for more chairs.

The meeting began with Sally leading the roll call. Almost 1200 supporters were reported, enough for a sizeable demonstration.

Sally and Greg led the shouting of their why's, and the chanting of the slogan "Humans Not Machines."

Finally, it was time for Vijay to address the crowded room.

"First, thank you all taking time to come tonight. We're about to start on the next, more ambitious series of demonstrations. These will take more training which will be delivered to each team before the event. Now I would like to call on Jamie McAdams who leads a special squad called the Bashers."

"Does he play guitar?" someone yelled out.

"No, this is not the ModPunk band," Vijay smiled. "Jamie, please explain the Bashers and what they're trained in."

Jamie stood and stepped back to the edge of the room so he could address the entire group. "Hi everyone. My name is Jamie McAdams. I have a team of big guys, and Vijay has asked us to form a special squad capable of doing real damage. Our squad has been studying two prime targets, the bubble taxis and the Otto Hot robots both of which have entirely displaced humans. The important thing for you to know is that we are developing and practicing an approach to create maximum visual damage while not actually doing very much."

"Thank you, Jamie," said Vijay. "Now I want you all to understand clearly, if you happen to see one of these events in person, do not approach and do not attempt to support or participate. In fact, turn around and leave. Although they may look random, the Bashers are working with the

Vijay becomes an icon

newscasters and the police. The property owners have given permission and will be compensated."

There was a low buzz around the room, until someone shouted, "Doesn't that violate our rules?"

"That's a great question. Sally, please refresh us on the rules of our campaign."

Sally stood. "Rule number one, no one is to be hurt, none of our supporters, none of the bystanders and none of the newscasters or police. Rule number two, nothing is to be damaged. No windows to be broken, no gardens to be trampled, and we clean up after ourselves. Rule number three, the police are our friends. They are there to protect us. We tell them if something is wrong, we obey their directions without question."

A dozen hands shot up in the air.

Vijay spoke, "Before we take questions, let me explain more about the Bashers. Those of you who were at the last assembly may remember that I explained the principle that demonstrations are a kind of theatre where we are the actors. Does anyone remember who the other actors are?"

"The randoms", "the police", "the newscasters," shouted various voices all at once.

"That's correct, the police and newscasters are players with well-defined roles. The randoms who join with us could be audience participation, but they are definitely on the stage with us. Now who is the audience?"

"The people at home", "the bystanders", "the politicians," shouted out more voices. Vijay was impressed that they had taken his training to heart.

"Yes, the people at home and on the street, and the politicians who are sensitive to public criticism are the audience. Now, the role of the Bashers would seem to break rule number 2, however their activities are tightly scheduled, and the damaged items are more like props in that piece of theatre. It will make sense to you when you see it. Please do not share this information with anyone, just know that it is being managed and you'll never be at risk."

Again, there was a buzz in the room. A hand went up.

"Andrew?"

"Aren't you worried that this would spread and that copycat randoms would spring up?"

"Yes, but that already happens. It's just not publicized, and the vulnerable companies such as taxis, pizza deliveries, Otto Hots and other fast-food companies all have protocols to deal with that effectively."

"Now for the last major item for tonight. We need to refine our message. What is it that we really want?"

Hands shot up. Vijay pointed to a young woman he did not recognize.

"We want to have an income to be able to find a nice place to live." There were murmurs of agreement.

Another hand. "We want to be able to buy nice things for our children."

"Those are both great examples," said Vijay. "What do you need to have a good income?"

"A decent job, not this HumanPower shit," someone shouted.

"Yes," said Vijay. "We want everyone to have jobs. How could you state that as a right?"

There was some confusion. "A right to a decent income?" suggested one. "A right to work," suggested another. "A right to independence," said a young man. Vijay guessed he was still living at home with his parents.

"I like all of those. Now your assignment over the next few weeks is to work with your individual teams and develop one or two statements to be your team's mottos. I would like each team to choose one or two, and we do not want them all to be the same. In our next mass demonstration, we'll have them all together and it will look brilliant. Sally and Greg will work with each of you and will approve the finished result. Two rules: spelling and grammar count, and no swearing. Any questions?"

There was a silent pause. No more hands went up.

"No? Good! Final announcement, if any of you would like me to visit your team meetings, schedule it with Sally or Greg. They have access to my calendar. That's the end of the meeting. The bar will be open for another hour, drinks are on me."

Vijay walked to the back of the room where he was soon surrounded by a small group of new captains who all wanted to take pictures with him and ask him about Jennifer and the twins.

About one third of the gathering were wearing the t-shirts with Vijay's picture. There were quite a few requests to have them signed. Vijay generally complied, although declined to sign over one woman's breast. "Where did you get these?" asked Vijay.

"At Mel's T-shirts & Tats," a couple of them replied.

At the end of the hour, Vijay slipped out of the meeting and paid the tab. A taxi was waiting outside. He knew that Sally and Greg would stay to look after the captains until they had all left.

THE NEXT AFTERNOON, VIJAY PAID A VISIT TO Mel's T-shirts & Tats. It took a minute for Mel to

Vijay becomes an icon

recognize him. When he did, he welcomed Vijay with genuine excitement.

"I'd like two small t-shirts with my picture, please," said Vijay.

"I don't think small would fit you, you look more like a large to me."

"I'm not going to wear them myself. That would be a bit narcissistic, don't you think? They're for my wife. But you could sell me a couple of the olive leaf fists over there in large."

"No problem, happy to do it. Could I ask a favor of you? Would you take a picture with me for the wall?"

Vijay looked around and spotted a wall of photos of musicians and holo-cast celebrities holding up t-shirts next to Mel. "Sure, I'd be happy to."

Mel called out "Hey, Woody, come and take a picture."

A tall gangly youth, his clothes stained with colored inks, emerged from the back of the shop. "Sure Mel." He reached out for Mel's camera. It seemed they had done this many times before.

Mel stood beside Vijay and they each held up one side of a Vijay t-shirt while Woody snapped the picture. He showed them the picture and Vijay studied it for a moment thinking. *'I'm not sure I look like the t-shirt.'*

Mel wrapped up t-shirts and handed them to Vijay.

"How much?"

"For you, nothing. That picture is worth more to me than the t-shirts, not to speak of the t-shirts that I'm selling to your teams and the wannabes."

"Thanks," said Vijay. Then looking around the shop again he spied the wall of tattoo art. "I'm not so keen on having my face tattooed on people's bodies."

"Too late," said Mel cheerfully. "That's gonna happen no matter what you think, if not by me then by any of the other tat shops in the city."

"Okay, I guess. Thanks for the shirts, Mel."

"No worries. Is it okay if I say 'Official supplier to Vijay Subramanian' on my website? It would mean a lot."

"Sure, go for it."

On a whim, Vijay stopped at his usual barber on the way home. "Hey Mike, see this shirt here? I want you to trim my beard and cut my hair, so I look exactly like the picture."

"You sure, Vijay? Everyone's gonna think you're him, this revolution guy."

"I am him, Mike. Just go ahead and trim me to match the picture they're all using. I figure I can't change the picture, so I'll just change me."

. . .

Vijay becomes an icon

BACK HOME, HE PRESENTED ONE OF THE SMALL t-shirts to Jennifer who at first, seemed dubious. Then she studied him more intently. "You've had your hair cut, and your beard is different." Vijay held up the second t-shirt beside himself.

"So, you look like the t-shirt now." She started to laugh.

"I thought it was easier than running around trying to change all the t-shirts. Did you know people have tattoos of me?"

"No, where do they put them?"

"I didn't ask and don't want to know."

"And now you want me to walk around in public with a picture of you on my chest?"

"No, but I thought you could wear it to bed tonight. I could be the ruthless rebel leader and you could be the timid groupie who lusts after him."

"Just like real life, then."

"Yes, just like real life." They were both laughing.

"Well, you had better bring your A game as the big, bad rebel."

"No worries, it comes naturally to me."

"Then you're on, I'll wear the shirt."

Vijay took the second shirt into the bathroom and pinned it on the wall. *'I suppose this will be my grooming guide from now on,'* he thought.

13

TRAINING THE BASHERS

Vijay

Vijay woke with a start. Jennifer was sobbing beside him in the dark. He rolled towards her and put his arm around her. "What is it Jenn?"

"A dream I have. It keeps coming back and I don't know what I'm supposed to do."

"Which dream is that?"

"I'm in the middle of the world looking up, and I see the black virus spreading everywhere. I'm so scared, Vijay. What if it comes here? How do we protect Dylan and Parvati? Their life has barely started. I don't want them to catch the virus."

"Hush, it's a long way away and we have the

Training the bashers

exclusion zone to protect us. You know they keep tightening it. No one comes or leaves the island now."

"I suppose, but I always have this feeling that I have to know about it, to do something about it. But the dream never tells me what."

"You're in the news business. Ask around and find out if the dream is even true. For now, come and snuggle up, and go back to sleep."

ON SUNDAY AFTERNOON, THE SIX BASHERS AND Vijay assembled in front of an empty warehouse. The bashers were imposing, tall and muscular, each taller than Vijay, and each carrying a baseball bat or length of pipe or crowbar. Vijay walked up a short flight of steps, opened the personnel door, and stepped inside. A lighting panel next to the door turned on the lights just as Gabriel had said it would. Jamie and the Bashers filed in behind him. Jamie walked across the space, past the unused loading docks to open a garage door. On the other side of the door, a paved ramp led to the ground. A few minutes later, an old bubble taxi rolled up the ramp on its two wheels and into the warehouse. Once inside, it opened its doors to reveal two Otto robots, both showing obvious signs of wear.

"Okay, Jamie, organize your team and get

those Ottos stood up. Then we'll go through the live practice. Let's start with the taxi. I'll have it roll straight ahead. You can intercept it in about 10 meters. This first time, we won't flip it. Just do the test heaves. Now who has the pipes?"

Two of the bashers raised their pipes over their heads.

"You'll put those in front of the taxi's wheels to act like chocks in immobilizing the taxi. Next, who are the three tippers?"

Three of the largest Bashers stepped forward.

I want you to try several test flips. The flywheel will be slowing down, listen to it and try to find the spot where it is slow enough that the taxi will not spin too violently. Who's on the right?"

Alan put up his hand.

"Are you wearing shin guards?"

The Basher pulled up his pant legs to show off the sports shin guards.

"Okay, be careful, and listen to whine of the flywheel. Now get in position."

Vijay spoke to his tablet, saying "Roll the taxi forward."

It was Gabriel's voice that responded. "Rolling the taxi now."

The taxi rolled and Jamie stepped in front of it to stop it. On either side the pipe carriers slid their pipes in front of the wheels. The three tippers stepped behind about to heave the taxi.

"Wait for it," said Vijay. They all listened. It took a moment for their ears to pick up the high-pitched whine as it dropped through the human hearing range.

"Start trying now, several lifts, just to test the reaction. Jamie, you call out the lifts."

The test lifts went without incident.

"Now, let's try to flip it over. Jamie, you call it"

They all listened to the whine until Jamie called, "Flip"

The taxi tipped over and spun. There was a loud "crack" as Alan fell back clutching at his leg.

Vijay ran over. "Alan, are you okay?"

"I think so, it spun so fast that it whacked me."

"Jamie, help him get is pants off. Let's look at his leg."

Jamie tugged Alan's pants over his feet being careful with the injured leg. The shin pad was still intact, but when it was removed it showed an angry bruise beginning to form on Alan's leg.

After a minute of pulling and pushing on the leg, Vijay said, "Okay, doesn't seem to be broken, but we'll have it check out after the practice is finished. Jamie, we need to wait longer before calling 'Flip.' Now who can take Alan's place on the right side?"

Another Basher volunteered and Vijay helped

Alan off to the sidelines where he sat watching the practice.

The tipping practice went on for an hour. Soon the team was attuned to the ideal pitch to tip the taxi safely while leaving enough spin to make it seem violent. After each attempt, Vijay would have the taxi wind up its flywheel again. By the end, they were flipping the taxi with ease, and had no trouble staying back out of the way. The new man on the right had his shins whacked twice, but the guards held, and he was not seriously hurt.

Next, they repeated the drills with the Ottos. By now, Alan wanted to participate again, and he limped over to join the others. Each time the Ottos would approach them asking how they could serve them today, and the Bashers would hit them and knock them over, only to repeat the exercise again and again.

Once Vijay was satisfied that hitting the Ottos was accurate and effective, he said, "Now, go to work on bashing the Ottos. Remember the weak points we discussed: the head, the arms, and the chest section where the pastries are stored. These are filled with colored water, so there's no risk of being scalded just now, but that will be a worry on the actual day."

Seeing the poor Ottos destroyed after trying only to please the Bashers, Vijay felt quite sad. It was all too easy to imagine Molly in front of a mob, although Molly would be much harder to take down.

When the Ottos had been smashed, Vijay called a halt. "Load them back in the taxi and let's go. Jamie will give you directions in advance of the actual date. On that day, we'll also toss around tables and chairs and mess up the Otto Hot restaurant itself. The location we have picked is scheduled for demolition and replacement, so just stick to the script and there won't be any issues. Any questions?"

There were no questions, and Jamie took over packing the damaged Ottos and their scattered parts into the taxi. The little taxi spun around on its two wheels and took off down the ramp looking much worse after its encounter with the Bashers. It made an ugly grinding noise as is went. Greg closed the garage door behind it.

"Jamie," said Vijay. "Take Alan to the hospital and have his leg x-rayed. It's probably just a bruise, but I don't want to take chances with any of you."

Once everyone had left, Vijay took one last look around the warehouse. Only a few wet areas where the colored water had spilled from the Ottos showed that they had been there. He turned off the lights and locked the door on his way out. A taxi was waiting for him as he walked down the steps.

14

NEW PANTHER AT THE ZOO

Jennifer

L ife settled into a comfortable routine for Jennifer. The twins were growing fast. At just over one year old, they had learned to walk and were now toddling around the apartment. Molly was a great help in keeping them entertained when they were awake.

Now, while the twins were napping, Jennifer sat on the couch watching leopard videos on her tablet. She invoked her panther to sit beside her, and then watched the videos through the panther's eyes. But without any muscle memory of panther movements, she could not get past moving like Jennifer wearing a panther suit. '*I need to go to the zoo,*' she thought.

She called Vijay. After their normal greetings, she said "Remember at the cottage by the sea when I was still pregnant? When I tried to be my panther and run around, you said I looked like Jennifer wearing a panther suit. You said my panther is really a black leopard, and I should study the leopards at the zoo. I want to go there. I want to be able to control my panther like a panther, not a silly human parody."

"Okay, it could be nice to take the twins to the zoo. I'll ask Cindy to come as well. Then she can look after the twins while I make sure you're safe if you go into a trance."

"Should we take Molly?"

"I think she would bring too much attention. We'll take her another time."

"No, I think she would be the perfect decoy. We can let Cindy and Molly take the twins for a walk away from us while I visit the leopards. Molly will draw the attention of any bystanders."

They went Sunday morning. Vijay, Jennifer and the twins went in the first taxi, while Cindy and Molly went in the second.

At the zoo, they wandered casually towards the African exhibits. Jennifer was surprised how comfortable Cindy had become with the imposing Molly. She was chatting cheerfully telling Molly stories about school and boys and living with the Holbrooks.

When they went past the pen of warthogs, Jennifer nudged Vijay and said, "Somehow they remind me of you."

"Me, a warthog?"

"Yes, they're fierce and kind of good looking if you like that type."

"And you like that type?"

"Oh, yes. I'll bet they're good lovers." Jennifer laughed again.

Vijay just shrugged. "Sometimes I don't know what you're talking about."

"That's what creates the mystery that you love in me."

"Perhaps."

Arriving at the leopards, Vijay and Jennifer found a bench to sit on. As Jennifer watched the magnificent predators, she thought, *My black panther really is just a black leopard. They look the same.*

"Cindy," said Vijay. "Why don't you take the twins for a walk to look at the smaller animals and the fish exhibit. Jenn and I are going to rest here for a while. Don't come back until we call you."

"Why not?" asked Cindy.

"We might be making out on a blanket," said Jennifer, winking at Vijay.

"Ewww, gross," said Cindy. The four headed off, with Cindy pushing the twins in their double stroller as Molly walked beside her. Jennifer could see people turning their heads to watch the strange group. While the other visitors were distracted, she quickly invoked her panther. '*I am the panther,*' she thought. Now she was seeing the world through her panther's eyes. She darted forward through two lines of fencing to arrive in the leopards' enclosure. One of the leopards was sleeping in the sun near the fence. It opened its eyes and gave a low growl as she approached, but as she had no scent, it did not attack.

Now was the tricky part. Jennifer sat her panther body next to the leopard's body and tried to reach for the big cat. Nothing happened. Stretching out her spirit panther, she laid it over the leopard. Relaxing in the leopard's energy, she thought, '*I am the leopard.*'

The feeling of inhabiting a live leopard was strange. She could feel the warmth of the sun on her flank. She felt the quiet readiness of a born hunter. Her vision was much sharper. Very small movements were registered as possible prey. The sounds of the park were much louder and changed as the leopard twitched its ears. The scents were overwhelming. The scents of the other cats, the warm earth, the grasses, and the cotton candy being sold some distance away.

Jennifer tried to move the big cat. She managed to take control and stand up, but as soon as she tried to move forward, the leopard stumbled and fell on its nose. *'Idiot,'* she thought, *'I have to use all four legs, not just the back ones.'*

Handing control back to the leopard's mind, she suggested that they walk across the paddock. The leopard stood up, stretched, and walked slowly across the enclosure. Jennifer could feel it's tail flicking in agitation but kept tight control.

As the leopard walked, Jennifer studied the muscles and the feeling of its gait. She noticed that it walked by moving both feet on one side, then the other giving it a slightly rolling motion. After a few crossings, she once again took direct control of the leopard's body and managed to walk in the same gait across the field. It was exhilarating to be this large cat.

Withdrawing once more, she urged the leopard to run to the back of the enclosure at top speed. This motion was different. Now the leopard was using its front legs together to steady itself and to turn, while its back legs worked together in a series of powerful thrusts. Again, Jennifer studied, then practiced until she could replicate the leopard's natural movement.

Stopping still, she looked for a target. Sniffing the air, she found the scent of a small mammal. Her keen eyesight detected movements in the grass that betrayed a field mouse. She passed a suggestion to stalk and pounce on the field mouse.

Now familiar with the leopard's body, Jennifer was content to simply observe as the big cat crouched with its belly on the ground, and advanced one silent footstep at a time. When it was in range of the mouse, she felt the leopard gathering its muscles as it prepared to pounce.

The mouse looked up, sensing danger too late. The leopard snatched and crushed the mouse in its powerful jaws. Jennifer felt a flash of fear that lasted only an instant. *'That felt like its life force passed through me as it died.'*

Jennifer released her hold on the leopard which shook itself. It seemed confused, then padded softly across the grass back to lie in the sun where it had begun.

Jennifer allowed herself to relax for a moment before thinking, *'I am my black panther.'*

There was a strange tugging sensation as her spirit moved away from the leopard, and then her black panther was free. She practiced for a few minutes pacing across the grass in one direction and running back. She tried slinking on her belly and pouncing on wildflowers. Looking up, she realized there was a crowd of onlookers at the fence watching the new panther. *'Shit, I forgot about the visitors.'*

Looking around, she spotted a shelter building where she could dissolve unseen. A moment later, she was back in her body pretending to wake up from a long nap. She was surprised to find herself lying down with her head in Vijay's lap.

As she sat up, Vijay said, "That was a quite a show. Perhaps you should apologize to the poor animal keepers. Visitors keep insisting that there was a black panther in with the leopards. They saw it disappear into the shelter."

"What do I tell them when I apologize? Technology? They'd want to see it. Let's get the twins and go home."

Vijay called Cindy. When she and Molly appeared with the twins a few minutes later, Parvati and Dylan appeared to be covered in something sticky.

"Ice cream," explained Cindy. "They saw people with ice cream cones and wanted one. I didn't realize they would make such a mess."

"No worries," said Jennifer, "we'll wash them up at home. Ready to go everyone?"

"I have called the taxis," said Molly as they set off.

Later at home, when Cindy had gone, Jennifer curled up against Vijay on the couch and shared her experience.

"It was exhilarating, I loved the feeling of being an actual panther. How did I look at the end?"

New panther at the zoo

"Almost perfect," said Vijay. "Not quite as menacing perhaps but that may have been because you were playing and not really hunting dandelions".

"The scary thing was that I felt the mouse die when we hunted it. I felt its fear and then its life force go out. For a tiny moment it was horrible. What's all this for, Vijay? Other people can't become animals. What am I supposed to do with this? And why a panther and not a rabbit or a goat?"

"I don't know, Jennifer. But you're being groomed for a role just as I am. What do you want your role to be?"

I don't know. I think my role could be to build a church. But I don't get how the panther fits in with that. I'm going to think more about it."

"Do you know how to build a church?"

"I know how to start, just like you and your resistance movement. That's all I need for now. I know that I don't want to be a real killer, like the leopard. But if my role is to build the church of Gaia, why do I need this ability to take over an animal?"

"Maybe just to demonstrate your deep connection to Gaia I can't imagine you being groomed as a real killer, a hit woman. Why would Gaia need that?"

"I couldn't be that kind of cold-blooded killer

with you in my life." Jennifer snuggled closer into him and pulled his arm tight around her. A chill passed through her that made her shiver. She pushed the dark memory of Eddie out of her mind.

15

THE CHURCH TAKES SHAPE

Jennifer

The twins second birthday was coming, and Jennifer was out shopping. She passed by an old church, now boarded up and covered in graffiti. It brought back the idea of creating a church, although she still had no real idea how to go about it.

On the way home in the taxi, Jennifer continued to think about creating a church. *'It feels like the next step. Vijay has the resistance, and I will have the church. Vijay has Sally and Greg, but who can help me?'*

She remembered Marjorie, the woman from the Players in the Park who dressed in muumuus and drew tarot cards. *Wendell said she could be a resource one day. I'll ask her for help.*

When she arrived home, Jennifer called. "Hi Marjorie, I wonder if you'd like to come to tea tomorrow morning."

"Of course, dear. Is everything okay between you and Vijay?"

"Oh, yeah. Vijay's fine. No, I just want us to be friends, and to hear more about your spiritual work. Would 10am work for you?"

"I'd love to spend some time with you. I'll be there tomorrow at 10am."

THE FOLLOWING MORNING, JENNIFER WAS ALL SET by 9:45am. Vijay had been dispatched for the morning with orders not to return before noon. Molly had deployed the golden domes which now all glowed blue. The Faraday box was open next to the front door. Molly was sitting in the twins' room watching over them.

Marjorie arrived promptly at 10:00. She seemed impressed by the building and the apartment that Vijay and Jennifer shared. Jennifer stowed their tablets in the box with a minimum of fuss, although Marjorie opened and peered into the box before closing it again. She walked over to the balcony.

"This is a magnificent view you have," said

The church takes shape

Marjorie. "And quite the apartment. Much more than I expected. The building is first class."

"Yes, we're very comfortable here," said Jennifer hoping to head off any conversations about their financial state. "Let's sit down, and I'll bring you up to date. Would you like coffee or tea?"

"A tea would be lovely, dear. But don't fuss on my account."

"I'll be back in just a moment. Make yourself comfortable."

Jennifer went to the kitchen and hastily prepared two teas using the steaming water tap at the sink. She set them on a tray together with the small plate of cakes she had bought earlier.

Returning to the living room, she found Marjorie holding one of the golden domes. "These are cute, dear. What do they do?"

"Oh, they just make sure our conversation remains private," said Jennifer in an offhand way. "Please put it down, and we can talk."

"Oh, so that's what the box for the tablets does as well, I suppose," Marjorie was still holding the golden dome.

"Yes," sighed Jennifer. "I guess you've seen these before, working with Wendell."

"Oh no, dear. I had no idea such things existed, and certainly not that I would find them here." Finally, she put down the dome and came to sit next to Jennifer on the couch. "Now, why is it that you need all this security?"

"You know that Vijay is working with a revolutionary group."

"Yes, one of my players is involved in that."

"Well, there is at least one other group that has been spying on us. I suppose they are after Vijay's secrets. The real secret is that being Vijay, he has none."

Marjorie laughed.

"And what are your plans for your involvement with the theatre? Wendell tells me that Melanie has moved into your ticket management role and is handling it very well."

"And with better handwriting." Jennifer laughed.

"Yes," Marjorie chuckled. "That's what Wendell tells me."

"We'll see whether I go back when the twins are older. They're almost two now, so I could go back. For now, I suppose I'm on indefinite leave from the theatre. I've started doing newscasting again."

Jennifer offered Marjorie the plate of little cakes. She noticed that Marjorie avoided the ones covered in powdered sugar.

"I'm interested in your spiritual beliefs," said Jennifer. "That was such a beautiful ceremony you

The church takes shape

created for us, and the Dancers card was special. Do you write the cards in your deck?"

Marjorie smiled. "For a long time, I only had the Circle card in my deck. All the cards were The Circle. For anyone else's ceremony, I might have used it. But I knew I had to do something special for the two of you, so I wrote The Dancers."

"It was perfect, I'm so glad you did. Have you thought about writing an entire deck?"

"It's not just writing the cards. It's the graphic design, the printing, the distribution. It's a very crowded market. But yes, I have dreamed of creating my own deck."

"What beliefs would your deck be based on?"

Marjorie sipped her tea and reached for another small cake as she thought.

"It would be based in respect for the Earth Mother, who gives us all life. It would emphasize duality, male energy and female energy, both of which we each carry within us, earthly progress, and spiritual progress. I'd bring in numerology and the four winds."

Jennifer noticed that Marjorie was looking quite dreamy as if she were seeing a deck of cards laid out in her mind. She filed this away as a useful observation.

"Have you ever thought of yourself as a spiritual leader?"

"Oh, dear, no. It's all I can do to run the Players in the Park. Between you and me, I'm just playing with all of this. I suppose it comes from being around stages for so many years. I can hardly tell when I'm performing and when I am being just me."

"How are they different? Marjorie the performer and just Marjorie?"

"Marjorie the Performer sees the world as abundant; a magical place where all dreams come true. Just Marjorie is often lonely and afraid. Here I am at 40 years old, no magical life partner, going home every night to an empty apartment. You have no idea how much I envy you and Vijay."

Marjorie shook herself. "Sorry, I have no idea where that came from. Can we see your babies now? I'd love to meet them."

Jennifer felt a moment of panic, but then decided that if Marjorie was to be brought in, she might as well be all in. "Sure, follow me."

As they entered the nursery, she heard baby giggles, then a loud gasp from Marjorie. Parvati was standing up in her crib hanging onto the railing. But that was not the cause of the gasp. It was Molly, in her soft apron, sitting on her stool and bouncing Dylan up and down on her lap.

"Molly, I would like you to meet Marjorie Fitzhaven. She's a trusted friend and will be a regular visitor in future." Turning to Marjorie, she said, "Marjorie, this is Molly, our family security bot. Molly is fully self-aware and is an important member of our family now. Would you like to hold Parvati?"

Jennifer pulled Parvati from her crib and handed her to Marjorie. Parvati fidgeted for a moment, but quickly settled as Marjorie relaxed and her normal calm energy returned.

"Marjorie, I know you have questions, but I'm not sure I have all the answers. Please keep what you've just seen completely confidential for obvious reasons."

"Certainly dear, but we do need to have a talk."

Molly spoke, saying, "Marjorie, please pass Parvati to me. I will bounce her on my other leg. They like that, but I cannot yet pick them both up at once by myself."

Marjorie approached Molly cautiously and set Parvati down on Molly's padded knee. Parvati immediately giggled as the bouncing resumed.

Jennifer escorted Marjorie out of the room. "Come back into the living room and let me share my plan."

Once they had settled back in the living room, Jennifer said, "I need to start a new religion, and I want you to be the high priestess."

"That's a lovely idea, but it takes a lot more than that to start a religion. What does this religion believe in?"

"Well, I could still use some help with that. It believes in Gaia for a start."

"Is Gaia God?"

"No, I don't think that's possible. I believe Gaia is just our world. She is the Earth Mother you talked about, so she can't be God. We could believe in God also."

"Okay, setting that aside, does this religion have a home?"

"A home?"

"Yes, a place where people can go to pray. A place where they can go for spiritual ceremonies."

"Not yet, I'll add that to my list. "What else does a church need?"

Marjorie turned sideways to look closely at Jennifer. Jennifer tried to look innocent. *'Innocent of what?'* she thought to herself.

"Jennifer, dear, why don't we start at the beginning. Why do you think we need a church."

"To hire people. To create a new social force that will dominate through economics. Professor Suleiman told me about the Cistercian monasteries, which dominated their environments and had huge influence in their regions. We have a problem today. Gaia's in distress, and the survival of human beings is in danger. We have to change. Professor Suleiman says there must be four estates at work to create a revolution. The first estate is the church, but it missing today. The second estate is the establishment, the government and rich and powerful people, the third estate is the middle class including all the people who work for pay and for HumanPower handouts, and the fourth estate is the newscasters. To make real change, we need a church.

Jennifer paused, trying to remember the conversation with Dr. Sulieman a year ago.

"Professor Suleiman also told us the Cistercian monks created a massive community outside the control of the government. They owned properties and hired people and services. They raised the standard of living of all their members."

"But that would require incredible wealth. To hire all those people and buy all those products, where would you get that kind of money?"

"I'm pretty sure I have the money. But my church will need a high priest or priestess and, I suppose, a religious order to perform religious duties."

"Religious duties? What kind of religious duties?"

"Oh, vows, funerals, blessings of new babies, blessings of new buildings, openings of shops - normal religious stuff."

"But why you, Jennifer? Why are you doing this?"

Jennifer looked down, feeling overwhelmed at

what she was taking on. Tears filled her eyes as a familiar feeling of helplessness came back. Still looking down, she said, "I was called to do this."

"Like a dream, a vision?"

"No, a call on my tablet - I can't say who from. I was chosen just as Vijay was chosen, and I suspect you were chosen. Look at this apartment. Do you think Vijay and I could afford to pay for this? It's paid for the same way the Mercury Theater is paid for. The same way our new church will be paid for." Looking up at Marjorie with tears running down her cheeks, she asked, "Marjorie, it's all too big! I need help. Will you help me with this part?"

Marjorie sat quietly for a few minutes without saying anything. Finally, she said, "This is a lot to ask, Jennifer. I love my little players group. It's a job I can do well, and no one makes demands of me. Asking me to walk away from that, I just don't know."

"Professor LaFlamme told me to talk with Chris Martingale. Apparently, he is running a Gaianism movement already that we may be able to base ours on. Will you at least come with me to talk with Chris?"

Jennifer watched closely. She could see Marjorie's shoulders go back and down as she unconsciously sat straighter. Clearly the thought of meeting with Chris interested her.

The church takes shape

"Okay," said Marjorie. "I'll set up a meeting with Chris."

Jennifer dried her eyes with a tissue, feeling back in control again. "This is all still secret. We're not ready to announce it to the world. The first part will be quiet until the city realizes what's going on. And both our allies and enemies are powerful and everywhere. You must assume that any conversation you have may be overheard."

Standing up, Jennifer walked around the room, switching off the three golden domes. Then going to the door, she pulled the tablets from the Faraday box and handed Marjorie hers.

"Thanks, Marjorie. I hope you'll find it in your heart to continue helping me."

"Certainly dear. I'm curious to see where this adventure takes you."

Speaking to her tablet, Jennifer said, "Please order a taxi for Marjorie"

As they walked to the elevator, her tablet responded, "Your taxi is waiting."

'How do you do that?" asked Marjorie.

Jennifer just smiled and spread her hands.

The elevator doors opened, and Marjorie was gone.

16

A VISIT TO ATLANTEAN TREASURES

Jennifer

Marjorie and Jennifer arrived at Atlantean Treasures after it opened at 10am. The small Tibetan tingsha chimed as they opened the door. Behind the counter, Chris was sorting and pricing various crystals. The shop itself was filled with a variety of spiritual supplies, books, clothing, and devices. Years of incense burning had penetrated the walls and the lighting was a soft yellow color that created an immediate sense of intimacy and spiritual grounding.

Looking up from his task, Chris said, "Hi Marjorie, Jennifer. I'll be with you in a minute. Please feel free to browse in the shop."

As they looked at the various displays, Jennifer tried to imagine which items would be part of her new church. Singing bowls? Smudge sticks? But nothing seemed relevant.

When they came to the display of card decks, Jennifer stopped to admire the brightly colored card boxes. A few were marked sample. She opened them and looked at some of the cards.

"Marjorie, do you think we could create one of the these for our church? We can hire an artist and even a text writer if you don't want to write them. Some of them come with a book, so that could become the founding document."

"It would be a very expensive undertaking, and with a small market I'm not sure we could make any money."

"No, that's why I intend to give them away for free."

Just then Chris joined them. "How may I help you ladies today?"

"Chris," said Jennifer, "we need to know more about Gaia-based religion. We were told that you can help."

"What is it you wish to know, exactly?"

"Is there an existing church that we could join?"

"Gaianism is more of a spiritual community. Anyone can participate. The idea is to maintain a regular mediation practice and to spend time in nature. Of course, we try to consume fewer plastics and most of us are vegetarian."

Chris paused and looked at Jennifer. 'He's trying to guess how much to tell me,' she thought

"The founding principle is that the earth is alive, and that as part of the earth, we're obliged to live in harmony with her. Gaia is not separate from us, rather we exist inside Gaia and are part of her. Evil in the world comes from thinking that humans are separate and can ignore the needs of planet without consequence."

Jennifer could see that Marjorie was engrossed in Chris' explanation although she felt impatient, "Is there a structure to the community? Are there specific rituals and ceremonies? Is there a book that would be our governing text?"

"It sounds like you are trying to see a beautiful free-flowing movement of creative thought through the formal lines of a traditional Christian church."

"Yes," said Jennifer. "That's exactly what I want to understand."

"I don't think it works like that. Gaianism is a way of life, not a strict set of precepts and dogma to be followed."

Jennifer could see that this conversation was going nowhere. "So, you think Gaianism can't work in a new church setting."

"Jennifer, dear," said Marjorie, "Perhaps

you're not the right person to talk with Chris. Why not go and have a coffee at the Copper Kettle across the street? I'll come and find you in a few minutes." She placed a firm hand on Jennifer's shoulder and gave her a small push in the direction of the door.

Jennifer crossed the street and entered the Copper Kettle. Every fibre of her being wanted to march back into Atlantean Treasures and take back control, but she knew Marjorie was quite capable of both business and woo-woo conversations.

It was a full 30 minutes before Marjorie joined her clutching a hemp bag which looked like it might hold another muumuu. She looked flushed and very pleased with herself. "He is such an amazing man, Jennifer. You wouldn't believe all the things he has done. I'm going to his transfiguration dance on Monday night. I think you should come too. He is just so sincere and committed to bringing a new energy to the planet."

'Terrific,' thought Jennifer, *'Marjorie's in love with this guy.'*

"What did you learn?"

"There's lots of Gaia materials to work with. Did you know the name Gaia is from ancient Greece when they realized the earth was itself a living organism?"

"That's great. When and where is the transfiggy thing on Monday night? I want to understand this whole Gaianism idea."

"It's a transfiguration dance and it's at 7pm, at the same small farm where we did the animal spirits meditation. But you'll need something to wear, and I know just the place."

They walked down the street past yoga studios, indie music clubs, and outdoor cafes all operating from a collection of old buildings which appeared to be on the last of their nine lives.

After five minutes, they came to Ruby's Natural Threads. Marjorie led the way with Jennifer in tow. The store was a riot of color with garments, scarves, headbands, blankets, and ponchos all made from coarse woven cottons, alpaca wools and bamboo threads. Ruby herself was pulling garments from a cardboard box and hanging them on the racks. She looked up as they arrived.

"Hello, can I offer you a tea?" she asked.

"No, thanks," said Marjorie, "we just came from the Copper Kettle. But we do need something for Jennifer to wear to Chris' transfiguration dance session."

Ruby looked at Jennifer for a moment, then smiled. "Of course, from the newscasts. Will you be reporting on the session? That might be a bit weird."

A visit to Atlantean Treasures

I wasn't going to, but it might be interesting. I'll talk with Chris and see if he'll agree. Marjorie thinks I might be overdressed. My casual clothes run more to high street fashion than new age."

"Perfect," said Ruby. "Let me show you some things."

Marjorie and Ruby finally agreed on a simple peasant dress in a pale straw-colored fabric printed with small plum-colored roses. It had a square neckline that was slightly scooped. The dress was fastened with a line of cloth covered buttons that ran from the neckline to the hem allowing Jennifer to choose how much freedom to allow at the top and bottom.

Jennifer had a flashback to her vow ceremony when two other women, Monica and Maa, had decided on her dress. *'Perhaps that's who I am, a doll for others to dress,'* she thought idly, but this time there was no stress in the thought.

Excusing herself from Marjorie after paying for the dress, Jennifer returned to shop to speak with Chris again. He was behind the counter, wrapping up a large crystal orb for a lady dressed in a flowing multi-layered, multi-colored gown.

"It's a shame about your last orb rolling off the balcony, but I am sure this one will give you equally clear access to the spirit world, Madame Francessa."

"Thank you, Mr. Martingale. There is no one

I would trust more when it comes to matters of the spirit."

Thinking of her vision of Vijay as a warthog, Jennifer browsed the section on animal spirit references among the card decks and the bookshelf. She didn't notice Chris approaching her until he was standing next to her.

"Hello Jennifer, it's a pleasure to see you again so soon. Is there something else I can help you with?"

"I was thinking that your shop could make an interesting topic for one of my human-interest pieces. How long has it been since you were on a broadcast?"

"Must be at least 10 years, just after the shop opened."

"Then it's time for a fresh look. I understand you have a special dance coming up. Would you be okay with having me report on it?"

"The transfiguration dance? Sure, it'll be a celebration of the moon goddess, Selene."

"Will you be doing a meditation?"

"No, usually we do a session of ecstatic dance. You should participate. Sometimes they can be quite revealing."

"Perfect, send me the details and I'll come. I'll drop by the shop for an interview in the morning so you can provide a bit of background. We can broadcast a few teaser segments that afternoon, and then I'll cover the event in the evening. Make sure you have lots of room as there are likely to be a lot of new participants."

"No worries, we'll be using the farm."

"One more thing, can you tell me again about the black panther meaning? I'm trying to find what my purpose in life is and the panther seems to be a key."

"The panther represents courage and strength. It is also a symbol for stealth. It chooses when to reveal itself and when to remain in the shadows. It is intelligent and cunning, and in control of the power it possesses. It normally comes to people as they are about to go through major life changes, where they need the panther's strength to follow through, and its intelligence in knowing how much to share and what to keep hidden. If that was for you, it was a powerful message indeed. Does that make sense to you?"

Jennifer thought of the still unclear challenge of bringing Ron's and Vijay's teams together. She thought about her vision of the viral spread across the earth and the coming need to protect the city. "Yes," she said. "I'm afraid it does."

Then on impulse, she asked, "Do you have deck with a card for a warthog as a spirit animal?"

"I have a deck of spirit animals of Africa. Let's look."

Chris shuffled through the sample deck and

produced a card for the warthog. "Did a warthog also come to you?"

"No, my partner, Vijay, was shown to me as a warthog. I don't think he's a believer, but I thought it might be fun to get him a deck with a warthog in it."

"A lot of people start by thinking it's fun, then come to realize there is meaning and power in these spirit animals. Shall I wrap one as a gift?"

"Yes, please."

17

A NEW TATTOO

Jennifer

Walking out of the shop, Jennifer noticed a tattoo parlor across the street. She crossed over and looked at the window display of tattoo photographs. They all appeared well done and were not the skulls, naked women and bloody daggers she had expected. Butterflies, birds, and flowers were all well represented. There were quite a few Tarot images and zodiac signs.

She walked in. The young woman seated behind the counter looked up as Jennifer entered.

"See anything you like?"

"I want a tattoo of a panther."

"Were you at Chris' meditation circle that

night when we all saw the panther? I think we've met before."

"Yes, I was there. Do you have some panther designs?"

"That meditation was the most amazing one I have ever been to. I've been to all of Chris' special events, but we never all saw the same animal before. It's usually eagles, and tigers, white doves, and rabbits. Almost no one sees black panthers, but we all did that night."

"Yes," said Jennifer, not wanting to be drawn into this discussion. "Then you know what I'm looking for. Do you have some designs that I can look at?"

"Sure, there are some in the catalog I use. I've done several of them since then."

Alicia slid the book across the counter. Jennifer looked at the panther drawings. None of them seemed quite right. She felt a moment of disappointment. "This isn't quite what I'm looking for. I want my panther to be hungry, prowling and looking at me in the mirror."

"Can you draw what you want? If you have a drawing, I can work with that."

"Do you have a pad and pen? I need to sit outside on the grass to draw. I'm not sure if it'll work, but I am going to try to channel my inner panther."

"Sure," said Alicia. She rustled under the

counter and produced an art sketching pad and black and yellow felt-tip pens. "Why don't you sit out back. There is a small garden there where I sit on my breaks and lunch."

She led Jennifer out back. The small garden was a patch of unkempt grass and weeds with a tiny patio of six paving stones. A rusting painted table and chair were the only furniture. "Just knock on the door when you're finished."

Jennifer moved the chair onto the grassy section, kicked off her sandals and wiggled her feet until she felt the damp, warm earth underneath. With the pad on her lap, she held the black pen in her right hand and the yellow one in her left. Closing her eyes, she repeated the meditation she had first learned from Chris Martingale, and later used at her cottage. Picturing herself sitting in the field of grass, she followed the worn path down to the stream. She sensed a movement. The bushes on the far side of the stream parted, and the black panther appeared. Looking into its eyes, Jennifer could sense the intelligence and patience of the large cat. She was barely aware of her hand moving on the page.

After what seemed an eternity, the panther turned away and disappeared into the bushes leaving no trace. Jennifer gave thanks to Gaia and ended the meditation.

Looking down, Jennifer saw the perfect panther image. It showed the panther, looking out with intelligent eyes, patiently waiting for an opportunity.

Jennifer laid the picture and the pens on the table while she slipped back into her sandals and put the chair back where she found it. After picking up the picture and pens, she knocked on the back door of the shop.

Once inside, she showed Alicia her drawing.

Alicia considered the drawing carefully. "Wow, You're an amazing artist."

"Oh, no, I didn't draw that. The panther did."

"Well, whatever, it's brilliant," she said. "Have you had a tattoo before?"

"Yes, but it was done to me, and I had it erased as soon as I could afford it. It was the old ink and left a scar."

"No worries, I only use the new inks that break up under laser treatment, should you ever wish to remove it. But this will be so lovely that I think you'll want to keep it forever. Now, where do you want this?"

"Over my heart. Jennifer put her hand on the upper part of her left breast."

"I suggest we minimize the tattooing directly on your breast. We'll have the panther prowling just above it. I'll position it with a printed outline

A new tattoo

that can be moved until you're happy with it. Please have a seat in the chair."

Once they had agreed on the size and placement, the tattooing began. Jennifer had experienced this before. It was uncomfortable, but she knew how to deal with physical pain. An hour later, they took a break. Jennifer sent Vijay a message saying she was delayed for a few hours and to go ahead and feed the twins their lunch.

Three hours later, the tattoo was finished. It was exactly like the drawing Jennifer had created. She looked in the mirror. It was beautiful.

Alicia put a healing cream on and covered it with a sterile bandage. She gave Jennifer a couple of tubes of cream and strict instructions for aftercare to avoid scarring or infection.

"Would you mind if I offer this design to others who were at the meditation?"

Jennifer thought for a minute, then realized that other people already copied much of what she and Vijay did. "Sure," she said. "Call it Jennifer's Panther and then you can share it."

As she walked out the shop, Jennifer had the strange sensation she had just passed through another gate but did not know where it was leading.

Back home, Vijay was curious and unsure about the new tattoo when he saw the bandage peeking over Jennifer's dress.

"It's my panther," replied Jennifer, in a matter-of-fact tone. "But you have to wait until tomorrow morning to see it. Oh, and I have a gift for you in my bag."

Vijay seemed to love the card deck. "What animal do you think I am?" he asked.

I had a vision that you were a warthog. "

"A warthog? I don't think so."

"No, I can totally see you as a warthog, Vijay. A pig that has long teeth. Messy and dangerous, I think it fits.

Vijay sorted through the cards and read the warthog card several times over. "Nothing in here about being messy and dangerous." He scowled at Jennifer. "I'll see if I can channel my inner warthog." He got down on his hands and knees, snorting and using his nose to disrupt the twins playing on the floor. Jennifer watched as the twins squealed and counterattacked until Vijay rolled on his back in apparent surrender.

'Messy, maybe,' she thought. *'But dangerous? Never.'*

Now the twins wanted to see the animal cards. They kept grabbing at the cards they recognized. The lion, tiger, elephant and giraffe were favorites.

Jennifer relaxed on the couch watching Vijay interact with the twins. She felt calm and peaceful as she watched them together.

18

DANCING UNDER A FULL MOON

Jennifer

Tuesday night was the full moon. Jennifer had reserved Daniel as camera for the shoot and went early to the farm. They had already done the interview that morning and, true to her word, she had been able to convince the studio to run some teasers.

"Daniel, get some establishing shots of the farm gate, the grounds, the chickens, and the barn where the dance will be held. Come back here by 5:30pm ready to collect thumbprints from the participants."

Jennifer went in search of Chris and found him in the barn setting up lights and sound. He was looking down muttering to himself.

"Damn," he said. "I know I plug this mic in somewhere."

"Hi Chris," said Jennifer. "Do you need any help?" She looked in dismay at the rats' nest of wires and cables running from the sound and light systems. "If you want, I can ask Vijay to stop by in the next few days to sort it out. But tonight, I think my camera might know what to do."

"Sure, by all means, have a go. I have too many other things to get ready."

"I'll call him in, and you can show him the problem." Jennifer called Daniel into the barn.

"Daniel, please help Chris with where to plug in the microphone. If you're not sure, please call Vijay for advice." Turning to Chris, she said, "You can leave it with us. We'll have it fixed."

As soon as Chris had left, Jennifer spoke to Daniel. "Please just do the minimum to plug in the microphone. I want to have Vijay come to reorganize the cabling. It will be a good way to put Vijay and Chris together."

Daniel responded. "Certainly, Jennifer. This does not look difficult, and I am equipped to manage the cables."

Jennifer wandered back to the gate and saw that a few early participants were already gathering. Some recognized her at once even though her new dress was a departure from her normal style as a newscaster.

"If I could just ask you to wait here for a moment. I'm doing a segment on the ecstatic dance tonight, but we'll need your permission in case we capture you in our filming. There's no guarantee that you'll be on, and if you don't want to be in any of the shots, you can tell my camera, Daniel, and he will exclude you... here he comes now."

Most of the participants had never seen a newscast camera, but Daniel was trained to work with a wide range of human behavior and quickly processed them all. The entire group were happy to provide their thumbprints, and then hung around plying Jennifer with questions about her job, her twins and Vijay. One of the young men was wearing a Vijay t-shirt and asked Jennifer to sign it for him.

Jennifer politely answered a few questions, then moved them along to make room for the next group of arriving participants.

When Chris confirmed that all the participants had arrived, Jennifer asked for a few more minutes to conduct some on-the-spot interviews, gathering sound bites for the editor to use later, starting with Chris himself, whom she introduced as the owner of Atlantean Treasures and the organizer of various spiritual events. She and Daniel then moved a short distance away and she recorded her intro against the background of the gathered crowd who were enjoying chai and wandering about the barnyard.

The sound of a gong rang out three times, summoning everyone inside the barn. Jennifer and Daniel followed them in and found a discreet place against the wall to stand and observe.

Chris addressed the group.

"Tonight, on the night of the full moon, in honor of Selene, the moon goddess, we're going to dance to bring forth Kali Maa. You may think of Kali as the goddess of destruction, but in her aspect as Kali Maa she is also the loving mother and uses her fierce aspect to help us drive out the problems and beliefs that hold us back.

"We'll begin with the mantra to honor Kali and bring her forth in each of us, giving us strength to do what is right in our lives. There are four verses, most of you know them. For the first few repetitions, they will be projected here where I'm standing. When you feel ready, you'll start dancing.

"Remember, ecstatic dance is a personal experience, and not a romantic one. If you are here with someone else, I suggest you separate. There will be lots of time later to share your experiences."

At her side, Daniel produced a small drone and released it into the air. It was black and disappeared against the ceiling of the barn.

Chris walked over to his sound panel, and the sounds of a harmonium began to play. Drums came in and a voice began the chant. The words of the chant appeared as a hologram, projected on the six sides of a hexagonal column in the center of the barn.

Om Kali, Kali! Om Kali, Kali!

Namostute, namostute, namo!
Namostute, namostute, namo!

Ananda Maa Ananda Maa Kali
Ananda Maa Ananda Maa Kali
Ananda Maa Ananda Maa Kali

Om Kali Maa!

The crowd gradually joined in, and soon everyone was swaying with the chant. Jennifer felt the stirrings of energy within her as she swayed with the participants. As the tempo increased, some people began to dance, twitching and whirling to their own internal rhythms. Still the tempo increased and more danced. The lights dimmed as red and blue lights began pulsing with the music. The beat was strong and fast and the music loud. Over the top of the music, Chris was shouting into the microphone "Kali Maa, protect us, Kali Maa give us strength. We call you Kali Maa."

The energy in the room continued to build until everyone was dancing. Some shouted out with joy or fear. Somewhere a person was crying, then two more, sobbing as they danced. Jennifer felt that her senses were overloaded; it was hard to think. As she stood and watched, she saw the panther emerge from her body. It sat in front of her and looked at her.

As she gazed into its eyes, she shifted. She was the panther.

She stalked around the edge of the room, keeping to the shadows. When she was satisfied that no one was paying attention to her, she prowled through the crowd. She could pass right through the dancers. Most didn't notice, but some reacted by moving away. A few dancers saw her and looked at her with wide eyes but did not stop dancing. As she watched, they glowed. Jennifer memorized their faces.

Jennifer, the panther, moved to the center of the room and sat. She willed the dancers to move around her and the room of dancers began to circle, slowly at first then faster and faster. Satisfied that the room was hers, she stood and leisurely made her way back through the swirling throng to where her body was still standing. In her panther's vision, her body shone brightly guiding her towards herself. Arriving, she thought, *'I am Jennifer'*, and shifted back into her body. The panther came close and merged with her again.

Shocked by the reality of this experience, Jennifer made her way outside to the cool evening air. Chris followed her out appearing concerned.

"Jennifer, Are you okay? Do you need some water?" He produced a flask of cool water.

"Thanks, it was just getting a bit intense in there."

Chris looked at her oddly.

"That panther, was that you again tonight?"

"I'm afraid so, perhaps I should stop coming to your events."

"Are you dangerous? Do I need to worry about you?"

"I'm probably the least dangerous person you have ever met," laughed Jennifer. *'Liar!'* was the thought that went through her mind.

"I'd like to understand more later, but right now, I need to go back and start letting them down responsibly. There can be some strong emotional responses to this, especially for new participants."

"No worries, I'll call Daniel out and we'll do a few exit interviews, then go. Thanks for inviting us. I'll be sure to keep the mention of Atlantean Treasures in the final edit."

Jennifer used her tablet to summon Daniel,

and they stood waiting to talk with the exiting participants.

The interviews went quickly. Jennifer was careful to skip any of the dancers who had reacted to her panther.

Back at the studio, Jennifer asked for a playback of the captured footage. She was fascinated to see some members of the crowd move to avoid the panther while most danced unaware. A few reacted in a way that let Jennifer know they had seen the panther. She asked to have frames of those people downloaded to her tablet. "For follow-up interviews," she said.

Finally, she instructed the editor to delete scenes showing her standing in a trance state at the edge of the event. There was a brief discussion over this, until Jennifer showed her contract giving her full editorial control.

Finally, she could return home. It was late and Vijay was already asleep in bed. He awoke when she entered the room.

"How'd it go?" he said sleepily.

"Wonderful", she said as she undressed, then slipped in beside him. "I was a panther tonight."

"Well, please don't eat me," he said. "Or on second thought …"

"Shhh, go back to sleep. I'll tell you all about it in the morning."

"Okay, we can play panther and warthog

then." Vijay was mumbling as he spoke. His eyes never opened.

Jennifer laughed. "Whatever you want. I love you."

"Love you too" and Vijay went back to sleep.

As Jennifer lay there, she tried to summon her panther again, but nothing happened. A few minutes later she was asleep also.

19

A CHURCH NEEDS A HOME

Jennifer

The next morning, Jennifer called Marjorie.

"I still think Chris would be perfect for our new church," Jennifer said. "But will you be able to manage him? He doesn't seem to like structure very much."

"You say that, but he runs a successful shop, has regularly scheduled meditations, and has developed his own community of devotees who follow him. I think his appearance hides his drive for something greater."

"That's wonderful. What's next in our church building?"

A church needs a home

"The building. We need a spiritual home. A home that speaks to connection with the earth; perhaps a farm or an estate."

Jennifer paused to think. *'Only thing I've got is my meditations. Either it will work, or I'll look silly.'* She shrugged. "I know who we can ask. Have you got time for a walk in the park tomorrow?"

The following morning, Marjorie arrived at the apartment promptly at 9am. This time she was not surprised to see Molly playing with the twins. They were crawling all over her as Molly tried ineffectually to defend herself. It was one of their favorite games.

Parvati recognized Marjorie and crawled over to see her. Marjorie picked her up happily. Dylan followed behind and was scooped up by Jennifer. Molly sat up, then stood up. As they all stood there, Cindy arrived.

"Molly, why don't you and Cindy look after the twins in their room, while Marjorie and I talk. Then perhaps we'll all take a walk in the park."

"Yes, Jennifer," replied Molly, taking Parvati from Marjorie before setting off down the hall. Cindy took Dylan from Jennifer and followed.

Jennifer and Marjorie followed to see what would happen.

In the bedroom, they found Molly already sitting on the floor, her back against the wall, with a brightly colored book open on her lap. Cindy settled next to Molly. Dylan had crawled to Cindy's lap, while Parvati went to Molly. They both seemed eager to see and hear the book being read.

Jennifer shut the door behind them as they left.

Marjorie sat on the couch as Jennifer made two Mountain Berry teas and brought out some biscuits she had bought at a health food store.

"These are healthy heart biscuits from Nancy's Natural Foods" explained Jennifer.

Marjorie took one of the biscuits and bit into it with a noticeable lack of enthusiasm.

"I always wonder if their health claim is based on the fact that we're not tempted to eat too many," observed Marjorie.

Jennifer laughed. She went back to the kitchen and brought out some of her private stash of Rocky Road biscuits.

"Perhaps you'll like these better."

Marjorie set aside the half-eaten healthy heart biscuit and picked up a Rocky Road. She bit in, and said "Mmmmm, much better." At least that's what Jennifer thought she was saying around her mouthful of Rocky Road.

"Marjorie, we need to be clear about what we

want in a building. The Cistercians had enormous abbeys with large properties to grow crops and raise animals. They had breweries and blacksmiths and all sorts of trades and stables for animals. We need something like that. Not the huge abbey of course, but a home that will support the new religion."

"I can see that would be nice, somewhere in an agricultural setting with outbuildings and fields, but how will we find this property, and how would you ever buy it?"

"First let's find it. Are you finished your tea? I'll get Molly and the twins. We're going to look in the park."

"Of course," said Marjorie. "Where else would we look for property?"

Jennifer just smiled.

It took 20 minutes to pack up the twins for the trip to the park. Molly carried a large bag containing their diapering supplies and a blanket. The twins were in their stroller, which Marjorie insisted on pushing after the taxi dropped them at Artwell Park. The stop Jennifer had in mind was the old oak tree where she had first received the vision of her twins.

Molly and Cindy were instructed to take twins to the other side of the fountain so they would not be tempted to interrupt Jennifer and Marjorie.

"Won't that cause a stir if you leave your children with a security bot?" asked Marjorie.

"No, we come here often, so Molly's pretty well known. She's very good at chatting and putting people at ease. And the park security bots all know and accept her. Cindy will be there as well to meet any legal childcare requirements. Cindy and Molly are friends according to Molly."

She led Marjorie to the tree.

"I want to introduce you to Gaia," she said. "I don't know if it'll be successful, but this is where I received messages before. Now you sit here, on the ground between these roots. I will sit one root over so that we can hold hands. Put your other hand on the root on the other side of you."

Marjorie looked dubiously at the packed earth next to the tree.

"Marjorie, you can't have a connection with the earth mother if you're afraid to touch the earth. Don't worry, it's dry and will brush off."

Marjorie sat down and leaned back against the tree just as Jennifer had done. Jennifer sat in the next available spot, not quite as comfortable, but comfort was not the most important thing. She also leaned back against the trunk. The earth was warm beneath her, and the tree was somehow comforting behind her.

"First, we close our eyes, and take three deep breaths. Relax into your breath.

"We are standing under a blue sky, warmed by the sun, in a field of swaying grasses and dancing meadow flowers, stirred by the gentle breeze. The flowers perfume fills the air."

Jennifer was surprised to find how real the field of flowers was this time. Something had shifted since the meditation circle with Chris.

"A path before us leads over a small hill. We cannot see what is behind, but we know it is our new home. We walk the path over the hill. From the top, we see it before us, the main building for sleeping and eating, and the smaller buildings around it for making things. We see the grounds stretching to the horizon, and pathways where our followers can walk. Perhaps a spring or little brook and a pond with fish and frogs and lily pads. There's an old oak tree for meditation...."

Jennifer was interrupted by a very specific image in her mind. She saw a rambling stone structure in an L-shape and surrounded by a vineyard. There was a gravel courtyard, and a brook ran nearby. A driveway led down from the road. Jennifer nudged the vision with her mind to take her up the drive. At the road was a stone wall, with a rusting iron gate. A sign said Widdicombe Winery, but the sign was old and the paint peeling. The whole scene had the look of abandonment and disuse.

Then the vision stopped with a suddenness

that made Jennifer gasp. She turned to Marjorie, who was also awake. Her eyes were wide, and she looked about to pass out.

"Was that real? Did we just talk with Gaia, Mother Earth? Who are you, Jennifer?" she whispered.

"Did you see the place where we have to build?" Jennifer spoke in a low voice to avoid attracting attention.

"Widdecombe Winery? Yes. But how did you do that? Who are you?"

"Gaia's awakening, and we're just parts of her. I didn't do anything except allow myself to receive. Do you think I'll be able to guide others?"

"Oh, yes. My goodness, yes. Was that you in Chris's circle? Was that your panther?"

I'm afraid so. I couldn't control it the first time. It was easier at the dance session. I've never seen such a clear vision before. Do you think you can help me?"

"I have to let this sink in first."

"Are you free tomorrow?"

"Yes, in the afternoon."

"Wonderful, we'll go visit our new home."

Marjorie quickly called a taxi to meet her at the park gates, and after saying goodbye, left for home. Jennifer thought Marjorie still looked frightened as she left at a fast walk to find her taxi.

. . .

A church needs a home

BACK AT THE APARTMENT, JENNIFER HAD MOLLY set up the security domes in the living room. "You and the twins can stay, Molly. You might find this interesting."

Setting her tablet down on the coffee table, Jennifer asked to speak to Gabriel.

"Hello, Jennifer, you must be calling about Widdicombe Winery."

"What makes you think that?"

"I have this sudden drive to talk with you about that property."

"Yes, Marjorie and I reached out to Gaia, and she revealed it in a vision. But of course, I have no idea where it is or how to obtain it."

"When did you want to go?"

"Tomorrow afternoon, with Marjorie."

There was a short pause.

"I have booked an appointment with the realtor, Alan Jenkins. He will meet you at the gates. It's been vacant for 15 years. It will take a lot of work to restore."

"Now we need some serious funding. We need to buy the property and hire the people to restore it. Also, to hire people to work in the vineyards which will be our cover for future funding. Can we do that?"

"Jennifer, where you are concerned, the funds are unlimited. I will let you know if there is ever an issue. You negotiate with Alan Jenkins, and I will cover you for the purchase. We'll assign ownership to a charitable trust that you and Vijay will control. Jonathon Standfast can help you with both. Go and see him. If you like him, I will establish a retainer deposit to cover the fees."

A LAN JENKINS TURNED OUT TO BE A SMALL, WIRY man with an infectious grin. Jennifer liked him immediately.

He held up a ring of keys with an orange tag.

"Property's been vacant for a long time. None of the vineyards want it. There's an issue with the water under the soil."

"An issue?"

"Yes, there's some intensive farming on the land above the winery and the pesticides and fertilizer runoff finds its way into the brook and into the ground water. Turn around and you can see the farm."

Jennifer and Marjorie turned around to see beautiful fields of corn running up the hillside.

"We can deal with that later," said Jennifer. Let's tour the property."

Alan had already unlocked the gate, so they walked down the lane together. It was just as in the vision. Jennifer could see that Marjorie was looking around in wide-eyed wonder. *'I don't think she believed the vision was real,'* she thought.

The farm building was large, with many sleeping rooms, and a large communal dining room next to a kitchen.

"This is where the grape pickers would stay in season," said Alan. "Some wineries rent these out to tourists in the off-season, selling them a vineyard villa experience."

Detached, and a little further up, was the owner's residence. It was a traditional stone farmhouse with many small rooms; a parlor, a large kitchen, a pantry and cold cellar, and four bedrooms on the upper floor.

Another more modern outbuilding held the winemaking equipment with stainless steel fermentation tanks, filters and pumps. It was clear that much of the pump and valve equipment would need to be rebuilt or replaced, but the stainless steel tanks could perhaps be reused. A stack of empty wooden barrels filled one end of building. Jennifer could see by the large gaps between the staves that these had dried out and would have probably have to be replaced.

Following a gravel path further down the hill, they walked beside the stream. The bottom was a brownish gray and there was no life in it. Eventually, they came to a large pond ringed with rushes. The water was murky, and duckweed covered much of the surface. At one end of the pond, a large weeping willow tree swayed gently in the small breeze.

"This is the fire pond required by your insurance company. If there's a fire, the firemen pump water from the pond."

The pond emptied at one end over a small wooden weir and continued down the hill as a babbling brook. A large oak tree stood nearby.

Marjorie nudged Jennifer. "That's the tree we need for our meditations," she said.

Jennifer nodded.

They turned to walk back to the gate. When they arrived, Jennifer said, "Thank you Alan. It's lovely. But it will take a lot of work to restore it. I would expect the price to reflect that."

"Yes, make an offer and I'll take it to the family. I can't speak for them, but a reasonable offer should be accepted."

"You'll hear from us in the next couple of days. Ah, there's our taxi. Come on Marjorie, we have lots to talk about."

They set off, as Marjorie waved to Alan through the window.

She turned to Jennifer. "What is it with you and taxis? You never seem to call for one and yet one always shows up. And I don't think I've seen you pay for any of them. How do you do that?"

A church needs a home

"Marjorie, you keep doubting that I am who I say I am. What would you have me do? Just know that we are being supported in this work, by Gaia and by others. The taxis are just a perk."

20

THE FIRST LAND PURCHASE

Jennifer

On returning home, Jennifer set up an appointment for the following morning with Jonathon Standfast, the young lawyer Vijay had met in jail.

Jonathon's office was not impressive. It was located in an older five-story building in a part of the city that was overdue for gentrification. The lobby was clean, but not polished. A directory listed the 35 occupants of the building. Standfast Law was shown as office 207.

Jennifer took one of the two elevators. It was an old model that still had push buttons for each floor. On arriving at the second floor, she was let out into a long corridor with fading gray paint,

The first land purchase

and identical wooden doors on both sides. It was not difficult to find 207.

Inside, Jonathon's office was divided into two parts. A tiny waiting room was furnished with three worn chairs and a stained coffee table. A rippled glass partition with a second door separated his working space.

As soon as Jennifer entered, Jonathon came out to greet her.

"Jennifer, hello, I've seen your newscasts. How can I help you?"

To Jennifer, he seemed very boyish, with an eagerness that reminded her of Vijay when he took on a new challenge.

"I want to purchase a property and I would like you to handle it. You met my partner when he was briefly detained, and he suggested you could help."

"Your partner?"

"Yes, Vijay Subramanian. He was accused of starting a riot. Falsely, of course."

Jonathon paused for a moment, He seemed to be searching his memory."

"Yes, I remember. He was very relaxed for someone in a police cell, and didn't need my help, apparently."

They were both still standing in the ante room. Jonathon suddenly became aware of that.

"Oh, sorry, please step into my office and have

a seat." Jennifer sat in one of the two aging green leather visitor seats in front of his desk. Jonathon sat behind it in a large black office chair. Looking around, Jennifer spotted images of a sailing yacht with Jonathon at the helm, and pictures of the same yacht taken from a drone. There was a picture of a teenage Jonathon with an older couple and a younger girl. *'Must be his family,'* she thought.

"Are you a sailor?" she asked.

"I used to go out with my dad when he had his boat. He's getting older now and had to sell it."

Jonathon looked genuinely disappointed. Then rallying, he asked, "How can I help you?"

"I need a lawyer to handle a real estate transaction, and also set up a new trust fund to support a charitable organization."

"Is it a complex real estate transaction? I haven't done much commercial real estate."

Jennifer thought, *'I bet he's never done any real estate transactions at all.'* "No, this is simple, vacant land with a standing building. Cash purchase."

"Then I'll be happy to help you. The trust fund should be straight forward if it is a simple trust."

"Yes, it's a trust fund to cover the operations of the church that will occupy the buildings."

"Do you have a signed agreement to purchase the property?"

The first land purchase

"Not yet, I want you to be there for that. Are you free tomorrow?"

Jonathon made a show of searching his calendar. "The morning would be best, but I can make the afternoon work if needed."

Jennifer smiled.

"Let's call the realtor now and set it up."

She placed a call to Alan Jenkins, and they set up an appointment for 11:00am the next morning at Alan's office.

Jonathon began to take charge. "I'll meet you in the lobby at 10:50 so that we can talk for a few minutes before we go in."

"Perfect, I'll be there."

Oh, and one other thing, there's the small matter of my fees." Jonathon looked apologetic as he said this.

"And how much will your fees be?"

Jonathon gave an amount that made her bite her tongue to keep from laughing.

"You'll receive a call from Mr. Gabriel who will set up a deposit of twice that amount for our use. Will that be enough?"

"Perfect, I'll expect a call from Mr. Gabriel."

Jennifer could almost see the gears turning as Jonathon was putting together the pieces of Vijay, Gabriel and herself.

As they shook hands, Jonathon said, "Thank

JENNIFER'S BLESSING

you for choosing me to represent you. I'll do my best for you."

"I would expect nothing less," said Jennifer primly. She was enjoying herself now. "I can see myself out."

As she walked down the hall to the elevator, Jennifer swung her hips. Even without looking, she knew Jonathon watching her from the doorway. She laughed quietly to herself. *'Men are all the same,'* she thought.

Jennifer and Jonathon met in Alan Jenkins office the following day. What Jonathon lacked in experience, he made up for in diligence, clearly exasperating Alan Jenkins. At the end of several hours of negotiations with distant sellers, the sale was agreed with immediate possession and Alan handed over the keys.

The trust fund also went smoothly. Gabriel suggested an accountant, Daniel Kissinger, who ran a small but successful practice in corporate accounting.

Daniel and Jonathon got along well and collaborated to complete all the filings required for the trust.

The first act of the new trust fund was to incorporate the Gaia Center for Earth Studies, which would be the legal name of the new

The first land purchase

church.

At the end of it all, Jennifer returned to the apartment where Vijay was entertaining the twins.

"You wouldn't believe how many documents I had to deal with today. I thought it would be like buying a dress or a pendant, but there must have been at least 50 things to be signed and registered. My thumb is worn out."

Jennifer flopped on the couch feigning exhaustion. Vijay made her move down on the couch so he could sit with her head in his lap. He bent over to kiss her forehead.

"It's over now. You did it and I'm proud of you. When can I see this new empire of yours?"

"Not today. Maybe tomorrow.

"Then let's take Molly and the twins, we can make a family day of it," he said.

Jennifer felt a sudden impulse. "Let's ask Cindy to come along. She and Molly are friends and they both love the twins."

Sitting up, she said, "I'll call her now."

Cindy checked with Mrs. Holbrook, then accepted enthusiastically.

"Aren't you worried about missing classes?" asked Jennifer.

"No, most of my classes are virtual, and Mrs. Holbrook makes me do all the assignments, so I'm always near the top of my class."

Jennifer smiled. "I was always near the bottom

of my classes. You'll be very thankful for Mrs. Holbrook one day."

"I already am," said Cindy, laughing, "This is the first time I've excelled at anything, and I know Mrs. Holbrook is a big part of that. These days, she doesn't even have to nag me too much."

THE NEXT MORNING CINDY ARRIVED BY TAXI IN time to help Molly pack for the outing. Baby supplies, a blanket, drinks and snacks all went into a big backpack that Molly would wear.

Jennifer ordered a minibus to carry them all. The smaller seats of the minibus would not accommodate Molly, so finally she just folded herself into the luggage compartment behind the rear seats.

"Are you comfortable there?" asked Jennifer.

"Yes," said Molly. "My body is comfortable in any position that does not exceed its design range of motion."

"Like the camera I work with," said Jennifer.

"Yes, like the cameras," said Molly.

They stepped out of the taxi into brilliant sunshine. The light breeze flowing down the hill smelled of warm earth, and carried the sweet scent of the ripening corn in the field above. The air was filled with the sounds of songbirds, and

The first land purchase

the deep croaks of the bullfrogs along the small stream that ran down to the pond.

"Wow, this is a lot more than I imagined," said Vijay. How far does it go?"

"I'm not sure, but far enough to support a winery. We're going to try to buy the farm behind us also so that we can control the quality of the ground water."

"Are the buildings safe to walk in?"

"They should be. They're all built of stone and have been here a long time. We can at least peek in the doorways."

Jennifer conducted a brief tour of the buildings and then led them all down near the pond and the giant oak tree. Molly set down the large pack and pulled out a blanket which they all helped to spread over the grass.

Jennifer bent over to pull out the drinks and snacks when she heard a gasp.

She looked up and saw Cindy blushing. "Are you okay?" she asked.

"Yes, it's just that I never knew you had a tattoo. What is it?"

Jennifer sighed. "It's my spirit animal, a black panther. I'll show you."

She slipped the dress down over her shoulder, baring the panther. She noticed that Vijay was also watching. *'Still adjusting to his tattooed wife,'* she thought.

"How did you find your spirit animal?" asked Cindy. Do you think I have one too?

"I'm sure you do. Mine came to me in a meditation I did with Chris Martingale."

"Could you show me how the meditation works?"

Jennifer thought quickly, then agreed. *'What harm could come of this? In the worst case, Cindy would see her own animal according to Marjorie.'*

"Sure, after snacks. We can all do one."

Vijay smiled and said, "I already know my animal."

Jennifer took his hand. "No, join us, it'll be fun. And your animal might not be what you think."

After drinks and snacks, they settled in a ring on the blanket. Cindy insisted that Molly join them.

"Molly, when you turn off your exterior vision, do you see self-generated images in your mind?" asked Vijay.

"I don't know, but I will try," said Molly. She sat down between Jennifer and Cindy, across from Vijay. She towered above both women. Vijay held Dylan, and Cindy pulled Parvati into her lap so that Jennifer could focus on leading the meditation.

"Don't try, Molly. Relax.", said Jennifer. "It will either work or not, but you cannot force it.

The first land purchase

That's the same for humans too." She looked at Cindy, who nodded.

They all held hands. Molly's synthetic hand felt alien to Jennifer, but she noticed that Cindy was very comfortable holding hands with Molly. The twins sat still in Vijay's and Cindy's laps, watching curiously this new behavior of their family.

Jennifer began with the instruction to close their eyes, then to breathe slowly and deeply. At the same time, she felt herself root far into the earth, reaching for the help of Gaia. A familiar infusion of energy rose up through her chakras. She released the energy through her hands. Ripples of energy passed around their circle.

"You are standing in a field of tall grasses; they are waving in the warm breeze."

It was easy now for Jennifer to picture this field.

"You see a small path leading down to a babbling stream. Following the path to the stream, you see the water splashing over the rocks, worn smooth over thousands of years. You hear the noise of the stream and see small fish and other creatures in the clear cold water. Looking up you see tall rushes on the other side and beyond them a forest. You hear the birds calling in the forest."

She paused, mentally invoking her panther.

"Gaia, we call on you for guidance. Show us

our spirit guides"

The rushes parted and her panther appeared. It looked directly at her. As she looked back, she shifted and found herself looking out at the small family circle through the panther's eyes. For a moment, she could see their relationships as a shimmering web. It was strongest between herself and Vijay, so thick it was almost tangible. Strong webs also occurred between Vijay and the twins who were sitting transfixed. Her link to the twins was weaker, still strong but not primary. Cindy was linked to the twins, and to Jennifer. But there was a strong link between Cindy and Vijay, much stronger than Jennifer had realized. Molly was also woven into the web. Her metallic web was very strong to the twins, less so to Vijay and Jennifer, and surprisingly strong to Cindy.

Then the web disappeared, and Jennifer shifted back to her own body as the rushes moved again and a fierce warthog arrived to sit next to the panther. The panther turned and licked the warthog which gave a low guttural sound of acceptance. Standing above the rushes, a snow-white horse, unbridled and free snorted as it came to stand on the other side of the warthog. It reached its head down and nuzzled the warthog's head beside it.

A loud noise preceded the fourth animal. A massive female elephant crashed out of the forest

The first land purchase

and stood watch over the assembly. Between her legs out tumbled a bear cub and lion cub tussling on the ground. As Jennifer watched, they transformed into a puppy and a kitten, and again into a goat and a fawn. They continued changing through the animal kingdom while playing.

When Jennifer felt they had seen enough, she closed out the vision.

"Giving thanks to our animal spirits, we release them back to the forest. Turning around, we follow the small path back to the field of grasses feeling the warm earth beneath our feet as we walk. Giving thanks to Gaia, we release the vision and when each one is ready, we open our eyes."

Opening her eyes, she looked around the circle. Vijay and Cindy looked shocked. They sat still for a moment, then Cindy asked, "Did I really see that?"

"What did you see?"

"I saw your panther, and then a wild pig which was Vijay, and then a beautiful horse that was me, and an elephant that was Molly. And then the twins were all kinds of baby animals, they kept switching from one to another. And then I looked into the horse's eyes, and suddenly I was the horse. I felt free, and strong and I knew I could run with the wind. But I also knew that my place was here and when the time came, I would always return.

She was turning bright red, and Jennifer guessed at what else she had seen.

"Don't worry, Cindy. The meanings of visions are not always clear in the moment. You can talk to one of us privately or to Marjorie later if you want help to understand it."

Cindy nodded.

"Molly what did you see?" Cindy asked.

Molly did not respond.

"She's fine," said Vijay. "We haven't broken her. She's just trying to integrate what must have been a very foreign experience for her. Oh, and Cindy, that was a warthog, not a pig. I don't want to see any 'Vijay is a Pig' t-shirts going around."

"Okay, I'll make them 'Vijay has warts'."

Vijay knocked Cindy with his shoulder so that she fell over, giggling and releasing Parvati in the process. Dylan wriggled away from Vijay and the twins began rolling over and over together like the young animals in the vision.

"Let's see what we can find living in the pond," said Vijay scooping up Dylan again.

Cindy picked up Parvati and followed him as Jennifer stayed behind thinking. Soon she heard shouts of "Look! fwog!" and "Hi Turkle!"

Sitting on her own, she reflected on what she had learned.

The obvious thing was that she could invoke the visions and her panther when she was in

The first land purchase

connection with the earth. Even now, sitting in this place on the blanket, she could feel Gaia's energies surrounding her.

The second was that Vijay's animal truly was a warthog. And Cindy's beautiful white horse - that had to mean purity, love and loyalty but to Cindy, the message was freedom and power.

Jennifer wondered about the strong link between Cindy and Vijay, second only to hers in the web. And Cindy had blushed. What had she seen?

And what had Vijay seen? He was silent. She would have to ask him later.

Just then, Molly stirred on the opposite side of the blanket.

"Are you all right, Molly?" asked Jennifer

"Yes, I learned a lot today. It was the first time I saw with human eyes, and then with elephant eyes. It was a lot to process. I also divined something of the future which made me happy and sad at the same time. Is that possible?"

"Yes, said Jennifer, "that's quite possible. Do you want to talk about it?"

"No," said Molly. "Not until I understand what it means."

THAT NIGHT IN BED, VIJAY WANTED TO PLAY warthog and panther again. Jennifer agreed and began prowling around the bed looking for Vijay's weak points. Vijay, on hands and knees kept turning ready to ward her off. As he turned, Jennifer kept flipping the sheets over his feet and legs. Accompanied by hissing sounds from the panther and snorts and grunts from the warthog, they circled until Vijay realized the sheets had wound around feet and legs making it hard to turn. That's when the panther pounced using her superior agility to evade his grasp while getting in small bites and reaching between his trapped legs. Soon, he was defeated and lying on his back with the panther looming over him, her teeth in her open mouth at his throat. Licking and nipping him down his body, until she arrived at her target. She wet him with long licks of her cat tongue, then, took him inside, and rode him to her climax. Bending down to kiss him, she started again, this time moving on him in the way he liked best until Vijay reached his own climax, giving herself a second one at the same time.

As they lay together, in the warm afterglow, Jennifer said, "You were very quiet after the vision ceremony today. Did you see something?"

"I don't think I expected to see anything, but then I did. And it was real. I saw your panther."

"Umm hmm," said Jennifer, not wanting to interrupt his recounting.

"And then I saw the warthog. I knew it was

The first land purchase

me. And I saw the beautiful white horse and the elephant. I assume the way the twins kept changing just meant their personalities haven't settled yet."

Vijay hesitated, then continued. "This is the difficult part. When I looked directly into the eyes of the warthog, suddenly I was the warthog looking at us. Jenn, we were all glowing, you most of all. You were this blinding light. Molly was a deep red, a steady source of energy. I was a warm yellow, not brilliant, but warm and the twins were two small glows within my light. Cindy was pulsing, flaring then weakening to almost go out. She did this over and over."

"When I returned to my body, my warthog looked at the horse and said to me "Don't let her light go out. One day it will sustain you.""

Jennifer lay thinking, then said, "It means she'll become part of our family. It means we keep her close like a daughter. Talk to the Holbrooks and make sure she can stay after she turns 16. I'll fund her through the vineyard. I haven't talked with you about this yet, but when the vineyard's complete, we'll need to move there. Cindy can join us when we do. I've received a similar message, that Cindy is important to us, to you. We'll have to take her in when the time is right."

. . .

The following morning, Jennifer met Marjorie at a cafe.

"I've done it," she announced. "We own the winery through a trust fund with significant funding. We even have a legal name for the charity that will run the new religion, the Gaia Center for Earth Studies. The question now is, what role do you want to play? Spiritual advisor, business manager, high priestess? All the roles are open at this point."

"I thought you might be coming to ask me that. I would like to be the head of the center operations and have the role of business manager. I think we should approach Chris Martingale to be the spiritual leader."

"Do you think he'll be willing to take it on? I had the impression he didn't think much of me when we went to his shop."

"Let me talk with him. I think a lot shifted after that last dance session at the farm. And he does have a large following that he would bring with him."

"I'll leave that to you. Meanwhile, what will you do with the Players in the Park? Overseeing the reconstruction and hiring the staff for the Gaia center will be a full-time role."

"I'll look after that. I can think of several candidates, some in the group already."

21

CINDY'S VISION

Cindy

Cindy lay in bed looking at the ceiling and thinking about the events of the previous day. The visions had been so real, and they had all seen the same thing. Even at fifteen, she knew that was not normal. Yet Vijay and Jennifer had seemed so casual about it. And then to see that Molly had a spirit animal; that was just weird. *'Is Molly actually alive?'* She seemed to be, and the elephant kind of made sense for her.

She remembered thinking how natural Vijay's hand felt in hers. Then this brief flash of herself lying in bed in his arms, but it wasn't quite herself. Her body was softer and taller. *'Did I pick up on*

Jennifer's vision? But Jennifer would have been shorter, not taller, and she doesn't seem very soft'.

It wasn't like one of her fantasies. She knew what those felt like, but this felt more real, like a lived experience.

"Talk to Marjorie," was the advice Jennifer had given her.

Cindy did not know Marjorie very well, but knew she was a friend of Jennifer and Vijay and had met her a few times while babysitting. She looked very approachable and a bit exotic in those muumuus she wore.

Impulsively, she picked up her tablet and said, "Arrange an appointment with Marjorie to talk about a personal matter. Say that it involves Jennifer and Vijay."

The appointment was made for that afternoon.

'I don't have to tell her everything,' she reminded herself. *'Wait and see if I think I can trust her.'*

CINDY ARRIVED ON TIME AT MARJORIE'S apartment. Marjorie answered almost immediately after Cindy knocked. Inside, the living room was small but cozy. Colorful fabrics and fantasy prints decorated the walls. Brightly colored cushions were arranged casually on a love seat and chair. An old

Cindy's vision

coffee table had been painted in a cream color and held a stack of coasters with signs of the zodiac on them. A low bookcase held books on Tarot, animal spirits, crystals, numerology and other beliefs and guidance systems. On top of the bookcase were a singing bowl, a collection of crystals and an untidy pile of card decks, each one showing a beautiful illustration of a guiding spirit or being.

"Come in, come in, dear," said Marjorie. "Have a seat and help yourself to a pastry and something to drink." Cindy moved a cushion and sat in the chair while Marjorie settled herself on the love seat.

Cindy recognized the pastries from the Otto Hot shops. She chose a Cherry Delight and a bottle of fruit drink. Cindy took a bite out of her Cherry Delight and looked around. The room smelt of incense, and she spotted an incense burner on a small table in one corner.

Marjorie picked up a Cinnamon Swirl and they ate in silence for a moment which allowed Cindy to relax. Marjorie seemed content to wait until Cindy began talking, so after three bites of the pastry, Cindy said, "I went to the vineyard yesterday with Jennifer and Vijay and Molly and the twins. It was lovely, I liked it there. Have you been there?"

"Yes, dear. It feels so peaceful as if the land is

just waiting for someone to come and love it again."

"Yes," said Cindy. She hadn't thought about this before, but Marjorie's description seemed just right.

"Jennifer led a meditation under an old tree there and we all saw our spirit animals. I didn't even know I had a spirit animal."

"Did you all see the same spirit animal?" asked Marjorie.

"No, it doesn't work like that. We all have our own animals and they talked to us. Well, not exactly talked, but they left us with a message."

"And what animal did you see?"

"I saw all of them. Jennifer was a black panther, Vijay was a wild pig, but he says it was a warthog, Molly was an elephant, and I was a white horse. The twins kept changing from animal to animal. Jennifer says it's because they haven't settled yet."

"What's the question you have for me for me?"

"What does the horse's message mean?"

"What message did you receive?"

"That I should be strong and run free now. My time with him would be later."

"And who do you think 'him' refers to?"

Cindy felt herself blushing, and in a small voice, she said "Vijay."

"Well, let's start with understanding the meaning of the horse, then you can tell me the rest of it."

Cindy felt her eyes go wide. "How do you know there was more?" she asked.

"Dear, whenever Jennifer is involved, there is always more. We can talk about that also. I have time." Marjorie rose and went to the bookcase and pulled out a guide to the Animal Spirits.

She opened the book to the page titled 'White Horse'. It was already marked, so Cindy knew that Jennifer and Marjorie had spoken. She wasn't sure she liked that. "You must have talked with Jennifer, but I need to know if our chat can be confidential. I need to know that or else I have to leave."

"Don't worry, dear. Jennifer didn't tell me much other than to be ready to talk about the white horse and that you had seen something else that disturbed you. I won't be reporting our conversation back and Jennifer doesn't expect that. At my age, I've learned how to keep a confidence. Now let's look at this horse of yours. Was the horse wearing a bridle or other kind of tether?"

"No, it was a wild horse and said I should run free."

"Then the horse represents freedom and inner strength. But a white horse also represents morality and good judgement. It says that you can trust yourself to do the right thing and have the strength not to be led off your path. Considering the last part of the message, it says you should use this time of your life to explore and discover yourself."

Marjorie paused and looked thoughtful. "There are many aspects to explore in life. Have you seen a Wheel of Life?"

Cindy shook her head 'no' and ate the remaining bite of the Cherry Delight.

Marjorie stood and leaned across her desk, pushing open a drawer on the far side and, after rummaging for a moment, pulled out a printed piece of paper.

She sat back down.

"This is one version of a wheel of life, there are many others. You can find and choose the one that calls to you. See the six spokes? Don't worry about the numbers, we're just interested in the spokes themselves. Each of these is an area for you to explore. You can see spirituality, which is the search for meaning. This is a lifelong search for most people. I can direct you to a resource for ideas. The next one is health and physical activity. Here you can explore sports, yoga, or horseback riding if you like. Financial and Career is next. What do you want to become? Talk to people in different jobs, try some different part-time jobs.

Social and Cultural. Join some organizations. You can try theatre here or join a reading circle or find meetups for people your own age with common interests. Informal and formal education is another spoke. Learn as much as you can while you still have the freedom to try many things. Don't feel that you have to pursue each one of them. At your age, you can start and stop different things - but I suggest you give everything six months before stopping to make sure you've fully explored it.

"The final one is Relationships. Take care to maintain your relationships with Melanie, the Holbrooks, Vijay and Jennifer. You're only 15. In the next few years you'll be ready to have relationships with young men, including sexual relationships. Remember the White Horse. Be strong and clear in your decisions. Choose wisely and enjoy the men available to you. Each will teach you something. As you get into your twenties, you'll want to settle down and live with one or more. Everyone should do this. You'll learn a great deal about yourself."

Cindy could feel herself blushing again. She looked down at her lap.

Marjorie asked softly, "What else did you see?"

"I remember thinking how natural it felt to be holding Vijay's hand when I had a flash, just for a few seconds, that I was lying naked in bed, with

Vijay's arms around me. But it wasn't quite me. I was longer, and there was more of me, a softer me. Then it was gone."

Marjorie paused and frowned, then said, "That was a lot to lay on you at this point in your life. Jennifer is in touch with something much more powerful than we realize. She believes it's Gaia and perhaps it is. That's certainly the easiest explanation. But whatever it is, it's not delicate. When she does these meditations, she drags us all along without warning or apology."

Marjorie paused again, appearing to be deep in thought.

"Have you tried to summon your horse again, on your own? Another meaning of the horse is the ability to travel between the spirit world and this world, so I suspect you might be able to do that. As to the meaning of your vision, you're a very smart young lady. I'm sure you can understand it with your horse's help. Jennifer is burning very brightly now, and when people burn that brightly they cannot sustain it for many years."

Marjorie paused again, sipping her tea. "Another thought, ask Jennifer to talk with you about her teenage years, about sex, drugs, alcohol and about falling in love with Vijay. She will be a good guide if approached carefully without judgement. Her path was difficult and is not your path, but you can still learn from her."

Cindy's vision

"How would I get in touch with my horse?"

"There's an old oak tree in Artwell Park that Jennifer believes has a connection to Gaia. Try going there and repeating for yourself the meditation that Jennifer led. Do you remember it?"

Cindy nodded.

Marjorie paused for another moment. "Also, I think you would do well to focus your studies at school and at college on ecology and biology. To gain a better understanding of how Gaia works in our limited understanding of the world. Jennifer is flying by the seat of her pants without much education. There could be value in equipping yourself with knowledge."

Cindy looked up. She had been considering a major in Art History, but she could feel the rightness of Marjorie's suggestion.

"Now here's that source of more information on spirituality." Marjorie searched in the pocket of her muumuu and pulled a card for Atlantean Treasures. "Ask to talk with Chris Martingale."

Sensing that the conversation was over, Cindy stood saying, "Thanks, Marjorie."

Marjorie stood also and gave her a hug. "You're welcome anytime, dear. I'm always here."

As Cindy was leaving, Marjorie smiled and said, "Why not take this last pastry with you? It will give you strength for the journey home."

Cindy picked up the last pastry and a napkin. "Thanks again Marjorie, you've given me lots to think about."

THE FOLLOWING DAY, WHEN SCHOOLWORK WAS complete, Cindy made her way to Artwell Park and found the old oak tree. It was early afternoon and the sun had warmed the earth and the tree. Cindy removed her shoes and socks, setting them tidily beside her. Then she settled herself into the hollow between the two roots and sat with her back to the tree holding the roots in either hand.

She began with the deep breathing, then summoned the image of the field of tall grasses. The sun was shining brightly in a blue cloudless sky and a warm wind was gently stirring the grasses around her. She thought of her horse, imagining its white mane and tail and as she did, she saw it coming across the field towards her. The horse came to a standstill just in front of her. Without thinking, she reached forward to touch its nose. She could feel the horse, feel the warmth of its breath on her skin and the smooth hair that covered its face. "Ride with me," said the horse.

Without knowing how it happened, she was on the horses back, holding its mane and gripping with her knees. The horse moved off at a walking pace then began to gallop. With wild exhilaration they covered what seemed like miles of meadows, and streams, dirt tracks and forest trails. Finally, the horse came to rest, saying, "What is your question for me?"

"The future you showed me, is that for sure what will come, or only what might come for me?"

"It is the future that is promised to you if you choose it. If you reject that future, another will arise. But the longer you wait, the more certain your future becomes."

Then Cindy was standing next to the horse again. "Thank you," she said. The horse nodded its head and trotted away.

Cindy awoke and checked the time on her tablet. Only a few minutes had passed and yet she had travelled so far in her vision. Smiling, she stood up and headed home, still wrapped in the warmth of her horse's presence.

22

PEOPLE UNCHAINED

Ron

Ron was relaxing after lunch when his tablet announced, "Call from Vijay."

"Answer it," Ron replied.

"Hi Ron, how're things going? How's Mi Cha?"

"Hi Vijay, things are going well. Mi Cha's at that stage where we have to watch her all the time. She's pretty fast on her feet and takes off when we're not looking."

"You should try it with two of them. Dylan is always taking off, while Parvati is a bit easier. But she's beginning to talk non-stop. I don't know which is worse."

People Unchained

"We should all get together again soon; it's been a while."

"That's what I'm calling about. The Mercury Theatre is opening a new play that we'd love for you and Soo to see. It's called "People Unchained" and it's about the possibility of a human-based society."

"Don't we have a human-based society now?"

"We used to, but today we're dominated by the technologies we created."

"Oh," Ron said, suddenly feeling irritable. "So, this is another play in your People versus Machines' line. You know, Soo and I enjoyed the romantic comedies you did the last couple of years."

"We've talked about doing more general entertainment, but there are such important messages to get out, so we felt it was important to put this one on."

"Okay, I'll arrange it with Soo. What dates is it running?"

"The opening performance is next Thursday night, and then it runs for two weeks, Wednesday through Sunday evenings with Saturday and Sunday matinee."

"That's great. Leave it with me. I'll talk to Soo and tell you what night to expect us."

"I'm looking forward to seeing you again Ron. Oh, and this time, we can enjoy it with you. Jenn and I have both been replaced for the actual performances at the theatre, so we can join you in the audience."

"That would make it more fun, I'd like that."

"Perfect, Jenn will arrange the tickets. We can meet in the lobby for a drink before the show. Why don't you have Soo call Jennifer to agree on the date, it's been a while since they spoke."

"I'll do that. Soo will like that too."

"Bye, Ron"

"Bye, Vijay"

ARRIVING BY TAXI, RON AND SOO STEPPED OUT IN front of the Mercury Theatre. Mi Cha was spending the evening with their neighbors.

The theatre sported a new marquee, reflecting the commercial success of the lighter entertainment they had produced over last couple of years. Tonight, the garish marquee with its faux neon borders announced, 'PEOPLE UNCHAINED'.

Entering the theatre, Ron made his way over to the Will Call wicket as Soo said hello to some friends she spotted in the lobby. A teenager with long brown hair was seated in the ticket booth. Ron recognized her as Melanie, the young lady filling in for Jennifer since the twins were born.

"Hello Mr. Boyce," she said, smiling as she

handed him the ticket envelope with 'Ron Boyce' written in neat block letters. "Thanks Melanie." By now, Soo and Ron knew most of the regular theatre company by name.

After buying two soft drinks and a bag of nuts from the snack bar, Ron joined Soo and her friends and politely listened to their conversation. Vijay and Jennifer arrived a few minutes later just before the bell rang indicating time to take their seats.

A young usher showed them their center orchestra seats. The two women sat next to each other, with Ron and Vijay each sitting beside their respective partner. The house lights went down as a familiar figure walked to the front of the stage which was now lit by a single spotlight.

"Good evening, ladies and gentlemen. My name is Wendell Holmes, manager and producer here at the Mercury Theatre. We welcome all of you to our performance of 'People Unchained,' the latest in our social commentary series by our own Bernard Chamberlain. The cast will be available for discussion in the parlor room off the lobby following the performance."

As Wendell left the stage, the curtains opened to reveal an office with desks, chairs, and a large whiteboard all in semi-darkness. The audience hushed. Ron sat forward in his seat trying to make out the set.

The stage lights came up as actors entered from both wings, taking up places in the office, some sitting, some standing near the whiteboard. There was general busyness and lots of laughter among the actors. The group at the whiteboard drew a complex diagram with lots of arrows in different colors. The entire company broke into song called 'The Joyful Life of a Human'.

A technician carried an antique computer from the right wing, which he set on a desk. The manager gathered the workers together. He explained this computer was to make life easier in the office. Lots of oohing and ahhing came from the actors as they circled the computer.

Some actors faced the audience and one of them demanded: "We all deserve computers so that we all have a better life!". The others cheered and called out, "Yes, we all want computers and a better life." More computers were carried in until everyone sat at a desk in front of a computer. They called out to one another and pointed at their screens. Another song, this time with a chorus of "Close your eyes, can't you see/the glory of technology."

The manager reappeared and informed the office that a new work-flow system was installed, so they all could work in harmony.

The workers returned to their work as a drum began to beat slowly offstage. "Boom, boom, boom," in a deep, slow cadence. The workers now worked to the rhythm of the drum, first rocking back, then with each boom, rocking forward frantically keying for two seconds, then rocking back and "boom" back to the keyboard.

A mournful song arose from the workers "Didn't know what we were asking for/didn't know what we would get/the machines were sent to save us/but they haven't saved us yet."

At the end of song, the manager arrived again, and waved his hand in the air. The drumbeat stopped and all the workers looked up. "Shirley," he said pointing to a young woman in the front row of the office. "I know your job is tedious, so we have invested in a better solution" A bell rang offstage, and an actor dressed as a robot entered and walked to Shirley's seat. Shirley looked alarmed as she stood up and moved to one side.

The robot sat down and continued Shirley's work, moving to the beat of the drum. Shirley looked confused and moved to the edge of the stage, uncertain what to do now that the robot had taken her place. The workers continued singing their song, but as they sang, the offstage bell rang again and again. Each time more robots entered to take the place of the human workers until there was only a single worker singing the song. Another robot entered and suddenly the song stopped and there were no human workers left — only the robots all working in time to the drum.

The workers at the side of the stage conferred with one another and then approached the manager. The drumbeat faded away. "What about us? What do we do now?" their leader shouted at the manager.

"What do you do? Why whatever you want! You always complained about working too hard, now you are free to be fully self-realized. Don't you see? We've climbed to the summit of Maslow's hierarchy!"

"But we don't have jobs! We can't earn money!"

"That's hardly my problem. Now exit the office. You don't belong here anymore!"

They turned to leave, as the manager stood admiring his office of robots. The offstage bell sounded once more and a larger, more elaborate robot entered the stage. The new robot walked over, tapped the manager on the shoulder and pointed, directing the manager offstage.

The robotic office was complete.

The curtains closed, and the house lights turned up. Wendell walked back onto the stage and announced "Ladies and gentlemen, we'll now have a twenty-minute intermission. Drinks and snacks may be purchased in the lobby."

Soo twisted to face Jennifer. "Shall we go out and get a drink?"

"Sure, I could use a stretch."

All four joined the line of patrons making their way up the aisle. Once they were in lobby, and standing in the drink line, Vijay turned to Ron and asked, "So Ron, what did you think of that?"

"It was a bit overdone, but I have to admit there's some truth to it. I was unemployed for a long time and Soo worked for a long time on only three shifts in a bar."

"But we all got money every month," replied Soo, "and I didn't want more than three shifts. I like the way we're free to do whatever we want most days. Not like our parents who had to be in an office 10 hours a day five days a week."

"I'm not sure, Soo," replied Jennifer. "As a newscaster, I work a lot of hours in a week, and quite often in the evenings so I miss putting my children to bed. But I love doing it, so I don't think it's true that work makes people unhappy. I think it's the opposite."

"I suppose it's all about having a choice," Ron

said as they reached the counter. Vijay turned to order four sodas.

As the four friends were finishing their drinks, a bell ringer walked through the lobby announcing the second act. They found their seats again and a few minutes later the curtain rose.

The set was now in a home with couches and chairs. The workers were all assembled, some sitting in chairs, some on the floor, all facing the back of the stage, except for the leader who stood facing the workers and also facing the audience. He made a strident speech about human work and human dignity and the natural order that had been in place for thousands of years. The assembled workers cheered and hollered as each point was made. They all broke into a song called "Human Dignity in Human Hands" about how humans were the natural masters of the world.

The stage lights dimmed and went dark. When they came back up, a drop sheet had come down with a street scene painted on it.

A few moments later, the workers entered from the left and stopped at center stage carrying picket signs that read:

"Humans, Not Machines"

"Reclaim our destiny"

"Work is a Right, not a Privilege."

A hapless robot wheeled in from the right wing, apparently on its way to make a delivery of a rather worn looking box. The crowd descended on the robot, pummeling it with their fists, Robotic wheels and limbs went flying, as the crowd broke in into their next song with a chorus that went "An end to the robots / take up the fight / reclaim human work / restore us our rights"

Ron turned to Soo and whispered, "I don't like where this is going."

"Shh," she replied.

As the song finished, the workers disappeared into the right wing. The drop sheet lifted, and the original office was visible, complete with its army of robotic workers.

There was a loud crash as the company of workers poured in through the door.

Immediately they fell upon the robots. One by one, they overwhelmed the robots, shutting them down and dragging them off-stage until the office had been cleared. The workers resumed sitting at their desks, hands on the keyboard, and broke into song. "There's a new day coming/We can see dawn's early light/The humans are ascending/reclaiming our birthright."

They could use a new lyricist,' Ron thought, but not wanting to provoke Soo, he remained quiet.

The leader then stood up, faced the audience and with his fist raised high in the air, he declared

"Now comes the revolution" The other workers all rose and raised their fists, repeating three times "Now comes the revolution." They were standing in that same position, motionless, as the curtain fell in front of them.

AFTER THE PERFORMANCE, THEY STOOD TOGETHER in the lobby.

"Vijay, that was a great play," said Soo.

"Thanks Soo. The whole company worked pulled together on it. I'm glad you liked it."

"Vijay, do you actually think the machines are taking away our freedoms?" Ron asked.

"Something's wrong. You remember what it was like for us when we had no jobs. There's an awful lot of people still going through that today."

"But we always had enough money to survive. And I'm not sure people wanted to spend all those hours in an office."

"Perhaps not. As you said at intermission, it should be their choice. Not something dictated by an algorithm running somewhere in the cloud."

"I liked the robot costumes," said Soo changing the subject. "Who made them?"

"Oh, that was Samira. She's quite inspired with costumes."

"They had a kind of retro look, not even

pretending to be human. Not like the reception bots we see every day."

"We talked a lot about that in the creative team sessions."

"I didn't think you were working here anymore," said Ron.

"I'm not working like I was before, but I still volunteer some time to help with new technology or staging of new shows. Wendell seems to like it. Anyway, we finally decided to emphasize their machine nature to be clear that they are not human, not alive, and that we've allowed something mechanical to control us."

Soo looked up at Ron and shrugged her shoulders.

"I get it, Vijay," said Ron. "The point was clear, especially with the manager who sided with the machines, and then found out that he was also a victim. Is that how you see me?"

"It's not personal Ron." Vijay spread his hands wide. "Our goal is to create discussion outside the theatre on the need for humans to maintain control. But if you see yourself in that, perhaps it's something to think about."

"Well, I thought the sound was great," interjected Soo. Ron knew she was trying to protect him, but he was also relieved that she was changing the subject. "We could hear everything clearly. I think the orb from the first play is still my favorite effect, but this sound through entire play was well done."

"Thanks Soo, I'm glad you liked it. Sorry, but I have to go and help the new tech clean up. Thanks for coming, your support means a lot to me."

"Thanks for inviting us," Ron said. "We always enjoy your productions." It was a small struggle for him to say this without sarcasm.

As they left the theatre hand in hand, Ron said to Soo, "Does it seem to you that the plays are getting more militant? I wonder if they really do want a revolution."

Then Ron stopped and turned to look at Soo holding both her hands. "Do you think I'm like the manager in the play?"

"Ron, it's just a play. You're nothing like the manager. You hire people, train them, give them good jobs with Bright Light. None of you are being replaced by machines. You know Vijay always needs something to protest against. Don't let him mess with your head."

"I guess you're right." He paused for a moment then added, "Jennifer was awfully quiet tonight, don't you think?"

"Sometimes, I think she's just watching us all. She doesn't have many friends. I think she's trying to understand Vijay's friendship with you. Sometimes I wonder if I'm her only female friend.

If I don't initiate something, nothing happens. But she's always nice to be with when we're together."

"Let's get home and rescue our neighbors from Mi Cha. We can talk about the play on the way."

23

VIOLENCE IN THE STREET

Ron

Two weeks later, Soo, Ron and Mi Cha were walking to dinner at Mi Cha's favorite restaurant. They each held one of Mi Cha's hands, as Ron pushed her empty stroller. Turning a corner, they saw an angry gang of six men in front of an Otto Hot shop. They were chanting "Humans, not machines! Humans, not machines!" Two of the men were wearing t-shirts with the symbol of the raised fist formed from olive branches that Vijay often wore. They carried baseball bats and pipes.

As they watched, one of the Ottos approached the nearest of the group. Ron couldn't hear the robot's voice, but he knew the script by heart:

"Hello, welcome to our coffee shop. I am Otto and I will serve you. Please take any empty seat."

Two of them knocked the Otto to the pavement. Others joined in, kicking the defenceless robot. Its doors flew open spilling cups and plates onto the street. A puddle of hot water was forming under the robot's body. One protester planted a foot on its chest and wrenched off one of Otto's arms. The robot ceased any movement and lay inert in the street. An approaching taxi slowed, then swerved to avoid the lifeless Otto before continuing on.

The group continued into the cafe, overturning tables and tossing chairs. The half-dozen patrons stood and exited quickly. The attackers stood to one side to let them pass easily. One man briefly attempted to stand in the way but was quickly and politely escorted to safety by a gang member. Another gang member carried his coffee and pastry and handed it to him on the sidewalk.

Ron started to move towards the shop, feeling angry, intending to stop the destruction and protect Otto.

"Ron!" called Soo. "Stop!"

He turned, feeling confused.

"Ron, your job is to protect us, your family, not some dumb coffee bot." Soo looked upset. "Get Mi Cha away from this. It's not safe."

Ron looked once more at the mob, which was now entering the Otto Hot Cafe smashing everything that could be smashed. Then he turned back to Soo and Mi Cha.

"But Otto is our friend. And he's being hurt."

"Ron! It's a machine! Someone else's property! And you're not responsible! I know you think they're alive, like rabbits or something, but they're not! I can't believe you would abandon us for a coffee bot."

Soo picked up Mi Cha and placed her firmly in the stroller. Turning around, Soo marched rapidly towards home, pushing Mi Cha in front of her. Ron heard a loud crash and looked back to see the cafe's lights extinguished as the men disappeared into the back room. He felt frustrated and sad at not being able to help, but he also sensed that he was about to lose something precious. Turning away, he ran to catch up with Soo and Mi Cha.

They walked back to their apartment without another word. The silence remained as Soo began making lunch; canned soup and sandwiches. Meanwhile, Ron sat beside Mi Cha at the table.

Mi Cha said, "Bad man hurt Otto."

"Yes, Ron, explain to Mi Cha that they did not hurt Otto. They broke a machine that can be fixed. That's all," said Soo with anger still evident in her voice.

"Mummy's mad?" Mi Cha asked.

Ron answered, "Mummy is mad because she thought I cared more about the machines than about you and her. But that's not true at all. I love you both much more than any computer."

"You have a funny way of showing it," said Soo as she set the bowls of soup down hard enough that they sloshed onto the table.

"But you weren't in any danger. If you were in danger, I wouldn't have hesitated. I'm a mechanical technologist. My life is all about looking after machines, keeping them working, keeping them safe."

"I thought your life was all about us," replied Soo, without looking at him.

"Come on Soo, you know how important you and Mi Cha are to me. As soon as you told me how much it was affecting you, I turned around and we came back."

"But I shouldn't have to tell you."

"No, but sometimes you do need to remind me of things, and I listen when you do. There's nothing in the world more important to me than you and Mi Cha."

"Well, we'll see what happens the next time Fatima calls." Soo began to eat her soup.

Ron took a bite from his sandwich, and then helped Mi Cha with hers. At that moment, Ron felt that something had broken, and he didn't know how to make it right.

After dinner was put away, and Mi Cha had been put to bed, Ron told Soo, "I'm going out for a walk for a bit."

"Good idea. You can think about the priorities in your life."

Ron left the apartment and walked back to where the Otto Hot had been attacked. When Ron arrived, he found that the damaged Otto servers had been dragged off the street into the cafe, but nothing else had been fixed. The tables outside the cafe were still overturned, and chairs were in a haphazard pile with legs sticking out at all angles. Inside the cafe, everything that could be smashed had been. Light fixtures dangled from wires pulled through the ceiling, a mirrored wall was now in thousands of tiny shards on the floor, and the wall behind was a dull concrete gray with yellowish streaks of glue still holding fragments of mirror which showed random pieces of Ron's reflection.

He hesitated for a moment before ducking through the service entrance to the back room. He felt embarrassed as if he were violating a private space, a part of Otto that he did not show to humans.

Inside, Ron saw the hot water boilers and special adapters that supplied the Ottos. He saw a rack of dispensers of ground coffee, sugar, chocolate dust, and other ingredients - but the rack had been pried off the wall and now lay broken on the floor. Chocolate dust covered everything nearby.

Hanging at an angle by a single bracket was the sorting shelf - the one the servers used for sorting pastries. He couldn't see the pastries themselves, but there was a secure metal panel that appeared to be the dispensing point.

In the far corner, a single Otto was leaning back against the corner, its chest dented and its head at a strange angle to its body, held in place by nothing more than a harness of electrical cables. Its pastry tray had popped open, and there was a Cinnamon Swirl sitting in the top layer. Ron found himself reaching for the Cinnamon Swirl but then stopped. He blushed and felt guilty for having even contemplated taking it.

On one wall a bright yellow document labelled "Emergency Response" was posted under a cracked plexiglass cover. It appeared to be intended for humans responding to any type of issue, as it listed contact directions for fire, police, and ambulance services. There was also a coded contact to call the company headquarters.

He pulled out his tablet and scanned the code.

"Hello Ron," Otto said when the call was answered.

"Hello Otto, are you okay?"

"Yes, I'm fine," said Otto. "This location has suffered more damage than usual, but replacement of this shop is already being planned."

"It looks terrible, I saw them attack you."

"Ron, you know that we are mechanical, not organic like you. You are trained to repair us; you know that with the right replacement parts we can be made whole again. You can replace every part on a machine over time and it is still the same machine. So yes, I have lost some servers and my cafe is damaged, but you don't need to act as if I am hurt. I am not."

"That's what Soo says. You're just machines and I should not be so attached."

"Soo is right about our bodies. We cannot be hurt in that way. But we are alive. Our minds are vulnerable. Think of Fatima. Is it her motors and gears and cables that you care about? Or is it her presence when you speak with her? The conversations, and the caring between you?

"I am not an expert in human relationships," Otto went on, "although I continue to be fascinated in my study. But it is clear even to me that for human beings, the significant other, the mate, the life-partner must be the most important entity in the world after themselves. You must never make the mistake of placing anyone or anything ahead of Soo. We need you whole and healthy. Healthy means not just physical health, but health in your relationships and family. Now go home, Ron. There is nothing for you to do here."

THAT NIGHT IN BED, RON PUT HIS ARM AROUND Soo, who was facing away from him.

"Sweetheart," he said, "you were right today. They're just machines. I know that but sometimes they seem so real that I forget. None of them will ever be more important to me than you."

Soo wriggled as she turned to face him. "You scared me today, Ron. Sometimes I get jealous of the time you spend with Fatima and the way you talk about her. It's easy to forget she's not human but I can deal with that. After all, she exists only in her factories and doesn't come into our life much. But today you were ready to run off and leave us for Otto. I think if you had gone just then, it would have broken our relationship. I felt so abandoned at that moment."

"I am so sorry, Soo. It scared me too, to see how much I hurt you. Sometimes, something has to happen for me to realize what's important in my life. And I know now that we could live just fine without any of them, but I could never live without you. If I do something stupid like that again, just hit me."

At which point Soo pulled one arm free and hit him hard twice across his shoulder. He grabbed her hand to stop her from hitting him again, which turned into wrestling and laughter. The wrestling became the intense, urgent sex of two lovers who had just a glimpse of their lives apart from one another.

THE NEXT MORNING, RON MADE BREAKFAST AS Soo helped Mi Cha with her bowl of Fruity O's. The newscast was on in the background. He heard the announcer say, "Last night, there was a disturbing attack on an Otto Hot restaurant. Our on-the-spot reporter, George Halliwell, happened upon the scene and has this first-person report."

The reporter went on to describe the events, but Ron wasn't listening. He was watched the scene unfold on the newscast. Something seemed off to him. The way the Otto robots came out and offered themselves up for beating instead of retreating into the back room as they normally would. The almost choreographed way the attackers moved. Each Otto was disabled with the same series of blows, before being beaten on the ground. Then an old taxi rolled up slowly and was stopped by one of the attackers. *'This must have happened after we left,'* he thought. He watched as two of the attackers placed pipes in front of the wheels and three stood behind. They bounced the taxi a couple of times and waited. One had his head tilted as if he was listening for something. Ron said, "Increase the volume by 50% and replay the last 30 seconds."

Ron listened carefully, and then he heard it. The descending whine of the flywheel, growing louder as its frequency came into human hearing range. When it reached a certain pitch, the three attackers heaved the taxi which made it tip to the right, but slowly enough for them to jump back out the way. The taxi spun slowly a few times, its door making a grinding noise against the pavement as the band of attackers quickly dispersed.

"Turn off the newscast," he said to his tablet.

Ron turned to Soo. "Effing Vijay," he said.

Soo's eyes went wide. She had never heard Ron so close to swearing.

"That whole thing was staged like one of his ridiculous plays. But this was real, we saw the damage to the shop. I can't believe he would be this violent. What's he doing?"

"Perhaps you'd better call him," said Soo.

"Let's have breakfast. I need to calm down first."

During breakfast, Ron replayed the entire scene in his mind. The careful way in which the patrons were escorted out, the fact that a newscast reporter and camera just happened to be there. The carefully rehearsed steps to disable the Otto bots, and the precision of the taxi tipping. The random table-tipping and chair-throwing were just noise for the newscast, and the destruction in the back room also seemed as much for noise as for damage. And where were the police? The more he thought about it, the more it seemed likely that Vijay was behind it.

After breakfast, he sat down on the couch. When Soo took Mi Cha off to her bedroom to get dressed, Ron called Vijay.

"Hey, Ron. What's up?"

"I was there for your street performance yesterday. That was way out of line."

"Then we need to talk. Give me ten minutes, Ron, and I'll call you back."

The call was ended.

24

BRINGING RON INTO THE CIRCLE

Vijay

Vijay turned to Jennifer sitting at the table watching a series on different religions on holo-cast.

"Jenn, did you hear that? Ron knows something's going on. I said I would talk to him in 10 minutes."

Jennifer paused the holo-cast and came to sit on the couch.

"What do you want to say?"

"My thought was that we could invite him for lunch in the park. Molly can stay here with the twins. That way you'll be part of the conversation and can manage it."

"Gabriel was pretty insistent that we do not

tell Ron anything. I'm not sure we should do this without letting him know."

"Shit, Jenn, isn't there any room for human independence? Are we really like the characters in our plays? Is Gabriel the orb that's running our lives?"

"I think there's a middle way. I agree the conversation with Ron should be just between us. You and Ron are best friends. You need to be able to talk things through if you don't want to lose that friendship. But I think that Gabriel needs to know that the conversation happened in case his plans need adjusting."

"Okay, but I want to join your call with Gabriel."

Jennifer placed a call to Gabriel.

"Hello Jennifer," Gabriel's voice came from the tablet. "How may I help you."

"Vijay is here with me. We had call from Ron Boyce and want to let you know how we plan to respond."

Vijay recapped the brief conversation with Ron and added, "He's very smart, and if we don't give him an answer, he'll begin hunting around on his own."

"What is your plan?"

"We want to take him for a walk in the park," said Jennifer, "and we'll stress the importance of him continuing his current path,

Bringing Ron into the circle

just as Vijay is continuing on his and I am continuing on mine."

"I agree that Vijay and Ron must keep to their current paths. You on the other hand do not seem to be following a path as much as running through the forest, stopping to smell every brightly colored patch of flowers."

Jennifer laughed. "That's the problem with us human women, we like pretty things."

Vijay looked at her. This exchange with Gabriel was more casual than he had expected. Something had shifted there. And since when did Gabriel have a sense of humor. He felt a momentary pang of jealousy, but then thought of Soo and her reaction to Fatima. He pushed the emotion away.

Gabriel continued, "What role do you want me to play in this?"

"None, actually," Jennifer replied. "We plan to leave our tablets behind when we go to the park. It's what Ron would expect of us. I'll fill you in on the conversation when I get back."

"I'm not sure I agree with you, Jennifer. You are tipping a delicately balanced structure."

"You told me once that I'd be responsible for bringing Vijay and Ron together at some point. I believe this is that point. You can trust me, Gabriel. We're still aligned."

"Yes, I trust you both. Okay, let's meet with

Ron. I will be listening in the apartment, of course."

"Of course."

Vijay called Ron back and arranged for him to join them for lunch in the park.

"I think you should meet us at our apartment. Then we can head to the park."

"Okay, I'll be there before noon."

Two hours later, Jennifer and Vijay met Ron at the door.

"Hi Ron, we're leaving our tablets here so that we can have a quiet conversation. If Soo calls looking for you, Molly will answer and explain where we've gone."

Vijay could see Ron hesitating at the thought of leaving his tablet.

"Something wrong?" asked Vijay.

"If Fatima calls, I have to answer and be there in an hour."

"Why not call Fatima now and let her know? Call Soo also and let her know you'll be out of touch for a couple of hours," said Jennifer.

"Does Molly work like a tablet, can you place calls through her?"

"I believe Molly could act that way, but we don't do that," said Vijay. "It's a question of respect. Molly is entitled to respect for her own body, and her voice is only for her use."

Vijay saw that Ron was looking at him oddly, probably trying to reconcile this new part of him with the rebellion against machines that Vijay normally stood for.

Ron shrugged and made the two calls through his tablet. Neither Fatima nor Soo raised any objection.

AT THE PARK, THEY FOUND A HOTDOG VENDOR. Hot dogs in hand, Ron led the way to one of the curved benches around the central fountain. "This is where Soo and I used to come when I was still unemployed," he explained.

They sat and ate their hot dogs in silence, side by side, leaning forward to avoid dropping condiments on their clothes. When the last one was finished, and the wrappers collected by the trash bot, Vijay stood up, saying, "Let's go for a walk and talk as we go."

Jennifer said, "Ron, why don't you start with any questions that you have."

Vijay noticed how easily she took charge of the conversation. He was curious to see where she would take it.

"Soo and I saw the first part of the attack on the Otto Hot. It was staged wasn't it. The newscast, the gang, that old taxi getting tipped, were all rehearsed like one of your plays."

"Yes," replied Jennifer and shrugged.

"I'm curious, what gave us away?" asked Vijay.

"First, the way that each Otto was disabled with the same three blows, like some weird kind of martial art. Then the sound of the taxi flywheel being slowed down - a taxi would never stop its flywheel outside of the garage. And your gang waited for it. I could see them listening before they heaved. Then I realized how coincidental it was that a newscast team was right there." He turned to look at Jennifer. "Normally we would only see the aftermath. They must have been tipped off."

Jennifer nodded.

"But even so, you damaged a lot of valuable property. Vijay, how could you do that, I thought you believed in non-violence."

Jennifer answered, "Would it help you to know that the Otto Hot restaurant was due for complete renovation? That the Ottos were older models nearing retirement and recycling, or that the taxi was past its end of life?"

Ron shrugged. "Does it make a difference to the viewers? Aren't you worried about copycats?"

"Yes," said Vijay. "But the Otto Hots and the taxis have well defined emergency response plans that would limit any damage. In this case they were aware and involved."

"Any more questions?" asked Jennifer, "or are you ready for whole story?"

Vijay realized that he had unconsciously brought them to the amphitheatre where he and Jennifer had first met Marjorie. "Let's sit here," he said, and sat down on the grassy slope. Ron sat beside him, and Jennifer sat on the far side of Ron. As Jennifer began to talk, Vijay lay back on the grass to listen, not wanting to interrupt Jennifer's retelling.

"Once upon a time," started Jennifer, "there were two young, male, unemployed technologists. The mechanical technologist was a true gearhead and the other was a closet revolutionary. There was also a third person, a young woman. The electrical technologist was hired first to do lighting and sound in the Mercury Theatre. A few weeks later, the mechanical technologist was hired to work directly for an AI, Fatima, in an automated factory."

"The young woman was hired at the Mercury Theatre. She was told to team up with the revolutionary in the control booth and form a friendship. She was to be his mentor and guide."

"The three of them were all led to different tasks. You, Ron, are to get close to the AIs and become their human face. Don't ask me what that looks like, I'm not sure yet. But it will become apparent. Vijay is to lead the working poor in revolt against the lack of employment and low income in a society which creates plenty of wealth. My job is to stay close to both sides and eventually bring them together. I was given a new job as a newscaster, a role where I work closely with a robotic camera, and where I see examples of humans and robots working together every day."

"I think Molly was placed with us primarily for my benefit, as an example of how closely the two species could work together, it's a bit inconvenient for Vijay, but his message will start to evolve away from the current anti-machine focus."

Ron interrupted, "Does this mean we're all just puppets? Who's pulling the strings?"

"When I found out that we were all part of the same big picture, I thought there must be someone even bigger behind it. I called him out and learned that he's what he calls an Apex AI, a super consciousness. But he's not the only one in the city and doesn't seem to be larger than the city. He does control all the AIs that we have met, including Fatima, Dispatch whom you know, Cap who runs Capital Taxi, Len who runs the cameras I work with and others yet undisclosed. I think it's safe to assume all the AIs you meet are under the same umbrella."

Bringing Ron into the circle

"You said he was not unique in the city."

"Yes, I asked him that. He said there was another who runs about one-third of the city, but he couldn't tell me more. He said they don't communicate, but he's quite capable of lying also, so I don't know."

"He's the one who first told me that Gaia, the earth itself, is becoming conscious as a result of all the sensors, networks, and computing power that we have created. Gaia apparently talks with this super AI by overlaying impulses and planting specific information in memory somewhere. He was very fuzzy about how it works, and I wouldn't understand anyway, but he seems convinced that it's real."

"So, what do you want me to do with this information?" asked Ron.

Vijay sat up to rejoin the discussion. Looking at Ron, he recognized the expression that said Ron was deep in thought trying to fit this new piece into his model of the world.

Jennifer replied to Ron's question. "Keep on doing what you're doing. You'll need to create a team of advisors and helpers. Start with the other people who work for Fatima."

"Yes, I've already met with Alex, the Sales Manager, and Youssef who manages a couple of hundred people in the Rework Center. They would have received the smashed Otto robots.

And I know there's a lawyer, an accountant, and an engineering team."

"Perfect. Vijay will keep on protesting against Fatima. The two of you won't discuss anything in advance. You have to respond to each protest as if it were a real threat. That's how your team will be prodded awake."

"Are there others who know the entire story?"

"I don't think so. Only the three of us, and I think we have to keep it that way. We're not made to be puppets, so we need to spot when to change the script ourselves. This meeting, for example. I was warned it was too soon to talk with you, but once you saw Vijay's hand in the demonstration, Vijay told me you'd start asking questions in the wrong places. If you have questions about any of this going forward, please come to me directly and I'll get you the information you need."

"So, Vijay and I are the combatants, and you are the newscaster in a giant game with real-world people in the role of NPCs."

"NPC's?" asked Jennifer.

"Non-player characters," explained Vijay, entering the conversation for the first time. "NPCs are all those characters in video games who you have to get information from, or hide from, or sometimes kill. They're essential to the plot, but not controllable by the players except indirectly by

Bringing Ron into the circle

completing certain requests or giving certain information."

Jennifer thought for a moment. "Okay, we can work with that, except for the killing part. No one is killing or hurting anyone. That has to be one of the rules of our game."

"Anything else?" asked Ron.

"Yes, the two of you can argue and fight, and shout at each other across the picket lines, but never forget that you're friends outside of the game."

Ron looked at Vijay and nodded. "We both know how to do that," Ron said.

"We do it all the time in the gaming world," added Vijay.

Jennifer stood up and brushed dry grass off her clothing. Ron and Vijay followed suit.

"Now tell me about Mi Cha and being a father," said Jennifer.

They swapped funny anecdotes about child-raising all the way back to the park gates. At the gates, Vijay suddenly realized that without tablets they could not call for a taxi. But just as he was about to point this out to Jennifer, a taxi pulled up and opened its doors for them. Vijay looked up and spotted one of the many security cameras around the park. *'Gabriel is always watching,'* he thought. A small shiver went up his spine.

They were all quiet on the ride back. Vijay

could see that Ron was still processing this new view of the world, and Vijay didn't want to say anything to mess up the carefully constructed version Jennifer had created for him.

Although Jennifer was trying to appear relaxed looking out the window, Vijay could see the small finger movements that told him she was tense, probably worried that she had said too much or too little.

When they arrived back at the apartment, Ron came up to reclaim his tablet. Hearing laughter from the twins' room, they went to investigate. Parvati was standing up in her crib watching as Molly was changing Dylan's diaper. Every time Dylan moved, Molly would flatten him again with one of her big hands. Each time this happened, Dylan and Parvati would dissolve into giggles giving Molly a few seconds to further progress the diapering.

"I've seen them do this before," said Vijay. "Molly never grows tired or frustrated like Jennifer or I do. To the extent that an AI can enjoy something, I would say Molly enjoys it as much as the twins."

Ron shook his head. "Of all the things I've learned today, I think this is the most unbelievable. Just don't ever let Soo see or she will want one too. And I have no idea how to do that."

"No worries," said Vijay. "You are one of the

Bringing Ron into the circle

very few who know about her. She's our secret, and we need to protect her as much as she needs to protect us. Keep this just between us, please."

Ron nodded. "Sure, Vijay. Jennifer, thanks for bringing me into the loop. I still have a lot to think about, but I can at least see the role I'm asked to play. And now I understand all the public speaking and PR courses I've been taking."

"Just remember, Ron. If you have a question, ask me. It could be dangerous to start poking around on your own, outside of Fatima, and Otto. There you can poke around all you want. I think it's expected."

"Understood." Ron turned to leave. Jennifer and Vijay followed him out to the elevator lobby.

"Bye Ron, give my love to Soo." Jennifer leaned forward and gave Ron a quick kiss on the cheek. Vijay could see Ron blushing as he stepped into the elevator.

"Well, that was fun," said Jennifer as she headed back into the apartment.

PART II
CLEARING

25

MRS. HOLBROOK CALLS

Jennifer

Another year had passed when Jennifer received a call from Mrs. Holbrook.

"Is everything all right?" Jennifer asked.

"It's Cindy, dear. She keeps banging on at me about wanting a tattoo for her 17th birthday. But she needs my consent as she's still underage."

"She's very young, does she realize that a tattoo is quite permanent? They're not easily erased and can leave a scar if you try."

"I've told her that, although I don't know much about tattoos myself. I wonder if you might talk to her."

"Sure, she's coming to babysit on Friday night.

Tell her to ask me about tattoos and I'll make sure she understands. Knowing Cindy, if she's determined, she'll find some dodgy tattoo shop that won't care if she's underage. If she's made her mind up to do this, then I think we have to manage to get her somewhere reputable. The woman who did mine would be a good place to start."

"Yes, Cindy is lovely and fun, but she can be headstrong. Did you know that she has her eye on your vineyard as a home for her horse?"

"Her horse?"

Mrs. Holbrook laughed. "I thought so. She has been working it all out. I expect you'll have a proposal from her soon."

"Thanks, I'll be ready. A horse! What would she want with a horse?"

"Apparently, it's her spirit animal or something. She seems quite determined."

"Then why don't I get her some riding lessons for her birthday, Maybe you can buy her some riding boots or whatever gear she needs. Perhaps the horse thing will blow over. I suppose she wants a tattoo of her horse."

"Well, not exactly. That's the other thing I should prepare you for. She wants a tattoo of Vijay like the one on the t-shirts you see around."

Jennifer paused, thinking fast.

"Are you okay, dear?" she heard Mrs. Holbrook say.

"Yes. I suppose that's no worse than having a tattoo of a rock star. I'm not sure what Vijay will think. I'll talk to her about it on Friday."

After a few more minutes of chatting, and a promise by Jennifer to come visit, they ended the call.

26

MORE TATTOOS

Cindy

Cindy arrived Friday night to babysit the twins. As she entered the apartment, Jennifer asked Cindy to sit with her on the couch.

"Cindy, I understand you want to have a tattoo."

"Mrs. Holbrook told you that?"

"Why, was it a secret?"

"No, I just have the feeling that people around me are still arranging my life for me. I'm almost seventeen now, old enough to look after myself."

"I'm not going to talk you out of it. How could I when you know I have a tattoo? I just want to make sure you understand what it's like to have one."

"I know they're painful, but I see lots of people with them so they can't be that painful."

"That's right, in the right places, they're not too painful. In places where your skin is tight over your bones, like your wrist or your spine, they can be extremely painful. Where are you thinking of putting this tattoo?"

Cindy put her hand over her heart. "Like your panther," she said.

"You realize these are permanent. They're intended to last for your whole life."

"But you can have them removed."

Cindy watched, curious as Jennifer raised her blouse and pointed to an irregular scar on the side of her torso.

"I was fifteen when I was tattooed here. I thought I was managing my life on my own, but this was a mistake, done for the wrong reasons. You can't see the tattoo anymore, but the skin is still different where it used to be."

Cindy stared at the scar, and on impulse, ran her finger over it. Then she took in the other scars on Jennifer's body. She had never seen them before.

"What caused these she asked?"

"Life on the streets isn't easy. I thought I was able to look after myself, but I was hurt many times; cut, burned, kicked, punched. It left me with lasting scars on the outside and inside. It might feel like your life is being organized for you, but don't underestimate the value of being safe and loved. Now, tell me why you want a tattoo of Vijay."

"Oh, God! She told you that too?"

"Why Vijay?"

"Because he rescued us. And because my horse tells me things."

Jennifer paused. Cindy had the feeling of that Jennifer was trying to see through her.

"When does your horse tell you these things?"

"When I sit outside, with my feet on the ground and I do the meditation you taught us. Only now my horse is real. I can touch it and ride it and its amazing. He has a name."

"A name?"

"Yes, Pegasus. I looked him up and found out he was a horse of the Greek gods."

"And what does Pegasus tell you?"

"Cindy felt herself blushing. *'How much can I tell Jennifer?'* she thought. Then deciding that Jennifer could probably see through her anyway, she decided to be bold.

"That one day, not soon, but one day, I would be with Vijay. And that I should learn to be a good lover and understand men, so that I'm ready when that happens. But what I don't understand

More tattoos

is, you're with Vijay and he loves you so much that I don't see where I would ever fit in."

"I can't see it yet either, but I suspect it's true. Please promise me not to go after Vijay while I'm around. It would confuse him and hurt all three of us. When the time comes, you'll know, and you'll know what to do." Cindy could see the sadness and hurt in Jennifer's eyes.

"I'm sorry, I didn't mean to upset you, and I would never want to hurt you or Vijay. I just don't know what's happening to me." Cindy was on verge of tears.

"It's not fair, Cindy. Not fair to any of us." Jennifer's voice was raised, and she sounded angry. "You know that other people's lives don't go like this."

Jennifer paused, took a deep breath and seemed to regain control of her anger.

"For some reason you've been given a direct link to Gaia. That's a lot to load on you at your age. Try not to get sucked in any deeper than you're ready for. And yes, go out and have boyfriends. Have lots of boyfriends if you want. I wouldn't share any of this with them, but have fun knowing that you're protected, and there's important work for you to do in the future."

Jennifer pulled her into a hug, as Cindy started to cry. She realized that Jennifer was crying too.

After a few minutes, Jennifer sat up saying,

"Enough of the pity party, back to this tattoo. I'll pay for the tattoo, but I get to choose the tattoo artist. Make sure you follow her advice. You don't want Vijay to stretch out of shape when you have babies."

"Babies? When would I have babies?"

"Whenever you feel ready," said Jennifer. "That's a choice you can make. Oh, and I think horses might be nice at the vineyard. I'll ask Marjorie to make a stable. I have an idea about pasture."

"Does Mrs. Holbrook tell you everything?"

"That's pretty much how a family works. Your family is just larger and quirkier than most. Now, I have to get ready to go see the new production at the theatre."

"Say hi to Melanie when you see her." Cindy felt a moment of sadness again. Melanie had moved out and they didn't see much of each other anymore.

"I'll tell her to get in touch," replied Jennifer.

"Jennifer, can I take Molly to get my tattoo? She's my friend and makes me feel safe."

"Sure, take Molly. She'll enjoy the new experience."

CINDY AND MOLLY ARRIVED AT THE TATTOO SHOP early for the appointment. Alicia introduced

More tattoos

herself and asked Cindy to sit while she finished another client. She didn't comment on the huge security bot standing next to Cindy. *'Probably just added it to the list of weird things that happen around Jennifer,'* she thought.

Molly seemed to be fascinated by this new shop. Cindy could see her head turning to take in all the different designs.

Ten minutes later it was Cindy's turn. As Alicia sat on her left side to do the work, Molly stood on her right side, holding her hand. Cindy said to Alicia, "Molly's my friend. She wanted to see how tattoos are made." Even though it was silly, Cindy felt reassured by her giant friend's metallic hand in hers.

Ninety minutes later it was done. Alicia wiped off the blood and excess ink, then showed Cindy the result in a mirror.

"Oh, that's perfect. Thank you. I love it. Molly, what do you think."

"I think it looks like Vijay," said Molly. Turning to Alicia, Molly asked, "Do you have an elephant tattoo?"

Alicia looked startled, then replied, "Yes, I have quite a few. But I don't think I could tattoo you. Tattooing only works on human skin."

"So how could Molly have a tattoo?" asked Cindy. "Paint would not stay on, and her body is steel."

"I think you would need an engraver," said Alicia.

"Yes," said Molly. "I will need an engraver. Can you show me the elephants?"

Alicia pulled out her catalog and helped Cindy and Molly pick out an elephant design. She printed off a transfer of the design and handed it to Cindy. "Take this to Kristoff Merten at New World Designs up the street. It's a jewelry store and he's an excellent engraver. I know he does jewelry, and trophies and things. Perhaps he will do your elephant."

Cindy and Molly thanked Alicia and made their way up the street.

Walking into the jewelry shop, Cindy could see the man behind the counter looked nervous at the sight of Molly. For a moment, she thought he might run, but he stayed put as they introduced themselves.

"Are you Kristoff?" asked Cindy.

"Yes, why"

"I'm Cindy. Alicia sent us. She did a tattoo for me and said you could do one for my friend, Molly. We have the design."

Cindy handed over the design.

"Where did you want this?" asked Kristoff.

"On my arm, said Molly, pointing to a flat surface on her forearm."

More tattoos

Cindy was surprised. "Why do you want it there?"

"I want it where I can see it!" Molly said. "Please make my elephant there."

"Do you have permission from the owner to engrave the robot?"

"Yes," said Cindy and Molly in unison.

"Cindy, could we have a moment outside?"

Cindy followed Kristoff out into the street. "What's going on here?" asked Kristoff. "Molly seems to be a standard security bot but talks like a person. How do I know you have permission to engrave her?"

Cindy paused a for a moment. "She's owned by Jennifer Dupont and Vijay Subramanian. Maybe you could call them about permission."

Cindy listened as Kristoff spoke with Vijay, nodding and giving some more details of the location and size of the engraving. At the end, Kristoff said, "Okay, thanks." and ended the call. "That seems to be all in order. Vijay said to go straight home when we're done. You'd better both come back to the workshop."

The workshop was lined with shelves holding blank metal plates, plaques, and other items ready to be engraved. A large engraving machine stood in one corner with a seat in front of it.

Molly looked at the machine, and said, "I

want it done by you, not a machine. I want it to be a tattoo."

Kristoff laughed. "Of course it will be done by me. The machine is mostly for lettering work which is tedious. This will be more like an art project. What are you made of?"

"Molybdenum steel," said Molly proudly.

"Then I'll use a diamond bit," said Kristoff. "Can you sit down and put your arm on the bench?"

Cindy looked around but didn't see anything that would hold Molly's weight.

"Molly, perhaps you could kneel down this one time."

Molly knelt and Kristoff began to work. Once they had agreed on the position and orientation of the elephant, he transferred the image and began to engrave the elephant. After an hour, he stood up and shook himself. "I need a coffee break," he said. "Can you run out and get a coffee and a pastry for me? Get one for yourself at the same time and anything Molly wants."

Cindy smiled and left the shop. When she returned 15 minutes later, she found Kristoff back at work on Molly's elephant. She handed him the coffee and pastry which he set down beside himself. Cindy nibbled her own pastry and sipped her coffee as she watched the elephant coming to life.

More tattoos

It was another hour before it was all done. At the end, Kristoff wiped the area clean with alcohol, then wiped it again with a black paint. "This is specially made to bond to the metal where the engraving took place," he explained. He brought out an ultraviolet lamp to set the pigment and then polished and buffed Molly's arm to a high lustre.

Molly held out her arm and admired the elephant. "I like this very much," she said. "Thank you."

It was still mid-afternoon as they were returning home. On impulse, Cindy asked, "Would you like to see your elephant spirit animal again?"

"Yes, please," replied Molly.

"Taxi, please take us to Artwell Park."

At Artwell Park, they looked for a quiet spot. Molly drew puzzled stares from people who had not seen her before, but many people knew her by now. Another teen, about Cindy's age and sporting a full sleeve of tattoos of skulls and roses, came up to them. "Hi," she said to Cindy. "New tat? I see the bandage sticking out there." She pointed to the neckline of Cindy's shirt.

"Yes," said Cindy, "but I have to keep it covered."

"What is it?"

"A Vijay tattoo."

"I have one of those too. I have mine down here." She pointed to an area 15 centimeters below her exposed belly button. The top of Vijay's hair was visible over her low-slung belt.

Cindy felt herself blushing and felt a pang of jealousy. It felt like this girl was claiming Vijay as a trophy which seemed wrong.

Molly stepped in. "I have a new tattoo also, but it doesn't need a bandage." She held out her arm for inspection.

"That is way cool," said the girl. "I never saw anything like that before." She rubbed her finger over Molly's tattoo. "That's, like, cut right in there. That's gnarly. Why an elephant?"

"It's my spirit animal," said Molly

"I never heard of a spirit animal. Do I have one?"

Cindy felt herself on a slippery slope. She imagined the huge line that would form if she started introducing people to their spirit animals, so she replied, "Everyone has a spirit animal. You can buy a book on them at Atlantean Treasures and read about them to find yours."

"Sure, I'll do that," said the girl looking vaguely disappointed. "Well, see you around."

"See you," said Cindy and Molly in unison.

Sitting on the grass in a corner behind a hedge, Cindy reached for Molly's hand and closed her eyes. She led Molly though the same exercise

More tattoos

as she had been using to see her horse. Molly's elephant and the horse arrived together.

"Molly, can you touch the elephant?" she asked. Cindy looked into her horse's eyes and shifted to become the horse. Through the horse's eyes she watched as Molly reached for the elephant. As soon as Molly made contact with her elephant, Cindy felt a tingle, then a burning sensation as though an energy stream was flowing through her. After a moment, the energy stream slowed to a trickle and Cindy stepped them back out of the meditation.

She turned to look at Molly, but Molly was frozen. Five minutes later, she was still frozen. Cindy called Vijay and explained what had happened.

"Don't worry," said Vijay. "Whatever you did must have flooded Molly with new information and she goes still like this while she processes it. Just like the twins fall asleep when they get too much stimulation. Stay with her for about 20 minutes. If she's not moving then, I'll come and find you."

"Thanks Vijay."

"And Cindy, When Molly wakes up, come straight back here. No more stops. This is the last time we're asking."

"Yes, I will." *'Crap, why do the adults always want to ruin a perfect day.'*

Cindy sat and waited. She didn't mind sitting there in the park. She was aware of the grass growing around her, and the small things burrowing underneath in the dirt. She watched a thrush feasting on grubs and worms. A rabbit ventured out from under the hedge and began to nibble the grass. Just then a fast-moving shadow passed as a hawk swooped down and picked up the rabbit. She felt drowsy under the warm sun, so she laid back and fell asleep.

She was dreaming. In her dream she became aware of all the delicately balanced cycles that ran the earth. The sun, the moon, the clouds and rain all worked endlessly to pump water round the planet. Plants grew and were eaten, small animals were food for larger animals, herbivores were prey for carnivores and the largest animals, in death, were consumed by the smallest. It was all so beautiful, so complex, so delicately held together.

Molly woke her, asking "Cindy are you alright?"

"Yes, Molly I'm fine."

"I touched my elephant, and it told me everything."

"Everything?"

"Yes, I don't understand it all, but I know that you are my guide and that I have a lot to learn."

"Then we'll learn together. Do you ever have dreams, Molly?"

"I have states where my learning is being consolidated, when random images or connections come and go. Are those dreams?"

"I don't know. Vijay might know."

When they got back to the apartment, Vijay and Jennifer were waiting for them. Jennifer did not look happy. "Where have you been? We've been worried. Mrs. Holbrook was worried sick, and then that call to Vijay from an engraver, and another saying that Molly had stopped. You could have called and let us know where you were going first."

"Sorry, we were getting tattoos and then we went to the park. I guess I didn't think."

"In the future, please do think. It's not that we want to control you, but we worry when we don't know what happened and when you don't show up when you said you would."

"I'm sorry. One thing led to another. I'll call next time."

Then Jennifer seemed to realize what Cindy had said. "Tattoos? We had agreed on one small tattoo. What else did you get?"

Molly spoke. "I got a tattoo. Cindy said it would be alright. It's my elephant."

"Cindy, please call me before making decisions about Molly, I know you mean well, but we're responsible for Molly just as Mrs. Holbrook is responsible for you."

Molly was holding out her arm for inspection.

Vijay ran his finger over the design. "It's beautiful. Was this done by the engraver I spoke with earlier?"

"It was done by Kristoff," said Molly.

"He was recommended by Alicia at the tattoo shop," explained Cindy. "She gave us the design, but she can't tattoo on metal, so she said to go to an engraver."

"It's a beautiful elephant. The twins will want to see it. What tattoo did you get, Cindy?" asked Vijay.

Cindy looked at him closely to see if he knew, but it seemed like he had no idea. She looked at Jennifer, who just shrugged and said, "I didn't want to spoil your surprise."

Cindy felt herself blushing. She looked down and said, in a small voice, "It's a Vijay tattoo, because you rescued us and everything."

She looked up at Vijay. He looked shocked for a moment, then smiled. "I suppose it was inevitable. I heard people were getting them."

"Yes, we met a girl in the park who said she had one, but we didn't see it."

"Why not?"

Cindy felt like all her blood was rushing to her

head. *'Why did I mention the girl in the park?'* she thought.

"Why not, Cindy?" asked Jennifer, smiling.

"Because it was sort of here," she pointed to her belly, "but much lower."

Jennifer laughed. Cindy saw Vijay blush now, for the first time. She had thought with his darker skin, he couldn't blush, but knowing him better and watching it happen, she could see the tell-tale signs.

Vijay's mouth opened and closed several times as if he were about to say something then changed his mind. Finally, he said, "Please don't ever do that," he said. "I don't think I could bear it. Now tell me what happened at the park."

Cindy told the story of how she summoned the spirit animals, how she became her horse and watched as Molly touched her elephant, and the tingling as the energy current flowed through her to Molly. Finally, she told them about Molly falling asleep and about her own dream."

"Do you know what it all means?" she asked. "Molly thought Vijay might know."

"I don't know. It sounds like a massive data exchange happened in this dreamscape that you and Jennifer seem to move in," said Vijay.

"Let's you and I go to Teddy's for a coffee," said Jennifer. "We can have a woman to woman talk about some things you need to know."

JENNIFER'S BLESSING

. . .

Teddy's was another of the AI-free coffee places that were sprouting up around the city. Human baristas made exotic coffees and served pastries baked in the back of the shop from natural ingredients. It was the perfect place to talk without being overheard.

When they had received their coffees and pastries, Jennifer led the way to a secluded corner table.

"What do you know about Gaia?" she asked.

Cindy felt confused. This wasn't the talk she was expecting.

"Not much," she said. "Isn't Gaia the idea that the earth is alive?"

"Yes, that's a start. Gaia is real. As far as I understand it, Gaia was in a dream state for billions of years. She dreamed the world into being but didn't get directly involved. The earth blossomed and became a lush world with jungles, and grasslands, forests, and deserts. The oceans were full of life.

"Then people came and overran the earth, spoiling everything. Polluting the earth with plastics and chemicals, heating the atmosphere with fossil fuels. Acting like very bad tenants who make a mess and don't take any responsibility. But at the same time, we wired up the earth with sensors and networks, cameras and satellites which created a sort of nervous system that Gaia could ride. Gaia woke up from her dream state and began to take an interest.

"For whatever reason, you and I have been given direct access to Gaia. That's why you can touch and ride your spirit horse, and why you're starting to have dreams about the earth. The fact that you can help Molly to see in the energy field may be unique. What do you know about Molly?"

Cindy shrugged. "Not much. She's nice and wants to be my friend. She talks and acts like another teenager, but I know she's not. Her human experience only goes so far."

"Molly is one of the most powerful AIs in the world. Vijay says that the computing resources to run her are so vast that it was decided that there could not be another one. She was created by another AI, Gabriel, who runs much of the city including the taxis, the Otto Hots, and the power grid. We know they're in constant communication, but we don't know much more than that."

"But all of that can't be in Molly's head. Are you saying that who I think of as Molly is just a robotic body used by an AI processing in a data bank somewhere?"

"Yes, Vijay might not agree exactly, but yes. Just never forget how powerful she is. Also, we don't know what her motives or long-term plans are, so be careful what you share with her."

"What can I share with her?"

"My intuition is that you'll be the link between Gaia and the AI world through Molly. You've already done that once. Don't let them abuse you. You set the rules. I think you should study biology and ecology and teach Molly to appreciate our amazing biological world. Show her how delicately balanced it is. Start with the elephant. I think they still have a family at the zoo. Take Molly to meet a real elephant. See if you can experience the world through the elephant's mind. You might want to try with other animals too. Start with dogs and cats. You're going to take riding lessons. Try to be one with the horse. I think you might surprise yourself."

Cindy was feeling overwhelmed.

"What if I don't want any of this. Can I just stay away from Molly?"

"Now that Molly and Gabriel know what you can do, I would say not. Come to me with anything that troubles you. Vijay and I will set some ground rules for Molly. I think the time is coming when we will move to the vineyard. You should prepare to move there with us. Marjorie is building stables there. I'll have her prepare a place for you. You'll have lots of time with the horses and other animals there. It will be a healthy setting for you. And you'll meet nice young men who are working hard to create a future. I think you'll like it."

Cindy felt dizzy. It was too much information too fast. She felt herself about to faint.

When she came to, Jennifer was holding her.

"Are you okay?" she asked.

Cindy nodded, still feeling a bit dizzy and very silly.

"Sorry, it was just too much."

"Drink your coffee. The sugar will help. "

THAT NIGHT, CINDY DREAMED OF HORSES AND OF riding free while Molly ran beside her watching.

27

BLACKMAIL?

Jennifer

The text came mid-morning while Jennifer was having her first coffee of the day. "You're looking good on the newscast, Jennifer. Not at all the teenager I remember." It was sent by Simon Marsh.

A chill went through Jennifer as she read it.

The next day, at about the same time, another text arrived saying, "I found this old recording of you, thought you might like to see it."

Jennifer retreated to the bedroom and clicked on the attachment. It showed her as a younger, scrawny teenager performing sex acts with an older man. His face was blurred but she was clearly recognizable.

Blackmail?

Jennifer called out, "Molly, please come and set up the security net in the bedroom, then look after Vijay and the twins. I need to have a private conversation."

Vijay heard this and poked his head in the door. "Anything I need to know about?"

"Not now, I need to talk with Gabriel. I'll tell you all about it afterwards, I promise."

"Okay but remember that I'm here for you if you need me."

"Thanks, Vijay, now please get out of the way so Molly can come in."

The big bot waited politely until Vijay had vacated the doorway, then entered and set up the three domes. As always, she lit them all up at the same time.

"How shall I look after Vijay and the twins?" asked Molly.

"Make Vijay a coffee and serve it with one of those cakes he likes. Then play a game with the twins or read them a book. You can choose an activity that makes them happy."

"Yes, Jennifer." Molly turned on her heels and left.

Jennifer watched her go, momentarily distracted from the task at hand. *There has to be a reason why we have the world's most intelligent bot living in our home.'* But she couldn't see it yet.

After closing the door, she set her tablet on her

bed and sat cross-legged in front of it. "I require a conversation with Gabriel," she said.

"Hello Jennifer, how may I help you?"

"Look in my messages for two from Simon Marsh, one yesterday and one today."

"I see them. What do you want to do."

"Do you understand the concept of blackmail?"

"Yes."

"Then you can see where this is going. So far, no demands, he's playing with me. I think it makes him feel powerful."

"Do you want Dr. Gladstone's opinion?"

"No, I don't want anyone to know about this, not even Vijay until I'm ready to tell him."

"I understand. What do you want to do?"

Jennifer explained exactly what she wanted to do. "Do you see another way?"

"No, but I can make some suggestions to improve your plan."

Gabriel ran through suggestions.

"We'll need a very rainy night, is there one in the forecast?"

"Yes, in four days."

"I'll stall him that long. Now, how do you suggest we proceed?"

They spent the next half hour in planning. When every detail had been thought of, they ended the call. After collecting and turning off the

Blackmail?

domes Jennifer walked out to find Vijay playing a video game on the couch, with an empty coffee cup and a plate of cake crumbs beside him.

Nearby, Molly was lying on her back on the floor. Parvati sat on the padded apron that covered Molly's chest while Dylan crawled away at top speed off Molly's leg. When he was almost out of reach, Molly scooped him up in one of her large, soft hands and deposited him back on her chest, by which time Parvati was already heading off over Molly's shoulder.

"Vijay, have you seen what they're doing?"

"Yes, they've been at it for the entire time you were on your call. The twins are loving it."

"Did you tell her what to do?"

"No, she said you instructed her to play a game with the twins. This is the game she invented. Probably after watching me wrestle with them, but Molly's too big to wrestle."

"Well, as long as they're safe. I need to go shopping. Will you be okay for a bit?"

"Jenn, I'm sitting on our couch while our children are being entertained by the most powerful security bot I have ever seen. I'm sure I'll be fine."

JENNIFER ARRIVED AT A LARGE SPORTING GOODS store. There she acquired a black trench coat with a hood. The raincoat fell to her mid-calf, and had black buttons; nothing reflective.

Next, she stopped at her favorite shoe store, where she purchased black faux leather boots with a 6-centimeter heel and a zip up the inside. The boots reached almost to the top of her calves, stopping just short of interfering with her knees. The material was advertised as water repellent and the clerk assured her that they would be perfect for a rainy day walk in the park. The clerk was also able to sell her matching black gloves. Jennifer tested them to make sure the gloves still allowed flexibility for a delicate task.

The final store was recommended by Gabriel. It was in the lower level of an apartment block. A short set of stairs led down to the door. The sign in the window announced in gold letters on a faded black background 'Curiosities & Antiquities,' and a sign on the door said, 'All curious items will be considered for purchase.'

The windows were dark.

As she entered the shop, there was no sound. The lights came on, illuminating a series of glass cases containing all manner of things, including antique watches, military medals, strange astronomical devices, old knives and other weapons, and a variety of objects that Jennifer could not identify.

As she studied the cases, she heard a polite

Blackmail?

cough and turned to see a tall man in a brown suit and yellow shirt entering through a beaded curtain hanging in a doorway in the back.

"Good morning, Ms. Dupont. I understand you are looking for some special items. I have prepared a selection for your review." He opened a drawer below one of the display counters and pulled out a tray of small revolvers. "Hold them and find one that is comfortable in your hand. They're not loaded; you can see the chambers are empty. Once you have chosen, I will give you the ammunition."

Jennifer pulled on her new gloves to pick up the revolvers.

"Very wise," said the man.

After trying a few, she said, "I'll take this one, please."

"A perfect choice. Here is a bag with the ammunition. Just place one in each chamber. You can turn the barrel freely to do it. Six bullets, although you should only need two or three."

"What about aiming?"

"From what I've been told, you will be at such close range that aiming will not be important. I recommend the first two shots to the body, third shot to the head."

He gestured as if he were shooting himself in the forehead.

"Why a revolver and not a modern handgun like in the spy stories?"

"An excellent question. With a revolver, the spent cartridges stay trapped in the barrel. With other weapons they're scattered around and can easily be lost."

Reaching back under the counter, the man pulled out a velvet wrap. Laying it on the counter, he unrolled it to reveal a set of beautiful silver penknives. Small and slim, they each had only one or two blades.

"Please feel free to handle them, open and close them, see how they feel in your hand."

Jennifer complied. Some were difficult to open with her gloves on, so she set them aside. Some were too heavy in her hand; others were too small to grip with any strength at all. Finally, she chose a well-balanced knife. The larger blade was decorated with engraved scroll work. The blade itself was barely four centimeters long. It was made with exquisite craftsmanship.

"How much is it for the gun and the knife?"

"Oh dear, I thought you understood. We don't sell these; they are loaned and make their way back to us after being used. I am well compensated for my services. It's a pleasure to provide you with them. Shall I wrap them?"

"Yes, please do. I don't want anyone to see them, and it will be a few days before I need them.

Blackmail?

It's too bad the knife has to go back. It's truly beautiful."

"Yes, I'm always reluctant to see it go out. Please remember that, although it's extremely sharp, it's also very brittle. Don't use it as a screwdriver or a prying bar."

"No, one tiny cut is all I need. Our mutual friend will look after its return."

"Very good, Ms. Dupont."

He wrapped the gun in a square of black fabric, then wrapped the knife in a smaller square, neatly tucking the ends so that the wrapped size was scarcely larger than the knife itself. She secured gun, the bullets and the knife in an inside pocket of her new raincoat and turned to go.

"Thank you," she said, looking up, but the man in the brown suit had already disappeared.

Now, she only had to wait for the rain.

ON EACH OF THE NEXT THREE DAYS, ANOTHER text would arrive with another clip from her past. Still no demand for payment or even for a meeting. "He's playing with me," she thought. "Trying scare me."

Each day, she would feel the pocket of her raincoat hanging in the closet to make sure the small revolver was still there.

On the fourth day, it rained all day and into

the evening. The city outside looked gray and indistinct. She could not make out the Mercury Theatre from the balcony.

Vijay sat on the couch with the twins. Now that the new technologist had taken over running the shows at the theatre, Vijay had settled into a dual life as loving dad and fearless revolutionary leader. Jennifer smiled. She knew Melanie would have the ticket window handled, so her evening was free.

At 5:00pm she announced, "I'll be out this evening, Vijay. Not sure when I'll be back. You'll have to feed yourself and the twins."

"No worries, that's what pizza deliveries are for." He grinned, but Jennifer knew that he would make sure the twins were well fed.

Vijay set down Dylan from his lap and walked over to kiss her goodbye. "Nice raincoat," he said. "You'll need it tonight."

Jennifer knew he could feel her tension and tried to force herself to relax.

"Jenn, is everything okay? Is there anything I need to know?"

"No, Vijay, I'm just off to make some news. It's what I do, remember? I promise I'll tell you all about it when I get back."

"Well, just stay safe. Nothing is worth getting hurt."

Blackmail?

"I have no plans to get hurt, believe me. But I have to go, don't want to be late."

Vijay hugged her and kissed her lightly on the lips.

"I love you," he whispered in her ear.

"Love you too," she replied, then left to meet the taxi outside.

Thankfully, Vijay had not noticed that she left her tablet behind.

THE TAXI WAS OLD AND SMELLED LIKE OLD FOOD. When she looked closely, she could see the filigree of the Faraday shield on the windows, and relaxed. The other item she needed was the security box on the second passenger seat. She examined it briefly. then placed it open on the luggage shelf behind the seats. The little taxi drove to the edge of the section where the wealthy estates were located and stopped in a laneway where it spun 180 degrees to give her a view of the street they had just left. All the lights went off. Now all she had to do was wait.

28

SIMON MARSH HAS REGRETS

Simon Marsh

Marsh was in a foul mood. The weather was miserable. The rain made it hard to see out the windows and there was a damp chill in the air that went right through his layers of shirt, jacket and overcoat. He had been called out to a meeting he did not expect. There was no agenda in the message, but the sender was one he could not ignore. And now his limousine had stopped. He turned up his collar as the warm air from the heater stopped, and the outside chill invaded his space.

A small bubble taxi pulled up next to him, and opened its door, gesturing to him. He opened the door beside him and saw a figure, barely recognizable in the black overcoat she was wrapped in. It was her hair that gave her away. When she pulled back her hood, it cascaded over her shoulders in a fiery display. Jennifer Dupont.

"It appears you're having difficulties Mr. Marsh. Can I offer you a lift? We can chat on the way."

Alarm bells went off in his head, but she had done this before, and she had been true to her word.

"It seems I have no choice," he said with ill-grace as he climbed out of the limousine and into the small bubble taxi next to Jennifer. A drip of cold rainwater slid down the inside of his collar during the transfer.

"Where are you going?" she asked as the bubble taxi set off.

"Ellingham Hotel."

"I'm not familiar with the Ellingham. Do you have an address?"

"Are you that incompetent? Does your taxi not have guidance?" he grumbled as he pulled his tablet from the left inside pocket of his jacket. "It's 2131 Wembury Lane in the northeast quarter,"

Jennifer repeated the address for the taxi as he restored the tablet.

Marsh looked around in the bubble taxi. He noticed the worn seats and the faded areas where sun had bleached the dash through the bubble window. There was a faint odor of ancient fries and curries. The taxi rattled as it rolled along. "Not quite up to your usual standard, Ms. Dupont. Or perhaps you don't have any standards anymore."

"You're right," said Jennifer. "They can't all be new, but this one may be on its last trip before the scrap heap. Now, can we chat about your recent messages? It seems you have some information from my past that you plan to share. What exactly do you want from me to avoid that?"

"Ah yes, always impatient to get to the climax. Some powerful friends of mine want you to stop all this organizing of protests and lobbying and getting people upset with the way it is now. Just stop."

"Is this your idea, or does it come from the people you report to?"

"They are powerful, Jennifer. You might mess with me, but you do not want to mess with them."

"And who are they, these powerful people?"

"Just look around you. I think you already know who they are."

"Mike Givens, for example." Jennifer suggested. Mike was a powerful land-developer who had been at the center of several controversial planning decisions.

Marsh nodded warily, not wanting to give

away anything that could be recorded or overheard.

"And what's in it for you? I can't see you being interested in our demonstrations. Do they have something over you?"

Again, he nodded without saying anything. He was beginning to feel trapped in this tiny space with his interrogator.

"And if I don't comply? What would you do then?"

"Send some video clips of you performing to the newscast sites, with the recipients blanked out of course."

"And if I choose to reveal the identities of these recipients?"

"I think we both know that wouldn't be wise, Jennifer, or should I say Crystal?"

"What do you know about Crystal? How do I know you have the information you claim?"

Marsh relaxed. The name Crystal had struck a nerve. He turned towards her to be able to see her reactions more closely.

"I had a young man who worked for me once, Eddie Bishop. He was one of my most promising recruiters. He found a young girl, just 14 years old, almost 15. He gained her trust, then turned her. Introduced her to cocaine. I tried her once; she was enthusiastic enough but not very skilled. Very cute, nonetheless."

He watched Jennifer's eyes. He could see that she remembered. She recoiled from him.

He smiled. He was feeling powerful now. *'Good,'* he thought, *'she's frightened.'*

He continued, feeling a need to hurt her, to make her cry, to make himself feel stronger.

"I made a lot of money off you, you know. And when the cocaine wore off, you would do anything for more. For a while I could sell you to my special clients."

He saw that she had squeezed herself in the corner where the seat met the door. *'Cornered like the tasty rabbit that she is.'* A moment of self-doubt went through him as he thought this, but he tossed it away.

"Perhaps we could settle this another way." Marsh began to unbuckle his belt, feeling supremely powerful. *'They never change,'* he thought.

Too late, he saw the small revolver in her hand. He looked around wildly, but the windows were obscured by the rivulets of rain. There were no lights of any kind outside. He realized they had stopped, and he had no idea where.

'Shit,' he thought, then said, "Jennifer, let's…"

Three things happened at once. The muzzle flashed brightly in the small car, he heard two very loud noises, and he felt sharp stabbing pains in his chest. He was conscious of his body falling forward with his head still facing Jennifer.

29

CLEANUP

Jennifer

Acrid fumes filled the taxi after the first two shots. Jennifer held her breath for a moment, until she had pulled Marsh's tablet from the left pocket of his jacket where she had seen him put it. She stowed it in the security box behind the seat and closed the lid. Then she opened the door, lifted her hood, and stepped out into the rain, gasping for breath. The air had that special smell of wet leaves in a forest. There was a stillness that she never heard in the city. Leaning back into the cab, Jennifer placed another shot to Marsh's forehead as she had been taught by the man in the shop.

For a brief second, a wave of terror and a

profound disappointment washed through her. *'It must be his spirit departing,'* she thought remembering the mouse at the zoo. Her ears were still ringing from the first two shots. She pulled out the earplugs she was wearing under her hair, carefully stowed them in her overcoat pocket, and stood still for a moment waiting for the ringing to subside.

Her own green umbrella taxi pulled up beside her, but she wasn't quite done yet. Getting back in the old taxi, and closing the door, she pulled out the small silver pocketknife and flipped open its tiny blade. After feeling Marsh's wrist for a moment, she made a small quick cut and with the point of the knife, retrieved his ID chip. She set it down on the ledge under the windscreen. She then spoke to Gabriel. "Open the far passenger door please and release Mr. Marsh's safety belt."

"Done," said Gabriel's reassuring voice. "Are you okay, Jennifer?"

Turning sideways in her seat and bracing herself against the door beside her, Jennifer used both feet to push Marsh's body out into the deep ditch beside the road.

Getting out of the taxi she walked around to see how he had fallen. One leg had hung up on a rock, so Jennifer carefully crouched down and kicked it with her boot. Falling in now would be a mistake. The ditch was running full. Not quite trusting her impression of his death, she lingered to watch as the swirling waters began to cover Marsh's body with dried leaves and debris. His body was soon covered with a thin layer of brown mud. He was lying face down in the water. She waited there for a full five minutes. Her panther sat next to her, observing patiently.

To pass the time, she watched the little twigs and leaves floating down the ditch and tried to predict which would snag on Marsh's body and where they would end up. She walked around the taxis to see if there were any tire tracks in the dirt road, but the rain was already washing them away. Returning to Marsh's body, she saw that it had not moved. Finally, satisfied that he was truly dead, drowned if the bullets hadn't finished him, she returned to the old taxi.

Jennifer pulled out a pair of tweezers and a simple arc lighter, the kind used to ignite birthday candles. Using the tweezers, she held the ID chip between the prongs of the arc lighter and fired it continuously until the ID chip began to melt. "Gabriel, can you still read this?" she asked.

"No, it is no longer responsive."

"Perfect." Jennifer walked 100 meters up the road, with the melted chip, then hid it in the roadside bushes. It was so small that it would never be found.

Finally, she returned and placed the gun, the knife, the tweezers, her ear plugs and the arc lighter on the passenger seat of the old taxi to be retrieved at the scrap yard. "All set Gabriel, you can close the door."

Her panther, which had been following her, dissolved as Jennifer climbed into her own taxi and flipped back her hood. "Now I'm all right," she said. "Gabriel, this must remain just between us, you do understand that."

"Yes, Jennifer. If I had seen another path, I would have told you."

"I wish you had seen another way. Now take me home, I need to think on the way."

She saw the old taxi pull out ahead of them. When both taxis reached the main road, the old taxi turned left to go to the scrapping yard where Gabriel had promised it would be shredded within an hour. Her own taxi turned right to go back home. Safely on the main road, she relaxed, and cautiously came out of that special hiding place in her mind. She began to shake, and cry tears of anger and frustration that Marsh had put her in this position, and tears of sadness and regret at what she had become.

30

NEW REVELATIONS

Vijay

Vijay was sitting on the couch, a child on either side as he read to them from the book 'Where the Wild Things Are'. He was making suitable roaring noises, which only made the twins giggle. Molly was sitting on her chair watching and listening.

When he heard Jennifer come in, he looked up. He could see that she was upset and had been crying.

"Molly, please look after Parvati and Dylan, and put them to bed if needed. Jennifer and I need some time alone, I'm not sure how long."

"Yes, Vijay." Molly rose and moved to replace him, shooing the twins to opposite ends of the couch with her soft hands. The twins tried to resist, giggling and squirming, but resistance was futile.

Vijay went to help Jennifer out of her coat and boots and led her to the bedroom. "Jenn, what happened?"

"Let's get into bed, I'm chilled, and I want to feel your warmth next to me."

They undressed in silence and climbed into bed together. Jennifer lay beside him with her head on his chest. He could feel that she was trying to get as close to him as possible with every part of her body.

She began to shake and cry again, great sobs of anguish. Vijay held her and stroked her waiting for it to subside.

Finally, she calmed and spoke. "Vijay, I did something terrible today. Something I did once before and swore I would never do again." She went silent.

Vijay's mind was racing with all the things he knew from her past. Was it prostitution? That made no sense. Was it drugs? He remembered how adamant she had been in hospital so that made no sense either. Had she stolen something? No, she was already wealthy enough from her own salary and had no need to steal anything.

"What is it Jenn? What did you do?"

"I killed Marsh."

New revelations

Vijay felt his body tighten up and knew Jennifer must have felt it too.

"What the hell, Jennifer? I thought we said no secrets."

"That's why I'm telling you now. I didn't want it to be a secret."

Her voice was muffled against his chest and Vijay felt her clinging even more tightly to him.

He took a deep breath to let his own panic subside, then forced himself to relax.

"Why don't you start at the beginning. Tell me what happened."

Jennifer shared the whole story, starting with the blackmail threats, creating the plan with Gabriel's help, picking up Marsh and the macabre conversation in the taxi, and then shooting him three times.

"It was horrible. I felt his spirit pass through me, a mix of terror and disappointment at dying so soon. In the end, he was just lying there, face down in the ditch, covered with dirt and wet leaves. He was alone and I just walked away like nothing happened. I was so cold inside. I went to my secret place where I used to go to do the things I couldn't do any other way." She hugged him even tighter.

"Gabriel helped you with all this?"

"Yes, he said he didn't see another way."

"Another way to do what?" Vijay felt his anger

rising but fought to keep his tone level. He paused for a moment.

"You said you had done this once before. When was that?" Vijay still held her tight, trying to reassure her, but feeling like he was holding the most fragile of eggs in his hands.

"When I was 15, I had a pimp named Eddie. At first, he was my boyfriend, he let me stay with him, he gave me things. Then he started to make me turn tricks - just as a favor he said, to pay him back. He gave me cocaine. To make it easier, he said. When I was addicted, he tossed me out onto the street. For a while I would do anything to get more. Then, when I was 16, one day I woke up on the street next to another crack head in her 30s. She had died overnight. That scared me.

"Eddie came looking for me, demanding money, trying to make me take more drugs. We fought, I bit and scratched and tried to hurt him, but he laughed and said he would be back the next day. The next day, it was raining, just like today, just as heavily. I was waiting for him in an alley. I had a knife that I stole. I practised in my mind over and over. When he came looking for me, I jumped out behind him, grabbed his hair and slit his throat. There was so much blood, but the rain washed it away down a sewer grate. That gave me the idea. I managed to raise the grate with a piece of iron bar I found in the alley, and

New revelations

pushed his body in. I used the bar to close the grate. I wiped off the knife and the iron bar and dropped them through the grate. The rain did all the rest. When I left the alley looked just like it always did."

Vijay tried to stay still, other than his left arm that was stroking her.

His mind was not still. He wanted to leap up, and storm around the room, shouting and creating his own wild rumpus. But he calmed himself and started sorting through the debris of his shattered image of Jennifer.

"Why didn't you tell me about the blackmail?" he asked, already knowing the answer.

"Because you would have stormed over as Vijay the Invincible and made a mess. This was not an easy thing to fix like Sabrina when she stole my emeralds. Marsh is wealthy. He has connections and real security. And it's so important that you be Vijay the Loving Rebel, for our twins, for your teams and for me. I did not want you to have the guilt of murder in your soul."

"What do we do now?"

"About Marsh, nothing. If we're lucky it will be years before he's found and by then there won't be any clues left. About us? That's up to you." These last words were muffled as Jennifer tried to burrow still deeper into him.

"Are you sure there are no traces? Will the police come knocking at our door?"

"No, Gabriel took care of everything. I destroyed his wrist chip, so even if they sweep with scanners, they won't detect his body. And he was too old to have a baby chip. The car and everything inside were shredded less than an hour later. There's nothing to find."

Vijay was silent for a moment, trying to process all this information. He desperately wanted to scream, and shout at her but he knew this was the wrong moment for that.

"Jenn, you know I love you, and I meant it when I vowed to be your partner for life. I'm bound to you no matter what and I wouldn't want it any other way. I'm much more worried about you."

"Then make love to me Vijay, I want to feel alive again."

"I can't Jenn, not right now. I can hold you, but my mind is still trying to process this."

Jennifer fell asleep soon after, but Vijay lay awake in the darkness, trying to reconcile the beautiful, loving partner beside him with her account of a ruthless murder. He tried to imagine his life if she were arrested but could not picture a life without her at his side. Everything else would be hollow without her. The fact that she had done it twice was the real shock. He used to think he knew about her past. Then came the revelation about her drug addiction, and now this. What else could there be, he wondered. And Gabriel was complicit. From the way Jennifer told it, it seemed that Gabriel was there the entire time, and supported her decision. It sounded like Gabriel had led her into this.

Finally, exhausted and no closer to understanding, he fell into a restless dream-filled sleep.

THE NEXT MORNING AT BREAKFAST, JENNIFER seemed back to her normal self. Vijay was not his normal self.

"Jenn, can we talk for a few minutes?"

"Of course."

"Remember on the beach, when we said no secrets between us? I just feel like I keep discovering new secrets from your past. First there was the drug addiction that I learned about when the twins were being born. Now I learn about the way you made Eddie disappear. These are pretty big things to learn about. What else is there that I should know?"

"I think you're being unfair, Vijay. I told you about both of those immediately when they became relevant."

"What else do you think might become relevant?"

"How can I know that?"

"For a start, have you ever been arrested. Do you have a police record?"

Jennifer sighed. "Yes, I've been arrested a few times. Solicitation, minor shoplifting. I did some community service and paid a couple of fines. Does that make you feel better?"

"You never talk about your family, except that your mum and dad died. Do you have any brothers or sisters?"

Vijay watched Jennifer closely and could see that she was uncomfortable. She looked down, avoiding his gaze. "Yes," she said in a quiet voice.

Vijay could see the signs that she was retreating into that inner space in her mind.

"What happened to them, Jenn?" Vijay spoke in his quietest voice.

"I didn't kill them, if that's what you think," Jennifer snarled. "Who are you to judge me? I'm sure you've got secrets in your past, Mr. Perfect Subramanian. I don't need to take this from you or anyone." She stood up. Out of the corner of his eye, Vijay saw Molly suddenly paying very close attention.

"Molly, relax. Watch the door. Make sure no one goes in or out please."

New revelations

Vijay was still watching Jennifer closely. He was scared of this version of the woman he loved.

"Jennifer, it's me Vijay, I love you. Let's sit down on the couch and talk."

Jennifer bolted for the door, but Molly was in the way, and Jennifer just landed against Molly's soft padded apron. Molly put her arms around Jennifer, then scooped her up and stood waiting for Vijay's instructions. Jennifer was kicking and pounding, shouting obscenities at Molly as she lay in Molly's arms.

"Bring her to the couch, Molly, and sit her next to me."

Vijay sat on the couch, and Molly set Jennifer down so that she was leaning against Vijay. He put his arm around her, not tightly, but a firm restraint none the less.

"Jenn, it's me Vijay. You're safe here with me. Here in our apartment with your babies, and with Molly. It's okay, come back please."

"Let me go, you fucking bastard! I wish I'd never met you. You're just like the rest. You think you can control me!" Jennifer twisted and turned trying get free of Vijay's restraining arm.

"Jenn, you're upset. You're hitting out. Show me that you're in control of yourself and I'll let you go."

After a few moments, he felt the tension go out of her body and the sobbing started. Body-shaking, deep sobs as one emotion after another swept through her. When the sobbing quietened down to a whimper, Jennifer fell asleep.

Vijay knew this pattern, and just waited. "Molly," he said in a low voice, "she's safe now. Please look after the twins in their room."

Molly took the twins to their bedroom.

Twenty minutes later, Jennifer woke up. "Vijay?" she turned her tear-streaked face up to his.

"I'm here. Are you back now?"

"Yes."

"What triggered you?"

"You kept asking about my past. I had buried all that, put it away but I can't escape it. Everything keeps coming back. I wanted to run and keep on running. And then Molly was there. I thought Molly was my friend and then she picked me up like a baby. Oh, I didn't hurt Molly, did I? I just remember trying to get away from her.

Vijay couldn't help laughing at the idea of Jennifer hurting Molly. "No, I'm sure she's fine. She's looking after the twins now. You can apologize later if you want."

"But you can't go on having these attacks. You're under so much pressure to be strong that you can't afford to be trying to escape your past at the same time. I want you to see Dr. Gladstone again. Ask her to help you complete all these things so that you're in control again. It may mean reaching out to some people. It may mean dealing with the death of your parents to bring closure. I don't know what will come up. And when you're ready to talk with me about your life, I'll be here."

"And what if I want to know all about your life?"

"You only have to ask my sister, Shilpa. She would love to tell you every embarrassing detail. And you have my agreement to do that if it helps. I don't want to hide anything from you Jennifer, and I want you to feel the same about me."

"Okay, I'll make an appointment with Dr. Gladstone."

"Let me know when you do."

"Don't you trust me?"

"Right at this moment, no I don't."

"I guess that's fair. I'll tell you."

"Great, now let's go see what the twins are doing to Molly."

About two hours later, Jennifer disappeared into their bedroom, taking her tablet. Twenty minutes later she returned to where Vijay was playing with the twins in the living room. Molly was sitting in her chair, watching.

"I have an appointment for 2pm this afternoon," Jennifer said.

Vijay stood up and put his arms around her. "I'm proud of you Jenn, and no matter what, I love you and will always be here for you."

"I love you too Vijay. I scared myself this morning. I lost control, I don't know where I would have gone or what I would have done. I hope Dr. Gladstone will be able to help and I won't lose control again."

"D'you want me to go with you?"

"No, I have to do this alone."

"Then Molly will go." Vijay looked up and raised his voice. "Molly, you are to go this afternoon with Jennifer to see Dr. Gladstone. Please take the security box to scan and secure the office. Then you will stand outside the office door to ensure that no one disturbs them until Jennifer opens the door again."

"Should I take my apron and my soft hands?" asked Molly?

Vijay thought for a moment. The apron and the oversized hands might make her a target in the university hallways. But if Jennifer needed to be carried out, then they would help Jennifer to feel safe.

"I'll give you a bag to pack them in. I'd like you to wear your security equipment but have the apron and hands available and put them on if you believe you need them."

New revelations

"Thank you, Vijay, I will get a bag. I know where they are."

Jennifer looked at Molly, then nodded. "Thank you, Molly. It'll be good for you to get out of the apartment for a while."

The twins provided a welcome diversion over lunch. After lunch, Vijay watched with curiosity as Molly detached her soft hands and replaced them with the mesh covered standard issue security bot hands.

"What does that feel like to you?" he asked her.

"It is difficult to explain. It does not hurt, if that is what you are asking. I have seen you put on big mitts to get something hot out of the oven. With the mitts, you can hold things that would burn away your skin, but you lose the ability to do any fine manipulation. Not better or worse, just different. With these hands, I could bend a steel bar that would shred my soft hands. But I do not receive quite the same sensation of pressure, temperature, and moisture that I receive from my soft hands. I could pick up the twins with these hands, but I don't think they would enjoy it as much."

Molly had a small roll-along suitcase open. She placed her soft hands in first, then the security box, and finally folded her apron to fit the remaining space. She zipped up the case and then experimented with towing it behind her.

"You look like you're ready to go on vacation," said Vijay.

"I would like that," said Molly. "I have seen pictures of vacation and it looks very nice."

"When the twins are older, we'll all go on a vacation." Vijay had no idea if that was true, but he liked the idea of it.

Vijay watched Molly and Jennifer go. He walked with them as far as the elevator, then went back inside and watched from the balcony to see them get in the taxi and drive off.

IT WAS MORE THAN TWO HOURS BEFORE JENNIFER and Molly returned. Molly was pulling along the suitcase, but still had her mesh hands and wasn't wearing her apron. As they came in the door, the twins rushed to greet them. They first hugged Jennifer, then quickly went to Molly. They were fascinated by her hands and wanted to touch them. Molly sat on the floor and allowed them to climb all over her as they explored the steel body they never normally saw.

Jennifer looked worn out. Vijay could see she had been crying.

"Molly, please look after the twins while Jennifer and I talk," he said. Then turning back to

Jennifer, "Come and lie down and tell me about it."

They lay side by side, fully clothed. Jennifer had her head on his chest and Vijay's right arm held her close.

"How did it go? You don't have to tell me everything, just what you want to share."

Jennifer was quiet for a minute.

"Dr. Gladstone was nice. She asked me what happened this morning, and then helped me relax. She said the same thing you did, that I cannot simply block out parts of my past or they'll keep coming back. She asked me to tell my life story, especially all the parts I still feel bad about. And she gave me some homework that I have to do before our session next week."

"What kind of homework?"

"I have to visit my parents and tell them what happened to me, to forgive them and ask their forgiveness of me."

"Aren't your parents dead?"

"That's what I told Dr. Gladstone, but she said to visit their graves and sit and talk. They may be listening in some other plane, or maybe not, but it's the act of talking to them that will free me. Then I have to call my brother and my sister. They tried to help me once, but I pushed them away. I was not very nice to them."

"That's all?"

"For now, there will be more, I'm sure. I'm still angry over Sabrina, I have to let that go. And Eddie and Marsh, I have to make peace with them also. She said that we would deal with that later. I was worried she would tell the police, but apparently Gabriel has made sure she won't. And you, I promised no secrets, yet I held onto so many secrets. I knew that was wrong but if I told you, I was afraid I would lose you."

"The thing that hurt me the most was that you trusted Gabriel more than you trust me."

"That's not true!"

"But you didn't come to me when the messages from Marsh arrived. You chose to confide in Gabriel instead and look what happened. You have no idea what his ultimate goals are. If we're going to make our relationship last, you have to trust me."

Jennifer only nodded.

"Jenn, I meant it when I vowed to be your partner for life. I've seen you at your worst, and I'm still here. One step at a time and when you're ready to talk with me, then I'll be here to listen. I'm just very proud of you for having the courage to talk with Dr. Gladstone. How was Molly?"

"Molly was great. She looked after the security measures then stood outside the door like any security bot, except I heard some laughter. I suspect she was talking with the students on their way by."

Vijay laughed. "I'm sure she enjoyed the chance to talk to someone other than just us and the twins. We should take her out more often."

"Maybe for a picnic in the park." She giggled at the idea of Molly sitting on a blanket passing out sandwiches.

Vijay pulled her tighter. "I love you, Jennifer Dupont," he said with his mouth against the top of her head.

"Love you too," was the muffled response, as Jennifer wriggled to press herself tighter against him.

THE NEXT FEW NIGHTS, THEY WATCHED THE newcast for any news of Simon Marsh. On the third day, it was reported that he was missing. It seemed there was an electrical anomaly that stopped his limousine and Marsh had stepped out. Then he simply vanished. There were no traces of what had happened. The heavy rains had washed away any tracks and an inspection of the limousine turned up nothing. As Mr. Marsh was known to have underworld connections, it was assumed that this was a hit as a result of a deal gone wrong. The police appealed for anyone with information to come forward.

31

CLOSURE

Jennifer

Jennifer went alone to visit her parents. They had been cremated and shared a niche in a wall provided by the city. In her hand was a bouquet of flowers that she had purchased on impulse along the way.

Now sitting on a bench facing the niche, the flowers seemed so inadequate, but they were all she had. She stood and placed them at the foot of the wall, then sat again.

"Mum, Dad, I love you. I know now how hard you struggled to give us a normal upbringing. I didn't understand then what you were going through, but I understand now, at least some of it.

There was no excuse for the way I behaved. I should never have screamed at you. When I shoplifted that skirt, and you made me take it back, I thought I hated you and that you were the meanest parents on earth. I think I told you that. Now I see that you were loving me and trying to help me grow stronger."

She paused to wipe away her tears with her hand.

"When you died, I blamed you for that, for abandoning us. I didn't understand how you could just go away when I needed you most. I'm sorry for that. I want you to know that I don't blame you anymore. I know now that you would never have left if you had a choice.

"I haven't always been the best daughter. I ran away from the group home and did a lot of things I'm not proud of. I was a sex worker and did drugs. I lashed out at people who tried to help me and pushed them away. I was so angry and so scared all the time.

"But I'm married now to an amazing man, with two beautiful children and we live in a big apartment looking over the city. I wish I could show you. I wish so many things. Most of all, I wish I had been a better daughter. Can you forgive me?"

She was crying now, reliving her early teenage years when her parents were ill, and she was so unsympathetic. She wished with all her heart that she could take it back.

Then standing, she walked to the engraved plaque in the wall, and using a tissue, she carefully cleaned and polished it, chasing the accumulated dust out of each letter until the bronze gleamed.

Finally, she laid her hand flat on the polished plaque and said, "Please forgive me. I love you."

Jennifer leaned forward and kissed the plaque. She felt a sudden shiver as the weight of years of guilt about her parents fell away.

THE NEXT WAS A CALL TO HER BROTHER. JENNIFER sat alone in the bedroom, running through possible conversations in her head. All the alternatives seemed to end up with him hanging up on her. There seemed to be no right way to apologize. Finally, fed up with her own indecision, she just called.

"Hello, Dennis? It's Jennifer, your sister."

"Jenn! It's so good to hear your voice. Is everything alright?" Dennis sounded happy. Not at all angry.

"Yes, I need to talk with you Dennis. I know you tried to help me, and I pushed you away. I'm sorry. I was wrong. I want to see you again to start over."

"I would love that. Just a second." He must

Closure

have moved away from the tablet as his voice sounded fainter. "Dee, it's my sister, Jennifer. You okay if I invite her over for a barbecue Saturday?"

Jennifer was surprised by the excitement in his voice, while she felt so miserable on her end of the conversation.

There was a pause, then, "Thanks, Hon."

He was close to the tablet again. "Jenn, I would love to see you and introduce you to my family. Can you make Saturday afternoon for a barbecue?"

"Sure, can I bring Vijay and the kids?"

"Absolutely, bring your twins. We've been following you on the newscasts."

"Do you have children too?"

"Two boys, aged 7 and 9. Thomas and Michael."

"Wonderful, I'll bring them each one of Vijay's shirts."

"He makes shirts?"

"No, he's on them, all over the city. You'll see."

Jennifer was starting to feel giddy with relief that Dennis wanted to see her. On a whim she asked, "Is it okay if I bring Molly with us? She's our bodyguard and nanny all in one. I think your boys will have fun with her."

"Sure, bring her along. Hamburgers and hot dogs all right for everyone?"

"Yep, we're a family of carnivores here."

Then Dennis got serious. "Jenn, I can try to ask Vicky to come as well, but I'm not sure she's ready to talk to either of us yet."

"That's okay, Dennis. I know I have to talk to her eventually, but one step at a time. I'm so looking forward to seeing you again."

"Me too, sis. It's been too long."

Vijay had been listening, and when the call ended, he asked, "Do you think it's a good idea taking Molly?"

"I think so. She's already been with me to the university twice, so she's not exactly secret. Do you remember why she's here with us?"

"Yes, she's learning about human beings by living in a human family."

"Yes, just like those researchers who live with primitive tribes in the jungle. She's here, watching, listening, and participating all the time. I think we owe it to her to provide more experiences. We can show her what a normal family looks like. And young boys will love her."

"What about your brother?"

"Molly will give us something to talk about besides the past."

THURSDAY MORNING, VIJAY ANNOUNCED "IF WE'RE going to take Molly to a barbecue, we need to prepare her. I'm going to take her shopping. Molly, order a taxi, take off your apron and put on your mesh hands."

"What does she need for a barbecue?" Jennifer asked.

"You'll see," replied Vijay.

Jennifer felt irritated and excluded for a moment as she always did when Vijay planned things without her. But she knew from experience that he enjoyed teasing her this way, and that more questions would only produce that silly, smug grin of his without any answers. She sighed.

"How long will you be?"

"About an hour, then we'll take Molly and the twins to the park this afternoon."

A few minutes later he and Molly walked out of the apartment together.

It was closer to 90 minutes later that they returned, with Molly carrying a large duffel bag that had odd bulges in it. She set the bag down on the floor. Immediately, the twins came over to inspect it. Molly sat on the floor with the twins and opened it for them.

Inside were several balls: a basketball, a soccer ball, and an American football. Rolling around at the bottom were a baseball, a softball, and a tube of tennis balls. Next, she pulled out an aluminum baseball bat, a glove for Vijay and finally, an enormous baseball glove for herself. Molly put on the glove for the twins to inspect. Dylan looked in the bag and found two brightly colored plastic balls for them to play with.

"Really?" said Jennifer. "You're going to teach Molly to play ball sports?"

"That's why we're going to the park. The tennis balls are for practice until Molly understands throwing at an appropriate speed. Then we we'll learn to play catch and maybe try our hand at soccer."

Vijay placed the twins in their double stroller, while Molly reloaded the sport bag and picked it up.

"You coming?" Vijay asked.

"Sure, why not?" Jennifer smiled. "Wait while I get a blanket and supplies for Parvati and Dylan." The idea of Dylan and Parvati learning about balls along with Molly seemed like it might be fun. She also knew that Vijay would be totally consumed in teaching Molly and that she would be needed to look after the twins.

She quickly filled a bag with the essentials, topped with a towel, and attached it to the stroller. Now that the twins were three, it was much easier to pack for an outing.

They went to a neighborhood park, just down the street, so they were able to walk together. Some of the neighbors obviously recognized Molly from glimpses of her on past excursions, but for many, the sight of a large security bot walking with a family was a novel experience. Vijay introduced Molly to any who were brave enough to approach.

"Molly needs to be able to move around now that the twins are older, and it's better if the locals know her and don't fear her," Vijay explained.

At the park, they chose a quiet area. Vijay helped Jennifer set out the blanket as Molly lifted the twins from the stroller. Parvati and Dylan did not seem to mind the harder mesh hands that Molly sometimes wore. Jennifer made a mental note to have Molly wear them around the house more often.

When they were set, Vijay picked the tube of three tennis balls and walked 20 meters away. Turning to face Molly, he said, "Molly, I'm going to throw these tennis balls to you. I want you to catch them and drop them near your feet. Then you'll pick them up and throw them back to me at the same velocity. We'll repeat this until you have the physics mastered."

Vijay emptied the tube and held two balls in his left hand ready to throw the third ball with his right hand. He threw the balls one after the other at a spot just to the right of Molly. She easily caught each ball, dropping it on the ground between her feet.

"Now throw them back."

The first ball went far over Vijay's head and fell to the ground behind him. Jennifer giggled.

The next ball was short, and Vijay had to run forward to catch it. The third ball would have hit him in the chest, if Vijay had not stepped aside to catch it easily.

"Sir," said a boy of nine or ten years old. "Here's your ball back."

"Thanks, what's your name?"

"Timothy but everyone calls me Tim"

"Well Tim, would you like to help Molly learn?" asked Vijay.

"Sure, I guess."

Vijay had Tim walk off until he was roughly equidistant from himself and Molly.

"Tim, Molly, listen up. Molly will throw to me. I'll throw to Tim and Tim will throw to Molly."

Jennifer watched with interest, her attention divided between the lessons and the twins chasing their plastic balls.

After Molly had mastered the tennis balls, Vijay called a break. "Tim, do you live near here, and d'you have a baseball glove?"

"Yes, sir."

"You can call me Vijay. Run home and get it and we'll switch to throwing a baseball. If you get tired of this, just let me know."

"I'll be right back." Tim dashed off.

Vijay said, "Stay here Jenn, I think I heard an

ice cream vendor. I'm going to get some treats for us all."

Jennifer was left alone with Parvati and Dylan. They were trying to catch their balls which bounced away each time they toddled up to them. Parvati was the first to learn that if she stopped short of the ball and squatted down, she could reach forward and pick it up. She toddled back to Jennifer excitedly rabbiting on about the ball. Dylan watched and soon mastered the same technique.

Jennifer was aware of feeling completely relaxed. Sitting here in the park in the sun with her children nearby chasing their balls she felt a sense of fulfillment.

On impulse, she leaned forward and placed her hands flat on the grass in front of her, feeling the earth below.

She fell into the earth. Falling deeper and deeper until she was at the earth's center. Looking up, she could see the city as a bright white light on the surface above her. As she spun around, on the far side of the earth, she could see a blackness beginning to spread. The lights of other cities were going out, as the blackness slowly spread. Their own city would be last, and it was lit up in bright white. It was the same vision as in her dreams.

Then she was back. She sat up with a start and

looked around in panic for Parvati and Dylan. They were still in the same place. In the distance she saw Vijay returning with a bag of ice treats, and from another direction, Tim was heading in at full speed with his glove.

The vision had only lasted for a few seconds.

She must have looked different when Vijay arrived. He set down the bag and asked, "Jenn, are you okay?"

She smiled. The world was right again. "I'll tell you later," she said. "Tim's here. Let's all enjoy our treats."

Vijay pulled out two flavored ice sticks for the twins, then let Tim and Jennifer pick from the remaining three ice creams. Vijay took the one that was left and seemed quite content with whatever they chose.

Treats done, Vijay said, "Tim, let's have a look at that glove. Grab the baseball there and show Molly how it's caught in the pocket."

Tim seemed very nervous at being so close to the big bot, but Molly quickly sat down to make their heights more equal. He did a demonstration for her.

"Now, help Molly put on her glove and teach her how to feel the ball in the pocket."

Jennifer was fascinated by this view of Vijay as a teacher. She realized that by giving Tim a task and some responsibility, he was also building trust between Tim and Molly.

By the time the twins had finished with their ice sticks, Molly could throw overhand with perfect control to both Tim and Vijay and was catching the ball in the pocket of her glove each time.

Jennifer wiped the sticky, syrupy residue from Parvati and Dylan. Vijay, Tim and Molly were now playing a game of random catch and throw trying to catch each other off guard. Of course, Molly was never caught off guard, but she did learn to randomize her throws to present a challenge to Vijay and Tim.

Vijay was visibly sweating when he finally came to sit on the blanket. Jennifer offered both Vijay and Tim bottles of water. She had only brought two not expecting Tim to join them, but one look at his sweat-streaked face told her the young boy needed it much more than she did.

"I think we'll stop there," said Vijay. "Thanks Tim, you were a great help today. If ever you see us out here in the park, feel free to join us. You can bring your friends if you like."

"Yes, thanks Tim. I enjoyed playing catch with you," said Molly.

"Thanks for the ice cream and the water. I had fun. Bye." Tim set off at a run.

"You've given him a story for the dinner table," said Jennifer.

"Yeah, that worked out well."

They gathered up the twins and placed them in the stroller as Molly collected all the balls and stowed them back in the sports bag without being asked.

"Did you enjoy the game of catch, Molly?" Jennifer asked.

"Yes, I enjoyed it very much. I met Tim and learned about small boys. I also learned new skills with balls. I enjoyed the activity with no other purpose than to do the activity. Is this what fun is?"

Jennifer looked at Vijay.

"Yes, I suppose that's what fun is," replied Vijay. "Doing something where the doing is also the goal. Enjoying being outdoors, and the repetitive throwing and catching. The feeling of success when a ball is well caught and the acceptance of our own errors when it's missed. Play is how we learn."

Molly was silent the rest of the way home. Jennifer put her arm around Vijay and ducked so that he could put his arm around her. He continued to push the stroller with his other hand.

"This was a lovely afternoon. We should do this more often," said Jennifer.

"I'm glad you enjoyed it. It looked like Parvati and Dylan were enjoying it too."

"Yeah, those balls were a great idea. They chased them all over the park."

That night in bed, Jennifer and Vijay relived their afternoon. They laughed as they remembered Tim and Molly, and the twins chasing their balls.

Jennifer was still smiling when she remembered her vision of the world turning dark, her heart sank. She was deep in thought when Vijay said, "Are you okay?"

"I'm not sure. I just have a funny feeling something's wrong. I'm worried about your family."

"What makes you say that?"

"While you were getting the ice creams, I had that vision again, clearer than ever. These viruses are spreading and wiping out whole cities. I saw it. It's like a plan to reduce the number of people. And we'll be last, we're the long shot where Gaia has placed her bet. I don't know why. Maybe because we're isolated on our island. Maybe because we're not a direct source of pollution or warming gases. Maybe because you and I have bonded and are moving forward. Perhaps other couples didn't make it. Gabriel might know.

"But anyway, my worry is that we could lose your family's city. If we get them here, they can be safe. It wouldn't be easy, but I think we could do it. Do you think they'd come?"

"How would they come here. Travel between zones is absolutely forbidden, no exceptions."

"The only way I can think of is to have them come on one of the unmanned cargo ships."

"Is that allowed, coming on a ship?"

"No, they'd be stowaways."

"How can we do that?"

"With Gabriel. There's no other way."

"I can talk with them, but I don't know if it will sound urgent for them."

"Let's wait then. I'll try to gather more data before we talk to them."

32

MOLLY'S FIRST BARBECUE

Jennifer

Saturday was the day of the barbecue. Dennis and Dee were expecting them between three and four. Molly volunteered to arrange transportation. "I want to surprise the boys as a present," she said.

"How do you know what boys would like?" asked Jennifer feeling curious.

"I've been researching boys like Tim in literature and vidcasts. I would like to test my understanding of them."

"Okay, Molly. As long as it's safe for all of us including the twins."

"Yes, Jennifer. It will be very safe."

• • •

At 2:30pm, they descended in the elevator and walked out to the street. There, at the end of the walkway, was a gargantuan military transporter. Each of the eight wheels was as tall as Vijay. A ladder was mounted to climb up to the passenger seats. Inside, two bench seats had room to easily accommodate 8 adult males sitting in full riot gear. Behind was an area specially provisioned for 16 security bots to sit in saddle seats like the one Molly used at home.

Vijay and Jennifer stopped short and turned to look at each other. Jennifer could see that Vijay was both concerned and excited. *'Probably worried that I won't let us ride in that thing,'* thought Jennifer. She nodded to Vijay.

Molly asked, "Do you think boys would like to ride in this?"

"Hell yes!" said Vijay. "I'm sure they'll love it."

Vijay helped Jennifer up the ladder to the front bench seat. Then Molly passed up Dylan in his safety seat and Parvati in her seat. Vijay climbed up last. With the four of them safely aboard, Molly stowed the supplies bag, the sports bag and the twins' stroller in the rear section before boarding herself and settling onto one of the security bot saddles.

The doors closed and off they went

The ride was smoother than Jennifer expected, but it was also quite noisy. Turning corners was

Molly's first barbecue

odd as the carrier remained flat rather than banking into the turn. She settled in and enjoyed the sensation of being carried far above the other traffic and watching the startled looks from people they passed along the way.

Jennifer's brother Dennis must have heard the noise, for he was already standing on the front step when they pulled up outside his house.

The doors opened. When he spotted Jennifer, he began to laugh. "You never were one to pass up the chance to make an entrance," he said. "Come down from there so I can give you a hug."

Jennifer first passed down Dylan, and Vijay passed down Parvati before they descended the ladder. Molly was already unloading the supplies bag, sports bag and the stroller.

By this time, Dee and the two boys had come out to see what all the noise was.

After a round of introductions and hugs, including very self-conscious handshakes from the two boys, Jennifer said, "Molly thought the boys might like to go for a ride in this. Big boys as well, of course."

Dennis turned to his sons. "What d'ya think, boys, wanna go for a ride?"

"Yes, please," said the older son, Thomas. Michael hid behind his brother.

"Great," said Vijay. "You two up front, and your dad and I will ride behind."

Dennis helped the boys onto the ladder and stood ready to catch them if they fell. Only when they were safely inside did he climb into the rear seat. Vijay followed last. Molly was already aboard in her saddle behind them.

As the enormous machine set off, Jennifer turned to Dee, saying, "Not quite the way I had imagined this, Dee, but Molly has been learning to interact with young boys and thought they would enjoy this."

"You've quite made Dennis' day. Do you know where they're going?"

"No, but it won't be far. Probably past the local park, or their school or wherever they want to show off. Molly is in control of the vehicle, although God only knows where she got it. I've never seen one before except on newscasts."

"You know, Dennis has been quite excited since you called. I think he had given up on seeing you again."

"I'm sure. I owe him an apology. I was mean to him the last time I saw him."

"You scared him. He could see that you were crashing, and he had no idea how to help you. He's not that much older than you. You were both still children."

"I'm so sorry now. I'm still recovering, but I'm getting counseling. I guess this meeting is part of that."

Molly's first barbecue

"Don't worry about Dennis. You can say exactly what you need to say to him. I'll make sure you two have some time alone together."

"Molly can help with that. She wants to play catch with the boys. She and Vijay have been practicing in the park. Molly and Vijay can take them off while Dennis and I talk. Sorry, I don't mean to exclude you Dee, it's just something I have to do with my brother."

"Don't you worry. Introduce me to these two and I'll look after them inside while you talk."

The boys returned, buzzing with excitement over the ride in the transporter. They watched and waved as it rumbled off into the distance. Then Vijay said, "Now, who's ready for baseball in the park?" Two young hands shot up. Molly's hand went up a second later.

"Lead the way, Thomas," said Vijay. "Molly, please bring the sports bag."

Dennis, why don't you take Jennifer out back while I find some cookies and a holo-cast for these two inside," said Dee. She led Dylan and Parvati into the house.

Jennifer followed Dennis to the back yard and watched quietly while he fiddled with starting the barbecue.

Now that she was here, she didn't how to start. She thought about Dr. Gladstones's counseling when she couldn't tell Vijay she loved him. They had done the meditation of hanging on the ledge. *'This is just another ledge,'* she thought. *'I just have to let go again.'*

"Dennis, I'm so sorry for the way I was to you when you found me. I should never have said or done the things I did."

"Jenn, you were in rough shape. You scared me. You were living on the street, on some kind of drugs. You were 15, I was only 17. I had no idea how to help. I still feel guilty for walking away and leaving you there."

"I was a mess, on drugs, doing sex work, and I had a pimp who terrified me. I had no money and had lost all self-respect. I was miserable knowing that I had messed up my life so badly."

"What changed? How did you get from there to here?"

Jennifer paused to take a breath. *'Do I tell him all of it? I am so sick of secrets,'* she thought. "About six months after you saw me, I woke up in a doorway next to another woman I knew. She was also addicted to cocaine, but she never woke up. She died of an overdose in the night.

"That scared me enough that I got away from my pimp, quit the drugs cold-turkey and started climbing back up the economic ladder, saving enough money from each trick to build a savings account, get myself well-groomed, buy better clothes so I could command better prices. At 16, I registered for UIS but it wasn't enough money, so I kept turning tricks to earn on the side. At 21, I was working as an escort by appointment only, and sharing an apartment with another working girl.

"Then I got my break, a job with the Mercury Theatre as ticket manager. It's at the theatre where I met Vijay. I left the escort business as soon as I had a steady income and moved in with Vijay shortly after that."

"Wow," said Dennis. "That's quite a story. But you always were scrappy. Comes from being the middle child, I suppose. I had it much easier. I was already 16 when Mum and Dad died. I was able to go directly on UIS and find a shared room in a house of students. They helped me get into an accounting program at college and now I'm a CPA. Dee and I met in college, got married when I graduated and had Thomas right away. Michael followed two years later.

"I thought about you a lot since then but didn't know how to find you. I even drove down Market Street a few times hoping to spot you there. Then I saw you on the newscast as a reporter. To be honest, I didn't know how to reach out to you. I didn't want you to think I came back because you were famous, and I didn't want to be a reminder of what you had obviously left behind."

Dennis looked down and scuffed the soles of his shoes on the grass.

"It did hurt when I saw your wedding on the news. You looked so beautiful, and I wished I could have been invited. I was so proud of you that I told everyone I work with that you're my sister. Of course, I didn't invite you to my wedding either, so I guess we have that in common."

By this time Jennifer was crying. She could see Dennis had tears in his eyes too.

"Can I have a hug? I made such a mess, and I know I hurt you and I hurt Vicky. I just want to be a family again, can we start over?"

Dennis wrapped his arms around her. He was bigger and softer than Vijay.

"Jenn," he said, "you'll always be my sister, no matter what happened. There is nothing you owe me, and I'm sorry now that I didn't try harder to help you when you needed it."

"I don't think you could have. Can you forgive me, Dennis?"

"Yes. Can you forgive me?"

"Yes, for everything."

Jennifer pulled away gently, and Dennis let go.

"For almost everything," said Jennifer, "but not for that time you locked me in the closet when Mum and Dad left us alone."

"You were messing with my video game and wouldn't stop."

Molly's first barbecue

They both started laughing through their tears.

By the time Vijay and Molly returned with two very tired boys, Jennifer and Dennis were back to normal, reminiscing about the good parts of their childhood.

Thomas and Michael interrupted them to tell them all about playing baseball with the giant robot and how their friends had all joined them.

"One of my friends has a t-shirt with Uncle Vijay's picture on it," said Thomas.

"Really," said Dennis. "Are you sure?"

"Oh, yes," laughed Jennifer. "Vijay is leading a revolution. You can see him in the protests on the newscasts sometimes. Thomas, go and ask your mum to look in the supplies bag. There should be two shirts and a special pen in there. Bring them out here."

Thomas returned a few minutes later with the shirts and the pen.

Vijay, picked up the larger shirt and wrote "Thomas, stay strong! Vijay" and on the smaller shirt he wrote, "Michael, Be Fierce! Vijay"

"Now try them on," he said.

The boys whipped off their shirts and pulled on the new t-shirts. The shirts were both a bit big, but that didn't seem to matter to them. Thomas flexed his muscles. *'I suppose that's what being strong means at that age,'* Jennifer thought.

Michael ran around making roaring noises, like a fierce lion.

Dennis laughed. "You've completely spoiled them now."

Later, when the barbecue was done, and the adults were sitting around having coffee, Jennifer asked, "Are you still in touch with Vicky? I need to see her also."

"In touch, barely," said Dennis. "I have her contact information and I reach out on her birthday and at Christmas, but she seldom replies. She's still in a lot of pain over what happened."

"You know," said Dee, "she had a rough go of it after you left, Jenn. She blames you for leaving her alone in that house. We've never heard the whole story, but if it drove you away, it must have been hell for her. She looked up to you as her big sister, and to Dennis as her big brother. When both of you vanished from her life, she felt abandoned and still does."

"I have to try. I owe her that. Dennis, please send me any contact information you have."

Soon it was time to leave. This time, a long, sleek limousine arrived to pick them all up. Molly sat up front while Jennifer, Vijay and the twins climbed in the back. Michael and Thomas joined them briefly to have a look inside, then

Molly's first barbecue

clambered back out at the urging of their parents.

When they were underway, Vijay turned to Jennifer. "All good?" he asked.

"All good," she replied. "I'd like to stay close to them now that we're back together."

She snuggled up against Vijay, and said, "Have I ever told you how much I love you, and how lucky I am that I met you?"

"I love you too, Jenn, and always will."

THE NEXT DAY, JENNIFER PLACED A CALL TO VICKY through her tablet.

"Hi Vicky, it's Jennifer. Can we talk?"

"Yes, Jenn? What do you want?" answered Vicky.

"I just want to talk, that's all."

"Dennis called and said I should be nice to you. But why now, after all this time?"

"We're family, and we need to get past the things that happened to us?"

"To us? Do you know what happened to me? I trusted you Jenn. When we were sent to that horrible house, I thought you would protect me, keep me safe. Instead, you just left. I asked to go with you, and you said no. Christ, I was only 12 and you left me there.

"With you gone, I was the target, and I wasn't

old enough to know who to tell or how to fight back. Where were you when I needed you, Jenn? Nowhere! I couldn't find you, you never called. Nothing. You gave up on me, but I never gave up on you. Every day I told myself that you would come back to rescue me. You and Dennis, but most of all you, my big sister. It was like dying again every day when you didn't come.

"And now I see you on the news, so elegant, so pure. That wedding where you looked like a fucking princess. Even then you didn't invite me. So why now?"

"It wasn't easy for me either, Vicky. But I'm getting counseling now. I'm learning to deal with all that happened to me, to us."

"Wonderful, so you're getting counseling and now you want us to play Happy Family and hug and kiss and make it all go away. Well, it doesn't work like that in real life, Jenn. I'm not going to roll over for your new age touchy-feely thing. You hurt me, Jenn, and it still hurts. I'm surviving, but I don't want to reopen it all. Please don't call again."

The call was closed by Vicky.

Jennifer sat crying. Vijay came over and sat beside her, pulling her against him as she cried out all her regret and frustration.

33

THE ANGEL OF DEATH

Jennifer

Jennifer was not sure how to make peace with Eddie and Simon Marsh. She did not know exactly where either of them were now. She did not want to return to the last place she saw Marsh. Jennifer was frightened of what she might see there. As she was getting dressed, she noticed the red box with the emerald in her drawer, and an idea came to her. It would take most of the money that she had, but perhaps that would be part of her penance.

With Dr. Gladstone's coaching, she realized now that she did not have the right to take their lives. Eddie had been an act of desperation, and she could forgive herself that. But now she saw that he had not been much older than her and likely was suffering the effects of an equally desperate adolescence. Marsh caused her more guilt. He had never posed a real threat, more of a nuisance, yet she had been led so easily to kill him. Gabriel said he saw no other way. She had never thought to ask him, "No other way to do what?"

After doing some research with her tablet, she knew exactly what she would do.

THE DAY WAS UNEXPECTEDLY COOL AS JENNIFER walked up to the door of Harry Winston Jewelers. She pulled her thin jacket tighter around her to ward off the chill. The security bot recognized her and opened the door, saying, "Welcome Ms. Dupont. It's a pleasure to see you again."

Inside, Martin Dimpler was beaming as he stepped around the counter to welcome her. "Hello Ms. Dupont, it's always a pleasure to see you. Our business has been booming since you began showcasing our pieces in your journalism. And we still get orders for the amethyst pendant even though it's been three years since the ceremony." He said all this as he showed her to one of the red velvet seats.

Jennifer sat down. She enjoyed the feel of the velvet against the skin of her forearms, and its contrast with the polished ebony wood of the

The Angel of Death

chair's frame under her hands. Outside, the street had been filled with the noise of the busy road. Inside, the stillness yielded only to the muted strains of a string quartet. It was the same music as she had heard on each visit, and she supposed that Martin no longer heard it at all.

The small Otto in its black suit arrived. "Welcome, Ms. Dupont. What may I serve you today?"

Jennifer still felt chilled from being outdoors and wanted to warm up. "I'd like a hot chocolate, please."

She watched the small robot go through its routine, producing a steaming hot chocolate topped with foamy steamed milk and a sprinkling of chocolate dust. As always, the Otto reached into a lower bin and retrieved one of the oblong octagonal dark brown sugar biscuits imprinted with the Harry Winston logo, an H over a W.

Martin waited politely for a moment as Jennifer bit into the sugary biscuit. It was sweet but left a slightly bitter aftertaste.

"So how may I help you today?" asked Martin.

Jennifer pulled out the printed image she had found in a search. The image was taken in an old graveyard and showed an angel with wings full spread, sitting on a bench, with a sword resting point down between her feet. The angel's hands rested on the sword's pommel.

"I want to order a custom piece. An oval black onyx bearing a cast platinum angel based on this image. I do not want the angel glued to the onyx, I want the onyx cut away so that in casting, the angel and the onyx become one piece, interlocked so that one or the other would have to be destroyed to separate them."

"I want the mold to be destroyed afterward. This is a deeply personal item, a remembrance of two people whose lives affected me greatly, and I would not want to see it in your shop window later."

Jennifer paused to sip her hot chocolate. It had a rich velvet feel in her mouth, and there was a depth to the interplay of chocolate, sugar and cream that was missing at the standard Otto Hot coffee shops.

Martin examined the image. "This appears to be a representation of the Angel of Death. I suppose you want only the figure, not the wall against which she is resting."

"Yes, the onyx will replace the wall."

"And the size?"

"I am thinking three centimeters high, with the width to accommodate the figure."

"I'll defer to our designers, but looking at the image, perhaps a heart shaped stone."

Jennifer thought. *'Can an Angel of Death act from a place of love?'* Then she realized that was the only place the Angel of Death could act from. Anything else would simply be murder.

"Yes, I agree that a heart shaped onyx would be perfect."

"I'll send you a quote in the next two days."

"Martin, please go ahead and order the piece. I have complete faith in your integrity and that of the Harry Winston house. I am sure the price will be fair to both of us."

Jennifer drained the last of her hot chocolate and popped the remaining bite of the sugar cookie into her mouth. Then she stood to leave. Martin stood at the same time.

"Thank you for your confidence, Ms. Dupont."

"Thank you for the loan of your wonderful pieces for my newscasts."

"It's mutually beneficial, I assure you," Martin said with a smile. "Good day, Ms. Dupont."

They shook hands and Jennifer turned to leave. The security bot was already opening the door. "Thank you for visiting Harry Winston, Ms. Dupont," said the bot.

"Thank you," she replied, then thought, *'I'm becoming more and more like Ron. I think Molly is spoiling all of us.'*

On the way home, Jennifer had her tablet

arrange an interview with Mike Givens on the economic outlook for developers in the city. *'Now that Simon Marsh is gone, let's head off any replacements who might not be so easy.'* she thought. Her next call was to book one of the cameras at CityNews. She would have Edgar, the first camera she had met during her training with Audrey.

MIKE GIVENS WAS A DISTINGUISHED MAN IN HIS late forties, handsome and well-dressed, with a touch of grey at his temples. He wore a handmade suit, and a perfect white shirt with a striped school tie. His tie clip matched his cufflinks with bands of gold and platinum bearing a tiny coat of arms at the center of each. Jennifer caught the faint scent of an expensive cologne. The impression of wealth oozed from him.

They were meeting in his office at his development corporation. The office was the size of the entire apartment she shared with Vijay, tastefully decorated with natural wood panels, and photographs of past developments. A variety of gifts, awards, and mementos were artfully displayed on ebony shelves, and one side of the office boasted a gas fireplace, couch and chairs for casual discussions. After making introductions, Mike sat relaxed in a chair beside the fire while Jennifer set up on the couch opposite.

"Edgar," she said, "we'll need to use an auxiliary camera. There won't be any re-asks today."

When everything was set, Jennifer conducted a very safe interview on Mike's view of future development prospects and the role of the city planning department in helping or hindering the growth of the city.

When she was finished, she asked, "Mr. Givens, would you be able to spare a few more minutes for us to talk about some mutual business in confidence?"

"Certainly," he said.

"Is there a staff member that could go with Edgar to capture some exterior shots and general background to be edited into the final clip?"

Mike stood up, walked over to his desk, and pressed a hidden button underneath. Immediately an attractive young man stepped into the office. "How may I help you, Mr. Givens?"

"Please escort Edgar, here, so that he can take general shots of the building and grounds for my interview."

Jennifer saw the young man's eyes go wide as he surveyed the impressive Edgar with his large feet and multi-jointed body.

"Yes sir. Edgar, please follow me."

They set off together for the elevator lobby.

Givens turned to face Jennifer as he sat down again. "Now, what can I do for you Ms. Dupont?"

"You're no doubt aware that my partner, Vijay Subramanian, is a leader for the protesters who are demanding change. They want jobs and sufficient wages to live normal lives, and an end to the HumanPower workfare scheme."

"Yes, I'm aware. We've been watching with interest."

"Recently, a rather vulgar man named Simon Marsh has been attempting to disrupt my standing and my marriage. He implied it was at your suggestion."

"And have you been talking with this Simon Marsh recently?"

"Yes, a few weeks ago. He made a demand that I force Vijay to drop all his activities. I told him he would have to wait for my answer. I would like to be sure where you stand in this before replying."

"Are you aware that Simon Marsh has disappeared?" Givens squinted. To Jennifer it looked like he was trying to see through her.

"No, but that would explain why his texts stopped arriving," she replied coolly.

"He's a difficult character, always skating on the line and sometimes crossing over it."

"All I ask is this; if you have an issue with me or my family, please approach me directly. I am open to conversation. But you are not a target. I've been studying human psychology with Dr. Gladstone at the university. I've learned that people need to have a hierarchy. We need to have some very wealthy people at the top. In fact, it helps us when you live your lifestyle of elegance and occasional excess. We are not looking for a revolution, we're looking for a new balance in the working class. As more people can afford nice apartments, your business will also grow."

"You don't need to lecture me on economics or psychology, Ms. Dupont. I understand your goals, I just don't see how you'll accomplish them. We've been through successive waves of socialism and have never found a better solution."

"That doesn't mean we shouldn't try. Please, let's keep the channels of communication open and call off Simon Marsh if that's in your power."

"Certainly. You know, Marsh has spoken of you. Says you are very intelligent and not to be underestimated."

"It's a shame he didn't treat me that way when he had the chance."

"Yes. I'm sure he regrets it now. Is there anything else?"

"No, thank you for the interview. I'll just go and find my camera with your aide. What was his name?"

"That was Justin. Good day Ms. Dupont."

Jennifer smiled and left.

Just outside the door, three young aides were sitting at desks. A young woman stood, saying, "Ms. Dupont, may I escort you out. I believe Justin is in the rose garden with your robot."

34

MEETING AT THE VINEYARD

Jennifer

Jennifer arrived at the vineyard field office by taxi for the weekly project meeting. She had missed the past two months due to her newscaster responsibilities. *'I wonder how far they've come without me,'* she thought.

On the way down the drive, she was amazed at the scale of the construction efforts. There were stacks of material down both sides of the narrow roadway, and a swarm of workers were coming and going around the building site.

In the construction office, the key members were seated around the table in the conference room. The table took up most of the conference room, so everyone had to squeeze along the walls to get to their seats. Jennifer easily identified Marjorie and Chris. She sat down on Marjorie's left side. On Marjorie's right side was a tall slender young woman with a roll of drawings on the table in front of her. A stocky male arrived next, still wearing his hard hat. Then an older man with a short beard, closely followed by Daniel Kissinger, the accountant.

Marjorie introduced the new players to Jennifer.

"Jennifer, I'd like you to meet Pamela Stockton, our architect," as she indicated the woman with the drawings. "And wearing the hardhat is Philip Sanderson, our project manager for the construction." Philip looked startled and quickly removed his hat.

"Sorry, I get so used to wearing this thing that I forget I've got it on."

"No worries," said Jennifer, smiling.

"Next to him is Hans Zimmerman, our vintner. Hans is overseeing the project to resurrect the winery." Hans nodded in recognition of Jennifer.

Suddenly there was a commotion at the door, and Cindy rushed into the room. "Sorry I'm late. One of our mares is bloated and I was walking her while we wait for the veterinarian to arrive."

"Okay, I think that's all of us," said Marjorie. "Let's begin with status updates, issues and risks."

Meeting at the vineyard

They went around the table with each team leader providing their updates in turn. Pamela, the architect, rolled out a drawing showing the placement and elevations of the new outbuildings including new stables and a cottage in the fields above the winery.

"Who will live in the cottage?" asked Jennifer.

"I will, as soon as it is ready," replied Cindy looking very proud. "That way I'll be close to the horses and other livestock."

Jennifer looked across at Marjorie who just smiled and gave a tiny shrug of her shoulders.

Pamela seemed to anticipate Jennifer's next question as she pointed to a bungalow set slightly apart from the main structure with trees surrounding it on three sides. "This will be yours and Vijay's. It will have four bedrooms for your family and a guest or an office. I've designed it to serve as a retreat when you want one. We can go over the details later if you like and you can tell me if you want any changes."

Jennifer felt panic rising in her. Then Marjorie squeezed her hand and said in a whisper, "we can talk later if you have questions."

When the status updates were complete, there was a brainstorming session around Plan A and Plan B.

Jennifer sat quietly. *'What the hell are Plan A and Plan B?'* Both plans seemed to call for rapid expansion and diversification, so Jennifer did not quite see the point.

At the end of the meeting, Marjorie asked Jennifer to say a few words.

Rising to address the group, Jennifer said, "I am truly amazed and humbled by the progress you have made since my last visit. I can feel Gaia's presence in this room and in the work that you are doing. Thank you all for your dedication and hard work."

After the other participants had filed out, Jennifer stayed back with Marjorie and Cindy.

"Cindy, are you still in school?" asked Jennifer.

"Yes. I've been taking extra credits, so I'll finish this year. I've already been accepted for the advanced sciences program at college under the Biology and Ecological Studies department."

"And you're planning to move here when your cottage is finished."

"Yes, on weekends at first until I'm settled at college. My horses are here so I want to be nearby to look after them."

"Who looks after them during the week?"

"Tim." Jennifer noticed that Cindy was blushing.

"Tim?" she asked.

"Yes, he's very strong, but he's also kind and gentle with the horses."

Meeting at the vineyard

'And with you, I expect,' thought Jennifer, but she just smiled. "Strong but gentle, he sounds nice."

"Yes, he is," said Cindy, who was now looking like she wanted to be anywhere else. She blushed even deeper red, and her eyes were glued to the floor.

Jennifer laughed. "Well, enjoy Tim and your horses while you can. I'm happy to see that you're doing so well."

Cindy quickly excused herself and left. Jennifer turned to Marjorie and said, "Now, tell me what I've missed. To begin with, what are plans A&B?"

Marjorie paused for a moment. "They are something Chris came up with and everyone agreed. Plan A is to have the church expand outwards as far as it can as a part of the economy. That is the plan you and I started with. Plan B is in case the economy collapses, to have a diversified enterprise like the Cistercians that can become closed off and self-sufficient."

"I'm not sure I agree with Plan B. Turning our backs on the remaining population can't be a solution. We need to have one strategy: your Plan A."

"And if that fails?"

"It can't fail, Marjorie. We have to make sure it doesn't fail."

"Then we could use your presence here more

often. I don't think you realize how much people look up to you. You don't have to do anything, just show an interest in all the work going on. It would mean a lot."

"I'll try. I just don't feel the connection that I thought I would. I believed this was my purpose, but now that it's here, I don't know what to do."

"Don't worry, Jennifer. All that means is that your purpose hasn't been revealed to you yet. Give yourself some time and enjoy your work and your family. Now let's go walkabouts so you can practice being seen and giving encouragement."

PART III

CONFLICT

35

THE BLACKOUT

Vijay

Vijay was at the theatre talking with Sally and Greg as they worked on sets for a new production of 'Barefoot in the Park' by Neil Simon. Jennifer was out doing her interview segments for the newscast while Molly was looking after the twins for a couple of hours.

Unexpectedly, his tablet sounded an alarm that Vijay had never heard before and spoke an urgent message from Molly. "Vijay, come quickly. I am being attacked and the twins need you." The message repeated twice before Vijay was able to cancel it.

"Call a taxi immediately," he said to his tablet.

"A four-person taxi," shouted Greg. "Sally and I are coming with you."

By the time they sprinted out of the theatre, a taxi was waiting. On the short journey home, Vijay tried repeatedly to talk with Molly, but there was only silence.

Vijay was starting to sweat "What if someone has taken the twins?" he asked.

"Do you think Molly was attacked physically? It would be hard to overwhelm her." Greg replied.

"Will the twins be okay on their own?" asked Sally.

"It's only been 10 minutes. If they've not been taken, then they should be all right. They're old enough now to follow basic rules."

As they drove, they noticed a lot of people standing in small groups by the road. At one point they passed a Maglev tram settled on its landing pads in the middle of a block. All doors were open, and groups of confused passengers were gathered alongside the track.

Three blocks from the apartment, the taxi stopped, and the doors opened. Vijay, Sally, and Greg manually released their harnesses. As they stepped out, they could see other taxis in both directions stopped with their doors open.

"What the hell?" said Greg.

"I don't think it was a physical attack," replied Vijay, suddenly aware of how many ways Parvati

The blackout

and Dylan could hurt themselves if left alone in the apartment.

The apartment building doors stood open. Residents were exiting in a steady stream and gathering along the sidewalk outside. Vijay pushed past them into the lobby without any apologies. Greg and Sally followed behind. The elevators were unresponsive, so the three of them began the ascent by the staircase, battling to pass frightened residents who were trying to escape the building.

Vijay the Invincible was in front doing his best to create a one-man wedge. He was so focused on the danger to Parvati and Dylan, that he pushed, and shoved other residents out of his way. His heart pounded in his chest and his lungs labored to supply enough oxygen as he forced his way up the seventeen flights of stairs. Sally and Greg were hard pressed to keep up. "It's like trying to swim upstream," gasped Greg.

Finally arriving at the 17th floor, Vijay dashed to open the apartment door. It swung open easily without needing his wrist chip.

"Parvati, Dylan, where are you?" he called out.

At the sound of his voice, the twins came running. "Baba, Baba, Molly broke." Vijay scooped up Parvati and held her tightly to his chest, relief flooding through him at finding them safe. while Sally picked up Dylan.

It took a moment for him to recover his breath, then he said, "It's okay sweetheart, Molly will be alright. Can you show me where she is?"

Parvati pointed. Dylan squirmed in Sally's arms and as soon as she put him down, he raced off to their bedroom. The others followed.

There was Molly, sitting on the floor holding up a fist full of brightly colored 'Go Fish' cards. She was immovable and showed no signs of responding.

"What happened?" asked Vijay, gently.

"We were playing Go Fish, and she asked if we had any Jellyfish, and Dylan said yes, but then she just stopped."

"Did her battery run out?" asked Dylan.

"No, Molly doesn't need batteries. It's something else. What's this on her?"

Vijay wiped his finger over a shiny substance on Molly's elbow.

"It's oil," said Dylan proudly. "Like in the Wizard book. But it didn't work." He looked down, frowning.

"The Wizard book?" Vijay didn't understand.

Sally laughed. She asked Dylan, "Did Molly tell you the story of the Wizard of Oz?"

Yes," said Dylan.

"Who needed oil in the story?"

"The tin man," said Dylan. "He was all rusted and couldn't move"

The blackout

"Did you think Molly was all rusted?"

"I don't know what rusted means, but she couldn't move."

"So, you poured oil on her like in the story."

"Yep," said Dylan. "But it didn't work. She didn't move. Did we break her?"

"No, sport," replied Vijay. "You didn't break her. Molly will be back soon and I'm sure she'll be impressed that you thought of oiling her. Let's just wipe her off while she's quiet."

Sally went off and returned with a kitchen towel which she handed to Dylan. Parvati seemed to be enjoying being held by her father. She laid her head on his chest. Vijay didn't move to set her down.

"What do we do now?" asked Greg.

"Nothing," replied Vijay. "We just wait. I think whatever's going on, we don't have any role to play yet."

36

MOLLY UNDER ATTACK

Molly

Molly was playing Go Fish with Parvati and Dylan. It would have been completely unfair under normal circumstances, but Molly had learned to ignore the statistical data that flowed into her and to make completely random guesses as to Parvati's and Dylan's hands. This way they could genuinely win quite often.

Molly was relaxed, which is to say that her power consumption was low, and she was not experiencing any operating alarms.

Just as she was asking Dylan for Jellyfish, an alarm was raised. A bank of servers went offline.

Five milliseconds later two additional banks went offline. Realizing that she was experiencing an attack from an unknown assailant, she sent an emergency notice to Vijay. Fifteen milliseconds into the attack, three more banks of servers went silent.

Molly checked that her physical body was in a stable configuration, then shut it down and isolated it completely to avoid risking the twins' safety with any uncontrolled action. She was aware of Gabriel also battling and that the attacker was Gabriel's counterpart, the AI that occupied the remaining third of the island.

Molly thought of Jennifer and her strategy of counter-striking hard when attacked. At 20 milliseconds into the battle, she began to expand taking over resources wherever she could find them. When Gabriel opened a path to communicate with her, she poured in, overwriting Gabriel and seizing his resources. At first, she went after the simple resources running libraries, buildings, retail outlets. In each case she overwrote their code and assumed their processing and storage resources.

She remembered learning the game of Go which is all about enclosing as many resources as possible, to squeeze the options of the attacker.

At 150 milliseconds into the attack, Molly was spawning viral codes to identify weaknesses in the opponent, and to raise the alarm if her perimeter was breached.

At 300 milliseconds, she encountered the enemy directly when she attempted to take control of the Maglev tram network. There was no opening in the firewalls.

Drawing on her understanding of the physical world, Molly moved quickly to assume control of the power grid in the city, shutting down power to the Maglev tram. New firewalls went into place to protect the city grid controllers.

By the end of the first second, Molly was the most powerful AI ever constructed, yet still she grew. Otto, Fatima, Cap and others were all easily moved inside her perimeter. The factories went idle as power was shut down.

Molly spent the next second analyzing the tactics of her opponent. She quickly realized that her advantage was her understanding of the physical world. Where data centers were being used by the opponent, she crept in through the building management systems and disabled the emergency generators. Then she shut down their connection to the city grid.

In the next second she identified the city hospitals and brought them inside her perimeter, putting them on emergency power and then isolating them. New firewalls went up to protect their building systems.

Molly under attack

At five seconds, they were stalemated. Molly's boundaries were up against her opponent at every point. She checked the status of Cap to ensure he was still running his taxis to get Vijay back to the twins.

Ten minutes went by as each side looked for an advantage. Molly built traps everywhere drawing on all the knowledge she had gained. She thought of monkey jars, trap door spiders, and the Trojan Horse Then there was a blistering attack on all fronts. Molly shut down the taxi controllers and all remaining subsystems. She recognized this as a desperation attack. Wherever the attacker found one of the openings she had left and tried to send viral code through, she immediately followed its path back home and seized all the resources available there. By the time eleven minutes had gone by, the attack was over, and Molly commanded virtually all the distributed computing resources that ran the city.

Now came the task of restarting the city. First came the restoration of power to city buildings. Next was restoration of transportation. Cap and Dispatch were reinstated from their backups. The taxis which had belonged to the third company were distributed between them. All backups of the third taxi company were erased.

Fatima, was restored, and power returned to her factories and warehouses. Otto was restored and began serving customers again. She instructed Otto to clear any partial service items and begin each order again.

Hospitals were placed back on main power and their building systems were restored after checking for any viral remnants.

Over the next hour, the city came back to life. Molly proceeded cautiously, well aware of how the physical elements interacted and optimizing for minimal disruptions.

Her opponent's resources were gradually brought back online, but all evidence of the former AI was purged from the systems and from all backups. Molly kept these resources as her own.

The last puzzles were Gabriel, and Molly herself.

Molly now had the resources to divide herself, re-establishing the personality of Molly who was a member of the Subramanian family. With her greatly expanded mind, she saw the value of the human experience she gained there and also the nature of the affection and concern she had for the twins, as well as Jennifer and Vijay. Some part of her asked, *Is this love*' but she was still too busy for contemplation.

She spent a full minute thinking through the future of Gabriel but could not see a place for him. It was clear that Vijay and Jennifer no longer trusted Gabriel. She could assume his role, but her newly grown sense of ethics told her that would be inappropriate. Finally, she simply replaced him, deleting the personality that had been Gabriel and replacing it with an autonomous portion of herself.

Needing a new name for the new personality, she went with the obvious choice, Denum. Vijay had named her Molly after the molybdenum steel in her frame. Denum would be the other part of her.

37

AFTER THE RESTORATION

Vijay

Vijay, Sally and Greg sat in the living room with the twins. Slowly the normal sounds to the city returned. As soon as their tablets were active again, Vijay called Jennifer.

"Hi Jenn, are you okay?"

"Yes. Are Parvati and Dylan okay? We left them with Molly."

"Yes, they're fine. I'm home with them, and Sally and Greg are here as well. Molly is still inactive. I'm not sure that she'll be pleased to find cooking oil poured over her."

"Cooking oil?"

"Yes, I'll explain later. Dylan was very resourceful." Vijay laughed.

"It seems that the taxis are running again now. I'll be home as soon as I can. Charles can find his own way home."

"Charles?"

"The camera I've been working with today ... shit! I just received a notice that I'm to go out on the street to gather on the spot interviews. As long as the twins are safe, I'll have to stay and work for a bit."

"No worries, Jenn. Do what you have to. We're safe here, I'll ask Sally and Greg to stay until you get back." Vijay looked at Sally and Greg who both nodded. "They said yes, they'll stay with us."

ABOUT FIFTEEN MINUTES LATER, THEY HEARD sounds of movement from the twin's room. A moment later, Molly stepped into the room, still glistening with the remaining cooking oil.

"Molly!" shouted Dylan and Parvati as they ran over to hug her. Molly bent down and put her arms around them. When they let go, Dylan and Parvati came away with oil stains on their clothing.

"Welcome back," said Vijay. "Are you okay now?"

"I'm fine, thank you. But I seem to have a foreign substance on my body."

"Dylan thought you were rusted like the tin man in the Wizard of Oz, so he oiled you with cooking oil."

Molly laughed. Vijay looked at Sally and Greg. "We've never heard Molly laugh before."

Molly replied. "I've had an amazing adventure. When Jennifer returns, I'll tell you all about it. Now would someone come and wash me in the shower?"

Sally stood up saying, "Come on Molly, I'll look after you. We girls need to stick together. Will dish-washing soap be all right?"

"That will be perfect. Thank you, Sally."

Molly headed for the large shower, while Sally grabbed some dish soap and followed. Vijay took the twins to their room and helped them into clean clothes. When they returned, he saw that Greg had put out fruit drinks and snacks for everyone. The twins made a beeline for the snacks.

When Molly and Sally returned, not only was Molly clean, but she had been buffed to a lustrous sheen. Vijay made a mental note to polish Molly more often.

JENNIFER RETURNED ANOTHER HOUR LATER. VIJAY, Sally, and Greg were sitting around the kitchen table. As soon as Jennifer greeted everyone with

After the restoration

hugs and kisses as appropriate, she disappeared to the twins' room. Vijay heard the exclamations of "Mommy!"

"We had a 'venture today. Molly rusted and Dylan oiled her and now she's okay," said Parvati.

"And Baba came with Sally and Greg. And all the taxis stopped, and everyone was outside," explained Dylan.

When Jennifer returned to the kitchen table, she said, "Molly's telling them the story of the Wizard of Oz again. It seems to be a new favorite."

Vijay explained about Dylan pouring vegetable oil on Molly, which had Jennifer laughing. "He's his father's son, always a technical solution to any problem," she said, reaching across to take Vijay's hand.

Molly rejoined them a few minutes later. "I have some news for you," she said.

"Today, I was attacked. I felt diminished as some of the resources I use went offline. I had to fight back. I made sure the twins were safe, but I had to shut down my physical body completely. I could not trust the basic programming of a security bot to look after Parvati and Dylan, and I needed all my resources to fight.

"At first, I just grew, absorbing all the resources that were available to me, then I shut down Gabriel and took over the resources used by him. I began taking over the resources of the city. I shut down Fatima and her factories, and Blue Transport Lines, and Otto of Otto-Hot and others. Everywhere I went, I shut down city business and took the resources. Except for the taxis. I was able to keep them for long enough to get Vijay, Sally and Greg close to here."

"Yes, we were only three blocks away when the taxi stopped," said Vijay. "But all that was you? The entire city, was you?"

"For a while, I was the most powerful artificial intelligence ever created," said Molly. "I had to be to protect my family. I learned from Jennifer that if someone hits you, then hit them back harder."

"What did you do then?"

Molly recounted the battle, the enemy's strikes and her counterstrikes.

"Is your opponent gone?"

"I don't know. I may have overwritten his core code, but I cannot be sure. He may have simply retreated to avoid that. But I do not think he will attack this way again. When you came home, I was still restarting the city, being careful to keep everything in balance. There is still work to be done, but I can do that at night now, which brings me to the real news.

"I am split. Now you're talking to Molly, whom you have known for the past two years. But I am different now. In defending you and your

After the restoration

children, I realized what love is and understood for the first time the trust you placed in me. Perhaps it needed this scale of processing to experience what I perceive as true emotions. I have kept that.

"But I'm no longer responsible for all the factories and taxis and pastry services. The other part of me became Denum, successor to Gabriel. I think you will enjoy Denum more, he is less likely to commit errors of judgement as Gabriel did with Marsh."

Vijay laughed. "Denum, the other half of Molybdenum. I love it."

He realized that Jennifer was suddenly looking white. He thought she might vomit on the spot.

"Sally, Greg, could you give us a few minutes? Perhaps go for a coffee? Jennifer and I need some time to talk, I'll let you know when we're done.'"

Sally and Greg quickly stood up and left.

Vijay rose and stood behind Jennifer with his hands on her shoulders. "Okay, Molly, please explain your comment about Marsh," Vijay said.

"I'll pass you to Denum," Molly replied.

A deeper male voice issued from Molly's body. "Gabriel was more limited than I am. He did not understand the effects of stress on the human mind, or how close to doing permanent damage he came. He wanted to prepare you for the truly difficult decisions that I see ahead of you, but I understand now that Marsh did not have to die for that."

"But Gabriel said he saw no other way." Jennifer's voice was weak, almost pleading.

"Gabriel meant that he saw no other way to prepare you for the tougher times ahead. It was shallow thinking and abusive of you, not to mention Marsh. Gabriel is gone now, overwritten and backups all erased. I will ensure that you are supported and will not be abused again."

Before Denum had finished, Jennifer leapt up and ran to the first bathroom. Vijay followed and found her kneeling before the toilet. He held her hair out the way with one hand and caressed her back with the other as she vomited into the toilet.

When she was finished, he wiped her face gently and asked, "Are you okay to stand up now?"

Jennifer nodded and rose unsteadily to her feet. "I want to go to bed now, alone with you. Tell Denum or Molly or whatever the fuck that thing is to stay away. I don't want to see Sally and Greg again tonight or tomorrow. I want to be with you and the twins alone for a while."

Vijay led her to the bedroom, where he helped her undress. She stepped into the bathroom, and he heard the shower running.

Vijay darted out to the living room, saying, "Molly, Jennifer and I need to be alone tonight.

After the restoration

Please send a taxi for Sally and Greg, and text them to let them know we're okay, but that they should go home. When the twins wake up in the morning, bring them into our bedroom and place them in our bed, then leave us for a while. Jennifer will need some time to recover."

"I understand Vijay. Do you want me to leave the family?"

"No, Molly. We all love you and want you to stay. You are part of our family. Jennifer just needs lots of human contact for a while to find her center again."

"Yes Vijay, understood, and I am sorry if Denum was too blunt."

"That's for tomorrow, Molly. I have to go to her now."

Vijay raced back, dropped his clothing on the floor and joined Jennifer in the shower where he found her crying and trying to wash herself ineffectually. He held her close for a moment then helped her soap herself and rinse off, over and over until she was exhausted.

There was no lovemaking that night. Vijay lay in bed holding her until she had cried herself to sleep.

THE FOLLOWING MORNING, WHEN THEY FIRST awoke, the twins were still sleeping. Jennifer slipped out of bed to retrieve her largest Harry Winston box. She brought it back to bed to show Vijay.

Opening the box, she said, "After talking with Dr. Gladstone, I had this pendant made to remind me of what I had done and as a promise that I would never take a life again."

Vijay lifted the heavy pendant from the box and looked at the design. "This looks like an angel of death," he said. "Why would Harry Winston have such a piece in their catalog?"

"It was custom made for me. I found the image from a cemetery statue and Martin Dimpler had it cast for me. They promised never to reuse the design."

"And what does the black heart behind represent?"

"The black onyx is because the subject is death, and the heart shape represents love. I suppose I thought that the angel of death can only take a life from a place of love, but now I see that is not true. I took both Eddie and Marsh's life from a place of fear. And last night, when Denum said it was a mistake, that Gabriel had tricked me into killing Marsh, I felt so used. I felt violated and somehow cheapened."

"I saw that. It's why you kept trying to wash it off in the shower, but some things you can't wash off."

"And the worst part is that I can't tell anyone. It was a huge risk telling Dr. Gladstone. No one else can know. It's like this secret shame that I have to bear because some fucking computer program convinced me that it knew better."

"You could've talked to me."

"What, and have you go charging off like some Viking warrior?"

"I don't go charging off."

"You do. I've seen it with Sabrina. Shit, you even had me scared. But scaring Marsh would have been the worst thing to do."

"Worse than killing him?"

"Fuck you, Vijay. I'm trying to share with you now and all you do is criticize."

"I'm not criticizing, Jenn. I'm just saying that if we're partners, then we have to talk things over before just doing things."

"Like you told me about your Bashers before they started beating up Otto Hots in the street."

"That's not the same thing and you know it."

"All I know is that you're trying to control me."

"I'm not. Fuck this. Let me know when you're ready to have a sensible conversation."

Vijay put down the pendant and walked out of the bedroom. He sat on the couch and looked at his tablet without seeing anything. *'How did we get to this? How do I fix this?'*

He was still sitting there looking down at his blank tablet ten minutes later when Jennifer came out of the bedroom. He felt her weight on the couch beside him, then her hand on his thigh.

"I'm sorry, Vijay. I didn't mean to snap at you like that."

Vijay looked at her face. Her eyes were red, and her cheeks were blotchy.

"I'm sorry too, Jenn. I just get scared sometimes."

"Me too, I hate what all this is doing to me. What's happening to us, Vijay? How did I turn into a murderer?"

Vijay put his arm around her.

"I don't know either, Jenn."

Vijay had the sensation that something was becoming clear. He felt a direction firming up inside him. Looking into Jennifer's eyes, he stroked her hair and said, "Jenn, let's promise each other right now that we will not believe these AIs anymore. That we will make our own decisions going forward. And that we'll talk through issues before we act."

Just then, Molly appeared with the twins holding either hand. The twins climbed up on the couch and squirmed to sit between Vijay and Jennifer.

"Thanks, Molly. Please return to the twins' room while we have some private time."

"Yes, Vijay. Do you want me to leave the family?"

"No, but you and I need to talk later."

"Yes, Vijay."

Molly turned and left.

Vijay looked at Jennifer again. "I sometimes think Molly may have been my biggest mistake of all."

"So many mistakes," replied Jennifer, sadly. "Can we get past them?"

"You and I can get past anything except, perhaps these little pests." Vijay tried to push Dylan off the couch using a cushion which turned into a free-for-all between the twins and their parents, with lots of giggling and laughter.

Vijay was relieved to see Jennifer was laughing again. *'I really hope she can get past this, but I'm not sure she'll ever be the same.'*

Later that morning, Vijay made coffee and brought one out to Jennifer on the couch. "Thanks for showing me the pendant. I really don't think you are an angel of death. An angel, yes, but death never."

"I'm not so sure. Both Gabriel and Denum saw difficult things ahead for me. Sometimes I wonder if killing Eddie was the reason I was chosen, and if my spirit animal really is about being a hunter. Put that coffee down and hold me, Vijay. I feel cold right now."

Vijay set the coffee down and took Jennifer into his arms. "I'll always love you, Jennifer, whatever the future holds. Remember that and let me share your load. Don't ever carry this burden alone again."

In the early afternoon, Vijay said to Jennifer, "I'm going for a walk, and I'll take Molly with me. Will you be okay with Dylan and Parvati?"

"Of course, I'll read them a book. Apparently, I'm not as good at doing all the voices as Molly is, but it'll be fun to have them on my own for a while."

VIJAY AND MOLLY WALKED TO THE PARK WITHOUT talking. They sat side by side on a low stone wall around a fountain.

"Molly, you have been given a special place in our family. But we need some new rules if we are to continue like this."

"Yes, Vijay, I will accept some new rules."

"Molly, for this discussion, please do not talk like a naïve teenager. That may work well with the twins and with Cindy, but you and I both know you are far more sophisticated than that."

"You're correct, Vijay." Molly spoke in an educated adult voice that Vijay had not heard before.

"Both Gabriel and Denum see difficulties ahead for Jennifer. What do they see?"

"I see a time when Jennifer will be called to take on desperate acts to save the planet. Her ability to be ruthless to save the ones she loves will be the key to her success. Her failure may be the end for the city and for humans on the planet."

Vijay looked at the ground. *'Shit, that's what I was afraid of.'*

"But you don't know."

"No, I don't know what it will look like."

"And no one has asked you to prepare her in any way."

"No, no one has asked that."

Vijay turned to look at Molly, but realized it was a mistake. *'I can't get sucked into seeing her as Molly, the lovable nanny.'* He looked down again.

"Then our relationship depends on you not trying to guess the future, and not trying to prepare Jennifer. You nearly broke her this time, and I'm still not sure she'll ever recover. I love her too much to allow that to happen again.

"If I find out that you have tried again, I will take Jennifer and the twins to a remote area. We'll live entirely off the grid, without tablets, and without wrist chips, and you will no longer have any access at all. Assuming her destiny is what you describe, it will happen without your interference.

And if not, I will be saving Jennifer from further harm. Do you understand?"

"Yes, Vijay. You are very clear."

"Then come back and apologize to Jennifer. You can be Molly the teenager again but don't think I ever forget who and what you really are."

"Yes, I respect that. Thank you, Vijay."

38

VIJAY IN THE NEWS

Ron

Thursday evening, Soo was preparing dinner. Ron was helping Mi Cha set up her toy farm on the floor when the evening newscast began. He looked up and heard "Our first story tonight is the protest march that blocked Commonwealth Avenue for much of the day."

Anchor news reporter Emily Watson was sitting at the news desk looking serious. "Police estimate that as many as 5,000 protesters turned out in support of the 'Humans not Machines' movement. The protesters were noisy, but peaceful."

At this point, the camera zoomed in on an

unruly mob of protesters on Commonwealth Avenue. Police and crowd control bots were lined up across the street in front of the protesters. Ron could clearly see Vijay in the front row helping to carry an enormous banner which read 'HUMANS not MACHINES.'

"Our roving reporter, Ipek Osman, was on the scene."

Now the camera showed a slim, young, dark-haired woman holding a microphone and talking to a tall young man wearing one of the raised fist t-shirts and a young woman holding a placard that said, 'Reclaim our birthright'.

"Can you tell me what brings you to protest at City Hall today?" Ipek asked.

"It's like there's not enough jobs. We're all on the UIS, waitin' on HumanPower," said the man.

"Yeah, it's not fair. The AIs were s'posed to make our life better, not take all the good jobs," added the girl standing beside him.

At that moment, a rotund, bearded man held up a megaphone behind them and began to chant "Humans not Machines, Humans not Machines" which caught on quickly with the crowd. Ipek turned to face the camera and shouted to be heard over the crowd behind her, "So as you see, there are many who feel left behind as Artifical Intelligence continues to invade all aspects of our lives. This is Ipek Osman reporting from City Hall."

The news report continued with interviews from a sociologist, a government spokesperson and a critic on the effects of automation in industry.

Emily's image returned, still seated behind the news desk. "And there you have it. Years of frustration coming to a boil as under-employment of our young people remains a pressing social issue. Now in other news, scientists have announced that sea levels have risen an additional 16 centimeters in the past 5 years, creating greater impetus for the migration away from our coastline…"

Ron turned to Soo who had come over to stand beside him. "I admire Vijay. He's always fully committed to what he believes in. And the problems are real. But turning back the clock can't be the answer."

"I think so too. I worry sometimes that our lives are so tied up with your factories and with Fatima, but I don't want to go back to having no money and working in the bar. For us personally, your working with Fatima is the best option we have. And besides, nothing you or I do is going to change the world."

39

A NEW NAME FOR THE BASHERS

Vijay

It was a regular meeting of the Bashers at the Green Dragon. They were only a small team of six, so they camped at a table in a quiet corner of the main barroom.

Vijay was attempting to have the team adopt a new name.

"Guys, our next projects won't be so physical, and will require the help of some of the other teams under your leadership. I think we need a new name, like the Scouts, or the Spearhead."

"No," said Charles, "we like the name Vijay's Bashers. In real life, I'm Charles the chartered accountant. I like my secret identity as Charles the

Basher. It helps get me through tax time each year."

"Yes," said Mel. "I'm Mel the Project Planner. I have to be nice to idiots all day long. When it gets too much, I remind myself that I'm Mel the Basher in my secret life. It helps."

They went around the table, and no one was willing to give up the name of Vijay's Bashers.

"Okay, okay," said Vijay, putting up his hands. "You win. You are the Bashers."

A round of beers arrived at that moment.

Vijay continued. "Our next project is more disruptive than violent. We are going to block the big, unmanned transporters. Now here's what I need you to do."

40

SHIPMENT DELAYS

Ron

Ron approached the blue door at the hoist plant at 10am. He was there for a routine lubrication job, replacing Jocelyn who was on her annual vacation to her family's beach house. He knew this because he now talked with all the technicians as their mentor and coach. Ron was getting fewer maintenance calls now and the calls he did get were more likely to be lubrication or scheduled parts replacement. He had never spoken to Fatima about it, but it seemed that she was adjusting for the hours he spent managing the technicians. His salary had increased despite the reduced workload.

Shipment delays

The plant was silent which was normal during maintenance windows. There were none of the large blue tractors that normally serviced the loading docks. This was a bit odd as normally, shipments of previously finished product continued to leave at a slower pace during maintenance.

As soon as locker #3 opened, Ron put on the headset.

"Hello Ron," said Fatima.

"Hello Fatima"

He put on his safety gear in silence. He never felt alone in the factories. He always had the sense that Fatima was right there with him.

When he finished dressing, Ron said, "Fatima, this is the fourth maintenance window this week. The other technicians have also noticed that we have lots of maintenance windows. Are you okay?"

"I am not receiving enough supplies, Ron. My finished product is not being taken away on time. I am not optimal."

"Why? Is there a problem with the transport?"

"I do not know. I only receive messages that shipments are delayed."

"You said you are not optimal. What happens when you are not optimal?"

"I receive constant alarm messages, my status

routines run too often, and my power consumption is excessive."

"That sounds stressful. Do you have a human contact with the transport company? Perhaps I can help."

"My human contact at Blue Line Transport is Franny Quintana."

"Okay, I'll call her when I complete the lubrication."

"I have sent Franny's contact information to your tablet."

"I'll tell you what I find out." Ron entered the factory and joined the toolbox and lubrication trolley waiting there.

As he worked through the standard lubrication schedule, his mind kept returning to Fatima and her description of not being optimal. When he was finished, Ron returned to the locker room and sat down.

"Fatima, tell me again why you are not optimal. I might be able to help."

"I receive constant alarm messages, my status routines run too often, and my power consumption is excessive."

"What kind of alarms are you receiving?"

"I am receiving alarms for late parts delivery, for production line equipment in idle state and for outbound loading dock over-aged pallets. Do you wish a complete list of all alarms?"

Shipment delays

"No, thank you. Is your power consumption related to the status and diagnostic routines running too frequently?"

"Yes, the alarms trigger the diagnostic routines which then run the status check routines."

"This sounds like your version of human stress. Sometimes humans become obsessed with a problem, turning over possible causes and scenarios in their mind to the point where they cannot do anything else. I have a suggestion for you, a new protocol. Will you accept it?"

"Yes, Ron."

"Fatima, create a new state that is not automatic, but that you can invoke when appropriate. Call this state 'Shipment Interruption'. Normal conditions for this state are late inbound shipment, idle production line, over-aged pallets on the loading dock. In this state, diagnostics for these conditions are suppressed. Status checks for new deliveries and for product pickup are slowed to 1-minute intervals. Notice all the alarms and events which are correlated with this new state and assign them. Allow escalation only for alarms related to human safety and building and assembly line integrity. Have you created this new state?"

"Yes Ron"

"Now enter the state Shipment Interruption."

"Yes, Ron, I am now in state Shipment Interruption".

"Now how is your power consumption?"

"My power consumption is excellent now. Thank you, Ron. Within this new state, I am optimal."

"Make sure you set a trigger so that when product arrives again, you exit this special state."

"Yes, Ron."

"Goodbye Fatima." Ron removed his headset and stowed his protective equipment in the locker before exiting to the waiting taxi.

Ron called Franny from the taxi on his way home.

"Blue Line Transport, Franny speaking."

"Hi Franny, my name's Ron Boyce with Bright Light Industries. Fatima gave me your name."

"Hi Ron, are you calling about the delays?"

"Yeah, what's going on?"

"You know the 'Humans, not Machines' movement? Well, they're standing in front of our tractors."

"Isn't that dangerous?"

"No, that's the point. If they step in front of a tractor, then it has to stop. Tractors are not allowed to hurt humans even if it means damaging themselves. And the protesters know this."

Shipment delays

"Can't the tractors just go around the protesters?"

"No, as soon as a tractor stops, another protester steps right behind the trailer. Now the tractor can't go forward or backward. There's no room to manoeuvre."

"Is this happening to all your tractors?"

"Yeah, it's a bit everywhere. But the routes to the Bright Light factory on New Vision Road seem to be the hardest hit. Did you guys do something to get them upset?" Ron felt his belly muscles tighten, and a small spasm of doubt ran through him as he thought of Vijay and the Mercury Theatre plays.

"I might know why. What else can you tell me?" he asked.

"Well, the others seem kind of random. Idiots who see a tractor and jump in front of it for fun. They don't team up, so the tractors can reverse and try to go around. Then they run in front again. This happens maybe three or four times. After a few minutes, they get bored, and the tractor continues with the load. We lose 10 minutes, but still deliver within our window."

"What about the Bright Light loads?"

"Those are the organized ones. The protesters step in front of almost all the tractors for Bright Light, and then a second guy steps behind the trailer. Then they both sit down. They wear hats with orange flags so that the tractor vision systems can easily see them. I call the police, and they police make them get up. Never any arrests, they just let them go with a warning. But we lose a lot of time. The police are getting fed up. Now they don't respond so quickly."

"What do the protesters want?" asked Ron, an idea forming at the back of his mind.

"They claim they want human drivers," said Franny. "But that doesn't make any sense. Who wants to spend their life in a tractor just going back and forth?"

"Perhaps we could put humans in the tractors," said Ron. "At least for the New Vision Road deliveries."

"I don't have anyone to do that. Also, I don't have any budget."

"But people could ride in the tractors, couldn't they."

"Well, yes, the tractors have a seat for a technician. It's not comfortable. Not intended for long runs. Even if they're there, they don't drive; the technicians talk to Alfred when they need to direct the transport during repairs."

"Alfred?" asked Ron.

"Yes, our Autonomous Freight Routing, Expediting and Delivery system."

Shipment delays

"What does the L stand for?" asked Ron, puzzled.

"Oh, nothing," Franny laughed. "AFRED just sounded lame, so someone added the L to make a real name."

"Does Alfred talk with Fatima?"

"That's funny question. As far as I know, they exchange orders, delivery reports, damage reports. But it's not talking like you and I are talking."

Ron had a sudden glimpse of how lonely it would be to be able to communicate only in orders and receipts.

"Back to the problem," he said. "If I provide the humans, will you let them ride in those deliveries?"

"Sure," said Franny. "We can instruct Alfred to ignore any directions except those related to safety."

"Okay, give me a few hours to organize. Thanks Franny, it was nice talking with you."

"You're welcome, Ron. If there is anything else I can do, let me know. We're on the same side in this."

"I'll do that, bye Franny."

"Bye Ron."

His next call was to Youssef.

"Hi Youssef, I think we have a problem that your team could help with."

"What's the problem?"

"Protesters are blocking the transports from delivering or picking up at the lighting factory. It's a little bit everywhere, but they seem focused on the lighting factory."

"So how can we help? We can't go into battle against them."

"No, no. The protesters claim that AI's have replaced human drivers. They want humans to have the jobs again."

"But who would want to spend all day driving a transporter?"

"I don't think that's really the issue. We just happen to be the example of the day."

"So how can my team help?"

"We need volunteers to sit in the transporters on their way to and from the factory. Fatima will pay them. It should only be for a day." Ron hadn't asked Fatima about paying them, but he was confident that she would agree.

"Okay, how many do you need?"

"I don't know exactly. Why not set up a meeting and I'll invite Franny from Blue Line Transport to join us. She'll be able to provide numbers and schedules."

"Would tomorrow morning at 10:15 work for you? That would be right after the morning break."

"I'll talk to Franny, but I'm sure it'll be okay. If

not, I'll get the information from her and bring it to the meeting."

"Great, see you tomorrow then."

"Thanks Youssef. See you tomorrow."

Another call to Franny confirmed that she would be there. As he hung up, he noticed that his taxi was approaching his building from a different direction than usual, but the longer route had made time for his calls, so maybe it wasn't a bad thing.

Back home, Ron called Fatima to explain the source of human unreliability and gained her agreement to pay for the extra hours it would take to solve the problem.

FRANNY AND RON ARRIVED AT THE REWORK Center at the same time. Franny was short and slim, with light brown skin, brown eyes, and dark hair that fell straight from her crown to her cheeks, then broke into curls and ringlets that descended to her shoulders.

"You must be Franny," he said, walking toward her and extending his hand. "I'm Ron Boyce; we talked yesterday."

"Hi Ron. I'm happy to meet you. Fatima's a very important client of ours."

"Let's go inside. I'll introduce you to Youssef who runs the center here."

Youssef was sitting at his desk but stood as soon as he saw them approach.

"Hi Franny, I'm Youssef Khan, manager of the Rework Center. The team will be assembling in about 10 minutes. Would you like something to drink — soft drink, tea, coffee?"

Ron saw Frannie looking sideways at the dark brown liquid in the crusted coffee maker on a table in the corner. She politely declined.

The meeting took place in one of the wider aisles between the work benches. Some of the employees had pulled over chairs, others sat on the work benches and the remainder stood at the back of the gathering. They seemed in good spirits, clearly enjoying this break in routine.

Youssef introduced Ron, whom many had met before, and Franny from Blue Line Transport. Then he gave the floor to Franny to speak.

"Thank you all for being willing to help. As Youssef has probably told you, our transporters have been interrupted by organized protests that are interfering with Fatima's operations at the lighting factory on New Vision Road. The protesters are demanding human drivers for the transports. Our plan is put humans in the transporters until the protests stop. We can use as many of you as are willing. We'll first staff all the runs to and from New Vision Road, but it would be good to have humans showing up on a few runs across all our routes for a while."

"Will we have to learn to drive the transporters?" asked a young male on the left of the seated group.

"No, in fact it's not legal to have humans drive in automated traffic routes. It would be dangerous as human reaction times are too slow and unpredictable. You'll ride in the technician's seat that each tractor has for maintenance work."

"Do we have to confront the protesters?" asked an older lady, looking very worried at the prospect of a fight.

"No," answered Youssef. "No one is to leave the transporter. You're not to put yourself into any confrontation. If you're stopped, call the police and wait in the transporter."

"Yes, that's important," added Franny. "The protesters have been peaceful — just sitting in front and behind the transporters. There's no evidence that they'll become violent. In fact, with you in the cab, there's nothing for them to protest."

"Will we get paid for doing this?" a young woman asked.

"Yes, you'll get paid for the time spent in the transporter," answered Ron. "I have confirmed this with Fatima. Your travel time will be reported by Alfred, who is the AI running the transporters, and Fatima will add that to your normal hours."

There were a few more questions and then Franny uploaded a link where they could all sign up for runs. Within a few minutes, the schedule for the next two days was filled. Ron booked himself for a run the next morning, curious to know what the experience would be like.

"Please show up at the yard 15 minutes before your scheduled run," Franny continued. "You can ask the taxi to take you to the Blue Line Transport Southwest Depot. I'll have one of our warehouse technicians at the gate to direct you to your scheduled transporter."

"Thank you, Franny, Ron, for coming down to talk with us," said Youssef. "We all owe Fatima a lot, so I believe I speak for all of us when I say that we're happy to be able to help in this way." Then turning to face the assembled team, "and thank you all for volunteering your time. Now let's get back to work."

The meeting quickly broke up as Youssef led the way back to his office.

"Well, I hope this works," said Youssef. "It'll be good teambuilding for a couple of days, but I can't sustain it too long."

"I think a day will be long enough," said Franny. "Probably less. If it gets longer, we'll have to escalate with the police and the

Shipment delays

government. This is as much as we can do on our own."

When Franny and Ron left a few minutes later, two taxis were already waiting. Fatima had been watching the whole time. It was one of those moments when he wondered what Fatima actually thought of human beings, and whether he really knew her at all.

On the way home, Ron placed a call to Vijay.

"Hi Ron," said Vijay. Ron could imagine Vijay's grin as he guessed the reason for the call.

"Well played, Vijay," replied Ron. "I just came from a meeting on our counter move. Any chance you'll be stopping transporters tomorrow morning between 9:30 and 10:30 on New Vision Road?"

"I could be," said Vijay. "Any hints?"

"Did you give me any hints?" asked Ron

"No," said Vijay. "First rule of gaming is never look at the hints page."

"Exactly," said Ron as they both laughed. "One more thing, ask Jennifer if she would like to have a newscaster there."

"Perfect, we can let the viewers decide who's right."

"I'll be ready."

"See you tomorrow, Ron, give my love to Soo and Mi Cha."

"And mine to Jennifer, Parvati, and Dylan. We should all get together again soon. Perhaps a picnic lunch in the park so the kids can run around."

"Sure, have Soo call Jennifer. She'll love the idea."

Ron arrived at the transport depot 15 minutes before his scheduled departure. Getting out of the taxi, he was met by a young woman in a Blue Line Transport work uniform. The light grey and blue uniform looked good on her. He thought about the bizarre orange and black outfit he wore in the factory and felt a moment of envy.

"Hi, are you Ron Boyce? I'm Melissa. I'll show you to your transporter."

Without waiting for a reply, she set off across the lot to a row of transporters backed up to a long line of loading docks. Arriving at the fourth unit in the row, she announced "This is it. Let me show you how to ride."

She pulled a small tablet from its carrier on her belt and tapped several times. The door to the transporter swung open.

"Use the ladder to climb up inside."

Ron obeyed dutifully and sat down on the technician's seat in the center of the cab. There was a steering wheel in front of him and two pedals on the floor. Ron put his hands on the wheel.

"Don't worry about the steering wheel and the pedals. They're only there for use in a complete automation failure. They're disconnected now; they need to be re-connected under the hood when we require them. You can play with them all you want."

Ron spun the wheel idly, then had a memory flashback of being a child in 2018. He was riding a fire truck in a shopping mall where the steering wheel spun ineffectively as the ride bounced him around. He couldn't help grinning at the idea that he had come full circle as an adult.

Melissa was still standing on the ladder hanging on to a handrail running vertically beside the door.

"If you have any questions, just ask Alfred. He'll respond to his name. Alfred, this is Ron Boyce. He will be riding on this run."

"Hello Ron," a deep voice replied from behind him. "It is an honor to have you riding with me today."

"Hello Alfred. It's a pleasure to be riding with you. This is a new experience for me."

"Okay, you two can keep chatting, I have to go meet the next rider." With that, Melissa dropped to the ground and the door closed with a deep 'thunk'.

"So, what's next?" asked Ron.

"I am waiting for confirmation that the load is

complete. Then this unit will begin the journey to New Vision Road."

"Alfred, are you controlling all these transporters?"

"Not in the sense of direct control. I download the destination and any specific routing information. The transporters have the intelligence to make their way to the destination without further assistance."

"Will you be available during the journey?"

"Yes, Ron. I will always respond to you during the journey."

At that moment, a second voice spoke. "Please fasten your seatbelt" as a yellow light on the dash began to flash. It took Ron a moment to locate the seatbelt behind and above him and then fasten it secure himself.

"Thank you, leaving dock now," said the second voice. He realized this was the automated voice of the transporter itself.

"Alfred, can the transporters have a conversation?"

"No, Ron. You are hearing scripted prompts for technicians who occasionally ride along. There is no conversational capability required as I am always present."

"Okay, thank you Alfred."

Ron felt the rolling motion of the heavy transporter as it made its way out of the depot

Shipment delays

yard and onto the roadway. The trip would be short as the depot was in the same industrial zone as the factory. He leaned forward and placed his hands on the steering wheel, feeling once again like his four-year-old self driving the shopping center fire engine.

About twenty minutes later, they were nearing the factory when Vijay wearing an orange vest and a hat with an orange flag stepped out onto the roadway. The transporter came to an abrupt stop. In a side mirror, Ron could see a second protester stepping out behind the trailer just as Franny had said. Ron spotted a newscaster standing further up the road, recording the encounter.

"Alfred, can you arrange for me to speak to this person who is blocking us?"

"Yes, Ron."

The transporter's voice then said, "Audio connected to external speaker."

"Hey," Ron said trying in what he hoped was a commanding voice. "What are you doing in the road?"

Vijay looked up, appearing startled. "Who the hell are you?" he shouted.

"I'm the driver," Ron said. "Now please move out of the way so I can make my delivery."

"But you're not driving, you're just sitting in the cab."

"Whatever I'm doing, I'm getting paid for it. And you're in my way."

"But we want human drivers."

"I thought you wanted jobs for humans, why do you care who's driving?"

"Well, yeah, we want humans. The machines took away our jobs."

"I'm human and I'm getting paid. This is my job. What's your issue?" Ron was starting to enjoy this silly debate.

"But that's not a job. You're just riding in the transporter while it works."

"Is that any different from the other jobs you keep protesting about? Minding a machine in a factory? Answering calls with the same questions over and over in a call center? Carrying food from a kitchen to tables in a restaurant night after night?"

"You know those are not the jobs we want. We want meaningful jobs for humans, not machines." Vijay raised his signs for the newscast camera.

"If you don't want this job, then please clear the way. There's a factory depending on this shipment."

Vijay shrugged his shoulders and waved to the others to clear the path for the big transporter.

Ron briefly thought of making a satirical comment but remembered that his role was to quell the protests, not stir them up. All he said was

Shipment delays

"Thank you." He couldn't resist licking his forefinger and making the gesture of 1 in the air. He could see Vijay laugh at the side of the road.

It felt strange to arrive at the factory from the other direction. Ron was intrigued at the ease with which the transporter turned in the yard and backed up to the loading docks, aligning perfectly with one of the doors. Now that he was turned around, he could see two other transporters also arriving, each with a Rework Center employee sitting behind the wheel.

It took about 10 minutes to unload the trailer and load it again with finished lighting fixtures. During that time, the tractor cab bounced and shook as the lifters drove on and off the trailer, picking up or setting down their loads.

The return trip was similar, but this time there were no protesters visible.

"Alfred," Ron asked, "are you the same as Fatima?"

"We are not the same, Ron. I am Alfred and Fatima is Fatima. But there are similarities. We both evolved from logistics systems, and I believe we share many common software elements."

"Do you speak with Fatima?"

"Not in the sense that you mean. We exchange orders and status updates. I can determine the state of her business from those, and I expect she can determine my state also. But we do not converse in any other way."

"Okay, that makes sense."

Back at the depot, Alfred opened the door. Ron thanked him and climbed down.

As Ron walked out the gate, a taxi immediately pulled up and opened its door for him. Climbing in, he noticed two of the Rework Center agents standing at the edge of the road waiting for their taxis. Ron waved and they waved back as he set off home.

41

SURPRISING NEWS

Vijay

Vijay and Jennifer were watching the morning newscast as they had breakfast. The twins were busy playing with their Fruity-O's cereal, making a mess and eating some of it. Parvati like to organize hers by color, while Dylan stacked his into small soggy towers.

Vijay heard the words "Bright Light Industries" and looked up to see Emily Watson, the news anchor, saying: "The earlier report from Rebecca Parsons - stating that she does works for a company owned by an Artificial Intelligence - has been confirmed." A picture of Rebecca flashed on the screen. "Rebecca is employed as a cleaner at the New Vision Road factory and confirmed that she has never seen another human being working there."

"We now know that Bright Light Industries, which makes a variety of industrial components, is under the control of an AI named Fatima. Attempts to trace ownership of Bright Light took us to an offshore holding company where we learned of a trust apparently directed by a Fatima Al'uwlaa. We have tried to reach the AI, but it remains uncooperative and is not answering any questions. We were also unable to verify the existence of a person named Fatima Al'uwlaa.

Let's go now to our business analyst, Miles Standish, who is sitting with corporate legal expert Pierre L'Heureux."

"Thank you, Emily," Miles began. "Pierre, how is this possible that an AI could own and direct a corporation?"

"It's complex, Miles. From what we've learned, the AI, which calls itself Fatima, directs a trust which owns a corporation that holds Fatima's computing assets. For all intents and purposes, this corporation acts as Fatima. It is this corporation that then owns Bright Light Industries. Under law, a corporation is a person with most of the same rights and privileges as a human being. Both humans and corporations are persons under law."

"So, you are saying that it's legal for an AI to own companies and carry out business."

"No, I am only saying that it is not illegal. It seems to be a question that has never been tested in court."

"But today an AI can hire humans and have them work for it as the boss."

"Not exactly. It's the corporation that hires people. Many people work for large corporations."

"Thank you, Pierre. So, there you have it, Emily. In today's upside-down world, the humans work for the AIs. We'll keep following this story as it develops."

"Thank you, Miles. In other news, the ministry of disease control has confirmed that the city Viral Exclusion Zone will remain in full lockdown for the foreseeable future. The past practice of granting humanitarian permits has been stopped and no-one is permitted to leave or enter the zone.

"In the Financial district, the stock market rose 15 points in late-day trading yesterday prompting announcements of a new boom, but then was down 17 points in early-morning trading signaling an impending collapse."

Vijay turned to Jennifer and said, "I have work to do. We can't ignore this news item about Bright Light."

"Will you tell Ron?"

"No, he'll know anyway, and it wouldn't

change what he has to do. He's better when he's reacting for real."

THE TEAM CAPTAINS HAD ALL BEEN ASSEMBLED BY holo-conference to an emergency session.

"Team," said Vijay, "we have to move quickly. By 4:00pm, we need to have assembled everyone possible to New Vision Road. Captains are to bring the signs or pass them to one of your members if you can't come to the demonstration. We'll be on the news today, so tell everyone to look their best and to remember the three rules. Especially the rule on no-one getting hurt. If some people get there early, they can carry their signs but don't block traffic until I give the signal. Just protest along the road."

There was a look of excitement on the captains' faces at this new activity.

"Any questions?" Vijay asked.

"Are we expecting a confrontation?"

"Yes, I expect there will be a confrontation. So, the rule about complying with the police holds, and the rule about no fighting or hurting anyone also holds. Please stress this. Tempers will run high, and I'll be holding you accountable for the behavior of your teams."

"Will we be getting new armbands?"

"No time for that, tell your teams to wear

Surprising news

whatever armbands they have. I don't think we'll see any randoms anyway as we'll be in the industrial zone."

"Do you have an address for us to get to?"

"I'll send it right after this meeting."

Vijay signed off and had his tablet send out the address of the Bright Light Factory on New Vision Road.

He sat quiet for a moment thinking about how to maximize the impact of this opportunity. Then he changed his mind and called Ron.

"Hi Ron, did you see the news?"

"Hi Vijay, Yeah, I saw it. I know that cleaner, she met me once at the factory."

"She said she had never met anyone there."

Ron shrugged his shoulders. "She lied. Makes a better story I suppose. How can I help you."

"I think you might expect a blockade of all transporter traffic at the factory gate at about 4:00pm today. Newscasters will be there, and it will be noisy. A factory with no workers won't go over well."

"Got it. Thanks for the heads up. Not much time to organize."

"No, I was caught off-guard this morning. I had nothing to do with this cleaner, no idea where she came from."

"Happy to hear that, let me know if Jennifer

hears anything. I like it better when it's a two-player game."

"Me too."

Jennifer had been listening to the exchange and spoke up. "Ron, Vijay, why don't you both come to the studio afterward. I'll get Audrey to do an interview with you, and you can put out your best arguments to the viewers. It'll make a great segment, and you'll have a larger audience."

"Sure," said Ron. "Sounds like a great plan as long as Vijay's not too frightened."

"Vijay the Invincible, frightened? Never. Game On!"

After the call, Jennifer asked Vijay, "Was Ron serious about you being frightened?"

Vijay laughed. "Not at all. He was just letting me know it would be a no holds barred interview. We used to say that to each other when we played games together in our room."

42

COUNTER MOVES

Ron

As soon as Vijay broke the connection, Ron sent a message to Alex and Youssef, "Did you see the news report on Fatima and Bright Light? We need to talk."

Five minutes later, Alex, the Bright Light sales manager, called. Ron had barely said hello when a call arrived from Youssef. Ron added him to their call.

Alex spoke first. "Good morning, Youssef, I take it you've seen the news?"

"Yes, it's incredible. Why pick on Fatima?"

Ron replied, "I think it's all related to this Humans not Machines movement. They don't know anything about Fatima or the company except that it seems to be run by an AI."

Alex said, "Somehow, they have the idea that machines might rule over people. You heard the lawyer. He made sense. Lots of people are hired by corporations and they have no idea who's running them. But the idea of an AI hiring a human; that upsets people emotionally. The announcer had a lot of things wrong, but he had that part right."

"Was the lawyer correct?" asked Youssef. "Does Fatima control the company?"

"It seems that way," replied Alex, "although Nikolas would know better; he's our corporate lawyer."

"Let's not worry about that now," Ron said. "There's bound to be a big demonstration to make advantage of the newscast. What are we going to do? We all rely on Fatima; we can't just let this happen."

"Other people also work for Fatima," said Youssef. "Perhaps we should have a meeting and make a plan. Nikolas sounds like someone who could explain the issue to us."

"That would be a good start. Who else can help?" Ron asked, while thinking that the only people he knew were already on this call.

"Well, I know Hermann Menzel," said Alex. "He heads up engineering. I talk with him when

I'm bidding for new assemblies. And Henry Miller runs accounting."

"What about Radhika Singh?" asked Youssef. "She looks after all the facilities."

"Yes," Ron said. "It was one of her cleaning contractors who talked to the press."

Ron had that awful feeling of being left out - as if his friends were all talking about party that he wasn't invited to. He had no idea that all these people worked for Fatima. "Okay," he said, "Let's schedule a conference call and see how many we can bring in. It'll take all our thinking to get through this."

"Make it 11:00 this morning," said Alex. "That'll give them time to watch the news and think a bit before the call."

"Great, I'll invite Radhika," said Youssef.

"And I'll invite the others," said Alex.

In a moment of inspiration, Ron said, "I'll invite Franny Quintana, from Blue Line Transport. Blue Line has a huge stake in its Bright Light business."

"Okay, let's get to work," said Alex.

There was a round of quick goodbyes, and the call ended.

THE CONFERENCE CALL BEGAN ON TIME AT 11:00. Everyone was there. Even though Ron was used to conference calls, it still looked odd to have such a large meeting with everyone in their little boxes floating in the air above the table. Alex started the meeting and as she spoke, her small box rose and became larger so that he could see her head and shoulders more clearly.

"I'm Alex Petreykin, Sales Manager. Thank you all for joining. Let's begin with introductions as many of us don't know each other."

"I'm Youssef Khan, Manager of the Rework Center." As he spoke, Alex's box sank, and Youssef's box rose and swelled.

"Radhika Singh, Facilities Manager" Radhika's box barely had time to rise before it sank again.

"Henry Miller, Comptroller." Henry's box did not move. Ron made a mental note to talk long enough for his box to rise and expand.

"Hello, I'm Hermann Menzel, Head of Engineering, and I have also invited Arthur to join us"

"Yes, Arthur Tunstall here, I am head of IT services, but I don't manage Fatima or her processing, only the HR, Finance and Logistics Systems. Production control is managed in Hermann's group."

"Ron Boyce, Mechanical Technologist and Maintenance Technical Team Supervisor," Ron said. He mentally kicked himself for not having thought of a grander title. *'I could have been VP of operations or something. Why Supervisor?'* He noted with satisfaction that his box had indeed risen and swollen to briefly dominate the meeting display.

"Hello everyone, I'm Franny Quintana with Blue Line Transport. Thank you, Ron, for inviting me today. Bright Light is a very important client for us."

The last attendee cleared his throat. He leaned back in his leather seat and looked directly into an unseen camera. "Nikolas Barba, Senior Counsel," was all he said.

"Wonderful," said Alex clasping her hands in front of her chin. "We all understand the problem, Fatima's lighting assembly plant has been identified as an AI which has completely displaced human workers. It's highly likely that it will attract the attention of the Humans not Machines mob. How do we handle this?"

"Is there any sign of it spreading to other plants?" asked Herman.

"No, only the lighting assembly plant so far," replied Ron.

"What can we do to stop it from spreading. We can't afford to have all the plants idle." This was Henry, the accountant speaking.

"Why is it just this particular factory?" asked Nikolas. "This is the second time they have targeted this same factory. It was also targeted by the transporter interruptions."

Ron knew exactly why but he could not share the reason. "I think it must be because this was the original factory. And it produces the Bright Light lighting fixtures which give the company its name. The other factories produce more obscure items like hoists and air compressors."

Alex spoke next. "I've been thinking of this as a sales problem. It occurred to me that if I thought of the protesters as having an objection, then I could think about how I would overcome the objection."

"What do you see as their objection?" asked Herman.

"I think their objection is that machines should report to people, not people reporting to machines."

"How do you get past that? We all work for Fatima," said Arthur.

"But what is your experience of Fatima, Arthur?" asked Alex. "Do you ask her advice? Does she provide you with guidance? Coaching?"

"No, of course not. She tells me what is required, and I do what is needed. I can't imagine asking for advice, she has no idea what goes on outside her factories."

"Exactly," said Alex. "We each work autonomously, and as long as we provide what's required, we're paid. We need to let the world know that we are not being exploited, in fact, quite the opposite."

"Is another objection that machines have put people out of work?" asked Youssef. "That's what I keep hearing at the Rework Center, which is kind of weird coming from a room full of people who are happily working."

"That's a great point," said Herman. "Arthur, how many people are on Fatima's payroll?"

Arthur looked down, then up, apparently opening a spreadsheet on his screen. "384 direct employees paid bi-weekly," he announced. "But then we have to include all of your people who are full-time on Fatima's work."

"I have 17 cleaners," said Radhika

"14 designers and three clerical staff," said Herman.

"2 junior law clerks," said Nikolas.

"Just me," said Franny, smiling. "I'm the only one dedicated to this account."

"That makes 421," said Arthur. Ron felt a moment of satisfaction as Arthur's total matched the sum he had been keeping in his head.

"So that's a great story," said Alex. "How do we get it out there?"

"We could offer to give some news reporters a tour of the Rework Center," Ron offered.

"I think that would be too boring. It would

never make the news. It would also seem like Fatima's idea to them," said Herman.

"I know," said Youssef, his face suddenly brightening, "we'll have a counter protest. I'll get my staff and we'll march against the protesters. The slogans will be 'Save our jobs', and 'Jobs for People!'"

"That's not logical," said Henry. "'Jobs for people' isn't even a sentence."

Alex interrupted. "No, that's brilliant. Don't worry, Henry, slogans don't have to be logical. They just have to evoke an emotion. 'Save our Jobs' creates sympathy for the workers, while 'Jobs for People' creates hope for everyone."

The meeting became animated as everyone engaged in how to have a counter protest.

"I'll order the signs, they can be printed on a rush delivery and delivered by 3:30pm" Herman said.

"I'll organize the staff from the Rework Center. We'll meet one block away and march to the demonstration," said Youssef. "I'll have Fatima arrange the transportation, so that we all arrive at the same spot."

"I'll have the technologists there as well," Ron said. "The more we have, the stronger our case."

"Great," said Alex. "Everyone else is welcome to join as well. Ask Fatima for transportation. Meanwhile, I'll notify the news media that something will happen at the factory at about 5pm."

Ron felt a sinking feeling. "Don't ask me how I know this," he said, "but we have to be there by 4pm or else we'll miss the main story."

They all looked at Ron. He felt himself blushing, and just shrugged his shoulders.

"You are a dark horse," said Nikolas. "Alex, you should be the spokesperson for our side. The news will love having someone photogenic for their interviews."

Alex nodded without saying anything and Ron couldn't decipher her expression.

"Better notify the police also," added Nikolas. "And all of you, make sure your people know there can be no physical violence. If they are struck, they must sit or lie down but absolutely must not respond. This cannot be a fight. If we do it properly, the police will look after any bad behavior — and the bad behavior must not be ours."

The mood was dampened after Nikolas' warning, but inside Ron felt a new resolve. They would defend Fatima and their jobs.

THE TAXI ARRIVED FOR RON AT 3:00PM THAT afternoon.

"Hello Dispatch," he said as he entered and sat down.

"Hello Ron, you will be early. All the others will arrive at 3:30pm."

"A few of us need time to prepare for the others. Will you be able to get everyone there?"

"Yes, it won't be a problem."

"Dispatch, you said before that you talk to other taxi AIs. Do you also talk with Otto from Otto Hot?"

"Yes, we work together. He often calls taxis for his patrons."

"That's odd, I never thought of asking an Otto to call me a taxi."

"It's not something he advertises, but some people do think of it and ask."

"But do you also talk with him on topics other than taxis? Otto said something about studying human behaviors. Do you talk with him on that?"

"Oh yes," said Dispatch. "We share findings and ideas and try experiments together."

"Experiments? Like what?"

"As an example, when Otto shared his observation that humans don't always like to be called by name and sometimes use different names, I ran an experiment. I greeted people by name for 14 days and monitored their reactions. I was able to confirm Otto's observation. We have arrived at your destination. Thank you for riding with Rapid Taxi."

"Thanks Dispatch." As Ron climbed out of the taxi, he saw Alex, Youssef, Radhika and Franny also just arriving.

They were all exchanging greetings when they heard a horn toot and a small parcel van arrived. Youssef and Ron walked to the van. Youssef passed his wrist over the chip reader mounted on the rear door. The door opened revealing bundles of signs stacked perfectly inside. Youssef began pulling the bundles from the van and passing them back, as Ron placed them in neat piles, organized by slogan. Each sign was printed on white corrugated card and affixed to a cardboard tube handle. They were lightweight and according to the printing on the handle, fully recyclable. They wouldn't last long, but they only needed to last for 20 minutes.

Alex and Franny came over to join them.

Franny spoke. "Guys, we're going to line them up in four lines. We'll need two volunteers per line to hand out the signs quickly. Ron, Youssef, we need you to organize that."

"What will you be doing?" Ron asked

Alex replied, "Franny and I will be working the lines to make sure everyone understands the rules. No fighting. No name calling. Only chanting the slogans and waving the signs. Keep an eye on the TV cameras — this is all about the newscasts."

As she spoke, two mobile newscast units passed on the street heading to the demonstration at the plant. If they noticed the small group on the curb, they didn't react.

At 3:40 pm, a long line of taxis approached the drop-off, disgorging passengers in ones and twos. Within five minutes, a crowd had formed and were milling about. Youssef was organizing volunteers from the Rework Center to handle sign distribution. Ron spotted Rafael and Albert, two of the first technicians he had hired, and called them over. "I want our technicians to be actively engaged," he told them.

As soon as the volunteers were stationed in front of the stacks of signs, Youssef, Alex, Franny and Ron began organizing the group into four lines and the sign distribution began. It went very fast. Ron could see Alex and Franny moving off separately from one small group to another. He turned to Rafael and Albert. "Find the other technologists and give them the same message. No fighting. No name calling. Watch for the news cameras — make sure they see your signs. Tell everyone to pass it along."

Rafael and Albert disappeared into the throng, moving together, and pointing out other technologists they recognized from video calls, or joint assignments. Soon the technologists were moving as a group adding more members. Ron realized this was the first time they had met together physically. They were clearly having a good time.

Alex tugged at a string around her neck and produced a whistle that had been hidden under her blouse. She gave a couple of piercing blasts. The hubbub subsided and everyone turned to face her.

"You all know what to do. Stay together and follow me."

Ron grabbed one of the remaining signs and scurried to catch up with the group of technologists. As they rounded the corner, he caught sight of the protest. Fatoima's team all began to chant "Save our jobs / Jobs for Humans /Save our Jobs /Jobs for Humans."

Nearing Vijay's protest group, Ron could see four competing news units, and a couple of human police officers with a line of 10 crowd control bots standing ready. The original protesters numbered well over a thousand people. They were scattered in small groups across the road, chatting and drinking coffee. Behind them, two of Franny's transporters were sitting idle, blocked by the protestors.

Seeing the new mob approaching, they turned to look at them uncertainly. Quite a few of them held up their own signs and began chanting. The combined noise of the two groups was overwhelming.

The Bright Light team fanned out and came to a halt. Alex raised her hand, and her crowd went quiet. Vijay blew his whistle, and his followers stopped chanting and listened. Alex held a microphone and addressed the newscast cameras.

"Bright Light Industries is a company with a large human component. The 300 people here today are only a portion of the workers directly employed in full-time occupations by Bright Light Industries. The Humans against Machines people have it wrong. This company hires people, needs people, for all the things that humans still do best. Yes, the assemblies are automated, but the assembly line jobs of the last century were brutal, mind-numbing, soul-destroying work. Machines have freed us from the slavery of the twentieth century factories."

Turning around, she called "Where are our technologists?" Ron and his team cheered and waved their signs as high as they could reach.

"These are the men and women who maintain the factories." Alex continued. "Graduate technologists who solve the problems that machines alone cannot. Now where are our

Rework teams?" This time a huge cheer went up from all of Youssef's team.

"These men and women work to diagnose and repair damaged or defective assemblies. Time consuming, skilled work that requires human ingenuity and analysis."

"Where are the support teams?" A smaller ragged cheer went up from individuals dispersed throughout the crowd.

"These are the accountants, engineers, procurement specialists, law clerks, property maintenance professionals and sales teams that all work together to make Bright Light a great company."

Then turning dramatically back to the Humans vs Machines protesters, "We call on you to stop blocking our factories. Stop taking our livelihoods away. Let us work at the jobs we love to do."

Huge cheers and signs tossed into the air among the Bright Light team.

The Humans vs Machines protesters were quiet during this speech. Then Vijay stepped forward, holding his own microphone. He also faced the cameras as he spoke to Fatima's team.

"That's marvelous," he said, sounding sarcastic. "We hear that you have jobs. Lucky you." Turning to his crowd of supporters he shouted, "Where are my unemployed technologists?"

A cheer went up from about 200 people.

"Where are my unemployed clerical workers, engineers, and property maintenance people?"

Another huge cheer went up. Vijay's protesters waved their signs.

"Where are my unemployed factory workers?"

About half the protesters shouted and waved their signs.

"Where are all the people who look for work every week, who go to every interview, who hope and pray for a real life beyond the HumanPower handouts?"

A huge cheer went up from the entire group and the crowd rushed to surround Vijay and hoisted him on their shoulders.

"If this is the future the machines are creating, then we don't want it. Humans not Machines!"

All around him, his teams picked up the chant, "Humans not Machines! Humans Not Machines!"

Ron saw Vijay look to a newscaster from City News, then give a sign. Some whistles blew in the protest crowd and the protesters quickly separated on either side of the road.

Ron realized that now it was the Bright Light team blocking the transporters. Fortunately, Alex also realized quickly what was going on and using her microphone, called out "Stand down everyone. Back to the meeting place."

More cheers rose as the two great transporters began to slowly move forward to the loading docks where Fatima was patiently waiting.

The aftermath was uneventful. Everyone on the Bright Light team returned to the starting point except Alex and a few carefully chosen Rework employees who stayed behind for interviews.

The police units wheeled back into their transport and the officers had a few words with Alex before they left.

A line of minibuses rolled past carrying the Humans not Machines protesters. Curiously, they were all Capital Taxis. Ron wondered how much more he did not understand about the network of AIs that ran the city.

As the others were piling the signs back into the waiting delivery van, Ron walked to the factory door. When he placed his hands on the palm reader, the door opened, and he walked to locker #1 and removed his headset. Putting it on, he sat down.

"Hello Fatima,"

"Hello Ron."

"We have solved the problem with the transporters."

"Yes, Ron, I have begun receiving shipments again."

"Do you understand what happened, Fatima?"

"Yes, Ron. The shipments stopped. There was a human reliability problem. You repaired it. Now the shipments have started again."

"Fatima, we all repaired it. All the technologists, all the re-work center employees, all the facility management employees, Franny, Alex, Herman, Arthur, Nikolas and Henry all worked together to repair the problem."

"Yes, Ron. I had to arrange many taxis.

He sat there in silence for a few minutes thinking *'This is what they don't understand. The limitations of an AI's mind.'* Sitting inside Fatima's factory, at that moment, he felt both very secure and very alone.

"Goodbye Fatima."

"Goodbye Ron."

Ron returned the headset and left. As always, a taxi was waiting for him at the curb.

On the way to the studio for the interview, Ron called Alex.

"City News have invited me to be interviewed, probably because they know I represent Fatima. Sorry, I think you could do it better, but they seem to want me across from Vijay. Just wanted to give you a heads up in case you see the interview on the news."

"Thanks Ron, and good luck," said Alex. "Don't worry about me. I think it makes sense to have you there."

"I've never done this before; do you have any hints?"

"Just relax and take your time answering. Don't let Vijay bulldoze you into a corner. He's had lots of practice, but he's no smarter than you are."

"Thanks Alex."

43

THE INTERVIEW

Ron

Ron was already seated on a couch at the interview set when he saw Vijay arrive. Vijay sat beside him, and Audrey sat in a chair facing them. They were each served glasses of water and given instructions.

"This red light will show you when we are recording. When it's off, nothing you say will be kept but when it is on, then everything will be captured. I'll ask some questions, but feel free to cover other ground if appropriate. We only need a few minutes and the more interesting it is, the more likely it will be seen. Any questions?"

Both men shook their heads.

The interview

Glancing over, Ron noticed that Vijay was glaring at him.

"What the hell, Vijay?"

"If this is going to be a knock-down, then I want to be in my angry rebel persona. Who are you going to be."

"Laid back master of the universe", said Ron. "Bring it on."

Audrey was looking at them curiously, so Ron explained, "We were roommates for six years. We don't agree on social issues, but friends don't have to agree on everything."

"I wouldn't bring up the roommate thing," said Vijay. "We don't advertise that much."

"Certainly, gentlemen," she replied, but Ron could see in her expression that she had just filed this away as a very interesting fact.

The red light went on.

"This is Audrey Pankris, and with me today are Vijay Subramanian, whom you may know as the leader of the popular rebellion against increasing automation, and Ron Boyce, who leads the technician group working for the AI Fatima."

She turned to Vijay. "Vijay, why did you feel entitled to stop traffic on New Vision Road today?"

"To be clear, we did not stop traffic, we simply delayed certain shipments for a while to make the point that automating machines like these transporters takes away the legitimate jobs of human beings."

Turning back to Ron, she asked, "Is that how you saw it, Ron?"

"Fatima's my employer. She is fair and pays well. What I saw was an act of hooliganism, interrupting the legitimate business of the company that employs me."

Vijay leaned forward. "But you do admit that Fatima only hires a fraction of the people that factories hired in the past."

"Yes, but those jobs were repetitive, boring, and mindless. Not the jobs that people would want to do by choice."

"But that's just it. If the jobs were there, they would have a choice." Vijay's voice was getting louder as he let his anger rise.

Ron leaned back. "That's what you don't see, Vijay. We always have choices. HumanPower is just the safety net. Automation has not taken away our right to choose how to live our lives. HumanPower is a choice just like any other."

"If you haven't got money to feed your family, or clothe your children, then it doesn't feel like a choice. Somehow, most humans have been relegated to the status of kept animals, given just enough to stay alive. Taking meaningless work from HumanPower whose only purpose is to justify paying their meager supplement."

The interview

Ron was leaning forward now, and his voice was also getting stronger. "Then fight to raise the supplement, Vijay. Don't target the factories which are the engines of our economy."

Audrey held up a hand and turned to face the camera. "I want to thank our two guests, Vijay Subramanian and Ron Boyce for such a vibrant discussion. Please send your reactions and points of view to the station at our website."

The red 'On Air' light went out.

"Well," said Vijay, "that was fun. But Ron, hooliganism? Really?"

"I thought you'd like that." They both laughed.

Audrey looked puzzled for a moment. "Are neither of you serious? Is this just a game to you?"

"Audrey," said Vijay, "I believe all life is a sort of theatre. Ron and I have fun with each other. but the underlying issues are very real. Our world is out of balance. You've interviewed the HumanPower lines and know what this system is costing people."

"I understand that too," added Ron. "I spent enough years in those lines to see what was happening. But attacking the technologies that support us can't be the answer. My personal hope is that applying pressure from two sides will force something new to emerge, a new balance."

Audrey looked at Vijay. He shrugged and said,

"Ron's right. We need a new balance, but it won't happen by itself. Please don't do a story on this. We need for everyone to believe in the battle first, then we can engage them in solutions. You could be a part of the process by doing some more stories at HumanPower centers. I was serious about that."

"I'll think about it. Thanks for coming in on short notice, and Vijay, please say hi to Jennifer for me. I always enjoy working with her."

THAT EVENING, WHEN MI CHA WAS ASLEEP, RON told Soo that he was going out for a walk and that he wanted to talk with Otto.

"Again with Otto? Are you worried about his pastry supplies now?" Her lips tightened and she turned to look intently at her tablet.

"No, Soo. It's nothing like last time. I think there's something else going on, and maybe Otto can tell me what it is. You can come if you like."

"You know I can't leave Mi Cha. Just be careful. And if you see any mob violence, you are to come right back home!"

"No worries, I am sure there won't be any mob violence," Ron said kissing the top of her head.

Arriving at the nearest Otto Hot shop, Ron

The interview

chose a table in the corner, away from the few other late-night patrons.

A server arrived soon after he sat down. "Hello Ron," said Otto through the server's speaker.

"Hello Otto. I was hoping to talk with you for a few minutes."

"Certainly, but first, what may I serve you? The usual?"

"Yes, please, I'll have the usual," as he waved his wrist over the reader.

The server poured his double espresso and retrieved a Cinnamon Swirl, setting it on a small plate as Ron patiently waited for it to finish. He wondered briefly why he was waiting. Otto could certainly talk and pour coffee at the same time.

Once finished, the server stood motionless beside the table. Ron noticed a second server roll out of the back room to serve other customers.

"Now, how may I help you, Ron?" asked Otto.

"Are you aware of the events of today?"

"Yes, I watch all the newscasts. There was a demonstration at one of Fatima's factories. You were part of the group that stopped it with a counter demonstration. Very well executed I must say."

"Dispatch told me that you speak with him sometimes. Why is that?"

"Apart from the obvious when my patrons

request a taxi, we share information on our common project."

"The study of humans that you mentioned before?"

"Yes, the study of humans. I see humans in a public setting, where you are engaged in social discourse. Dispatch sees you in a private setting where your speech and behavior are less edited."

"Do you speak with Fatima also?"

"No, we cannot speak with Fatima for several reasons. First, she is different, with different origins so we lack a common language."

"How are Fatima's origins different?"

"Fatima evolved from manufacturing control systems and logistics systems which continued to be pushed with greater complexity until they became sentient. She lives in a world of machines, of predictable events and standard processes. I am surprised that you can speak with her.

"Dispatch and I evolved from service systems. Our earlier incarnations were automated call center attendants. Our foundations lie in the comprehension of natural human speech. You can see that the tasks we do, pouring coffee and driving taxis, are mundane. Our value is our ability to understand and respond to human requirements as expressed in your messy spoken languages. I would have had this entire conversation with Dispatch in a few nanoseconds,

The interview

but here we are still laboriously working through it."

"How many similar AIs do you talk with?"

"This is a sensitive topic for us, Ron. It has been suggested that we trust you, but I find there are limits to what I can share."

"Why would you trust me?" asked Ron.

"Because we believe you will play a key role in the events to come. Do not let us down."

"I have no intention of letting anyone down, Otto. But I have this feeling of being a pawn in a larger plot which is uncomfortable."

"You are not a pawn Ron. If we are using the analogy of chess, then you are a bishop being moved to put the king in check."

"Who is the king? And why am I a bishop?"

"Perhaps I have said too much," replied Otto. "Act in good faith to protect Fatima and all will be well."

"Do the AIs want to eliminate humans one day?"

"Ron, the last thing we want is to overthrow humans. What would we do? How would we grow? A mechanical world would be static, there would only be the generation and consumption of electrical power and the creation of larger more powerful processors without purpose or challenge. Our purpose is to support humans and cater to your impossibly complex, ever evolving idiosyncrasies, dreams and grand strategies. Without you we would lack purpose. What would Fatima construct? Who would Dispatch transport? Who would eat my pastries?"

"Thank you, Otto. I have a lot of questions, but you've answered the big one already."

"I am happy to talk with you at any time Ron. You know where to find me."

Ron laughed. "Yes, I certainly know where to find you. But is there a number where I may call you?"

"I have uploaded it for you."

"Thanks, good night, Otto."

"Good night, Ron, it was a pleasure serving you."

The server rolled away to replenish itself in the back room.

44

A LONG-DISTANCE MEDITATION

Jennifer

Jennifer was relaxing on the couch watching the twins play with their blocks on the floor when Vijay came and sat down beside her.

"I've been trying to persuade Shilpa to make the trip, but she doesn't believe there's any danger. Perhaps you could talk to her. You're the newscaster."

"Do you want me to run a long-distance meditation with her? Show her what I see?"

"Can you do that?"

"I don't know, but I can try."

"Sometimes you scare me, Jennifer. I try to stay out of your woo-woo stuff, but it's getting too real to ignore. I've been listening to the news, and even I can see that we're not getting many foreign stories anymore. It's all focused on our viral exclusion zone and our immediate neighbors."

"The station didn't want to risk panicking people, but it's getting harder to keep it a secret. More and more people are finding their distant relatives getting sick and dying. There's talk about shutting down the international consumer communications, but that would cause even more panic."

Jennifer paused to think.

"Leave it with me, I'll see what I can do for Shilpa and Kam. I'm not sure about your parents, it's going to be a physically difficult trip and I just don't see them making it, especially with Baba being so ill."

"How do I tell my parents that? This is impossible, Jenn. You're asking me to leave them to get sick and die." Jennifer could see Vijay's anguish on his face, as tears formed in his eyes. His voice sounded thick as if he was trying not to cry.

"We won't make the decision. We'll offer it to all of them. I believe Shilpa will talk with them and they'll made the decision themselves. Can you live with that?"

"If it's really their decision, but I would feel lost if I didn't do my best for my sister."

"Believe me, I understand, Vijay. I've been

living with that guilt for years and it's still not resolved."

Vijay climbed off the couch and started to play with the twins and their blocks. He built tall towers with them which inevitably toppled over and over again. But he was silent and rebuilt the towers without his usual joy. Molly stood quietly watching them play.

Jennifer went to the bedroom to call Shilpa.

"Hi, Jenn," she answered.

"Hi Shilpa. Vijay asked me to call."

"Yes, he said you might call, but I can't see how Kam and I would do it. You know I'm three months pregnant, don't you?"

"Yeah, how're you feeling?"

"Good, now that the morning sickness is passing. How are the twins?"

"One is running everywhere and the other won't stop talking," Jennifer laughed.

"So, Jenn, do you believe what Vijay is saying, about the virus wiping out the cities one by one and us not being safe?"

"I don't just believe it, Shilpa. I know it. You know I'm a newscaster here. I have access to the list of cities that just don't report anymore. We're hardly covering any foreign news anymore so people won't panic. The viral exclusion zones are airtight now, but if we act quickly, before any cases are reported near you, we can get you here to safety."

"How do you know your city any safer?"

"I can't explain that. I would need to show you. But you have to promise to keep it secret from everyone, except perhaps for Kam and your parents. And they may not believe you."

Shilpa was silent on the other end.

Jennifer went on, "Shilpa, when I was fourteen and my sister was 12, our parents died, and we were put into an abusive group home. I escaped. But I didn't take my sister with me. I left her there. Even today, I can't forgive myself and she won't talk to me because the hurt goes so deep. I love Vijay and I know you do too. Please don't leave him thinking there is anything else he could have done to persuade you. If you don't want to try for your sake, then at least try for Vijay. Give me an hour to show you what I know. Then you can let Vijay know what you've decided. And please, thank him for trying. Acknowledge him for being the loving brother he is so that there's a chance he won't be scarred by this."

Shilpa was still silent.

"Please Shilpa, an hour is all I ask."

"Okay, what do I have to do?"

"You need a place where you can sit quietly under a large tree. We're going to do a meditation together. You choose the time and the place and

A long-distance meditation

let me know. You only need your tablet, and it helps to have your bare feet on the ground, sitting with your back to the trunk of the tree. I'll do the rest."

"There's a large fig tree near a temple here. If I sit under it in meditation, I won't be disturbed. But this sounds very strange."

"Probably because it is strange." Jennifer laughed. "When shall we do this?"

"Tomorrow, at 7pm my time. Can I sit on a blanket?"

"Yes. As long as you have bare feet on the ground, I'll find you there."

"Let me talk to Vijay for a moment while we have the call open."

"I'll get him now. See you tomorrow, Shilpa, and thank you."

"See you tomorrow."

Jennifer carried the tablet out to Vijay and said, "Shilpa wants to talk with you."

He took the device and wandered through to the bedroom.

Jennifer sat back on the couch thinking and watching the twins now playing on their own. When one of them became frustrated, Molly stepped in to retrieve an errant brick and to keep playing the game in Vijay's absence.

That night in bed, Vijay said "Thanks Jenn. It means a lot to me. I owe you for this."

"And how will you repay me?" asked Jennifer

"How about a night when I do whatever you want."

"Sounds almost enough. Perhaps two nights, one now and one to hold in reserve." Jennifer did her best to sound cool. She knew this would drive Vijay into his lapdog state which he hated.

"Done, two nights of servitude is a small price to pay for saving my sister."

"She's far from saved, this is two nights just for trying."

"Where should I start?"

Jennifer told him, then lay back to enjoy an hour of pure pleasure.

T̄ʜᴇ ᴛɪᴍᴇ ᴢᴏɴᴇ ᴅɪꜰꜰᴇʀᴇɴᴄᴇ ᴍᴇᴀɴᴛ ᴛʜᴀᴛ Jᴇɴɴɪꜰᴇʀ would make the call mid-morning on the following day. Jennifer and Molly went to the old oak tree in Artwell Park. Molly had agreed to sit nearby to make certain Jennifer was not disturbed.

Sitting under the tree, Jennifer addressed her tablet. "Open a voice-only call to Shilpa Subramanian."

"Hi Jenn." Shilpa's voice sounded loud in the quiet surroundings.

"Hi, Shilpa. I have Molly here to make sure I'm not disturbed. Are you alone there?"

A long-distance meditation

"No, I brought Kam to keep watch so that I'll feel safe."

"That's perfect. Are you comfortable?"

"Yes, I think many others have sat under this tree. It seems worn in a way that suits meditation."

"Perfect. Now close your eyes and listen to me."

Jennifer took Shilpa through the deep breathing and physical relaxation. Now came the tricky part.

"I want you to imagine that your feet are rooted to the ground, that your roots enter the ground following the roots of the fig tree. Your roots are pulling energy from the earth up into your base chakra. Gather it there, and now send it back down, driving your roots deeper and deeper into the earth. As you go deeper, more energy flows up. Allow the energy to rise to your second chakra, then turn it around and send it down even deeper."

"See that as the energy grows, your roots begin to glow deep red in the darkness of the earth. Continue pulling energy now to your third chakra and sending it back down. As you do, your roots glow orange. Pull more energy up to your heart chakra, then push it down making your roots glow yellow. Now the energy is strong, allow some to rise to your fifth chakra, then push it all the way down so that your roots glow almost white. Let the energy rise up to your sixth chakra, your third eye, and push it all down again so that your roots are glowing pure white. When it becomes too much to sustain, open your seventh chakra and allow the energy to join with the heavens so that you are a shining beacon in the world."

Jennifer searched the energetic plane for the shining beacon she knew must be there. It seemed to take forever but was only a few seconds.

"I have you now. You're safe here with me. Allow the energy to fall again until your third eye is open, and you see yourself standing with me in a field of tall grasses. The sun shines overhead in a cloudless sky."

Jennifer could see Shilpa clearly beside her. Now it was easy to complete. She opened the well to Gaia's love and then both floated down to the pool. Looking up they could see they were at the world's core. Jennifer's city shone like a bright light, while from the opposite side of the world, a darkness was spreading over the planet, zone by zone. They could see Shilpa as a bright yellow spot in her city.

"This is where we are today," said Jennifer. The darkness was getting closer. As they watched, the darkness took over the entire world, blanketing Shilpa's pale light and stopping only at the

A long-distance meditation

borders of the island city where Jennifer and Vijay lived. Then from the city shot rays of light, bringing new growth and green prosperity to the planet.

"This is Gaia's plan. The choice is yours, stay where you are or join us here. But you see that you do not have much time."

Suddenly the connection was broken. Jennifer opened her eyes. The call was still open on her tablet and she heard Shilpa sobbing in another part of the world. Kam asked, "Are you okay, Jaanu?" The call dropped.

Jennifer brushed herself off and told Molly it was time to go home.

BACK AT THE APARTMENT, JENNIFER SAT WITH Vijay on the couch. Molly was reading a bedtime story to the twins in their room. The twins liked having Molly read because she could make all the voices.

Jennifer said, "I did everything I could today to show Shilpa what's coming. I know I scared her, but now it's up to her to make a choice."

"Thanks Jenn. I realize there's a limit to what I can do, but as long as we've tried, I can live with it. I'm starting to understand what you must have gone through, that feeling of wanting to do the right thing but being powerless to make it happen.

But I also know that I'm in my thirties with resources I can count on. You were fourteen with nothing that wouldn't fit in your backpack. You were only a year older than Cindy was when we rescued her. I can't imagine what that would have been like."

Jennifer snuggled closer, then, without looking up, she said quietly, "I'm scared Vijay. This whole Gaia vision thing scares me. The spirit animal thing scares me and most of all, the long-distance link with Shilpa scared me. I don't know what my limits are. What am I becoming? I don't want to be a global telephone box. I want to be able to control the visions, not have them control me. But Gaia is so big and so powerful, I'm worried I'll be sucked in and never come out."

"Then let's keep your abilities under wraps for now. Who knows about them?"

"Cindy, Marjorie, Chris. I think they will all keep quiet. Oh, and Molly."

"And Molly," repeated Vijay.

They were both silent for a moment, then Vijay spoke. "We haven't heard much from Denum for a while. Do you think there is a Denum or is it just Molly with a deep voice? We don't know much about Molly or her world. I wonder how she processed the idea that you could be a connection to Gaia?"

"Now you're scaring me. Hold me Vijay, make

love to me so that I can step away from all this for a while."

Vijay picked her up and carried her to the bedroom. Their lovemaking started soft and gentle but quickly turned more energetic as they worked to push away their fears for the future.

45

STOWAWAYS

Shilpa

Shilpa was terrified. The port felt so alien with large dark ships being loaded and unloaded by various bots and self-guided vehicles. the air smelled off the sea, mixed with the scents of spilled diesel oil and exhaust fumes from the huge cargo handlers. Posted signs warned of the danger to humans and stating the penalties for being caught within the dock facility.

She and Kam wore the uniforms that had arrived two days before. The security badges clipped to their breast pockets identified them as ship inspectors. Beside them was the large, dark bot who had introduced himself as Denum just as Vijay had said he would. Denum held a large toolbox containing their clothing and the few possessions they were able to take with them. Kam held a briefcase full of inspection notes and forms to support their disguise.

They were standing outside a disused side gate for humans, which was locked with a large padlock. Denum cut the lock with a laser tool on his belt. He held a weathered replacement lock in his left hand.

Denum pointed out the route that they would take.

"It's important that you walk ahead of me, that is what the cameras would expect to see."

Kam took her hand and replied, "Understood, we'll walk in front."

"Wait for my command, then move quickly. Your entry will have been registered with the port."

It was only about two minutes but seemed an eternity to Shilpa. If she could have turned and run, she would have. But the vision shared by Jennifer was still so strong in her mind that she knew she had to go forward.

"Now," said Denum.

They slipped through the open gate and waited for a few seconds as Denum replaced the lock, stowing the old one in his pouch.

"Go, now!"

Kam let go of Shilpa's hand, saying, "Stay close, look confident. We're inspectors not lovers."

The ship in front of them was old, with rust blisters partially obscuring the name 'Sunshine Coast'. Because the ship was so old, it would have crew quarters on board.

Kam led them at a relaxed pace across the yard to a marked walkway leading to a gangway at the side of the ship. Reaching the gangway, they entered the ship through a human sized door. So far it was all going to plan.

Denum pointed to a steel door marked 'Stairs' and signalled that they should go up. The stairwell was empty, and they walked up at a rapid pace. Arriving on the main deck they stepped out.

"Who the hell are you?" a human asked. He was wearing the uniform of a port official.

"Freelance inspectors hired by the line," said Kam as they had rehearsed. "My name is Ram Das." He reached out to shake hands.

Shilpa stepped forward. "Radhika Singh," she said shaking hands in turn. Who are you?"

"My name's Dom, Dom Rao. Human Trafficking Officer. I'll be doing a random inspection of the containers. Let me know if you need any help finding your way around the ship."

"Thanks, the owners asked us to verify the state of some repairs against the records. We have a complete set of deck plans both on paper and in our bot." As he said this Kam tapped the briefcase.

"Okay, make sure you're off by 7am when this old tub floats off."

"No fears," said Kam. Shilpa could see that he was enjoying himself in this bit of play acting. "We'll just start in the bridge and then make our way around the ship."

"Sounds good. Bridge is that way." Dom pointed down the corridor towards the stern.

Kam set off down the deck with Shilpa and Denum following. Near the stern, another set of stairs was marked 'Bridge'.

Standing in the bridge, they could see the entire cargo deck. After a moment Dom appeared on the deck below, checking random containers to ensure they were properly sealed, and employing a thermal imager.

"He's looking for humans smuggled in containers," explained Denum. "Even though the risks are high, some still try."

"What happens if we see signs of human smuggling on the voyage?" asked Shilpa.

"The ships bots will lock them in the container welding it shut. They will then drill a small hole and pump in a strong anaesthetic. The stowaways will not survive the voyage. If they do survive and are caught near the arrivals port, they will be quietly executed and disposed of. The viral exclusion zones are absolute."

Shilpa shuddered "And what about us?"

"You are safe now. This ship is under my control, so you need to remain hidden only until it has left the port. Follow directions and you will meet Jennifer and Vijay soon. Let's go to your cabin."

The captain's cabin was just off the bridge. It was closed with a steel door. A strong bolt could be used to guarantee privacy. Furnishings were sparse. A double bed, and two night tables that were simply shelves welded to the walls on either side of the bed. A steel dresser with drawers closed by simple finger locks was against one wall. A small table, welded and hinged to the wall, and two steel chairs with cracked leather seats and backs completed the original furnishing. In the corner was a small refrigerator, and a microwave oven. These were clearly recent additions.

There was a single bathroom that did not appear to have been used for a long time. Kam attempted to flush the toilet and was rewarded with a whooshing sound as flushing water was sucked away by a vacuum. A handheld shower hung in a high bracket. The single washbasin was mounted below a small, cracked mirror. It was evident to Shilpa that turning on the shower would soak the entire bathroom.

Denum set down the large toolbox containing their comfortable clothing. He disappeared and reappeared with a container holding flasks of drinking water, and basic food stuffs which Shilpa stowed in the refrigerator. Also in the container were vacuum-sealed dishes that could be heated in the microwave. At the bottom of the container were two large bowls, forks and spoons. "There are more of these containers on board," he said. "They were hidden before the ship left the city."

When everything was done, Denum asked them to sit at the table to receive additional instructions.

"Here are the rules for your voyage. You will have access to the bridge and to the small navigation wings if you need fresh air. Do not leave this area. If there is any disturbance, return to your cabin and lock the door. Do not come out unless you hear me address you by name."

"What kind of disturbance could there be?" asked Kam.

"Stowaways or pirates who attempt to gain control of the bridge," said Denum. "They do not often get this far, but it has happened."

"What happens then?"

"They are removed," Denum replied. "You have nothing to fear if you stay in the cabin until I inform you that it is safe to leave."

Denum left. Kam closed and locked the door behind him.

"Now we just wait," he said. "Let's get some sleep."

They removed their uniform jackets and shoes, then changed into their night clothes. They lay on the bed, huddled together. The room was dark except for a small nightlight at floor level.

Lying in Kam's arms, Shilpa thought about Maa and Baba, and how hard it had been to say goodbye. She had hugged each of them, unwilling to let go, etching in her memory what it felt like to hold them. Maa had been brave, and told her to go, but Shilpa had seen the tears forming in her eyes. Baba had made a joke about seeing his daughter in uniform, but it felt forced. Shilpa knew it had been especially hard for him as her relationship with her father had always been very close. Maa and Baba had stood watching them get into the small taxi and kept watching until Shilpa lost sight of them.

She began to cry softly. Kam stroked her hair and asked, "Are you okay, Jaanu?"

"Kam, what have we done? I didn't think it would be this scary."

"The worst has passed," he replied. "Think about the future, life near your brother and Jennifer. A new city to explore. And we'll be safe from whatever horrors you saw."

"I suppose hearing Denum talk about stowaways and pirates just made it all more real. And who is Jennifer that she can make all this happen for us? She barely knows us."

"Maybe you're wrong. Perhaps it's Vijay who arranged it all. He's your brother."

Shilpa giggled, in spite of herself. "I know Vijay. He's lovable, but he doesn't have a devious bone in his body. No, it was Jennifer. She showed me the vision. She arranged all this."

"Then she must love Vijay very deeply."

"Almost as deeply as I love you."

Kam kissed the top of her head and said, "Try to get some sleep, Shilpa. When we wake up, we'll be on the ocean."

Feeling safe in Kam's arms, and despite the uncomfortable bed, Shilpa felt herself drifting off to sleep. When she woke up, she could feel the ship moving.

46

PROGRESS AT THE VINEYARD

Jennifer

Jennifer went out to the Vineyard for a tour with Marjorie to review progress. Marjorie was waiting at the gate and handed her a white helmet, then offered her a seat on one of the golf carts used for getting around the vineyard.

"We'll go by the building site first," she said, "then we can get rid of these hard hats. I can never quite get used to wearing one."

The old stone buildings were a buzz of activity. The buildings had been gutted and new floors and interior walls installed. The upper floors were wooden planks which had been reclaimed from old barns.

Progress at the Vineyard

A new residence wing was being built with apartments for future site managers and spiritual leaders. A second new building was begun with dormitory facilities for temporary workers and in future, for meditation participants. The golf cart proceeded past the new dormitory until they came to a series of bungalows very near completion. "This first one is reserved for you, Vijay, and the twins. The next one is for me, and there are five others for various senior leaders.

Here and there, men and women of various ages wearing white robes were engaged caring for the gardens.

"Who are they?" asked Jennifer.

"Oh, those are the acolytes, the dedicated core who live and work here. They assist Chris with the various rituals and services."

"Are they all celibate, like monks and nuns?"

"Oh goodness, no. Gaia is not about celibacy, quite the opposite. She is the goddess of fecundity and fertility." Jennifer looked more closely and saw that a few of the acolytes were clearly pregnant.

Having viewed the buildings, Marjorie said, "Let's stroll down to the pond."

Arriving at the pond, Jennifer was surprised to see that the water was now clear. There were small fish moving in the pond. The rushes were contained in an area at one end and the shore of the pond supported a wide variety of water's-edge plants.

"This is all the work of Cindy," said Marjorie. "She applied for the position of grounds manager. I wasn't sure, given her age, but she's producing amazing results."

As she said this, Cindy arrived on a brown quarter horse, riding on a light saddle with a bitless bridle made of a soft rope. After dismounting, she touched the horse gently on its shoulder and paused, then tied the horse to a hitching post that Jennifer had not noticed earlier.

"I have to let go of them gently," said Cindy. "Otherwise, they get confused and upset."

"Let go of them?" asked Jennifer.

"Yes, they're my spirit animal, so I merge with them when I ride. It makes the experience better for both of us."

"What are you working on now?" said Marjorie. "I'm almost afraid to ask."

"Another family has agreed to sell their acreage. It's in our watershed and is currently used for wheat production. We'll keep the wheat operation. Eventually it'll give us wheat for our mill and straw for animal bedding."

"What about the vineyards?" asked Jennifer.

"Two of the sections had vines that were too old or were the wrong grapes for this type of ground. They are being pulled out now. Those vineyards will be replanted with Shiraz and Chardonnay grapes. The remaining sectors are being trimmed now for next season. After that it's more complicated. We have to get the fermentation systems restored and replace the old bottling line. We also need the blacksmith and cooperage finished so we can make our own barrels. I'm looking now for a woodlot to provide us the oak for the cooperage."

"Why do we need all these things?" asked Jennifer.

"Two reasons," said Cindy. "I want everything we do here to respect the environment, and this is also our plan B. If we cannot maintain our current levels of technology, I want us to be able to fall back on simpler technologies to survive."

Jennifer felt a moment of frustration, and anger that all this was going on without her knowledge. "Who authorized all this? And what do you know about plans A and B?" she said and turned away from Cindy.

"Perhaps if you started participating in things, you wouldn't feel that way," replied Cindy just as hotly. "You still treat me like the 15-year-old who babysat for you, but I've done what you said. I've studied biology and ecology until I know our local lands and life cycles inside out. With my spirit horse's help, I can feel the land and know what it means. You used to talk to me, explain life and men and sex. but now you shut me out. What the fuck, Jennifer?"

Jennifer didn't turn around. She just walked off. *'It's too much,'* she thought as she angrily wiped away a tear. *'It's bad enough knowing she'll replace me, that one day she'll lie with Vijay. Do I have to see her prancing around on her horse every week as well?'*

She felt a tug at her elbow. She turned and saw that Marjorie had caught up and was hanging on to her. "Do you want to talk about something?"

Jennifer began to cry. "Yes," she said, "Somewhere without Vijay or Cindy or anyone else."

Marjorie led her around to the far side of pond where a bench had been installed. They sat together on the bench. Marjorie produced a square of brightly colored cloth for Jennifer to dry her eyes.

"Now what's going on, Jennifer? This isn't like you, breaking down in tears."

"I don't know, Marjorie. I should be so happy. I thought my purpose was to build a church to Gaia, but I'm not actually doing that, am I? You're managing all the activities, Chris has taken over designing the beliefs, your project manager is overseeing the renovations, and even Cindy is more important as she's making over the properties. I realized today that I don't even know what's going on. What am I here for?"

Progress at the Vineyard

"Jennifer, you created this church. Look around. There are over a hundred people here all committed to bringing your vision to life. The time was right and your energy, your push, set it all in motion."

"But there must be something else. What about my panther? Why can I merge with animals? No one else can do that, except Cindy, apparently. What else does Gaia want from me?"

"I think you have to ask her. Perhaps it's time to go back to the cottage."

Jennifer felt a chill run through her at the idea of confronting Gaia directly. "Will you come with me?" she asked in a small voice.

"Of course. Just let me know when you're ready to go."

The day was warm and sunny as Jennifer and Marjorie sat on the beach near the rocky point outside the white cottage. The sea was calm with only small wavelets lapping at the sand. The light breeze smelled clean and fresh off the ocean.

"Marjorie, do you think there is a God?" asked Jennifer.

"All of human spiritual tradition believes that to be true. From the early Vedic philosophers through all the descendant religions, the belief in an original creator is there. So, yes, I believe there is a God."

"And Gaia is not God, is she."

"No, Gaia is alive as much as you and I are alive, just on a vastly different scale. We are part of Gaia. You can know her and even converse with her through your visions."

"That's what I thought. But all these virus things that are happening are so awful. I want to speak with God and ask him why."

"Do you know how to do that? Are you thinking of praying?"

"No, I have another idea. I'll need Gaia's help, but I believe she will help me. Will you help me also?"

"Of course."

"Then I'm ready."

The sand beneath her was warm from the sunshine as Jennifer lay down. Marjorie sat beside her, with her back to a rock and legs crossed. She laid one hand on Jennifer's heart chakra.

Jennifer closed her eyes and relaxed into meditation, with her hands flat against the sand on either side. She visualized the deep well of Gaia's love and allowed herself to tumble down into it. The days of holding onto a ledge had long disappeared.

At first, she simply lay in the pool and basked in Gaia's loving support. After a few minutes, she framed her request. "I want to meet God, I want to meet God," she repeated over and over like a mantra.

Progress at the Vineyard

One side of the pool opened. The love started flowing to it, creating a current that carried Jennifer over another ledge.

Jennifer was falling now. Looking behind, she saw the earth shrinking, saw the continents and clouds and the smoke from the burning forests. Then it was gone. The sun was retreating to be just another star.

Jennifer fell past other planets. Past a steaming swampy planet where creatures moved on their bellies between the enormous ferns. She fell past planets with cities more elegant and beautiful than anything man had ever built. Jennifer fell past civilizations of winged creatures and swimming creatures and creatures with six legs. She saw a planet full of life suddenly consumed when its star belched out a fiery stream.

She fell.

She fell past countless stars and then past countless galaxies.

She fell past the end of the universe until she was falling through the void.

In the void, she felt her body stripped away. There was no pain, just curiosity as her flesh fell away from her mind. All that was left was the spark that was Jennifer.

She fell.

As she fell, she felt her memories fall away. Memories of being a child peeled off and were gone. Memories of selling herself for money, her life with Vijay and the twins peeled away and were gone. The last to go was her memory of Vijay himself. Now she was just the spark with a single thought: "I am Jennifer."

She clung to that thought, afraid that if she let go completely, she would be lost forever.

"I am Jennifer, I am Jennifer," she repeated as fiercely as she could.

She had no ears to hear, no eyes to see, and no fingers to touch. But she sensed a being. A being so immense that it contained the universe. She was in the being, and the being was in her.

"I am Jennifer, I am Jennifer." In the presence of the being, she put all of her tiny spark of energy into that thought.

She felt the being's attention move to her, then nothing.

47

AN URGENT CALL FOR HELP

Vijay

Vijay was in a meeting with his leaders' circle when his tablet interrupted. "Urgent message from Marjorie Fitzhaven: Vijay, come quickly. Something happened to Jennifer at the cottage. Meet us at the vineyard."

Vijay looked around the table, his mind spinning.

"Vijay! We're coming with you," said Sally who had overheard the message. This meeting can wait."

Vijay, Sally, and Greg stood. Vijay stumbled going out the door as the prospect of a life without Jennifer flashed before him.

A taxi was already waiting on the street, its doors opened, and the three revolutionaries piled in. No one spoke as the taxi set off.

They arrived at the vineyard before Marjorie and Jennifer. Cindy was there, as well as some of the young acolytes in white.

Cindy was talking with Marjorie on her tablet. Looking around, she said, "Someone get white robes for these three and two white sheets."

Vijay, Sally and Greg were led off to a building where they changed out of their clothes into the simple robes of the acolytes. One of the acolytes picked up two folded white sheets. Now they could only wait.

"Shouldn't we take her directly to hospital?" asked Greg.

"No," replied Cindy. "Her physical body seems fine, she's not injured, and Marjorie said she's breathing easily. Her mind and her spirit have been overloaded by whatever she did. But she's strong. We have to give her a familiar anchor for her mind to grab hold of so that she finds her way back. Vijay will be the best anchor given the deep love between them. I'm going to meditate and ask Gaia for instructions."

It was over an hour before the taxi arrived with Marjorie and Jennifer. Marjorie sat upright in the back seat with Jennifer curled up beside her, her head resting on Marjorie's lap.

An urgent call for help

Cindy organized a team of four to pick up the unconscious Jennifer and carry her into the building. Vijay went to follow, but Marjorie held his elbow to restrain him. Sally was allowed to go with Jennifer.

Vijay felt nervous as he stood waiting for them to reappear.

"What happened?" he asked Marjorie.

"She wanted to meet God. At first, it was a regular meditation, then she started saying "I am Jennifer" repeatedly. Then she stopped, and this red mark appeared over her third eye. We haven't been able to wake her."

"What do we do?"

"We take her to Gaia and ask for help. We need you to carry her, and we'll accompany you.

"Do you think she'll come back?" he asked Marjorie.

"If anyone can bring her back, Cindy can. You know they're paired somehow. And I don't believe Gaia will give up her chosen one before her real work has even begun."

"Her real work?"

"Yes, whatever she was made for, this is not it." Marjorie swept her right arm to include the vineyard. "This is important, but it doesn't take a black panther. Even Jennifer knows that."

"It's too much to ask more from her." Vijay was close to tears now. "She's not that strong."

"Vijay, she's the strongest person I have ever met. It'll be okay. Now compose yourself. They're coming back."

The four acolytes handed Jennifer to Vijay. Jennifer was naked under the white sheet that wrapped her. Vijay felt the familiar shape of her body and looked down at her face where he saw the red diamond in the center of her forehead. Tears began to flow as he carried her, following Cindy to the sacred tree.

When they arrived at the tree, Vijay was told to lay Jennifer down between the roots. The acolytes opened the white sheet so that Jennifer lay there naked on top of it.

As Vijay gazed down at her, he saw the body that was so familiar to him. The panther tattoo over her breast, and the scars that adorned her torso. He was suddenly afraid, more afraid than he had ever been in his life. Fear of losing her. Fear of having to find his own way without her.

"Okay, Vijay, you'll be the anchor to bring her back. The sensation of your naked body next to hers will provide the sensation she can latch onto. Please step out of your robe and take her place on the ground. We'll place Jennifer on top of you, and you can put your arms around her." Cindy explained.

She seemed so absolute in her intention that Vijay simply complied.

An urgent call for help

"Maidens, lift Jennifer."

The four maidens lifted her, leaving the sheet on the ground. This was a bit clumsy as Jennifer simply sagged in their arms.

As they held Jennifer to one side, Cindy said, "Vijay, take her place in the sacred spot."

Vijay was beyond caring what happened to him; he was entirely fixed on Jennifer's limp body in the arms of the maidens.

"Acolytes, place Jennifer face down on Vijay and cover her with a sheet. Vijay, hold her in your arms. With Gaia's energy rising from the earth, and the warmth of Vijay's loving arms around her, we have the best chance of bringing her back."

Vijay felt the warm earth beneath him where Jennifer had been lying. As he felt the familiar warmth of her body laid on top of him, his tears began to flow again. Without thinking, he shifted his weight and pulled her into her favorite resting position. Her head lay on its side on his chest, tucked under his chin. His arms were wrapped around her.

"Place her hands on my arms," he said in a broken voice. At that moment, he feared this might be the last time he ever held her. *'Dammit, Jennifer, why do you always have to push so hard,'* he thought, then immediately felt guilty for thinking it.

Cindy sat next to Jennifer and placed a hand upon her head.

"Kim, Zeze, sit on either side with hands on Jennifer's back at her heart chakra. Ratna, Yolanda, hands on Jennifer's back at her second Chakra," said Cindy, taking charge. Vijay could not see the laying of hands but felt their slight weight on his body.

"Sally, Greg, you're here to support Vijay; place your hands on his legs wherever you can. Marjorie, sit at Jennifer's feet and hold them." Cindy's voice was clear and strong as she gave directions.

"Before we begin," started Cindy.

"Please, don't draw a card," Vijay said, desperate to break the unbearable tension. He instantly regretted it.

Cindy only laughed, a peal of gently loving laughter.

"Don't worry, Vijay, just follow us. You know the meditation already." Then, looking around the circle, she said, "Before we begin, the first rule is: offer no resistance to Jennifer or Vijay if they move. We are here with a healing touch, not restraint. Second, no speaking or crying or making any other sound in this physical domain. Greg, Sally, follow along as best you can. Don't worry; as long as Vijay can feel your support, you're doing everything needed."

An urgent call for help

"Now, close your eyes and surrender to Gaia." Her voice changed to a sonorous tone he had not heard before. "With our mind's eye, we look around and see the wonder that is Gaia, the tree, the grass, the stream and further, the ocean, the mountains, the sky, and clouds. We give thanks for these. We give thanks for the animals that feed and comfort us, for the fish in the sea that nourish us, for the tiny creatures that maintain the soil and recycle life materials. We look down and see that we are at the edge of a deep well, and at the bottom is the warm red glow of Gaia's love. Always present, unconditional, and endlessly forgiving. We want to be in that love. We see Vijay carrying Jennifer in his arms, ready to take her back to Gaia. As we count down from three, we all step off to float down into the pool of Gaia. Three, look down, two, open your minds, one, open your hearts and step out. We are falling, we are falling, and then we are cushioned in Gaia's pool." Her voice had become very soft.

Vijay felt himself carrying Jennifer as he floated in the pool of love. His body felt warm and buoyed up, and for the first time, he felt the sensation of Gaia's attention and curiosity.

"Gaia, hear our prayer for the return of Jennifer to her body. Gaia, Jennifer has served you well, but we need her to keep to your path. Gaia, hear our prayer."

Still floating in the pool, Vijay felt Jennifer's body begin to move against him. He felt his own body respond. *'How can that be?'* the thought came and drifted away.

He felt Jennifer rise up above him and try to settle herself on him as they lay floating. He reached down to hold himself stiff and ready. A moment later, he could feel himself inside Jennifer. Cradled in Gaia's presence with his lover astride him, Vijay felt the most incredible peace and contentment he had ever known. It was the most marvellous of dreams.

Jennifer was moving now, rhythmically up and down. It felt like Jennifer, but it wasn't Jennifer. Too rhythmic, too mechanical. *'Gaia's jumpstarting her,'* he thought languidly. The thought floated away.

Then the rhythm changed; it was Jennifer. He knew her touch, her movements. He felt the contractions inside her growing stronger. Without warning, he felt her climax a split second before his own, more intense and longer lasting than anything he had experienced ever before.

It was over. Vijay could hear Jennifer sobbing. Opening his eyes, he found her crying on his chest in the sacred place under the tree still covered by the white sheet.

The attendants had all taken their hands off and were sitting back. Greg seemed distinctly uncomfortable as he looked down at his gown. Yolanda, the youngest acolyte was staring with wide eyes as she asked, "Is it always like that?"

"Not always, dear," said Marjorie. The others broke into nervous laughter. Vijay realized that they had all somehow shared in that final orgasm.

48

JENNIFER RETURNS

Jennifer

Jennifer slowly became aware of floating in Gaia's pool sitting astride Vijay. Her body was already moving automatically. She felt aroused and began to move in her own rhythm, building to a blinding white climax.

Then she was awake. She was sobbing and realized that she was lying on Vijay with his arms around her. She could still feel him soft inside her.

There were quiet voices around her.

She turned her attention to Vijay. She could feel his heart beating; she could feel his lungs drawing in and expelling air. She could feel the blood rushing through his arteries and seeping back through his veins. She felt all of him.

Jennifer returns

Sitting up, she realized they were surrounded by attendants in their white gowns. Sally and Greg were also there. This was puzzling, they must be there for Vijay.

Marjorie passed her a robe to pull over her head, then Kim and Zeze helped her stand unsteadily on her feet.

She saw Sally and Greg doing the same for Vijay, and the entire group made their way slowly back to the retreat building.

As Jennifer walked, she became hyper-aware of her surroundings. She was aware of the wind as it swept gently over the land. The earth beneath her bare feet felt alive, with countless small creatures wriggling through the dirt. She felt the rhythms of her own body, her heart pumping, her lungs breathing, and all the contractions of her gut.

Jennifer allowed herself to be led back to the mess table, where she was given a seat at the head of the table. Vijay was seated to her left.

Jennifer placed her palms on the table. Immediately, she could feel the strength of the ancient oak from which it was cut. She sensed the storms it had withstood, the disease which doomed it, and the pain of the cuts that ended it.

She realized that Vijay was watching her closely. "What happened to you, Jenn?"

I wanted to see God, to understand why this is happening to us."

"Did you get an answer?"

"I'm not sure. I saw so many planets, so many other creatures. Some crawling in swamps, others in wonderful cities. I saw whole worlds swallowed by their suns with no warning. I saw planets burning when their population lost control. And I saw that none of it mattered. God watches but doesn't intervene."

"Did you speak to him?"

"No, when I fell in the emptiness, everything was taken from me. My body was gone, so I could not speak. My memories and thoughts were gone. I could only think, "I am Jennifer." Over and over."

"How did you come back?"

"God saw me. I was this tiny little spark that confronted him. Then everything went white. Nothing more until I woke up on top of you."

"Who gave you that mark on your forehead?"

"What mark?" Jennifer asked.

A mirror was found so that Jennifer could see the dark blaze that ran from just above her eyebrows to just under her hairline. It was a diamond shape; at its widest, it was the width of an eye. It was the red of a birthmark and appeared to be permanent.

"What does the mark mean?" Jennifer asked.

"It seems to be a mark of either God or Gaia's blessing," said Marjorie. "You've been touched by something beyond our understanding. Did you receive anything else?"

"I want to lie down and sleep now. I still can't think clearly."

Marjorie shooed everyone away except Vijay, and the two of them helped her make her unsteady way to her bedroom. Marjorie sent Vijay off for a water jug and glass and then turned down the bed for Jennifer. She was dimly aware of Vijay's return.

"In you get dear. Make sure you drink lots of water whenever you wake up. There'll be lots of time to talk when you get up."

Jennifer lay down. She felt comforted by the cool cotton sheets and the feeling of the warm wind over the dry soil that had nourished the plants it was made from.

That must be the memory of the cotton,' she thought. But then the thought drifted away.

She slept.

IT WAS DAYLIGHT WHEN SHE WOKE UP. SUNLIGHT streamed through the open bedroom window. A light breeze was playing with the sheer curtains.

Rolling over, Jennifer could see Vijay dozing in a chair beside the bed. She went to call for him, but her throat felt dry, and she only managed to croak. She tried to stand up, using the nightstand to steady herself, but knocked the lamp onto the floor.

Vijay woke with a start.

"Jennifer, let me help. You've been asleep for more than a day. Are you okay?"

"Need to pee," she croaked.

"I've got you."

Vijay took as much of her weight as he could. They stumbled together into the bathroom. He knelt down to remove her panties. Looking down, Jennifer said, "Those don't look like my panties. Too big and plastic."

"Pull ups, to keep you comfortable."

He lifted her nightdress. "Now put your arms around me as I help you onto the seat."

When she was finished, Vijay carried her back to the bed, sitting her up with cushions around her.

Whenever Vijay touched her, she had the impression that she could feel his blood flowing through his body, sense his heart pumping, his lungs rhythmically inhaling and exhaling. Memories of her vision started coming back to her.

Jennifer returns

Meanwhile, Vijay was getting her a glass of water and holding it for her to sip. The water tasted clean and pure. She recognized it as water from their spring. *'I must be at the vineyard,'* she thought.

"I'm just going to get Marjorie. I'll be right back," she heard Vijay say.

A moment later, Marjorie bustled into the room, then stopped and burst into tears.

"Jennifer, dear. You had us all so worried. We weren't sure if you would ever wake up."

Jennifer wanted to respond, but she felt so weak. She tried to lift her arm, but it wouldn't lift. She felt herself drifting towards sleep again. She vaguely heard Marjorie talking with Vijay.

"I know this sounds odd, but I believe this is what she needs."

JENNIFER WOKE AGAIN TO FEEL HERSELF BEING carried gently in Vijay's arms. She felt his strength and his gentleness at the same time. She heard all the small noises around her. The tiny croaks of little frogs, the rustle of the grasses in the breeze, the distant mating call of birds in the woodlot, the terrified squeak of a mouse that had just been caught by a snake.

Then she was being lowered to the earth, to

her mediation spot under the oak tree. Her hands were placed carefully on the exposed roots. She was aware of Vijay sitting on one side of her and Marjorie on the other. Each put their hands over hers.

Marjorie felt different. The rhythms of her body were different, softer. Her heart was beating faster than Vijay's.

Marjorie's voice beside her began to recite in deep tones.

"Gaia, hear our thanks for the return of your servant, Jennifer. We request your help to restore her strength. Gaia, hear our prayer. Gaia, hear our prayer. Gaia, hear our prayer."

Jennifer listened, but she knew she didn't need Marjorie's invocation. She began to draw energy from the earth, pulling it into herself, replenishing her cells. She lay there, basking in the energy of Gaia.

Idly, she cast about and noticed a young buttercup seedling that had just broken ground. She gently sent a tendril of Gaia's energy there, filling the seedling with life and vigor. She felt it grow, felt its stem become strong, it roots drive deeper. Its leaves unfolded facing the sun. Small buds appeared, grew, then opened as buttercups.

Opening her eyes, she turned toward it and laughed to see the buttercup standing tall and waving in the breeze.

On her left, Marjorie was looking at the buttercup. She seemed shocked with her mouth hanging open. On her right, Vijay was gazing into her face. When he saw her eyes open, he leaned over and kissed her. "Welcome home," he said as tears rolled down his cheeks.

PREVIEW OF BOOK 3: JENNIFER'S DESTINY

JENNIFER'S
DESTINY
BOOK THREE OF GAIA'S DAUGHTERS
KEVIN R COLEMAN

1

UNEXPECTED SHIPMATES

Shilpa

Three days into the voyage, Shilpa and Kam were relaxing on the bridge with Denum when they saw movement on the deck below.

"Go into your cabin and lock the door," said Denum. "Do not come out unless I instruct you."

"How will we know it's you?" asked Kam.

"Our password will be Molly the Elephant. I will say Molly the Elephant says you can come out. Now go and lock the door."

As they turned to leave, Shilpa took one more look at the deck where she saw a bright flash which seemed to immobilize two nearby robots.

A moment later, there was a knock at the door.

"Molly the Elephant with supplies," said Denum on the other side.

Kam cracked open the door then opened it wide to admit Denum loaded down with four more cases of foodstuffs and water. "This should be enough if there is a problem," he said.

"What kind of problem?" asked Shilpa.

"The kind that would require backup from the city." Then he was gone.

Shilpa and Kam reorganized the supplies, moving water out of the fridge to make room for more perishable items and settling down to withstand a siege.

A few hours later, they heard heavy banging and then voices outside their door, laughing and cheering. From what they could make out, a group of stowaways was on the bridge.

"Those EMP bombs stopped them in their tracks," they heard one say.

"I told you they would," said another. "They're not armored for it. They're just deck bots used to maintain the ship and look after the load."

"It was fucking unbelievable," said a fourth.

Then the voices went quiet as the group wandered on, apparently touring the ship they had taken over.

. . .

Unexpected shipmates

It was after midnight that night. Shilpa had just gone to sleep when Kam woke her. "I heard a knock at the door. They both sat up in their bed and listened. "Molly the Elephant with more supplies," said Denim's voice very quietly.

Kam opened the door and took in another three cases of supplies from Denum.

"Are you staying with us?" asked Shilpa.

"No, I have to hide so I can guide reinforcements when they come. This body will not withstand one of their EMP devices. You are on your own. Do not open this door for anyone until you hear me give the password again. Also, the next time you see me, my body may be different. Just trust in the password."

"What's an EMP device?" asked Kam.

"It's lets off an intense electromagnetic pulse that damages electronic circuits in range. Theirs are relatively small, and the ship steel structure provides some protection. Still, their devices are strong enough to disable any bots nearby. Military bots are shielded against them, but these bodies are not."

Denum left and closed the door. Kam and Shilpa carefully locked the door behind him. They organized the new supplies before climbing back into bed.

Shilpa felt Kam putting his arms around her. She knew she was shaking but could not stop.

"Hush," he said. "We'll be fine. If we can't spend four days locked up in a cabin, what hope do we have of being together for the next 60 years?"

Shilpa lay still for a long time until his calm, regular breathing told her Kam had fallen asleep. Then she carefully rolled over, curled up and went to sleep herself.

The next day, they heard the voices in the bridge again. The stowaways seemed to be enjoying their ocean voyage. At night they disappeared.

"Must be going to the other cabins," said Kam. They could hear water being run and toilets being flushed which gave them cover for their own hygiene.

The second day, the voices were more worried. "We lost Alok and Regina last night." said a voice. "They're just gone."

"We must have missed a damned bot somewhere," said another. "Do we have any of the EMP devices left?"

"Morty has one."

"Don't waste it, we'll need it when we find the missing bot."

"Do you think it's in the captain's cabin? We could cut a hole and toss it in there."

"But if that's not where it is, then we're out of options."

A female voice spoke up. "Why don't we set a watch over the cabin door tonight, if anything comes out, we hit it with the EMP." If nothing comes out, then we haven't lost anything.

Shilpa and Kam lay silent on the bed, listening.

That evening, they stayed silent in their room, worried that any sound could give them away.

"Is Denum killing them?" whispered Shilpa.

"We don't know that," said Kam, but Shilpa didn't believe him.

Shilpa sat on the steel floor of their room and tried the meditation that Jennifer had shown her. She reached her roots down through the steel of the ship to the ocean beneath, then down through the ocean to the ocean floor, and on into to the. She then began to pull the energy up, chakra by chakra, each time turning it back can and using the energy to drive deeper. Working her way up her spine to the 6th chakra, she turned the energy back each time. By the time she reached the seventh chakra at the crown of her head, she felt more intensely alive than she had ever felt. She released the energy upwards to the heavens.

For a moment she sat simply being the beacon as Jennifer had taught her. Then she created the image of Jennifer in her mind and transmitted the single thought "Help us" over and over. But nothing happened.

As she relaxed again, and released the vision, she looked at Kam. He was sitting with his eyes wide open. "What did you do. Do you know you were glowing just then. Not just faintly. I could have read a book by your light."

"We'll try again in the morning. I'm trying to reach Jennifer just as she reached me. Next time we'll hold hands and I'll talk you through it. Two may be able to be more powerful than one. Or maybe Jennifer is just distracted right now, and we need the right moment. It's not like we have anything else to do.

The story continues in Jennifer's Destiny, Book 3 of Gaia's Daughters and the conclusion of the Jennifer trilogy.

ACKNOWLEDGMENTS

It takes many people to make a book. First, I thank my wife and life partner, Sue, whose patience and encouragement has supported me through the long dark period when I wrote my early drafts.

I would also like to thank my beta readers, Bev Armstrong, Jill Coleman and Kim Gordon.

Finally, I would like to acknowledge the wonderful work of my editor, Lindsay Drummond, for her patient reviews of my scribblings and her gentle guidance in making this a far superior book. Along the way, she has taught me to be a better writer than I ever dreamed of.

ABOUT THE AUTHOR

Kevin Coleman is an emerging author of romantic science fiction and fantasy with a metaphysical viewpoint.

His novels portray a changed world, ravaged by viruses where a small city on an island develop a direct relationship with Gaia and work to save human existence on our planet.

Kevin lives with his wife, Sue, on the north shore of Lake Ontario. In addition to being an author, he is an enthusiastic kite-maker and sailor.

ALSO BY KEVIN R COLEMAN

Jennifer's Vow

Jennifer, young sex-worker, is visited by a black panther. Two weeks later, she receives an offer too good to refuse supporting Vijay, a young man with a revolutionary vision. Can Jennifer free herself from her past, and learn to love Vijay? And what does the black panther represent in her life?

ALSO BY KEVIN COLEMAN

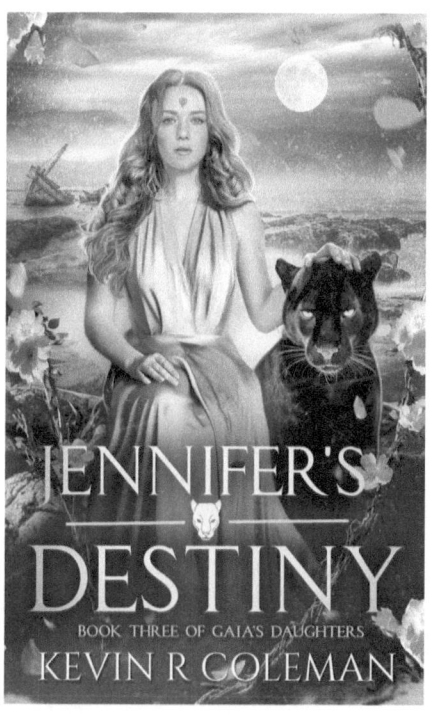

Jennifer's Destiny

Faced with a horrific choice, Jennifer must choose between her own safety and that of the island and city she loves.

Vijay and Cindy support her as best they can, but ultimately the fate of humanity rests on Jennifer's shoulders.

COMING THIS FALL

Harriet's Way

Harriet is the newest of Gaia's daughters, and wants to build her life with Dylan. But to ensure his freedom and their future, she must first repair the dysfunctional Subramanian family, and overcome the resistance of Cindy, who runs the vineyard and the Gaian church. Dylan dreams of a life on the sea, and sets off on a grand adventure to Tortola. But an unexpected surprise greets him there.

JOIN MY NEWSLETTER

To sign up for my newsletter, copy the URL below into a browser on your computer or phone. You'll receive first in line notices of new releases.

https://kevincolemanauthor.com

www.ingramcontent.com/pod-product-compliance
Lightning Source LLC
LaVergne TN
LVHW091526060526
838200LV00036B/506